Crowned

a novel

Christina Coryell

Books by Christina Coryell:

The Camdyn Series
A Reason to Run
A Reason to Be Alone
A Reason to Forget
For No Reason

Girls of Wonder Lane
Simply Mad
Crowned

Facebook: www.facebook.com/AuthorChristinaCoryell
Twitter: @c_tinacoryell
www.christinacoryell.com

Crowned

To Britten,
For words and faith that have inspired me
and influenced this story

Chapter One

"Something stinks, and this time, it's not the sewer."

Pulling the microphone away from her face, the trim yet shapely young woman brushed a strand of dark hair from her eyes, taking care to keep one wave falling gracefully across her shoulder. "For the sake of our city and its population, might we have a frank and open discussion? Let's cut to the facts, fellow citizens: It *is* the sewer, isn't it? If the members of the City Council would open their eyes for five seconds, they would see that the man they placed in charge of this mess is not doing his duty. But ignorance is not the only thing that blinds; occasionally it is a willingness to ignore the simple facts. That is what we are wrestling with in this particular case, because this is cronyism at its worst. Whose brother is he again? Or was it cousin? And does anyone really care what I'm saying, or have they already gone back to eating their fish sticks and macaroni and cheese because the weather has been dissected and the sports scores are played out, and they're not interested in this drivel? Why do we keep getting sent on these stench-hole assignments, Kenny?"

She slipped her hand sleekly across her tresses—two parts dark brown to one part cherry red—meticulously colored the perfect hue. Her crowning glory, hair that cascaded across her shoulders in flawless, shimmering waves.

"Go again," she ordered, stretching herself taller and taking on an aura of poised resolve. "Something stinks, and this time, it's not the sewer. After taking complaints from many members of the public and thoroughly assessing the situation, such is the finding of the personnel in charge of the situation: the sewer system is not to blame. While the City Council works with local environmental agencies to discover the source of the unfortunate mess, rest assured that Channel Six Action News will be here to uncover the story. In the meantime, perhaps Summer and Denton can provide a breath of fresh air from the studio."

Mitch Penner paused the video and stretched his arms to the back of his head as he leaned farther in his leather armchair behind his workspace, tilting enough that the mechanism under the chair clicked and creaked. Just as it appeared about to topple, he sprang forward and placed an elbow on his desk.

"Did Kenny have any comments as to why you keep getting sent on stench-hole assignments?" Mitch asked.

Twisting uncomfortably in her chair, she fought the urge to speak her mind. "A bit of a joke. That is allowed, right?"

"Harley..."

"Look, I'm professional, am I not? I give you the slant you want on these stories, and I manage to make them interesting somehow. I'm your most popular reporter, and you're allowing me to languish on the flybys."

"You're young and you haven't been here that long yet," he argued, bringing his left hand up to rub his brow thoughtfully.

"Almost two years now. I've more than proven myself— enough to avoid sewer trips, anyway."

"The story is where the story is. I don't mind you having a bit of fun, but what if that accidentally made its way to the air? It's better if you don't give people ammunition."

"Ammunition? I'm not worried about ammunition." Would somebody really use something like that against her?

Mitch stood and jerked on the waistband around his pants that were half a size too small, tightly pinched under his protruding stomach. If his white button-down shirt were any smaller, the buttons holding it precariously closed might have launched across the room, destroying innocent lives in their path.

"Just do the stories you're asked to do, Harley. I don't need any drama right now, so don't create any."

He doesn't need any drama, she thought. *Harley Laine doesn't create drama, she makes the stories dramatic. There's a huge difference.*

"I assure you I'm a consummate professional, Mitch," she murmured as she rose to exit the room, heading down the hall in search of the turncoat cameraman who had most certainly stabbed her in the back. Passing three familiar locations where he might have been lounging, she finally found him standing next to the coffee bar, swirling the contents of a stack of artificial sweeteners into his cup.

"'Sup," he drawled casually as she took the coffee from the countertop in front of him and moved it out of his reach. "Hey, my joe."

Adjusting her thin frame so that she looked her most intimidating, she gave him a frosty glare. "Consider your joe confiscated until you explain why you gave Mitch a video of my snide sewer remarks."

Despite the fact that he was taller, he was lanky and awkward, and he looked slightly intimidated. Reaching a hand up slowly, he scratched the front of his unruly head of auburn hair. "Whaddya mean?"

"What *do you* mean?" she corrected, folding her arms across her chest. "Please, Kenny, work on losing that ridiculous hillbilly accent. Your constant drawl is going to affect my speech pattern one of these days, and I'm going to be judged harshly because you choose not to speak like an educated person."

"One of these days, huh?" Kenny surmised, eyeing his coffee. "Sure, one of the local people's gonna care if you say 'hey' instead of 'hello' right?" Laughing, he shook his head with a condescending grin. "What'd I do, Harley? I'm not into playing guessing games; I just want my caffeine."

"Mitch called me into his office to show me video of the sewer segment, where I mentioned stench-hole stories…"

"Oh," he muttered, realizing his part in her dignified anger. "Should have erased that, I suppose. It's all good, though. Mitch loves ya."

"He certainly should," she retorted, making sure he didn't take her posture too lightly by stepping forward a couple inches and placing her hands on her hips. "It's not Mitch I'm worried about. 'It's better not to give people ammunition,' he said. He meant Summer, of course."

"Summer Davis doesn't care what you do," he insisted, glancing at his coffee again.

"Doesn't she? She knows I'm better than her, and that I deserve the desk. It's just a matter of time before someone else notices, and then her number will be up."

"People love Summer." Reaching a long arm past her frame, he clasped his cup and pulled the coffee towards him. "She's been 'round a long time."

"Too long," she offered, stepping back and allowing him some space. "They're going to need new blood, and when the time comes, I want to make sure it's mine."

Hurrying down the hallway, Harley sidestepped a box dropped haphazardly on the floor and tried to make a hasty exit. She was late, and that wouldn't do. Her royal blue Manolo Blahniks with the pencil-thin heels were not making matters easier, and she attempted to push her body momentum forward so she was almost on tiptoe rather than clomping along roughly on those spindles.

"Hey, Harley, can I get your opinion on this phrasing?" she heard Denton ask as she sped by. Normally she would make time for the handsome blond newsman six years her senior, but she was already late.

Pausing only a second, she glanced in his doorway. "Can it wait, Denton? It's Wednesday night, and I have an appointment."

"Of course, the elusive Wednesday appointment," he added with a chuckle. "Please tell me you're not secretly dying or something. That would ruin my weekend plans."

"Not dying," she insisted as she picked up her pace and walked further down the hallway. Denton had recently begun flirting with her, which she would have appreciated were it not for the fact that she had too many irons in the fire already. Now was definitely not the time, because if she was late the whole thing would go awry.

Trying to run across the parking lot, she mentally cursed those Manolos, even while admiring them as she glanced down. Not wearing them hadn't been an option that morning; she wanted everyone to know she was the best-dressed person in the building, and her appearance that day could have left no doubt. Popping open the door of her shiny black BMW, she swiftly tossed her Prada handbag into the passenger seat and started the ignition before she even had the door closed. A glance at the clock on the dash confirmed that she was running dangerously behind.

Fourteen blocks she had to drive from the studio to her destination, and she squealed the tires twice as she turned, racing against the clock. The final traffic signal switched from yellow to red just as her car reached the white line, but she ignored it and gunned the BMW forward, desperate to arrive in time. Pulling up at the back of the little strip mall, she parked her slick black automobile dangerously close to a large green dumpster and flung herself out of the car, trotting the few steps to the back door with the pink lettering. Three times she pounded her fist against the door, hoping she wasn't too late. When a few seconds passed, she put her arm against the side of the building and allowed herself to slump against it a bit, trying to catch her breath.

The Revolving Closet, the block letters on the door read. Thinking about the name made Harley chuckle at its simple honesty.

With a click, the door opened, and Annie Jessup gave Harley a wary glare. "I'd almost given up on you."

"I'm so sorry," she attempted to explain, stepping into the cluttered space. "Mitch was on my case, and then Denton tried to hit on me—"

"Don't worry about it," Annie insisted, shaking a head adorned with a mass of fiery-red curls on one side and nearly shaved with her natural black on the other, lifting her pierced eyebrow just a tad and causing the tiny gold-hoop to rise. "Denton, huh?"

"Not worth discussing," Harley told her as she closed the door behind her. Every Wednesday, like clockwork, she visited The Revolving Closet. It was one of Louisville's premier resale locations, where most of the city's elite women brought their handoffs. Since the new merchandise hit the shelves on Thursdays, Annie allowed Harley private viewings the evening before. The first time she visited, Harley wondered why the city's most prestigious clientele would bestow their business on someone who looked like Annie; soon after, though, she found out she was one of them—the daughter of a business tycoon. Her rebellion against her parents looked like piercings and wild hair, and as long as she didn't proceed to anything worse, they told all their friends to give her their patronage.

Harley would have likely tried to befriend Annie anyway to score the clothing perks, but the two had naturally become close when Harley started visiting the resale shop—close enough that Harley considered the red-haired shop owner her best friend in all of Louisville.

"Human Barbie dropped by yesterday," Annie said cryptically, causing a slight grin to form on Harley's lips. Her best hauls usually came from Faith Cooper, whom Annie casually referred to as Human Barbie. Faith's husband owned the prestigious Cooper Corporate Financial, and apparently Faith's daily routine involved buying overpriced clothes, wearing them once, and then bringing them to Annie. Harley and Faith were roughly the same size, so she usually only had to take the pants up by about half an inch. She also shared Faith's foot size, which was a special bonus and had scored her many sweet pairs of shoes, including the Manolos she had on her feet at that moment.

"Someday I will meet Faith Cooper, and she's going to accuse me of robbing her," Harley added with a slight giggle, sliding her handbag to the ground by the door and slipping out of her shoes. "I can almost guarantee that Faith has never run in those Manolos, and probably for good reason. I'm lucky I didn't break my neck. Or ankle."

"Crazy girl," Annie chided, shaking her head and causing those curls to dance. "I would have stayed here until…"

"…six o'clock, I know."

Annie played the bass guitar for her church group on Wednesday nights, and although Harley hadn't been to see what kind of crazy church Annie attended, she was always slightly intrigued. *When I get a spare minute,* she would tell herself.

Annie stepped forward and grabbed a pair of Rock Revival jeans and held them out toward Harley. "What are you going to do when you get the desk? There won't be any sneaking out of there before the six o'clock news when that happens."

"Spoken like a woman with inside information," Harley answered, lifting an eyebrow mischievously as she took the jeans from Annie's fingers. "I'm sure I could ask my wonderful friend to let me in here at midnight, right?" She winked for good measure. "Do you honestly think Faith Cooper wore these?"

"Um…no. Not a chance. Probably some jeans of the month club or such nonsense. Anyway, they still have tags."

"Maybe she has a daughter," Harley offered as she unzipped the back of her skirt and slid it down, stepping out of it deftly.

"Oh, she does have a daughter," was the response as her friend assumed a slight accent. "Her name's Audrey. No way would that girl fit in those jeans, though."

"I love it when your southified speech slips out, Annie."

"Says the only customer who undresses in the middle of my store. There's a little bit of hillbilly under that cherry cola hair of yours."

"You're in a hurry, and I am saving you valuable time trotting back and forth to the dressing room. Besides, you love me and you know it."

"I do, darn it," Annie said, pilfering through the pile of clothes. "God only knows why."

"It's because I see your authentic self and we connect on a soul level." Zipping up the frayed jeans and fastening the button, Harley gave her friend a sly grin.

"Girl, I almost threw up in my mouth a little. Save your fancy speeches for your newscasts and your boyfriends."

"Newscasts and boyfriends," Harley complained, prying the jeans off her thighs. "Newscasts would imply that I'm at the desk, which I'm not. I'm a beat reporter who had to do a story from the sewage plant today. So gross. And boyfriends... Don't even get me started." Accepting a black pencil skirt with a Dolce & Gabbana label, she stepped into it and pulled it to her hips. "Why couldn't Denton show an interest in me a few weeks ago, before Kip? Not that I'm entranced by Denton—far from it—but a little headway with him could land me the desk. Kip could be helpful in the long run, but not at the present moment."

"And what about that guy from the country club...what was his name again?"

Harley's eyes went wide as she stopped and turned to her friend. "Oh, I didn't tell you about that? The nerve of that guy! He asked me to drinks and I went to the club to meet him, which thankfully no one knew about except you, because while I was politely waiting for the hostess to acknowledge our reservation, someone introduced me to his wife."

"Nuh-uh," Annie blurted, showcasing just the level of surprise that Harley expected.

"Oh, I assure you, it happened." She withdrew the skirt from her ankles, unbuttoning her blouse and accepting a Carolina Herrera blue floral sleeveless dress. "Thankfully I hadn't said anything yet about who I was meeting. 'Confirming a reservation for Harley Laine,' is all I got out, and then we were introduced. She comes from a long line of horse-breeding families who have participated in the Kentucky Derby for decades. I had absolutely no idea he was married. And before you say anything, I have to get my foot in the door somehow, even if it means kissing a few frogs."

Looking at the dress on her frame, Harley suddenly straightened and glanced at her friend again. "Not to insinuate that I kissed him—I wouldn't dare. It was simply supposed to be a drink and a little flirting, to try to get some influence with the powers that be."

"Honestly, Harley, you should have more self-respect than that."

Sliding the dress back down to her ankles, she placed one hand on her hip as she gave her friend a weary sigh. "I have oodles of self-respect. Oodles." Glancing down, she suddenly laughed. "I don't suppose Faith brought any bras in her delivery today? I could use a couple new varieties."

Giving the once-over to her skinny friend who was standing in the middle of her store wearing only her undergarments, Annie simply grinned. "If she did, Human Barbie's brassiere would not fit you, dear."

"Ugh. You have wounded me to the deepest parts of my being, my anarchist friend. I cannot be cheered without the bestowing of fancy, overpriced shoes."

Without a word, Annie handed Harley a pair of Christian Louboutin pumps, black leather with several straps across the toes.

"Forgiven," Harley stated with a wink.

Headed south out of Louisville on I-65, Harley glanced toward the passenger seat of her BMW and her Wednesday score. Annie never charged her what she would have charged other store patrons, and for that Harley was grateful. Sweat began to bead on her upper lip, and she rolled the window down slightly to catch a breeze on the unseasonably warm autumn day. Her air conditioning had gone out on her car a couple months before, so she had learned to drive only in the morning and on her way home, so as not to wilt in the heat of the black leather interior.

For a split second, her eyes rested on the dark piece of tape stuck to the back of the seat next to her. Her car had once belonged to a drug dealer who had stabbed someone in the passenger seat and left a couple slash marks in the leather. It had become her car after a crash involving a police chase landed the vehicle at a junkyard. The man who worked there sold it to her with a salvage title, and had his kid brother perform most of the work for next to nothing. The outside looked perfect, but the inside?

It got her from point A to point B, usually while turning a few heads in the process, so it was of no consequence.

Living in the city would have been preferable, but on her salary, that would have meant a tiny studio apartment. She was ahead of most young women her age because she didn't have any student loan debt, which had enabled her to put forward a nice down payment for her home in the suburbs.

Pulling onto Wonder Lane, she paused her car for a young boy riding his bike down the middle of the road. Just past that, she came upon a woman hugging her little white dog to her chest like he was an infant. As she rounded the hill, a third person slowed her progress—this time a woman with a mass of auburn hair piled into a ponytail high on her head. When she didn't move over quickly enough, Harley gave her horn a quick blare and directed her gaze momentarily toward that jogger, noting that her face was slightly red and she looked rather winded.

Exactly why I do my interval training in my own home, Harley thought. *Don't want anyone to witness me looking bedraggled like that!*

Wonder Lane didn't offer any bustling city life; no, it was a boring center-of-America street with families and children and pets running loose. At the end of the street, though, tucked into the cul-de-sac, was the crown jewel of Wonder Lane: a stately Victorian-style white home built in 1903. Adorned with a two-story pedimented front porch with Corinthian columns and double doors on both levels, it rose like a watch tower over the smaller and more ordinary homes on Wonder Lane. It once belonged to a doctor, who built it for his wife in a secluded spot where she could plant her garden and her rosebushes. His granddaughter sold it to Harley for a fraction of what it could have been worth.

Parking the car in front of the home, Harley glanced up at the windows of those double doors that looked like they belonged on a palace for an antebellum southern belle. The exterior of her home was perfection, just like her car and her clothing. Grabbing her handbag and the items she picked up at The Revolving Closet, she locked her BMW and headed up the walk.

Unlocking the door to her little mansion, she stepped through into the foyer, looking at the hardwood floor and the large mirror on the wall. Everything about her home spelled grace and sophistication. She hung her handbag on a coatrack peg and slid her heels off to hold them in her fingers.

Home, sweet home.

To the left of the foyer sat the dining room, with the same hardwood floor and a large solid cherry dining table with an antique vibe. Those areas were all that could be seen without advancing further into the house, and the staircase to the second floor sat to the right, where Harley had a door installed when she moved in. She wanted to separate the two areas of the house, she said.

Pushing open the door, she grabbed her slippers from the first step. She didn't dare to walk up the stairs without something on her feet, since they were bare to the plywood and liable to give her splinters. Climbing up the stairs, Harley stopped at the first open door, which should have been a bedroom but served as her closet. The walls were vacant, with some of the beams exposed by rotting wood, and she had several metal clothing racks randomly placed throughout the room—her designer fashion collection hanging on them like prizes. A trail of shoes lined the wall, one next to the other like an army lining up for the catwalk.

She grabbed a couple hangers to add today's finds to her collection, then stepped down the hall into the next room, which served as her bedroom. One twin-sized bed sat along the corner, with a pink bath rug directly under it to protect her from the plywood.

The bed and the dining room table were her only pieces of furniture in the house. When she decided to make the purchase, she had enough for the down payment and the minor repairs on the outside of the home. She barely had enough left over to make the foyer look presentable, but that was the extent of her funds. Until she could afford to make improvements, at least she could keep up appearances should someone stop by.

Sitting on the bed, she flipped on her tiny television that was sitting on the floor near the wall, settling on a reality vocal competition. She would probably have to eat ramen noodles again that evening, but she didn't mind. One of her professors in college had given her advice that she took to heart: Dress for the job you want, not the job you have. Well, she was living the life she wanted, on the outside anyway. With any luck, the inside bits would follow shortly.

Chapter Two

Mornings always came early, but that was part of the life, and Harley didn't mind. In fact, she usually stayed at the station well after her hours were over, immersing herself in anything and everything imaginable. If she was going to earn the desk, she had to make herself indispensable. Since Mitch chastised her the day before about the sewer clip, she was especially interested in making a good impression.

Her Gucci python sandals seemed to be a good choice, so she paired them with a simple black shirt dress and a skinny red leather belt, topping it off with some red baubles around her neck. If the desk was given or taken away based on personal style, she had earned it ten times over. Unfortunately, Summer Davis was entrenched and seemed impervious to attempts to topple her from her throne.

Fifteen years Summer had been at the desk, and her age was beginning to wear on her. She no longer had that youthful glow she'd possessed when she was hired, and attempts were being made to cover the wrinkles about her eyes and adjust the harshness of the lights in the studio. She wasn't as svelte as she once was, either, and that didn't escape Harley's notice.

For her part, Harley avoided any weight gain like the plague. Some of the camera guys had a habit of bringing doughnuts into the break room, and she had witnessed Summer helping herself on more than one occasion. Her coworker wasn't what Harley would call overweight by any stretch of the imagination, but that didn't matter. Being in the public eye meant being subject to extra scrutiny.

Not long after she landed the reporting gig, Harley had been waiting on takeout at a local Chinese restaurant while some patrons were watching a weather report on one of the competitor stations.

"Looks like Millie needs to lay off the pizza," a young woman commented with a sharp laugh.

"No doubt," her companion agreed, all the while stuffing an eggroll into her mouth. "Look at the size of her booty. Yikes."

Poor Millie was a perfectly average weight. Sure, her situation wasn't assisted by the too-tight pants she was wearing, or the angle she had to maintain to point at the weather map, but she was significantly smaller than both those snippy women shoveling the orange chicken at their faces. Harley learned then and there that she never wanted to be judged in that way. Morning smoothies, meal replacement shakes at lunch, and ramen noodles for dinner were her usual meals after that point. She might indulge in some vegetables or lean meat during a date, and she allowed herself one slight splurge a week, but she wasn't about to be judged for her booty.

Well, unless it was in a complimentary way, and if...

No, not even then. Yuck.

Strolling into the studio, Harley slung her bag onto the floor next to her chair and settled before the desk to check her e-mail. She had been working on a couple public interest stories with the city and was waiting on some contacts to return to her with information, but so far no luck. What she did see, however, was an impassioned plea from a local resident forwarded from Mitch with the express wish that he would like to see her cover the story. Intrigued, she moved the arrow with her mouse to point it over the subject line. Need Help In Unfair Fight With City. Now that could be the ticket. She clicked twice.

Morning, Ms. Laine. Thought this would be right up your alley.
Mitch

A little buzz of excitement went through Harley's veins at the thought that this might be a great story, and she crossed the first two fingers of her left hand in anticipation.

Dear Channel Six... My name is Agnes Tuttle. Me and my husband have been fighting with the city about what we do on our own property. We want to tell you our story before they force us to... "Face palm. She should have known. "*...before they force us to take our chicken coop out of the yard. Please call me ASAP.*

So this was to be her punishment for yesterday's little slip of the tongue—she would be running around town chasing chickens. Perfect.

"Mrs. Tuttle, I presume." Harley stood a good two inches taller than the woman from a step below on her porch, partially aided by those Gucci heels.

"Yes, I'm Agnes Tuttle," the slight woman responded, shoving her screen door a little wider.

"I'm Harley Laine from Channel Six Action News."

"Oh, I recognized ya," she blurted quickly. "You look smaller on TV."

"Naturally, being in a relatively small box tends to make a person look...smaller, I suppose. I'm sorry, but I thought you were expecting us."

"Uh-huh, they told us you was coming."

Twisting her mouth slightly to the side, Harley bit her tongue. It seemed to her that, had her subject known the news reporters were coming, she might have taken care not to open the door in a faded blue t-shirt with Tweety Bird in the center, but she kept that thought properly locked deep within her brain.

Agnes ushered her inside, and she stepped timidly up into the house, glancing to make sure Kenny was behind her. The befuddled look on his face was not assisting matters, so Harley quickly assessed her surroundings. Brown and orange-speckled shag carpet that was permanently crushed in high-traffic areas covered the floor, assisted by two old worn-out forest green recliners and an off-white loveseat that looked like it was woven with brown and orange fibers right out of the carpet.

Harley fought the urge to shudder as one of two overweight, lazy Welsh Corgis was brushed off the loveseat by its owner. The other remained in the corner, taunting and perched like royalty atop a small red pillow.

"It's okay, Tipsy won't hurt ya none," Agnes insisted.

I'm going to kill Mitch. Sending me on this fool's errand to meet with a woman wearing a cartoon shirt and... Are those boxer shorts? Dear heavens, the woman's wearing boxer shorts with the flap propped open and the whole bit.

"Hello, Tipsy," Harley forced through her lips, settling herself gingerly next to the dog, who didn't even bother to glance in her direction. "Mrs. Tuttle, will your husband be joining us today?"

"He's at work." Plopping onto a recliner and tossing off her flip flops, she stared at her houseguests. "Can I get y'all something? Tea, maybe?"

"Certainly not," Harley instinctively reacted, immediately hearing Kenny's throat being cleared. "I mean, we're on the clock, Mrs. Tuttle, so we'll just stick with the business at hand so we don't waste your time. What can you tell me about the problem you're having?"

"Her name is Mildred Prescott."

Thank goodness I said no to the tea, because I would have just choked.

"Pardon me? I thought you had a problem with the city."

"Yeah, and it's all because of that Mildred Prescott. She lives across the street, and she's all the time complaining 'bout the noise and such. Been complaining 'bout the smell, too. There ain't no smell."

Harley's hesitance to breathe in was begging her to give a retort to that statement, but she lifted her hand to her face and pretended to be scratching her nose while she quickly inhaled.

"So, what you're saying is that your neighbors believe your pets are a nuisance?" Harley prodded, trying to get some pertinent statements quickly recorded so she could hastily depart.

"No, they don't have a problem with my pets. It's the chickens."

"And when you ask what the issue is with the chickens, what is the answer?"

"The noise and the smell, mostly."

"Your neighbors don't appreciate the fact that the chickens are loud and don't smell very pleasant."

"Seems now I told you that twice already."

It would seem that someone wearing boxer shorts to appear on television should not appear quite so smug.

"Yes, of course you did. Might we go outside and get a look at the problem?" Harley rose and began to walk toward the door, and Kenny quickly shot her a look and brushed his hand across his leg. "What, Kenny, are we playing charades?"

"No biggie, you're just covered in dog hair."

Looking down, Harley gasped audibly and began feverishly brushing against her black shirt dress, which was sporting tiny tan colored wisps of hair that appeared to be multiplying at an alarming rate.

"Don't just stand there, Kenny, help me!" Those lanky arms began pawing at her in a way that normally would have made her sock him in the eye, but she was frantic enough to allow him to smack at her hips and her backside in an attempt to swipe that hair away.

"Need some duct tape?" Agnes suggested. "It works wonders."

"Duct tape on my clothing?" Harley huffed as Kenny finally stood erect and widened his eyes. "Is it off? Please tell me it's off."

"Mostly," was Kenny's short reply.

Mostly. This is an even bigger nightmare than I imagined.

Without another word, Harley stalked out the front door, straight onto the lawn, where she let out her breath quickly and angrily. The instant she began to suck it back in, though, she clamped her hand over her mouth. The stench was truly horrible.

Turning, she locked eyes on Agnes coming down the steps. "Where are the chickens?"

"Just behind the house." She pointed towards the back of the yard, and Harley obligingly followed, even though her instincts were telling her to point those heels in the other direction.

"Kenny," she whispered, facing the cameraman, "you remember what I said yesterday about the sewer?"

"Um, yeah."

"I take it back. Every word." Stepping carefully, she barely avoided a pile of dog waste. At least, she thought it was dog waste. She wasn't entirely confident of that fact.

"We keep the chickens back here," Agnes informed them, standing with her legs slightly apart so the little flap in her boxers was sure to slightly open. "See, they sure ain't bothering no one."

Um, they are assaulting my senses as we speak. Eww.

"How many chickens do you have, Mrs. Tuttle?"

"Thirty-seven," she answered quickly. "'Twas thirty-eight, but one died last week. Bit by Tipsy."

Oh, the agony.

Harley gazed at the chicken wire wrapped around four metal posts, with one makeshift wooden lean-to chicken coop in the center. The site was certainly not impressive in any way, shape, or form. "Thirty-seven is certainly a large number of chickens for such a small area, don't you think?"

"Well, no, I don't think so. They have plenty of space."

"So, you're going to have to do what about the chickens?" Harley glanced down at her shoes and brushed a stray dog hair off the bottom of her dress.

"If Mildred gets her way, then the city will make me 'clean it up.'"

"Clean it up, that's all?"

"Who knows what 'clean it up' means?! For all I know, it means get rid of everything."

"I see," Harley muttered, glancing around at the disastrous mess. "Thank you very much, Mrs. Tuttle. I think I've got the information I need."

"That's it?" she complained. "You gonna go grill that Mildred?"

Fighting a chuckle, Harley stilled herself. "I will speak with Mildred, yes. I think I have enough to get started with the story."

"Alright." With a slight shrug, her "chicken victim" stepped toward the house, and Harley pondered the situation a moment. Thinking quickly, she turned to Kenny.

"We ready?" she asked, and Kenny nodded stoically. "In the game of life, what happens when a neighbor calls foul on the play? In this case, f-o-w-l. Agnes Tuttle believes her neighbors have no reason to complain, but do they have something to crow about? I'll have the full story at the top of the hour."

Allowing the camera to slide down a bit, Kenny gave her a questioning smile. "The top of the hour, huh?"

"He better give me the top of the hour. I'm pretty sure Mrs. Tuttle fertilizes her yard with chicken dung."

"Oh, yikes, that's sick."

"Tell me about it. Come on, let's go across the street and get to the bottom of this fiasco before I catch some sort of bird flu." Daintily stepping out of the yard, Harley wiped the bottom of her shoes against the street pavement, cringing at the harsh treatment of her beautiful sandals. They made a staccato tapping sound as she marched to the other side of the road, continuing their tap-tap up the sidewalk in the center of an immaculately groomed lawn. Stepping up to the front porch, she rapped on the door twice.

A moment passed, and then a woman of about fifty with a brown pixie cut opened the door a couple inches.

"Oh, good Lord," she breathed, shaking her head. "It's come to this, has it?"

"Good morning. I'm Harley Laine from Channel Six Action News, and I'm assuming you're Mildred Prescott?"

"The same."

"I was wondering if you might have anything to offer, other than the neighbor's yard is noisy and smells like feces? That was her stated complaint, and I certainly can't argue with those two issues."

"Are you going to be taping this? If so, can I at least put on some makeup first?"

"Spoken like a sane person," Harley stated with a laugh. "Sure, we'll wait."

Mildred walked back inside, and Harley cautiously lowered herself to the porch and dared a glance at the bottom of her shoes. Snapping a quick picture, she sent it to Mitch: *Thanks for the lesson, but next time, an actual stench-hole is not necessary.*

"Don't think I could live here, man," Kenny said, glancing back across the street. "That's just plain gross over there."

"Ya think?"

"Careful, you're slipping out of your careful reporter speak."

"Oh, shut up, Kenny. I have poop on my shoes. Surely that deserves a bit of a reprieve from being poised and polished. How is one supposed to be professional and unaffected when she's standing in fecal matter? That is a question I'd like to pose to Barbara Walters."

"Meh, she wouldn't stand in it. She'd throw a fit."

She probably would throw a fit. Oh, to be at the stage in my career where I could throw a fit and get away with it!

"Sorry about that," Mildred stated, returning to the porch. Kenny reached a hand out to haul Harley to her feet, and she turned toward her hostess.

"Mildred, can you give me your side of the story regarding these chickens?"

"Most certainly," she stated, appearing completely reserved and professional. "The homeowner's association clearly has a rule that states that no animals are allowed in the neighborhood besides dogs, cats, and inside pets. No horses, no goats, and no chickens. The Tuttles don't have a couple chickens—they have well over thirty. Does the smell bother me? Of course. Anyone who moves into the neighborhood and utilizes manure as a yard fertilizer would be a bit of a nuisance, but the Tuttles' complaint is not with me. Their complaint is with the homeowner's association, in violation of the agreement they signed when they purchased the home."

"Are there other members of the association that would attest to that?"

"Councilwoman Stewart is a part of our association. She would confirm our complaints, I'm certain."

"Very good. Thank you, ma'am, for your time. You don't need to worry about the story. I'm not sure what she's trying to prove, but she doesn't have much to stand on here."

"No, she doesn't. Thank you, young lady. You're my favorite reporter—you always have the cutesy little sayings that you throw in before the stories. I bet you'll do one on this, won't you?"

"Already done," Kenny tossed out.

"It's been a pleasure," Harley stated, shaking the woman's hand before stepping back to the van. Looking down at her phone, she caught a glimpse of Mitch's reply:

Drama, drama. Hope you got the story.

"Boring story, Harley. You made it sound good in the lead-up, but there's nothing there." Mitch flipped the video off and stared at the feisty young reporter across his desk.

"What do you want me to do, disparage the poor neighbor? That place smelled to high heaven. The woman had the bird feces spread all over her yard like fertilizer."

"I know, I saw the shoe." Chuckling, he crossed his arms over his protruding stomach. "Make the lady look crazy, then. Whatever works."

"What's your angle? You gunning against that councilwoman or something? Or trying to protect her?"

"Always so skeptical," Mitch muttered, grabbing a handful of peanuts from a glass jar on his desk. "No angle, just wanted to send you after the chickens. Now get out of here."

"That's cruel," she stated, pointing a finger at him accusingly. When all he did was grin, she rose and walked out into the hall. Passing the first office, she slipped by Summer standing in the doorway discussing a story with one of the producers. Harley knew Summer's form well—two inches taller, twenty pounds heavier, blonde hair cut into a bob that slid around her chin like two hands gently cradling her cheeks. Every day she wore a camisole covered by a blazer along with a pair of slacks—gray, brown, or black.

Summer's star was fading, and Harley could tell, but she was still the one with poop on her shoe. Summer would never be sent to do such a ridiculous story.

"Harley, got a sec?" Denton's voice broke into her thoughts. She paused in the hallway, taking two steps backwards.

"What's up?" she wondered as she stopped in his doorway, and he waved his hand for her to step inside.

"How's Kit?" Denton leaned back in his chair and placed his hands behind his neck, giving her a teasing grin. He was so quintessentially news anchor material, with his polished look and his handsome guy-next-door face. Sandy blond hair, light green eyes, always buttoned up and professional with a tie around his neck.

"His name is Kip, but to you he's Christopher," Harley told him with a sly grin. "He's perfectly fine, by the way. Thank you for asking."

"You practically have to be a Senator's son, with a name like Kip. His parents certainly labeled him well."

"As though you have room to talk, Denton Price. Your parents practically groomed you for the anchor desk the minute they gave you that moniker."

"And what about you, Harley Laine? You were certainly destined for the spotlight. Maybe not on the evening news, that name sounds more adult film industry—"

"Shut up, Denton. Did you call me in here to insult me?"

"Would I do that?" He gave her a winning smile and motioned for her to sit, which she did reluctantly. "What are you doing tomorrow night?"

"I have plans," she said simply.

"Kip plans?"

"As a matter of fact, yes. And please don't call him Kip. I have a feeling he would be perturbed if he knew I called him that here."

"No worries. I don't plan on calling him. I might call you, though."

"I won't be home, Denton," she told him again, rising from her seat.

"I might call anyway."

Pausing in the doorway, she gave him a flirty glance over her shoulder. "Get me the desk, and I might answer."

Chapter Three

Christopher Stanton knocked on the door promptly at 6:00, just as promised, and Harley swung the door open enthusiastically.

"Good evening, Kip," she said formally with a smile tugging at her lips.

"Good evening, Miss Laine. Are you slumming tonight? What gives with the outfit?"

Looking down, Harley took in her Rock Revival jeans, fitted black blazer over a sequined black tank, and open-toed booties. "Am I inappropriate?" It seemed like such a ridiculous question, but Kip seemed to be giving her a bit of a glare. His eyes were most definitely narrowed, and he wasn't grinning to hint of a teasing tone.

"I'm taking you to the club. Maybe a skirt?"

She instantly bristled, but attempted to remain breezy.

"Yeah, okay, I'll be right back down."

Disappearing through the doorway, she headed up the steps, tiptoeing in her boots so she wouldn't clomp on the wood. The club. She didn't even have to immerse herself in the Stanton world to know what it felt like—all political and posturing and putting the best foot forward. Apparently that foot could not go forward wearing jeans at the club.

As she slid the jeans down over her hips and grabbed a white skirt from a nearby rack, Harley glanced at the full length mirror and stuck her tongue out at her reflection. Stupid club. It would be really nice if Kip would take her on a real date for once, instead of forcing her to visit with his dad's stodgy business acquaintances. Still, networking could be good for her, and knowing a Senator's son could prove invaluable in the long run.

Giving herself a long glance in the mirror, she switched her shoes for some simple black pumps and sighed. Another Friday night of pretending, but she was dressed for the life she wanted, right? Something like that, anyway.

Heading back down the stairs, she pushed the door open at the bottom and emerged to find Kip standing there, patiently waiting in his standard gray suit and blue tie. She tried to remember if she had ever seen him in anything other than a suit, and couldn't recall a single instance.

"Better?" she wondered cautiously.

"You're a vision of perfection," he indicated, stepping forward to gently brush his lips against her cheek. "Shall we?"

Harley allowed him to lead her out onto the porch and in the direction of his Cadillac Escalade, which was parked next to her BMW. He opened the door for her to step inside, and she pulled herself up into the vehicle. Daring a slight glance at him as he opened his own door, she gave a quick smile. Kip wasn't what she would call dazzlingly handsome, but he was definitely passable and distinguished. He possessed very fair skin, which caused his caramel brown eyes to stand out more than they probably would otherwise. His nose was slightly crooked, but not to the point that it was distracting. He was pleasant and well-versed in current events, so there was usually easy conversation.

So why did dating him feel like an extended job interview?

Brushing the thought aside, she peered out the windshield to the front of her home and smoothed the skirt across her knees.

"I saw your piece about the chickens, darling. Riveting stuff."

Harley wrinkled her nose, not particularly about the chickens, but more in response to the affectionate phrase. Kip's habit of calling her darling was beyond annoying.

"Oh? Riveting, Mr. Stanton? Pray tell what you found so riveting about poultry."

Glancing over his right shoulder as he backed out of the driveway, he offered just enough of a pause that Harley knew he would be teasing her.

"Poultry I could not care less about, to be honest, but you looked stunning in that black dress you had on, going on about fowl and having something to crow about. While I was watching you, I thought, 'Now there's a woman I can feel proud to have by my side.'"

"Well then, I suppose one good thing came out of that chicken nightmare, although I'm sure I'll have a hefty cleaning bill for getting all the dog hair off that black dress."

He laughed—a slight, reserved laugh, but she supposed it was all she could expect from the buttoned-up Christopher Stanton. The only thing that ever surprised her about him was that he allowed her to call him Kip, but she suspected he wouldn't have done even that if she hadn't heard his mother use the nickname first.

On the way to the club, he regaled her with tales from his past week of practicing law, which included two business deals gone awry that admittedly could not hold her interest past the first couple sentences. She didn't find his profession boring, to be truthful, but she absolutely found his manner of relating the relevant facts less than interesting. It was like picking up a much-hyped audiobook only to find the narrative was all given in monotone.

Staring at the passenger window, Harley gazed into her own eyes, raising them to accentuate her own little private joke.

Can you believe he's droning on and on about business law?

Come on, let's pop open the door and hop out into the street.

"That is the important thing, don't you think, darling?"

Raised from her stupor, she turned her eyes back to her companion. "Oh, of course. Certainly." He sounded like he wanted her to agree with whatever it was, and surely he hadn't proposed anything too ridiculous.

"You seem slightly distracted tonight. Not mulling over an ambush of city leaders or anything, I hope."

"Would that be so terrible?" she suggested, knowing full well that he absolutely *would* think it was terrible.

"I like that you're driven, but I do hope you'll tone it down for a bit. Especially after tonight."

Her first instinct was to be annoyed at being ordered to "tone it down," but his cryptic mention of the evening's future piqued her interest.

"What's happening tonight?"

"You'll see," he stated, reaching over and placing his hand atop hers against her knee. "I think you'll be pleasantly surprised."

"Harley, dear, when are they going to give you a nice studio job at that station, instead of sending you out after ridiculous stories?" Mrs. Stanton asked, fake kissing Harley on one cheek and then the other. As the elder woman grabbed Harley's wrist, it took every ounce of strength the younger woman could muster not to gawk at the gaudy new diamond on the woman's right hand. "It's just such a waste, my darling, when they could have you doing the real news stories. Covering politics and such—that should be your focus instead of chasing frivolities across the city."

She happened to wave her hand in front of Harley's face at that precise moment, mentioning frivolities as the ring danced in front of her eyes.

"From your lips to God's ears, Mrs. Stanton," Harley answered politely, offering a pageant-approved smile. "Perhaps if Senator Stanton put in a good word for me, I'd make some headway."

"If he were around for five minutes at a time to do so..." she trailed off, glancing around the large room for her husband. "Thank heavens Frankfurt's not too far from Louisville, or I might never see the man."

Harley pretended to laugh as she scanned the room herself, not seeing Senator Stanton or his lookalike offspring. Instead, they were interrupted by a couple of Mrs. Stanton's acquaintances, and the night took to idle prattle.

Thirty-five minutes later, when the two couples finally settled down to dinner, Harley had barely taken a sip of her sparkling water when Kip's fork tapped delicately on the side of his wine glass, a small smile appearing on his face.

"Mother, Father, Harley," he began, "I have an announcement. I've been doing some serious thinking about my future, and I've come to a conclusion about possibly the biggest decision I'll have to make in my life." Her breath caught in her throat as Harley realized she sincerely hoped he wasn't talking about her. "I'm thirty-two years old, and I'm not getting any younger. There just comes a time when you have to go after your dreams, and not hold anything back." For some reason, Harley's mind shot back to the gaudy diamond she saw just a while before, and her blood nearly froze in her veins. Afraid to look at Kip, she stared at her plate. "That's why I want to share this moment with you three, who I care most about. I've decided to enter the election for the U.S. House of Representatives."

Oh, thank God.

Realizing she was nearly prepared to hyperventilate, Harley grabbed her water and took a cautious sip as the Stantons congratulated their son on his wise decision. If she needed any realizations about her relationship with Kip, the fact that hearing him talk about his life's goals sent her into a near panic might have been a wake-up call. Nearly trembling, she placed the glass back on the table.

"What do you think, Harley?" Kip looked at her expectantly, so she swallowed and reminded herself to choose her words carefully.

"Of course I think it's wonderful, and you'll do well."

"You won't mind being thrust into the public eye with me? I would imagine Mitch would keep you well away from political stories, so there wouldn't seem to be a conflict of interest."

No! I'll be relegated to chickens forever.

"Maybe Harley should leave reporting entirely," Senator Stanton piped up. "You'd be great as a lobbyist, young lady. I'd be happy to make some contacts for you."

"Thank you, Senator, but I'm sure some arrangements can be made." Schmoozing patrons of the club was bad enough—she couldn't imagine having to sit around with fake politicians for a living. The mere thought made her want to go running into the hills.

"We'll discuss it later," Kip insisted, placing his arm around her shoulders, his hand resting limply against her back.

"Of course, there will be plenty of time for that," Senator Stanton agreed. "If you all will excuse me, I have some business to take care of."

"As do I," Mrs. Stanton added, rising from her chair. "Do enjoy the rest of your dinner, you two."

Harley barely noticed their retreat, because she was imagining the next year of her life: Fundraising dinners, press conferences, public forums. She would be forced to stand on the sidelines, politely nodding and keeping her mouth shut. What if Kip said something ridiculous? She would just have to pretend that she agreed.

And she hadn't even given any thought to being Lady Stanton—Kip was simply a diversion who allowed her to press her own flesh in the game of high-powered politics. She wanted to report on the races, not be involved in them. If he wanted her to be by his side, he obviously had long-term plans that involved her. He wouldn't want to appear at his speaking engagements with a woman he was casually dating.

What if he believed something that was totally against her beliefs? Something she was passionate about?

Was she even passionate about anything, other than getting her foot in a door? Any door?

And the occasional fantastic fashion score?

"What ticket?" she asked cautiously.

"Ticket? What do you mean?" He withdrew his arm and reached for his wine glass.

"I mean, are you running as a Republican? Democrat? Independent? Libertarian? For the Green Party? Constitution Party? Communist? Anarchist?"

"Very funny," he told her with a smirk. "Republican, naturally."

"Because you agree with Republican principles? What's your platform? What are your fundamental beliefs?"

"Fundamental beliefs," he repeated in a mocking tone. "My fundamental belief is that Kentucky is a predominantly red state, so if I want to get elected, I'm presenting myself as a Republican. Take off your reporter hat for the evening, would you?"

"I'm sorry, but that statement amounts to an egregious breach of trust to anyone who would dare to vote for you. You have to stand for something, Christopher. If you don't, you're going to be nothing but another one of the faceless weasels who will do or say anything to remain in power."

"Which ticket would you have me choose, then? I should go all idealistic, I suppose, and forego winning as a matter of principle?"

"I can't believe we're having this conversation." Turning in her chair, she faced him. "I'm not telling you to be one party or another, I'm telling you to have some values. Deep inside, in your soul and in your heart, you have to believe in certain things—espouse certain things. When you know what those are, then you can champion your cause confidently, no matter which ticket it is."

"Even as a Communist?" he asked, narrowing his eyes. "Honestly, Harley…"

"I'm just saying you shouldn't be disingenuous. Are you a Republican?"

"Some parts of me might be."

"Then you're a Democrat?"

"On some issues…"

She fought the urge to let out an annoyed sigh. "So run as an Independent. Why is that so difficult?"

"Because I don't intend to lose."

"Yuck," she blurted, rising from her seat. "How can you expect me to stand by and support you when you don't even know what your principles are? Or when you won't be honest about them, anyway?"

"Give me a break, Harley. What do you stand for?"

"I don't know," she blustered with exasperation. "Truth. Justice. The American way."

"So you're Superman?" he asked with a sharp laugh. "Harley Laine, not Lois Lane. You've got your first name confused, I believe."

"Well, at least you *believe* something," she retorted, grabbing her water and draining the glass before she turned to step away. "Don't bother getting up, Kip. I'll get a cab."

Chapter Four

Harley couldn't put her finger on what exactly set her off at dinner, but the minute she reached the lobby of the club to call for a cab, she felt slightly foolish. She hadn't heard anything over that table that she didn't already know, but the thought of standing idly by while she pretended to agree with Kip's political positions hadn't rested well. To add insult to injury, the fact that the Senator actually suggested she give up her reporting career, when she wasn't even in a committed relationship with his son…

No, Harley had goals and dreams of her own, and none of them included being a trophy girlfriend for a future representative.

The cab arrived quickly and took her towards home, and Kip didn't come looking for her. He didn't call, either. In fact, by the time she was halfway to Wonder Lane, she had glanced at her phone several times in disgust. When there were only a couple miles left, she finally felt it buzzing against her leg, and she picked it up with a smug grin on her face.

"Harley Laine," she stated haughtily, waiting for Kip's apology.

"And you said you wouldn't answer the phone."

Not the voice she expected.

"Denton. I told you I was busy this evening."

"And yet you answered the phone. Where is the heir to the political dynasty?"

If Kip did run for office, he would be the third generation to do so. Harley didn't relish the reminder.

Pausing to ponder her response, she squinted her eyes. "I cut him loose…for the evening, anyway. He was boring me to tears."

"Come out with me, Harley. I'll pick you up. Tell me where you live, and I'll be there in ten minutes."

"I don't live in the city, Denton."

"Then I'll be there in twenty minutes. Thirty at the most."

Laughing, she shook her head. "Good night, Denton."

"I won't stop asking. Good night, Harley."

Pushing the end button on her phone, she wondered why she had been hesitant. Just a couple months before, she would have welcomed a phone call from Denton. Coming off the heels of the evening at the club, though, the thought wasn't appealing.

The cab pulled into her driveway at the end of Wonder Lane, and she almost handed him a few bills as she slid out of the car, but then she thought better of it. Asking him to wait for her, she strolled back up to the front porch in her heels. Her stomach growled in protest before she even reached the house, and she groaned to herself when she realized she'd barely eaten two bites of her salmon at the club.

Every Friday night it was the same—she would go to some ridiculous function with the Stantons, and then when she was returned to her home, she would hesitate only long enough to make sure Kip was safely gone before venturing back out into the night.

She carefully unlocked her front door and stepped inside, closing the door and locking it behind her. The stairway always seemed precarious and creepy in the dark, with only the exposed light bulb hanging overhead. She removed her shoes at the foot of the stairs and held them with her first two fingers on her left hand, sliding her toes into the slippers before she marched upwards. Stopping in the first bedroom, she returned the shoes to their spot along the wall and carefully shrugged out of the skirt, hanging it back where she had hastily grabbed it earlier. She slid off the blazer as well, placing it on a hanger. She momentarily considered continuing to wear the black sequined tank, but decided to discard it also.

Wearing only her underthings, she stepped across the hall into the bathroom and stared at her reflection in the mirror. Harley Laine-Stanton. She could already see the entire non-future stretched out in front of her like a boring Stepford wife nightmare. Releasing a shudder, she plunged her fingers into her cheap cold cream and began rubbing it onto her face.

As soon as her skin was cosmetics-free, she pulled out her eye makeup remover and began gently erasing any traces of mascara and eyeliner. When she was in full "mask" she could convince herself she was truly a great reporter who deserved the news desk and had great potential in life, but stripped bare, all she saw in the mirror was innocent Harley—a slightly nervous teenager who wanted to make something of her future but felt inadequate and ill-prepared. Staring back into those amber eyes, she simply studied her own face.

"What do you believe, Harley?" she whispered.

Truth, justice, and the American way. You might as well be running for political office yourself.

Taking a deep breath, she bent over and flipped her hair forward, pausing upside down as she wound an elastic band around the base of the makeshift ponytail, twisting it around itself until she had a little topknot that had wisps of hair poking out haphazardly. She wasn't Harley Laine when she looked that way—she was Harley *Elaine*, and she knew it.

Giving herself a knowing grin, she slipped back into the closet/bedroom and reached for a pair of ratty boyfriend jeans, pairing them with a simple white T-shirt and a military jacket in olive green. A quick grab of her black Converse, and she was ready.

Normally she drove her own car to town, but she didn't feel like being alone, so she would spend the night with Annie in the city. She didn't want the hassle of finding a parking spot near Annie's building, so taking the cab would be much easier.

Twenty minutes later, the cabbie glanced up in his rear view mirror.

"You sure this is the place?"

"Of course I'm sure. I come here every Friday night."

Glancing at the man sitting outside on the park bench, gray-streaked beard reaching halfway down his chest, wearing a slightly dirty blue t-shirt with a bald eagle screen print, the cabbie merely shrugged his shoulders.

"Okay, miss." Harley dutifully handed him the cab fare and exited the door, stepping in front of the bench the cabbie had just been eyeing.

"Harley, that you taking a cab?" the grizzly gentleman wondered. "Where's that car of yours?"

"It's safe at home, Duke."

"You drunk?"

His bluntness caused Harley to laugh. "No, I'm not. Are you?"

"Life would probably make a heap more sense if I was. But I'm not. Date didn't feed you enough again?"

"They never do. Why is that?"

"You need to find yourself a real man's all," he called to her as she walked toward the front of the building.

"Well, if you happen to see one, send him my way," was her reply. Grabbing the door handle, she pulled it open and walked across the little hole-in-the-wall restaurant, stepping up to the bar.

"There's my little friend," she heard from her left. Turning, she grinned up at the man she visited every Friday night.

"Tiny, what have you got for me tonight? It's been a ramen noodle week. I think I had yogurt twice. Oh, and two bites of salmon earlier."

"Miss Harley, you make me sad," he said, hulking over her with his big frame. Nearly 6'5" and built like a building, he made her feel like a child. "You oughtta come by here more often and let me feed you, girl."

"It's tempting, believe me, but I don't want to be as big as a house."

He grinned, his white teeth a stark contrast against his dark skin. "You don't got no worries there, I'd imagine. Don't worry though…I'll get you fixed up right quick." He rubbed a large hand against his shaved-smooth head, and she merely nodded.

One splurge a week she allowed herself, and it was always Tiny's. He had the best home cooking she had found in all of

Louisville—on a shoestring budget, at least. Most meals were under ten dollars, but lately Tiny hadn't been asking for payment at all. She realized he probably thought she was down on her luck, or practically starving, and she never divulged any information. Tiny and Duke might have been the only two people in town who hadn't seen her on television enough to recognize her face.

"I'm thinking you look like you need a cheeseburger with a big pile of bacon on top," Tiny offered, twisting his mouth slightly in a questioning manner.

"Keep talking like that, and I'm liable to fall in love with you," Harley joked. Tiny chuckled and headed back to the kitchen. Locating a seat directly behind her, she slumped into it and slid down, her knees stretched out in front of her and her head resting against the wooden chair's back. She hadn't expected the life she was creating for herself to prove so difficult, but some weeks she felt more like an actress than a reporter. It felt like a true release to just slouch like a goofy kid for five lousy minutes.

"I think we got a bit too much grease on this thing," Tiny stated when he reemerged carrying a plate holding a delicious-looking cheeseburger in his hand. "You not gonna want this burger, right?"

"Please don't torment me," Harley begged, sitting up straighter. "That burger looks about perfect from where I sit."

"You sure? I can have him make another one." He didn't wait for her to answer, but simply placed it in front of her as he settled into the other chair at her table. "Salmon, huh? When you gonna bring one of your dates 'round this place?"

"Oh, no," she stated around a mouthful of food, lifting her hand to her lips so she wouldn't feel quite so self-conscious about talking with her mouth full. "The guy is supposed to take me on a date, right? So far none of them have suggested this place. I tell you what, though—if any one of them ever did, I might marry him on the spot."

"You shouldna told me that. What if I go find all the young men I know and tell them to ask you to dinner at old Tiny's?"

"I'd be having a lot of really good meals then, I suppose. You know a lot of young men, do you?"

"I'm sure I'd know a lot more if they knew you was in here." An easy smile spread across his cheeks as he wrinkled his nose a bit. "Most young men I know wouldn't let you be alone at eleven o'clock on a Friday night, though. Seems like a waste."

"One night is just like any other, right?" She paused as she thought about the fact that she sounded a little cynical. "Anyway, maybe I like being alone. No guy would sit here and watch me eat this slab of beef with a straight face."

"They'd have to tell you that you got mustard on your cheek."

"Why would they do that?"

"Cause you do, hon," he stated with a laugh. "You got mustard on your cheek."

"Oh," she muttered, grabbing her napkin and swiping at her face. "Thanks."

"You want anything else, or can we close up the kitchen?"

"I'm sorry, Tiny," she said with an apologetic sigh. "You must think I'm incredibly selfish, always popping in here when you're about to close up."

"Are you kiddin'?" He grinned as he stood, reaching one large hand over to pat her on the shoulder. "I'd have closed up an hour ago if it weren't for waiting for your pretty self. You're my favorite customer, my little friend."

"You just made my night." Tears inadvertently filled her eyes, and she blinked to fight them back. "Now why would I need to find some date when I can come here and have you butter me up like that?"

"Why indeed?" he wondered with a smirk. "Milk or dark?"

"Surprise me," she said with a grin. Reaching behind the counter, he pulled out a purple-wrapped bar of dark chocolate. "Thank you, Tiny. You know I love you. Will you let me pay you this time?"

"You know your money's no good here, Miss Harley. Just take care of yourself and keep visiting me on Friday nights, and we'll call it even."

"I can do that." Accepting the candy from his palm, she gave him a winning smile before walking back to the front door. "Next Friday?" she asked as she turned to glance at him. He merely waved and smiled.

Stepping back out into the night, Harley walked to the bench beside the sidewalk and parked herself next to Duke, not saying a word. Without bothering to look at him, she reached her right hand toward him and offered the candy bar, just like she did every Friday night. And, just like every other Friday night, Duke took it from her and broke it in half, passing one section back across the bench.

"How you managing to get home?" Duke wanted to know, popping a piece of the chocolate into his mouth.

"I was kind of hoping *you* might drive me home," she slyly stated, turning her head slightly to the left so he wouldn't see her smile.

"Now I would, if I could remember where I left my bike." She laughed, and he chuckled a bit in return.

"Because you're a 'Harley man,' I know. That never ceases to be funny no matter how many times you tell me."

"The dripping sarcasm would tell me otherwise."

Allowing a slight laugh to slip out, she really studied her companion.

"What can I do for you, Duke? Is there something I can do for you?" Continuing to peer at his face, she stared at his eyes—steel gray and gazing into the distance.

"You're good people," he finally answered. "I can tell good people. I don't need anything. I got the clothes on my back and the kindness of friends, and the good Lord saw fit to keep the air pumping into my lungs today."

"All about perspective," she acknowledged.

"That it is. That it is." Turning to appraise his seatmate, Duke reached up to scratch his cheek under his beard. "You never did tell me how you're getting home."

"Going to call a cab." At that verbal reminder, she pulled her phone out of her pocket. The screen was black, and when she hit the button to try to power it back up, nothing happened.

"Problem?" Duke wanted to know.

"Dead phone." She laughed sardonically at her misfortune. "Figures."

"The Lord works in mysterious ways," Duke added cryptically.

Mysterious. Guess I'll find out how safe the streets of Louisville are at night, because it's several blocks to Annie's from this point.

A humming noise broke into Harley's thoughts, and a hand shot down between her shoulder and Duke's, offering a familiar smelling delight wrapped inside aluminum foil.

"Here you go, brother," the voice said, handing Duke the burger.

"Thank you," he replied, brightening a bit. "Harley, have you met my friend, Ryan? You need a traveling companion, and Ryan is most likely available."

Shaking her head, Harley let out a sigh. "Being pawned off on strangers as a hopeless case is my favorite type of introduction," she began, turning slightly.

"You're in luck, because I have a soft spot for hopeless cases." The new individual reached his hand out toward her, and she twisted enough to offer him her hand in return. "Ryan Temple." The firm handshake was the first thing she noticed, right before her eyes lifted casually up his arm until they rested on the edge of a rather large-looking tattoo near his shoulder, the bottom of which was peeking out under the sleeve of his black T-shirt.

"Harley Laine," she stated cautiously. Lifting her eyes a few more inches revealed a thin line of facial hair under his bottom lip in a dark-chocolate shade, but an otherwise clean-shaven face accentuated by friendly dark blue eyes.

"So you're Tiny's reporter friend that he dotes on every Friday night," Ryan assessed with a laugh, removing his hand from hers. "Nice to meet you."

The verbal acknowledgement that Tiny definitely knew exactly who she was greeted Harley as a bit of a shock. She continued to gaze curiously at the man in front of her, noting the dark hair that rested near his shoulders underneath a gray stocking cap.

"So, what's this about needing to travel?" He tried to avoid a smile as he asked the question. She wasn't sure how she realized he was avoiding said smile, but she definitely realized it, and it made her feel somewhat defensive.

"My friend Harley needs a ride home," Duke spoke up, eliminating her need to say anything.

"That's all?" Ryan asked breezily. "You want to come inside for a minute, I'll get you taken care of."

"If you're sure…"

"He's a good guy, I promise you. No worries." Duke obviously meant his comment to make her feel at ease, but accepting a ride from a man she just met didn't seem particularly intelligent. Still, if she went inside, maybe she could convince him to let her use a phone.

Rising, she followed him into the restaurant, where he began wiping down the counter while she stood uncomfortably near the door.

"It shouldn't be a minute. Tiny seemed tired, so I sent him home and told him I'd lock up."

"I've never seen you here before."

His shirt sleeve moved up as he rubbed his rag over a stubborn spot, revealing more of his tattoo and scrolling letters. "I'm never here on Fridays. Tiny's brother's usually in the kitchen, but he's under the weather tonight. Anyway, it's all good, because now I've finally laid eyes upon Tiny's favorite customer. I can sleep a little more soundly tonight."

"Funny," she muttered, crossing her arms over her abdomen protectively. "What days do you usually work, then?"

"Every day," he offered, but then laughed when she squinted in his direction. "Not here, though. I'm only here on special occasions, when Tiny needs some extra assistance. Plus, I need the cash."

"He wouldn't let me pay him for the burger. Can I pay you?"

The suggestion caused him to let out a quick breath, and he shook his head. "If Tiny said you don't pay, what kind of man would I be if I let you pay me after he left the building? You *are* his special friend, after all."

"He said that?"

"No, but he stayed open an extra half-hour after everyone else left waiting on his little reporter, so I surmised as much."

Feeling guilty, she glanced at the floor. "I'm really sorry about that."

"Why? I thought it was fascinating. Now I'm wondering if *you're* fascinating."

"Because?"

"Because Tiny's right." He straightened up and gazed over at her, staring her right in the eye. "There's got to be some story behind you showing up here every Friday night."

She wasn't overly fond of the way he was looking at her, as though somehow he saw directly through her.

"Or maybe I just like greasy food," she offered.

"Perhaps," he agreed with a slight twinkle in his eye. "Here's the thing, though... You don't look like you usually eat a lot of greasy food. Also, I happen to be a pretty good listener, and I have ice cream."

"Ice cream."

"Yep. You haven't had ice cream until you have a Caramel Delight via yours truly." He offered up an irresistible grin, and she couldn't help but return a small smile. "You can't say no." Stepping toward the kitchen, he turned back and pointed to her in an effort to gauge her answer.

"What? I thought I couldn't say no?"

"Yes," he said with a wink, disappearing around the corner. Feeling slightly flustered, she pulled a chair out and sat down gingerly, placing her elbows on the table. She should have wanted to get to Annie's so she could relay the events of the evening and make sure she hadn't overreacted to Kip's announcement, but she strangely felt planted to that chair.

"Okay, I know you like chocolate," he stated, returning from the kitchen. "Well, Tiny said you always get a chocolate bar after you eat. But he also said that you give it to Duke when you leave, so do you not really like it? I should have asked you that before."

For the first time he looked a little unsure of himself, and she tried not to smile. "I love chocolate, actually. I had no idea Tiny did so much spying on me. Here I thought I was incognito."

Rather than reply, he set a glass bowl in front of her. "Caramel, chocolate, secret ingredient." Sitting across from her, he pulled off his stocking cap, revealing hair that was falling to his shoulders in the center but short on the sides, like a massively overgrown mohawk.

"Wait, secret ingredient? No, I can't eat it. I mean, I'm allergic to nearly everything imaginable. What's the secret?"

"What specifically are you allergic to? I can't give away my secret." One corner of his mouth crept upwards, and she glanced at her ice cream.

"Honestly, nothing. I just wanted to see how easily you'd crack."

"Well played," he said with a shake of his head. Reaching for his spoon, he paused when he heard her laugh quietly. "What's funny? Is it my hair? I have hat hair, don't I?" Lifting both hands, he raked his fingers from the front to the back of his head.

"No, your hair is very...whatever vibe you're going with there."

"Ouch." Dragging his spoon over the ice cream in his bowl, he mixed the flavors together. "I take it you don't approve."

"Hmm..." She lifted her index finger to her lip and pretended she was thinking. "Are you a tattoo artist?"

"No."

"Are you with the carnival?"

He began laughing as he put his hand on his cheek. "Um, no."

"Are you now, or have you ever been, in a rock band?"

"Perhaps. Does that make a difference?"

"No, actually," she said, offering a manipulative smile. "I just wanted to torment you a bit."

He appeared to think things over while he placed a spoon of ice cream in his mouth. "So, wait... Does that mean you like it, or you don't?"

"Yes."

"You are a horrible person, you know that? You're easy to talk to, though."

Harley paused with the ice cream partway to her lips, because his comment came as a surprise. No one ever accused her of being easy to talk to. He was looking down at his bowl, so she took a few seconds to study his face before she answered. He wasn't classically handsome in the traditional sense like Denton, but there was something about that face that told her she could just stare at him for hours. Unnerved by her own thoughts, she shoved the spoon in her mouth and paused while the trio of flavors melted against her taste buds.

"I'm not a horrible person," she finally told him. "I mean, I hope not. I was trying to be funny, but I actually really like your look. Not for the masses or anything, but on you. It sort of fits."

"As long as I work in a tattoo parlor," he retorted with a grin. "Oh well. At least I'm not one of those news reporters, you know, running around stepping in chicken poo all day."

"Now you're making fun of me," she said, digging into her ice cream again.

"Sorry, I couldn't resist. What's a girl like you hanging around here on Friday nights for anyway? You don't have some high-powered lawyer or doctor boyfriend to take you out on the town?"

"Oh, I go out every Friday night," she stammered, feeling a bit of heat rise into her neck. "Usually, but then I come here afterwards. It's my end of the week reward, so to speak."

"Reward for?"

Yikes, I'm not sure. Keeping up pretenses?

"A job well done, I guess. A good week. Anyway, I do have a boyfriend, or I did, but I'm not sure if I do now."

"Do I want to know?" He offered a smile that caused a little flip in the pit of her stomach, and she tried to pretend she didn't notice.

"Why am I talking to you about this? I don't even know you." When he took that opportunity to wink, she rolled her eyes. "Okay, if you must know, he decided that he wants to run for political office."

"How could he?" he teased, shoving a heaping spoonful of caramel into his mouth.

"And," she continued with a slight glare, "he wants me to stand by his side and be supportive."

"The nerve of some people."

Laughing, she slapped her hand on the table. "Will you let me get through the explanation without a running commentary, please?" He gave a sheepish look, and she mentally regrouped. "So, as I said, he wants me to be supportive. The problem is, when I asked him which ticket he was running on, he said he was going to choose the one he imagined was most likely to get him elected. He has no backbone. He's not willing to stand up for what he believes, if he even believes in something. That feels like a deal breaker. Am I overreacting?"

He sobered a little and looked like he was giving the idea some serious consideration. "So he's basically being a politician."

"Would you date a wishy-washy politician?" she wondered, feeling a need to defend herself.

Shaking his head, he stopped eating and focused solely on her. "No, I wouldn't."

"Well, then we have something in common," she muttered, going back to her ice cream. For a moment he was silent as they both spooned through the last of their caramel, and then he stood to retrieve her bowl. Without a word, he leaned down just enough that she noticed a faint hint of cologne along with the greasy food smell, and a warm feeling rushed over her as she inhaled quickly and turned her face the other way.

I know you did not just get all swoony over a guy who smells like a hamburger. Wake up, Harley!

"I stink, don't I?" he asked with a quick chuckle, and she turned precisely in time to find herself inches from his face.

"Um, no." Thinking quickly, she glanced at his arm. "How many tattoos do you have?"

"Wow," he breathed, leaning his backside against the table and remaining dangerously close to her. "That's a pretty personal question."

"I'm sorry," she whispered, averting her eyes.

He began pulling his shirt up over his abdominal muscles, and she fought the urge to bolt.

"One," he stated, pointing to the side of his ribcage. "Anchor, I think it's kind of cool. And hope, because hope's the anchor for the soul and all that."

So my attempt to distance myself wound up with him placing his bare abdomen in my face. Nice.

Leaning back, he lifted his shirt higher, until it was almost to his neck. "Two, forgiven." He pointed to the word that started at one collarbone and stretched to the other. "Pretty self-explanatory."

With one deft move, he had the front of his shirt down and had lifted the back over his head, so it was bunched around his neck. Twisting, he turned his back to Harley. "Three, eagle—rise up with wings like eagles." He gestured to indicate the tattoo on his right shoulder blade, as though she didn't already know. "And four...the cross. Saved." When he turned and motioned to the final tattoo, she could see that it stretched from his upper arm all the way up to his shoulder and halfway to his neck.

"A simple 'four' would have sufficed," she mumbled, watching him replace his shirt. "You obviously have no filter."

"Sorry," he said, dropping his head and shaking it solemnly. "I'm not usually so forthcoming, but you're just..."

"...easy to talk to, I know."

Rather than respond, he simply carried the bowls into the kitchen, and Harley stood and put her palms on either side of her head.

Knock it off, Harley. You are not allowed to be attracted to a fry cook who is covered with tattoos and has an unconventional hairstyle. Are you insane?

Gazing out at the street lights, she looked toward the bench on the sidewalk and noticed that Duke was gone. Her mind drifted back to Ryan giving him the burger, and the thought made her feel a little warmer inside.

"Ready?" he asked, startling her enough that she jumped a bit. "I'm all done in here, if you are."

"Yes, of course. Listen, thanks for the ice cream."

"Any time, seriously," he said with a hint of a smile, and Harley had a sneaking suspicion that he meant it. He led her out the front door and locked it carefully behind them before dropping the keys in the pocket of his jeans. They strolled a few feet down the sidewalk, and then he swung himself over the park bench, sitting at the top with his feet resting on the seat. "So, back to this boyfriend of yours."

"Ex-boyfriend," she insisted, feeling immediately ridiculous for having done so.

"Ah, I like this turn of events, I think," he added flirtatiously, practically begging her to sit on the bench just by pulling her in with his eyes. Unable to stop herself, she sat along the edge, far enough away that she couldn't see his face. He countered by lowering himself to the seat and sliding a little closer.

"What about him?" she wanted to know, feeling slightly nervous at his closeness.

"Why him? What was it about him that first got your attention?"

"Honestly, I don't know. It never seemed serious, so I didn't give it a lot of thought. He was just a diversion, really." She could feel his eyes upon her, and she responded by focusing her gaze out onto the street.

"You don't seem like the kind of person who would go after diversions."

"What's that supposed to mean?" she questioned, turning to face him. "I'm a fun person when the opportunity presents itself."

"Whoa, who said you weren't fun?" he wondered, wrinkling his brow. "I just meant you don't seem like the time-wasting type."

She fought to drag her eyes away from his, and when she managed to do so, she realized with a jolt that her gaze was drifting across his cheek, his nose, his lips...

"No," she said more forcefully than she intended. "I'm not really the time-wasting type."

"You like music?"

"Why do you ask?"

"You asked if I was in a rock band, so I thought maybe you were a closet groupie or something."

"Very funny," she said with a short laugh. "No, I'm not a groupie, but I like music. Quite a lot, actually."

"What are you passionate about?"

Her heart leapt to her throat, and she fought to swallow. At the moment she couldn't quite work past the passionate desire to drag her finger across that little trail of hair under his lip. Fighting a blush, she attempted to smile.

"Wow, I don't know if anyone's ever asked me that," she began, pausing to collect her thoughts. "I guess I'm passionate about finding out the truth, uncovering things, digging under proverbial rocks, so to speak."

"Why?"

What was it with this man?

"Why?" For some reason she thought back to dinner at the club, and she had to stifle a giggle.

"What's funny?"

"I was just thinking about my first dinner tonight, with the ex, when he asked me what I believed in. You want to know what I said? It was so stupid. 'Truth, justice, and the American way.'"

"You're Miss U.S.A."

"I know, it's so pathetic," she whispered, shaking her head. She glanced at him, and those blue eyes were locked on her in an entrancing way that broke through her defenses. "You want to know what I'm passionate about, Ryan? I want to be important enough to make a difference."

"Except you don't have to be important to make a difference," he replied, looking at her pensively again.

"Maybe not, but it sure makes things easier." Taking a deep breath, she dared to stare boldly at him. "What about you? What are you passionate about?"

The corner of his mouth stretched into a hint of a smile, and she could have sworn he inched closer.

"I just want to help people, really," he said. "To be there in their moment of need."

Like with Duke, she thought.

"Miss U.S.A.," she muttered teasingly, and he laughed as he exhibited a full, straight-toothed smile. "Actually, in reality, I like that. Very noble. Most guys your age would say they're passionate about football or making money or getting lucky." He continued looking at her, and she started to feel self-conscious. Brushing a strand of hair behind her ear, she averted her gaze. "Quit staring at me, you're making me nervous."

"Sorry, but you're..." Breaking off, he turned his head and looked at the street.

"I'm what?" she prodded. His eyes returned to her face in a way that penetrated her attempts at resistance, and she couldn't pull her own away.

"You're beautiful."

"On TV," she offered, completing his sentence.

"No. I mean, yeah, on TV of course, but not like right now. Without the makeup and the hair and the clothes, you've just got this ethereal quality about you."

"Ethereal?" She hadn't meant to repeat him, but she was entranced enough that she couldn't help herself.

"Please don't make me explain that."

"You don't have to..." she began before a lump rose in her throat. "Thank you."

"Maybe I should just get you home," he assessed with a smile, rising to his feet. He reached for her hand, and as she took his, the pulse of electricity that flowed through her veins surprised her. As though he sensed it himself, he stood there for a moment, her hand in his, both awaiting something.

"Harley..."

Ugh, why can't I feel this way with Kip? Or Denton? Or someone...appropriate?

"Ryan, this has been a really, truly lovely conversation." Her words brought a smile to his lips.

"Okay." He breathed out quickly. "I get it. I'm parked out back." Releasing her hand, he led her to the back of the restaurant, where she glanced around to look for his car. Instead, he stepped over to an older model motorcycle, grabbing a black helmet.

"You don't have a car," she stated the obvious, staring at the bike.

"No," he answered with a shrug. "I had a truck, but I really needed some capital in a hurry, so I sold it and picked this up. It works for now."

"Do you live far from here?" Lifting an arm to her neck, she covered her heart as though she could shield herself from the truth.

"About five minutes. I had an apartment not too far, but..."

"Let me guess," she interrupted. "You needed some capital."

A flicker of disappointment crossed his face, but he forced a smile. "Yeah, I'm with my parents for the time being."

Of course. A fry cook who doesn't have a real vehicle and lives with his parents. Nice one, Harley.

He offered her the helmet, and she reluctantly took it, pulling it onto her head. He started his bike and then motioned for her to move behind him while he asked for the address. She gave him Annie's street name and then settled against him. Within seconds, they were rolling down the street.

She knew it was in her best interest to remove herself from the man as soon as possible, but her arms were wrapped around his stomach and his warmth creeping through the front of her own T-shirt was alarmingly comforting. As she held herself tightly against him, she wondered if he was thinking the same thoughts about her.

Tears pricked her eyes as she thought about the kind of man he was. Kip wouldn't bring anyone dinner. Denton wouldn't offer to give anyone a ride home. Well, scratch that—he might offer an attractive woman a ride home, but not without expectations. She was on the back of a motorcycle with a fry cook who stated his biggest passion in life was helping someone in their moment of need.

As he pulled the bike to Annie's street, she took a deep breath.

"You live here?" he asked as she pulled the helmet from her head.

"No, a friend," she answered quickly. She was preparing to make a quick goodbye, but he turned off the engine of his motorcycle. "Thank you for the ride. And the ice cream, and the talk. Thank you."

"You said that already."

"I know, I don't know what else to say."

"Harley, you and I are pretty different, but do you think..." The intensity in his eyes made her breath catch in her throat. "I'm not going to stand here and try to pretend that I'm not attracted to you, because I am. Immensely. It's more than that, though. I can't remember the last time I felt so at ease talking to someone I just met."

"You're pretty easy to talk to yourself," she managed to reply as he reached for her hand. Pulling it upwards, he brushed his lips softly against her knuckles and her knees threatened to buckle beneath her.

"I can't leave without asking to see you again."

Looking down briefly, she took a deep breath.

"I like you, Ryan—a lot, actually."

"But…"

Her eyes returned to his, and her heart squeezed a bit inside her chest.

"But we're just too different. My world consists of appearances and perception, and you…"

"I'm not good enough." Nodding his head, he released her fingers and ran his hand through his hair. "Yeah. Well, I suppose that's an answer."

"That's not what I was going to say."

"But it's what you're thinking, right?"

"Of course not, we're just not in the same place in life. I don't think we would have anything in common."

"It's all about perspective," he surmised, shaking his head.

"I'm sorry," she whispered, fighting her own instincts. She wanted to reach for his hand again. Tell him that whatever he was going to ask her, the answer was yes. Instead, she willed her hands to stay by her side.

"Maybe I'll see you around." With that, he pulled the helmet onto his head, started the engine, and peeled into the street. Cringing inside, she turned around and headed to her friend's door, slightly brokenhearted.

Chapter Five

"Harley?" Annie looked surprised as she opened the door, her red curls slightly askance. "Girl, it's nearly one in the morning. What gives?"

"You don't mind, do you?" She stood on the stoop, waiting for an invitation. "It's been a trying night, and I didn't feel like spending the remainder of it alone."

"Of course not. Get in here." Obligingly, she stepped into the entryway as Annie locked the door behind her. "How did you get here? Where's your car?"

"Motorcycle," she muttered. "Long story."

"Chocolate milk? A couple episodes of *The Office*, maybe?"

Giving a small laugh, Harley smiled at her friend. "Yes, and yes."

Harley walked into the living room and prepared to sit on the couch, but Annie's throat-clearing abilities caused her to turn toward the kitchen. "You smell like a big grease pit. Go get some of my pajamas before you plop onto my furniture, please."

"I'm going to rifle through your drawers in your bedroom," she warned.

"Go right ahead."

Rather than filtering through all of Annie's clothes, she hastily grabbed the first articles of clothing she could find and tugged them loose from their drawers—a purple t-shirt with sorority letters on the front and a pair of striped white and pink pajama pants. As she was pulling her shirt over her head, however, the familiar scent of food and cologne assaulted her senses, most likely attained from body-hugging Ryan on the back of the motorcycle. Holding the fabric against her nose, she imagined him being close to her again.

Why do I have to be so darn impractical?

Rather than existing in her fantasy, she finished dressing and promptly plopped onto the couch as Annie predicted.

"What did Kip do?"

"Ugh, Kip, I'd nearly forgotten about Kip."

"Well, this just got all kinds of interesting. Still want the chocolate milk, or should we upgrade to straight hot fudge?"

"Ha, ha. I just ate a whole bowl of caramel ice cream, so don't tempt me."

"Where have you been?" Annie settled next to Harley on the couch, facing her with her legs pulled up to her chest. "And don't tell me with Kip, because he wouldn't take you to any restaurant that smelled like your clothes smell."

"I'm pretty sure I broke up with Kip. And if I didn't, then I intend to. He wants to run for political office, and they actually mentioned me giving up my job so I won't interfere with his plans."

"You've got to be kidding me," Annie muttered.

Harley responded by leaning her head back against the couch cushions. "So I went to Tiny's for a burger, and I was going to get a cab, but my phone was dead. So the fry cook had to bring me here."

"The fry cook," Annie repeated. "The smell is starting to make sense."

"I am such a dolt, Annie. Tell me I'm a dolt."

"You're a dolt," she replied bluntly.

Harley reached up and untwisted the knot atop her head, allowing her hair to fall over her shoulders. "I liked him. Seriously, really liked him. He tried to ask me out, and I stopped him, but I didn't want to."

"Who?"

"Who else? The fry cook!"

"Oh, girl…"

"His name is Ryan Temple. He's maybe 5'10", dark chocolate brown hair that looks like the longest mohawk I've ever seen, multiple tattoos."

"Sounds like just your type," Annie retorted with a snort.

"He has the cutest little strip of hair under his lip." Rather than reply, Annie simply stared at her. "I know I'm being ridiculous, and he's not really even that great looking, but he just had this animal magnetism."

"This is truly hilarious. You are honestly sitting here telling me you are wild-animal-drawn to a man who flips burgers for a living?"

"Yes."

"I love it," she said with a laugh, staring into Harley's eyes. "So go out with him. What do you have to lose?"

"A lot. Anyway, it's too late for that. I'm pretty sure I insulted him about living with his parents and not having a car."

"Ooh, yeah, I can see where that could create a problem." Annie seemed far more pleased about the turn of events than Harley expected.

"I'm glad you're finding this humorous."

"You're actually human, Harley! Some days I wonder, you get so far into your reporter act. I know you let your hair down occasionally with me, but it's nice to see this side of you."

"He said I was almost ethereal without my makeup on," Harley continued, gazing across the room at the wall. "He asked me what I was passionate about, like he honestly cared."

"Girl, stop being so stupid. Go over to Tiny's tomorrow and figure out how to get ahold of him."

It was easy to believe that things were really so simple while staring at her wild-haired friend, but deep inside Harley knew that she couldn't see things in quite the same light.

"I'm not sure I want to," she admitted, cringing a bit. "Things are different for me, you know? You grew up being part of the movers and shakers in this town, and I have to claw and fight my way into their ranks. What am I going to gain if I throw away everything I've given my heart and soul for in order to have…what?

A fling with some guy who lives in his mom's basement? You asked what I had to lose, but the truth is, the answer is not much. Not much, so I have to cling to everything I have."

"You're right," Annie said solemnly.

"Really?" Despite her hopeful tone, Harley looked dejectedly at her friend.

"Yep. You *are* a total dolt."

Chapter Six

"Morning, Kenny," Harley stated hesitantly when she saw her accomplice saunter up to her desk. "What's going on today?"

"Zip." He dropped himself into the chair facing her desk and sprawled out like he was getting ready to take a nap.

"Hectic weekend?" she wondered uninterestedly.

He must have sensed her reluctance, because he opened the corner of one eye and peered at her. "Naw, man, just hanging out with my girlfriend."

The fact that lanky, scrawny Kenny had a love interest and she didn't rankled her just a bit, but she reminded herself to be pleasant.

"What did you do?" he asked.

What did she do?

After a solid week of no contact, Kip showed up at her house at 6:00 Friday night dressed to the nines and expecting to take her to the club. She answered the door wearing a tank top and yoga pants, and promptly told him that he could hit the road. He hadn't been happy, and told her she should probably avoid showing her face at the club for a while.

"I had no idea you were so fickle," he growled. "Imagine if you'd pulled this stunt while I was on the campaign trail. Dad told me you were just a nobody. I should have believed him."

His feelings hadn't bothered her in the least, but the thought that the Senator called her a nobody really ticked her off. Immediately after he left, she plaited her hair down the side of her shoulder and drove her BMW to Tiny's at the unheard of hour of

7:00, when there will still plenty of other patrons inside the restaurant. She had a plate of fried chicken, and Tiny sat with her three separate times asking if she was okay. She drew a few stares from some of the other diners, and she surmised that they either realized she was "that news reporter" or they simply felt sorry for the lonely young woman in the corner.

When she was finished eating, she carried her milk chocolate bar to the park bench and handed it to Duke. They talked about the weather and Tiny and the fact that the city needed to repair the potholes in the road, but the one thing she really wanted to ask about never came up in conversation. She couldn't make herself ask Tiny, and she darn sure wasn't going to ask Duke.

For whatever reason, she couldn't remove Ryan Temple from her mind.

"Nothing," she insisted to Kenny. "It was a really boring weekend." Grabbing her paper coffee cup, she rose and straightened the hem of her gray skirt. "I'm going to go hassle Mitch—see if we can find something important to do today."

As she walked away, she threw a look at Kenny, who had his eyes closed as though he were really going to take a nap right there next to her desk.

Meandering down the hall, she made a point to glance in every office and give a slight nod. If Mitch was insistent on keeping her on ridiculous throwaway stories, she had to make a connection somehow. As she passed Denton's office, she couldn't help but notice Summer lounging by his desk, telling him an animated story.

Summer was enigmatic on the camera in her heyday, Harley had to give her that. She wasn't interesting up close, though. Like an old friend who made you feel comfortable when she was around, but who wouldn't turn your head in a crowd.

Stepping up to Mitch's door frame, she tried to offer a winning smile.

"Hey, boss, what do you have for me today?"

Glancing up, he waved her into his office. Just a couple steps and she was settled into a chair, staring at him expectantly.

"Harley, I try to run a tight ship here, and I'd really like to avoid the appearance of bias or favoritism."

"Naturally," she agreed politely, crossing one leg over the other. He already had a huge coffee stain down the front of his shirt, but she tried to avoid noticing.

"I can't have anyone at the station going all politically rogue and inserting their own views into the reporting."

"I should say not."

"Which is why I'm pulling you from any political stories for the time being."

A tremor of panic seized her entire body, and she uncrossed her leg and leaned forward in her chair. "What are you talking about?"

"I've been made aware of your bias regarding Senator Stanton," he began, not looking her in the eye.

"That's a blatant lie. The only problem I have with Senator Stanton was that I wouldn't follow the little path he had planned out for me as a proper romantic partner for his candidate son. I don't put bias into my news reports, and you know that very well." She realized that her voice had risen significantly, and she fought to regain control.

"Be that as it may, I don't need people breathing down my neck." He began tapping his computer mouse as though he were dismissing her, and she placed her hand on his desk in earnest.

"Mitch, we're here to report the news. Not the politically correct news, or the pleasant news, but the honest, brutal truth. If we were doing that the way the public expects us to, politicians *would* be breathing down your neck on a consistent basis."

"Careful young lady," he warned her, giving her a wary look. "I've got a couple human interest stories I'll send you. Elderly roof repair scam. Family complaining of insurance fraud. They're right up your alley."

Every inch of ground she had gained felt like it had been pulled from beneath her in a split second. She thought she could use the Stantons to her advantage, but instead they had set her back. How far? Weeks? Months? A whole year?

"This isn't right, Mitch, and you know it," she whispered, rising from her chair.

"Television isn't right or wrong, Harley—it's entertainment. You might want to remember that in the future."

She wouldn't have been angrier if he'd slapped her in the face. She wasn't in her job to be an entertainer. Clenching her fist, she stepped out into the hall, marched straight to the back of the building and pulled open the bathroom door, jerking open a stall door and locking herself inside. Trying to calm her breathing pattern, she placed her fist against the cold metal wall beside her and closed her eyes.

"...not what I had in mind at all," she heard as the door swung open. "I thought we would make steaks, but then he brought the bratwursts."

Summer Davis—an easily recognizable voice for not only Harley, but probably most of Louisville.

"Of course, they never do anything right," another voice responded. Karen Richards, weather. "And what about that project Mitch asked you to work on? Any luck?"

"No. He really wants an exclusive with that bizarre bestselling author Camdyn Taylor when she's here this weekend, but I've called her people several times and they're absolutely refusing. I haven't made any headway at all."

"Well, I could hardly blame her. Her last appearances on television were kind of strange, to say the least. She's probably a little leery of anything television-related."

The door opened again, and the sound of their laughter followed them out of the bathroom.

Standing calmly inside the stall, Harley allowed a new line of thought to begin formulating in her mind. So Summer couldn't get an interview with this Camdyn Taylor person, whoever she was? Harley would do it herself. She would study her to find out what was so strange about her television appearances, discover what made her tick, and then figure out a way to get close to her.

How could she convince Mitch she was worthy of the desk?

Prove that Summer Davis was an amateur.

Spending her mornings discussing illegal repair scams with their victims wasn't what Harley had in mind for an enticing news week, but she did her job with a smile on her face. It was impossible not to feel for those who had been swindled, but she also held a little hope—deep inside, she felt that she was really about to turn a corner. She had an inside scoop thanks to Summer, and she was determined to land the elusive interview.

As it turned out, studying Camdyn Taylor was interesting enough to keep her involved in the work until the wee hours of the night. Hers was, indeed, a strange case. She was presented to the world as the face behind best-selling author C.W. Oliver, which was fascinating in and of itself simply because two of Oliver's books were being bandied about as potential future movies. Into that debate, enter a charming, witty, very pretty blonde who made her first television appearance sitting next to her dashing husband and pretending to know the names of her fans in the audience. It was bizarre, really. Then, she somehow managed to react calmly and coolly on The Tilly Show while she was playing a ridiculous karaoke game. Obviously rehearsed.

In fact, the whole persona seemed designed to bring as much attention to the books as possible. If the game show bit hadn't been enough, the next day she appeared to throw up in a plant on one of the morning shows. Harley studied each of her appearances one by one, looking at her mannerisms and her patterns of speech. She came across as slightly goofy and charismatic, but Harley was skeptical. It certainly seemed possible that it was an act.

Her reporter's tendency to lean in that direction was further solidified when she began researching Camdyn's publisher, Fairmont Publishing. They were operating in the red, and their one solid investment in the last couple years had been C.W. Oliver. Of course they would capitalize on that by hiring someone to take on the role publicly, and who better than a fantastic actress who had the uncanny ability to somehow come across as klutzy and loveable at the same time she was poised and gorgeous?

Honestly, the entire sideshow was fairly brilliant.

It was a shame she was going to have to pull back the curtain.

Chapter Seven

Summer had been correct about one thing—scoring an interview with Camdyn Taylor was proving to be a bigger challenge than Harley anticipated. She was able to get plenty of face time with the conference organizer and even some of the other attendees, but couldn't score an interview with the woman herself. She had Kenny on standby at the hotel just in case an opportunity presented itself, but when Camdyn finally arrived on Thursday night, she was ushered straight into her room and no one could get close to her.

She managed to sneak over to the megachurch where the conference was being held on Friday morning to try to figure out where the weak spots in her defenses might be, but she was met by a very firm Lex Fairmont from Camdyn's publishing company, definitely doing his best to handle his star. Harley attempted flirting with him to no avail. Even when she asked him to lunch (not for business, but for pleasure), he had an excuse. "No interviews," he kept insisting. "Camdyn has a lot of work to do, and I don't want her to have any interruptions."

All the blockading of the rising star caused Harley to believe that her assumption was correct, and they were attempting to hide Camdyn from the public eye. Still, there seemed to be no getting past Lex that morning, so she left to finish the rest of her daily assignments and vowed to return later in the evening.

Sneaking out of work a bit earlier than normal, she returned to her house and dressed in a very ordinary pair of jeans, pairing them with a purple t-shirt claiming "I Am Not Ashamed" that she got from a youth lock-in at a church when she was in high school. If she wanted her plan to work, she needed to look like she might work at that megachurch. Not that she had any idea what that church's workers would dress like—she hadn't even been inside a church for at least five years, if not more.

She began to drive the BMW toward her destination, but soon realized her car was running on fumes. Pulling up at the first gas station, she exited the vehicle and grabbed the nozzle on the gas pump while she punched the buttons on the keypad. Mentally plotting her attack plan in her brain, she heard the roar of a motorcycle pull up on the other side of the pump, and she turned quickly to avert her face, in case someone saw her wearing that ridiculous getup.

The muffled sound of someone humming came from the reverse side of that pump, and she tried to ignore it. After a second, though, she turned her head just a bit and dared a peek around the side of the island only to see a very familiar old bike. Taking a step to her left, she nearly ran straight into the man she couldn't seem to forget.

"Ryan," she stammered, backing up a tad. The tattoo across his chest was visible at the top of his white V-neck T-shirt, and although it was a rather warm day, he was wearing a black leather jacket.

"Harley," he acknowledged. "Wait, I guess I should clarify—it *is* okay if we use the same gas pump, right? I wouldn't want to taint you or anything."

"What?" She felt her cheeks burning and was immediately angry that he could instantly cause such a reaction.

"Where are you going dressed like that?" He stepped closer as her eyes widened in response. Tonight he didn't smell like food. He smelled one-hundred percent like heaven, or at least like masculine body wash and some kind of sporty deodorant.

"I'm undercover, of course," she blurted, feeling about ten years old and completely ridiculous.

"Are you ashamed?" he wanted to know. Glancing around to make sure no one was overhearing their conversation, she reluctantly returned her gaze to his cobalt-blue eyes.

"Why should I be?" She couldn't determine what was causing her more frustration—the fact that he was taunting her, or the fact that her heart was pounding.

"Your shirt," he said with a sideways smile, pointing down. Glancing at her clothes, she let out a short sigh.

"Very funny." He was looking at her intently enough that she felt like shrinking. "Are you..." Edging towards him, she pulled herself within inches of his face. "Are you wearing guyliner?!"

Rather than reply, his warm fingers wrapped around her upper arm. "Come with me tonight," he entreated softly, his scent clouding her mind. She forced a shaky breath, and he responded by stooping a bit so they were eye to eye. "You don't have to ride the bike. Follow me with your... Wow, you have a Beemer. Come with me? Please?"

"I can't," she managed to whisper. "I've got this very important work thing—"

"On a Friday night?" The feel of his fingers against her skin was threatening to change her mind in a hurry.

"Yes, undercover, remember?"

"Of course, undercover. I forgot. Are you raiding a prayer group? Infiltrating a church camp, maybe?" He smiled, but he didn't back away. She tried to balance being slightly annoyed with being enthralled by his nearness, but it wasn't working the way she intended.

"Are you going to an all-night rave with that guyliner?" Her jab didn't have the punch she planned, because he laughed, his breath hitting her cheek and sending her emotions into overdrive. "I have legitimate work to do, I'm not trying to be a jerk."

"You mean I'm wearing you down?" When she didn't answer and attempted to look away, he tipped her chin up and forced her eyes toward his. "The universe is pulling us together."

"The universe...that's completely preposterous."

"Yeah, I know," he admitted, releasing her arm, "but it was worth a shot."

Pulling herself away from him, she grabbed the nozzle from the gas pump and shoved it back into place, twisting her gas cap closed. For a few seconds he stayed on his side of the pump, and she was slightly afraid that he would drive off without another word. The thought was jointly terrifying and unbearably disappointing.

"Hey," she said awkwardly, poking her head around the side of the gas tank. "Um, just so you know, I like the guyliner. On you, I mean—not for the masses."

He was leaned over messing with his motorcycle, so she stood there awkwardly until he straightened and turned his eyes toward her.

"Bonham Station," he stated with a near-perfect grin, "if you change your mind." Shoving his wallet in his pocket, he straddled his bike and grabbed his helmet. "Change your mind, Harley." He gave her a parting wink before placing the helmet on his head, and then he was gone.

Getting into the megachurch wasn't difficult, and she managed to pretend to be part of the catering team to sneak her way into Camdyn's dressing room. Unfortunately, the lady of the hour wasn't in the room at that moment, so she snuck out and investigated the back hallways, trying to make an escape plan should she need one.

Eventually she retreated into a side hallway where she had seen some of the others congregating earlier, and as though she were witnessing a miracle, the bathroom door swung open and out popped a pretty blonde, rubbing her hands together like she had just washed them. Recognizing her instantly, Harley moved forward to take advantage of the opportunity, but she suddenly halted when a couple other reporters appeared, chanting Camdyn's name and trying to get her attention.

She knew Camdyn wouldn't recognize a local reporter by face or name, but the others might, and she didn't want her cover to be blown. Leaning forward, she allowed her hair to fall over her face as she rushed toward her prey, grabbed her by the elbow, and shuffled her toward the back hallway and the escape alley she had just been examining.

While the supposed authoress looked a little startled and uneasy for a moment, she relaxed as Harley explained that she was a church volunteer and had been catering her dinner. In fact, lying came very easily as she stated that Lex Fairmont had asked her to supply the items for the room, and she felt a little guilty when she realized Camdyn was buying her story hook, line, and sinker.

As they stepped into the room together, Harley studied the pretty blonde with the random curls who seemed grateful for the assistance while also coming across as slightly awkward and nervous—nothing like she seemed on television. In fact, with Harley in the room, she almost appeared to be mentally crying out for help as she scanned the room. Something was definitely making her uneasy.

Smiling to herself, Harley began recording their conversation on the device she held in her pocket. "Can I get you anything?"

"No, everything is great." The presumed actress sat in front of her laptop as Harley leaned against the wall and studied her. On television she appeared so self-assured and confident. In person she looked much the same, but her personality seemed different somehow.

"Aren't you going to watch the conference?" It was just a little prod, but Harley hoped it might get her talking.

"I doubt it. I've got way too much work to do."

Sensing an opening, Harley settled into a chair. "I figured that's why you didn't want any of those reporters bothering you earlier."

Camdyn glanced up from her laptop and laughed quietly. "Maybe someday I'll have something useful to say, and then I'll talk to them."

"You don't think you have anything useful to say?" Harley wondered, feigning surprise. "I'm sure they wouldn't have asked you to be the speaker tomorrow if that was the case."

Something in that statement must have clicked with Camdyn, because she seemed to visibly relax and let her guard down a bit. "They probably have expectations for me," she admitted, "but I'm not sure I'll live up to them."

Is she going to flat-out admit to everything? Wow, it sounds like it.

"But you're always so funny on television," Harley tried, seeing if she could get her to bite.

"That's the thing," she replied breezily, as though she were chatting with a friend. "It's a fluke. Everything I do is a complete accident. Practically televised miracles, if you want to know the truth."

Fluke, fake—the words are very close. She almost admitted the whole thing is a sham.

"That can't be true," Harley protested, adding a slight laugh for good measure. "I saw you on the set of *Almost Midnight with Jamie Price*, and it was obvious he thinks the world of you."

Maybe not the best direction of the conversation, because Camdyn sobered a bit at the mention of the television appearance, visually withdrawing a bit. In fact, her mood darkened quickly enough that Harley wondered if she had overstepped her bounds.

"Do you mind if I have a bottle of water?" Harley tried to stall as she considered the best way to reword her attack. A sad smile seemed a good way to indicate that she was in solidarity, so she gave it her best shot. "I feel for you, really. People are so cruel. I've heard some of them saying you made the whole thing up. Some think your whole persona is a publicity stunt. They think you're a fraud. In fact, I've even heard people say that you're not the one who writes the books—that you're just an actress hired by Fairmont Publishing." Taking a breath, she waited as those words sunk in before she continued quietly. "You've got to admit, from the outside looking in, it looks pretty strange."

She seemed to take that criticism to heart, because she reached up and grabbed a fistful of curls and paused before she spoke. "I guess I've never really thought about it."

"And that picture on that blog with your doctor…"

The mention of the doctor must have hit a nerve, because all hints of friendliness slipped off of Camdyn's face.

"You really seem to know a lot about me," she leveled at Harley, eyeing her suspiciously.

Fake you're a crazy fan, Harley.

"Of course. We're all huge fans around here. If I'd known I would bump into you in the hall, I would have brought my book in for you to sign."

Will she buy it?

Harley stared at those blue eyes for a split second before adding to the conversation. "Do you know what you're speaking about tomorrow night?"

"No." It was a quick reply, and Harley was so surprised by it that she leaned forward slightly in her chair.

"What do you mean? They haven't given you the speech yet?"

This is it! She's going to admit it!

Laughing, Camdyn rolled her eyes a bit. "I only wish they'd give me a speech! Then I wouldn't have to write my own."

"Well, why haven't you written it yet? It seems to me that a bestselling author like you could have a speech done in nothing flat."

Cause you're not an author, right? That admission will have Summer's head spinning.

"It's not as simple as that," she said, twisting her wedding ring around in circles on her finger. "Writing a fiction work is taking me out of myself—pretending to be someone else. Giving something worthwhile as Camdyn Taylor is a little more difficult."

"Why?"

"Because I don't know what I have to offer anyone," she admitted with a sigh, and Harley thought she saw a sheen of tears building in her eyes. "I'm here in this huge church, and they think I have words of wisdom, or hilarious stories, or some kind of insight into pop culture or the media. The truth is, though, I don't have anything figured out. Lately, I've barely been able to pick myself up off the floor most days. I'm not even sure who I'm supposed to be."

The sincerity with which she spoke those words pricked Harley's conscience, and she felt a stab of guilt cross her body.

"But you know you're supposed to be Camdyn Taylor," Harley suggested gently, chiding herself for asking the question when Camdyn seemed slightly distraught, but she could see her own chance at the exclusive floating right out the window. All her preparation and presumptions would be for nothing, and wasn't that what good reporters did? Push into the forefront when things got uncomfortable?

While Harley was wallowing in her own self-loathing, Camdyn simply wrinkled her nose a bit as she stared at the woman she thought was a volunteer. "Well, I know I *am* Camdyn Taylor, like it or not. I've just got to figure out what that means."

The statement that she was trying to figure out who she was struck Harley at the heart as though the question ricocheted off Camdyn and somehow penetrated her own soul.

But you know you're supposed to be Harley Laine.

And who is that, really? A sneaky reporter trying to pull the rug out from under a seemingly nice person? By lying? In a church?

"I guess I better get out of your way so you can get your writing done," Harley quickly announced, rising to her feet in an effort to escape the room. If she stayed much longer, she might wind up being the one to confess.

After politely shaking Camdyn's hand and exchanging some pleasantries, she pulled the door closed behind her and leaned against it briefly while she thought about her intentions. Did she really want to try to destroy someone simply to rise above Summer Davis? The woman behind that door didn't seem fake or manipulative. No, she seemed rather sad and slightly confused. She almost wished she could go back in and try to help her, or see if she honestly needed something.

"What are you doing?" she heard from her right, and she turned her neck to see the representative from Camdyn's publishing company rushing toward her. "I told you no interviews today."

"Don't worry, Lex," she assured him, stepping away from the door. "Just a friendly conversation. Nothing newsworthy, I promise you that."

Chapter Eight

Feeling rather frazzled, Harley departed the conference and headed across town to Tiny's, merely looking for a little normalcy. It briefly crossed her mind that her version of normal had become being fed greasy food by a giant man who called her Miss Harley and sharing chocolate with a homeless person.

With her green military jacket pulled tightly across the T-shirt that she would not be caught dead wearing in public, she slowly ambled up to the sidewalk where Duke was sitting on the park bench. She had often wondered what his story was, but he was tight-lipped. When she dared to ask him the week before, he responded by saying, "Sorry, ma'am—Duke doesn't give interviews. Besides, I prefer the art of listening to talking about oneself."

It was obvious he could see her coming, because those steel-gray eyes followed her movement as she stepped to the bench.

"Your date must have ended early tonight," he surmised, his gravelly voice containing a hint of playfulness. She sat beside him, staring out into the street.

"Actually, I'm still looking for a date, as it turns out."

"Well, Ryan's not here tonight," Duke offered, causing Harley's pulse to jump at the name. She had no idea whether she was simply transparent or Duke was trying to be funny, but she felt terribly self-conscious either way.

"That's very interesting, of course, but I had another date in mind."

"Pray tell who that lucky young man is, Miss Laine."

"My friend Duke," she breathed quietly. His eyes lingered on her, and she attempted to give him a tremulous smile. "Would you do me the honor of eating dinner with me?"

Reaching up to stroke his beard, he cleared his throat. "Now, you don't want to eat your dinner with this old codger."

"You're mistaken. Besides, you're not going to make me eat alone, are you?"

He wrapped his arms around his broad frame under his charcoal-colored jacket, pondering her request. "Now what will people think if they see you eating dinner with me, young lady?"

Standing up, she placed herself in front of him and shrugged her shoulders. "I'd imagine they'd think that I'm a very lucky woman. Now are you getting up or aren't you? Begging is not something I do for just anyone."

"Please, don't stoop to begging," he insisted, grunting a bit as he rose. "I wish I had a suit jacket since I'm accompanying such a beautiful woman to dinner."

Laughing, she latched her fingers onto his arm. "I dare say Tiny would kick anyone out who showed up in a suit jacket." He didn't bother replying as they strolled toward the front door, where he pulled it open and held it for her like a gentleman. She breathed a short "thank you" as she located a table and stepped forward. Duke was insistent upon pulling out her chair, so she let him do so before he sat down across from her.

"Why, Miss Harley, you're here early again tonight. Special occasion?" Tiny maneuvered his bulking frame close to their table, causing her to smile up at him.

"Very special," she insisted. "Duke and I are here to share a lovely dinner together."

"I'd say that *is* special," Tiny stated. "Two of my very favorite people."

"So what do you have for me today, Tiny? And don't hold out on me. I've literally only eaten three crackers since breakfast."

Tiny placed his hand on his hip and directed his eyes toward Duke. "Do you see what I put up with? How am I supposed to go to bed at night not worrying about this one when she tells me things like that? You tell her, Mr. Duke, that she outta come on out here every night and let me feed her."

"Don't bother, because I won't listen. If I was out here every night, it wouldn't be as special. Besides, you wouldn't miss me during the week and you'd stop treating me like a queen when I walked through the door."

"You'll always be a queen here, and you know it," was all Tiny replied. Sensing a bit of emotion rising inside her at his unconditional acceptance, Harley decided it best to change the subject.

"So, what do you have for us then?"

"Tonight I got a big chicken fried steak smothered in gravy, with—"

"You can stop," Harley interrupted. "You had me at that whole 'smothered in gravy' bit. I'm in. Duke, how about you? 'Smothered in gravy' sound appetizing?"

"Suppose," he muttered. "That girl always eat like this?"

"No, she don't," Tiny said, giving Harley a slight glare. "Only once a week, and she gonna waste away to nothing if she ain't careful. But she eats when she's here—I see to that."

With that he wandered out of their sight, and Harley grinned across the table at Duke. "So, what should we talk about? Most of my dates talk about politics and current events, but I'm sick to death of those things."

"I don't know," he replied, looking up as though he were thinking. "What did you and Ryan talk about the other night in here?"

"Why do you keep bringing him up?" she asked with an exasperated laugh as she felt her neck getting warm. "I don't know... We talked about his weird haircut, and he inappropriately showed me every tattoo on his body. Thank God he only had them on his torso, by the way. And then..." She hesitated, because she knew she was saying too much.

"Then?"

"Then he asked me what I was passionate about." Placing her elbows on the table and clasping her hands together, she leaned closer to her companion. "Duke, have you ever done anything you've really been ashamed of? I came this close to doing that tonight." She held her fingers up a hair's-width apart to punctuate her point. "I thought I wanted to be important to really make a difference in the world, you know? After tonight, though... What if I want to be important *just* to be important? It's pathetic."

"I'd say we all have things we're ashamed of, if we look hard enough. You don't have to be important to make a difference, though."

Feeling her eyes fill with tears, Harley pulled her hands back and folded her arms across her chest. "That's the same thing he said."

"Who?"

"Ryan."

Laughing, Duke nodded his head. She hadn't heard him laugh before—it was a low, rumbling chuckle that instantly made her feel more at ease.

"So what kind of tattoos does he have?" Duke wanted to know.

Harley couldn't avoid exhibiting her own sheepish grin. "A bunch of Bible verses and Jesus stuff about being saved and all that. It's weird, right? Just tell me it's weird to appease me."

"Why do you need to think it's weird?" He shifted a bit in his chair and reached up to scratch his beard. "I have a tattoo, you know, from back in my younger days when I was a biker. It's across my upper arm."

"Oh my word, please tell me it doesn't say Harley."

"Little lady, I keep telling you I'm a Harley man. One of these days you're going to believe me."

Tiny returned at that moment, setting two steaming plates on the table. Rather than continue to focus on her tablemate, she inhaled the aroma of her food and looked down at the large portions of chicken fried steak, mashed potatoes, and green beans. Placing her napkin in her lap, she prepared to cut into her food when Duke broke the silence.

"Mind if I say a prayer?"

Of course she minded. Wasn't he paying attention during her very recent "tell me it's weird" comments?

"Um, I guess," she stated hesitantly. He bowed his head and prayed internally, she supposed, because he made no external utterances. When he was finished, he simply began eating, and she did the same.

"So, I have to be honest with you, Duke," she interrupted their meal, slight grin on her face. "I've never been on a date where someone prayed over their meal. That's a first for me. Also, I've never eaten dinner with someone who may or may not have my name tattooed on their arm."

"Well," he said, twinkle in his eye, "maybe if you hang around Ryan a little more you can convince him to do it."

Choking on her food, Harley lifted her fist to her mouth as she coughed a few times. "Seriously, Duke, warn a girl when you're going to say something like that! And that wasn't funny, by the way."

They ate the rest of their meal with comfortable conversation, him occasionally bringing up Ryan in attempts to embarrass her, and of course the occasional mention of Harleys just to get her ire up. When they finished, she told him she needed to talk to Tiny for a moment and wandered up to the bar, waiting on her friend.

"Get enough to eat?" he asked when he noticed her, stepping up until they were face to face over the counter. His grin was always easy, and she loved the way it lit up his countenance.

"More than enough, of course. How much do I owe you?"

"Now your money's no good here and you know it."

"You know I love you, don't you?" she asked, giving him a smile.

"Well, I didn't know that, but it's mighty nice to hear."

"Then let me do this, please. I've not had such a great week, to be honest, and I feel a need to redeem myself a little. This may be a ridiculous way to do it, but let me have this, okay?"

"Miss Harley, I'm proud to call you my friend, you know that? Darn proud. You give me ten dollars and we'll call it even."

Shaking her head, she pulled her wallet out of her purse. "I'll give you thirty, and we'll say I still owe you a great deal. And I'm proud to call you my friend, too. Darn proud, even."

Leaving her money on the counter, he stepped around the end and folded her little frame in his big arms, wrapping her in a hug. "I meant what I said, girl. I'd feed you every night."

"I know," she told him, squeezing a little tighter. "Thank you." He handed her a chocolate bar, and she returned to Duke and they walked outside, where they could sit together on the bench and split their chocolate just like they did every Friday.

Sliding into the driver's seat of her BMW, Harley picked up her phone and dialed Annie's number, listening as it rang three times.

"Why are you calling me on a Friday night? I could be on a date."

Turning the keys in the ignition, Harley checked the mirror and pulled out into the street. "Hello, Annie. It's nice to hear from you, too. Are you on a date?"

"No, I said 'could be.'" Giggling a bit, she let out a sigh.

"So what are you doing tonight?"

"No plans, why?"

Harley paused as she looked at her own eyes in the rear view mirror. "I have an urge to go to Bonham Station."

"Do I want to know why we're here?" Annie asked as they stepped up to the outside of the building, listening to the pounding drumbeat and the thump of the bass.

"Aren't we allowed to have a little fun?" Harley told herself it was only curiosity that had drawn her to Bonham Station, but deep inside she knew better. If it had been curiosity, she wouldn't have taken the time to go home and put on extra mascara. She also wouldn't have exchanged her "church volunteer" clothes for the Rock Revival jeans she recently scored. She wouldn't have put on her black sequined tank, and she wouldn't have added the black leather jacket to top it off. For whatever reason, it wasn't until she was at the front door of the building that her obviousness dawned on her.

She stopped walking, and Annie drew up beside her. "What gives? Aren't you going inside?" Annie looked quintessentially herself, with her gauzy black long-sleeve shirt and her camouflage jeans, naturally accentuated by those red curls on one side of her head. The hoop in her eyebrow rose, and Harley knew that meant she better get to explaining.

"Maybe we should just go somewhere else, do you think?" Her hesitance was enough to practically send Annie into a tizzy.

"Oh my gosh, that guy is here, isn't he?! The fry cook who thought you looked like a goddess?" Grabbing her arm, Annie propelled her forward. "We are definitely going in. I have to see the guy who has you all worked up."

Before she knew it, Annie had shoved her past the bouncer and they were inside, the thump of the music so loud they could barely speak.

"Where is he?" Annie yelled, leaning as close to Harley as she could. She only shrugged in response, glancing around the crowd. Try as she might, she couldn't see him among the faces, her attempts made more difficult by the people jumping up and down and the slightly dark atmosphere of the room. Five minutes of honest effort in gazing at every guy in the room left Harley in a state of disappointment, so she reluctantly turned her attention to the stage and the lead singer. He was halfway bent to the ground singing in a raspy voice, wearing a baseball cap and a t-shirt with the insignia of a metal band.

"Great singer!" Annie told her, but Harley barely heard her because her eyes had just drifted past the lead vocalist to land on the drummer, and she froze in her spot. As if sensing her lack of movement, Annie grabbed her arm. "The singer is the guy?"

"No, the drummer," she told her friend, daring to stare openly at him. As she did so, she wondered if he did the same to her when she was on television, and the thought unnerved her a bit.

"Seriously, *that's* the guy?" Annie wanted to know.

"What's wrong with him?"

Shaking her head, Annie glanced back up at the stage. "Nothing's wrong with him, he's just not what I expected."

The comment rankled Harley, but she merely turned her attention to the band and tried to enjoy their music. They weren't exceptional, but they were good for a bunch of local boys, and she liked some of the song lyrics. The ones she could understand, anyway—many of them were screamed so loudly she couldn't make sense of them. One song in particular was subdued and quiet, and the lyrics were hauntingly beautiful, enough so that Harley couldn't drag her eyes off the lead singer for that one.

At the end of the set, the band began to disperse and go their separate ways, and Annie poked Harley in the side. "What are you waiting for?"

"Nothing, let's just go home, okay?"

"Harley Laine, I never would have figured you for such a coward." Annie latched onto her arm again and jerked her forward to the lead singer, who was standing near a couple other laughing young men. "You guys were great up there—really good. I'm Annie Jessup, and this is my friend, Harley Laine."

Harley wanted to fade into the wall, but she forced a slight smile onto her face.

He adjusted his ball cap slightly before he responded. "Wow, it's really funny that you're here, because we were just talking about you earlier. Sorry, I'm Matt. I guess I should have said that already."

"I'm just fascinated that you were talking about me when you don't know me," Annie said, winking at Harley.

Matt seemed to think that was funny, because he laughed heartily. "I'm thinking it's a shame that I *don't* know you," he joked. "You ladies want to join us?"

"Sure," Annie stated breezily, giving Harley a smug grin. "What were you saying about my friend Harley, anyway?"

Glancing behind him, he leaned closer. "Don't say anything, but my friend Ryan has a little crush on you."

"You're kidding." Annie kicked Harley, who gave her a quick glare.

"No, totally serious. In fact, it would probably make his year if you just went up and introduced yourself. He's over there, messing with his drum kit."

"You should definitely go introduce yourself," Annie repeated, about to laugh.

Rolling her eyes, Harley excused herself from their presence and moved nearer to the drums, feeling extremely self-conscious. He had shed his jacket and was only wearing the white V-neck T-shirt, which was just damp enough that she could see the contours of his tattoo through the white fabric. Turning and reaching down to grab something off the stage floor, his eyes managed to find her as he rose. Moving slowly and deliberately, he walked to the edge of the stage and knelt down, lowering himself to a seated position. A slow smile spread across his face as he stared into her eyes.

"I really must be wearing you down," he teased. "Or is this another undercover assignment? Let me guess...you're investigating my murder of the drums tonight?"

It was difficult to miss the fact that he was slightly sweaty, and he shoved his hair away where it was clinging to his cheek.

"Actually, your friend Matt wanted me to introduce myself to you, because he's convinced that you have a crush on me."

"I don't know where he'd get an idea like that." Holding out his drumstick, he looked at her curiously. "Have you ever held a drumstick?"

"No." Despite her inner protests, she let a little smile break onto her face.

"Take it," he insisted, and she wrapped her hand around it. Instead of letting go, he gently pulled it towards him, causing her to take a step. "See what I did there? I just wanted you closer. Pretty clever, huh?"

"Naturally. You could have just tried asking, though."

"That's not as much fun."

Boosting herself up to sit next to him on the stage, she avoided his eyes by looking around the room.

"So, you guys were good. I especially liked that sort of slow song."

"Really? You liked that one?"

"The lyrics were gorgeous. I'd love to hear it again."

Leaning back and reaching into his bag, he pulled out a CD. "Here. I'm sort of glad that you liked that one, because it's mine." She glanced at him with surprise, and he laughed. "You're shocked that I wrote that?"

"No, I'm just..." She took a quick look at the blank CD case and then brought her eyes back up to his. "Yes, actually. I'm a little surprised, but mostly because I had no idea you were even in a band."

"Just for kicks," he insisted, not taking his eyes off her face.

"Sing the song for me," she requested, causing him to shake his head.

"You don't want that," he assured her firmly, adjusting the drumstick in his hands. "Completely tone deaf. Trust me. Not pretty." She pretended to be disappointed, and he gently prodded her with the stick. "Hey, be honest—were you already planning on being here tonight, or did you show up just because I asked you?"

"What difference does it make?"

"Well," he began, looking down at his hands, "if you were going to be here anyway, then it's really cool that you took the time to come over here and say hello. If you're here because I asked you, though..." Twisting slightly, he looked at her face. "That means you dressed up and drove down here and disrupted whatever plans you had this evening. You wanted to see me. You invested something into this back and forth we have. That sort of feels like a game changer."

"I'm just having some fun with my friend Annie, that's all."

Looking toward Annie and Matt, Ryan pointed his drumstick. "That your friend over there? Keeps staring at us? With the half-shaved head?"

"Yes," she admitted with a smile. "Apparently I have a soft spot for people with unconventional hairstyles. And I should get back over there, since she's waiting for me."

"Give me your number," he entreated. "I won't be able to wait even twenty-four hours before calling you. You might not even get out of this building before I call you."

Sliding off the stage, she shot him a flirty glance. "I've really got to go."

"Take my number then. Come on, or I'm going to embarrass you."

She paused for a second to determine his intentions, and when he lifted his eyebrows teasingly, she shook her head. "Thanks for the show, Ryan. Maybe I'll see you around."

Taking a few steps over to Annie, she grabbed her friend's shoulder and nodded towards the door. They politely said their goodbyes and then turned to go. She dared a glance back at Ryan, who was still sitting on the edge of the stage.

"Harley Laine, my heart aches for you!" he called, pointing the drumstick in her direction. "I'm serious! You're killing me!"

Raising her hand to her chest, her breath caught in her throat as she hurriedly tried to pull Annie from the room. Laughing, Annie gave her a teasing shove.

"Girl, you are in *big* trouble with that one. And he's not even someone you would normally look twice at. I don't get it."

Harley didn't understand it herself, but she knew Annie was correct—she was in way over her head.

"What is with you, man?" Matt stepped up to his friend Ryan, placing a hand on his shoulder. "I manage to score you a meet-and-greet with a girl you can't stop talking about, and you're acting crazy."

"I already met her a couple weeks ago," Ryan told him, staring at his friend to gauge his reaction. "And I ran into her when I was on my way over here today."

Taking the drumstick from Ryan's hand, Matt used it to whack him on the arm. "What do you mean, you already met her?" He laughed as Ryan attempted to shrug it off. "So hang on a second. You don't think the reason she came down here tonight was to see you?"

Ryan took his drumstick from Matt and began twirling it in his fingers as a smile started to form on his face. "Yeah. As crazy as it sounds, yes."

"She's way out of your league, buddy."

Ryan slid off the stage and stood, gazing at the door through which Harley had disappeared a moment before. "Out of my league?" he asked with a laugh. "Forget that—she's out of my stratosphere." He shook his head as he thought about her rather obvious attempt to match his look with her leather jacket. "You know what she does on Friday nights? As a reward for the week, she goes to Tiny's. Tiny's, can you imagine? And not dressed like that, either. She dresses down like she's a penniless college student and takes all her makeup off. Oh, and when she's finished... Remember Duke, that guy that always sits on the bench over there that I told you about? When she's finished with her dinner, she asks for chocolate and then she takes it outside and sits next to him and shares it with him."

"Wow." Matt appeared pensive as he sat on the stage. "She actually sounds really cool."

"Very cool," Ryan agreed. "More than that, though—she's good. I don't even think she realizes it."

Slapping him on the back, Matt gave him a knowing grin. "You're due for some good, man. Overdue. Life owes you that much."

Nodding, Ryan looked at his friend. "I don't know that life owes me anything, but I'd take some good." Glancing back at the door, he pictured Harley in his mind again. "I'd gladly take some good."

Chapter Nine

Mitch didn't soften on his intention of sending Harley after human interest stories, and she handled the situations with more grace than she felt. The pet rescue facility needed donations? Harley was sent to investigate. It happened to coincide with a story she was doing about a bone marrow drive at the local hospital, where she met a young man who had lost his father. She had taken time to get to know the little guy, made a point of getting her cheek swabbed and being added to the donor registry mostly for his sake, and then took the boy and his mother over to choose an adorable rescue pup.

Perfect piece of reporting, Mitch called it, right before he sent her on another non-news assignment. A local car dealership doing a car giveaway to raise money for high school graduates was naturally Harley's story. While she was there, she made a point of talking the dealership into donating a used vehicle to a mother of four who didn't have transportation. She was quite pleased with her accomplishment.

Still, Mitch wasn't adequately impressed. Community-wide blood drive on Halloween, complete with gimmicky theme and nutty costumes? Who else would report on that event? She spent her time there making mental notes of a new Cooper Corporate Financial company spokesperson who was young, spunky, and offered a fresh outlook on corporate giving. Harley had even written the young woman's name down when she arrived back at the office—Madeline Heard. If the two of them partnered on human interest news stories, maybe she could convince CCF to fund some high-profile things in the city. Of course, she would have to steer clear of any black-tie functions involving the company, so she could avoid face-to-face meetings with Faith Cooper. She wouldn't want to be accused of stealing her high-end fashions, after all.

Although she was making the best of a bad situation, Harley had grown more than sick of the constant drivel she was required to report. She expected Mitch to relent after Senator Stanton let up on the Harley embargo, but suspiciously that didn't happen. Either Mitch had his own reasons for holding her back, or Kip's embarrassment reached farther than she imagined. Either way, she was stuck with the fluff while Summer sat next to Denton, smiling like a cat that had eaten a canary. She even looked like a canary one day in a solid daffodil-yellow blazer that was boxy and very unattractive, but Harley kept her opinions to herself.

To make matters worse, she hadn't accidentally bumped into Ryan at all. After she visited him at Bonham Station, she figured he would show up at Tiny's the next Friday night or search her out somehow, but no such luck. When she worked up the nerve to ask Tiny about him, he said he hadn't been by in probably a month, or at least since the night she met him there.

When she was about to convince herself that her work life couldn't get much worse, the week before Thanksgiving rolled around. She was out on a trip to a turkey farm when she had a text from Summer asking her if she would mind providing a quick on-location spot with a man who was trying to earn the world record for most consecutive days spent listening to Christmas carols. She thought about sending a snarky response, but instead she leaned her head back against the seat of the van and took a deep, cleansing breath.

Fighting her gut instincts, she looked down at her phone to text a two-letter response: OK.

The problem was, she accidentally fat-fingered the numbers and the word came out as oik. Naturally, the phone decided to autocorrect her spelling mistake, so the response she sent to Summer was simply one word:

Oink.

Oink, as though she were snorting like a pig. Or worse—calling Summer a pig. Even though she immediately texted and apologized for the mistake, when she was back at the studio, Mitch scolded her for her thinly veiled insult.

"What were you thinking?" Denton asked as she left Mitch's office and walked down the hall. He was standing cross-armed in the doorframe of his office, and when she didn't stop, he grabbed her arm. "Get in here, spitfire."

"You know that wasn't on purpose, Denton. I'm sick of being treated like garbage because of Kip and the senator. And Summer, telling on me like we're in junior high. I'm just over it."

"You don't deserve it," he insisted, not releasing her. "What can I do to help? Should we discuss it over dinner tonight?"

Recognizing his blatant attempt at flirting, she jerked her arm away. "It's not going to happen, Denton."

"What if I can get you the desk?" he prodded. A month ago his attempt might have worked, but she had grown weary of the office politics.

"It's not going to happen." She walked down the hall, but he remained a step behind, trailing her all the way to her desk. When she finally stopped, he leaned close to her so they wouldn't be overheard.

"Don't roll over and play dead. You're Harley Laine, aren't you? The Harley I know is a fighter."

The day before Thanksgiving, a scandal erupted involving one of the local judges accepting bribes, but was Harley allowed near that story? Of course not. Instead, Mitch sent her down to a local shelter where they were hosting a food drive and would have a hot meal for those in need on the holiday. She decided on a white blazer and a brown suede skirt complete with knee-high boots in a camel color that morning, and she checked her hair as she stared at her reflection in the passenger's side mirror of the van.

"Oh, check out the paper today," Kenny interrupted her sulking. "They've got the annual favorites list." Harley hastily grabbed it out of his hand and folded it in her lap. Every year around Thanksgiving they sent out the same survey: favorite local restaurant, shopping excursion, sports team, doctor... Basically, the best of the best. Scanning the list for favorite local newscaster, she nearly held her breath. Last year she had been number three behind Taylor Kennett and Shawna Mitchell—not bad considering how new she was to the scene. This year...

"It's me," she whispered, staring in disbelief. "Did you see this, Kenny? Favorite local newscaster—Harley Laine."

"Sure I saw it. Why'd ya think I handed it over?"

"Don't you see what this means?" she asked, laughing in delight. "Mitch won't be able to argue with this! How can he? The city has spoken, and they've decided for him. Even relegating me to the sidelines, he couldn't keep me out of the top spot."

"Star reporter right here," Kenny agreed, pretending that he was announcing her at some sort of event. "Have you met the star reporter, Miss Harley Laine?"

"Oh, please, Kenneth. You know I don't meet with the riffraff."

"Just don't go getting a big head over it," he warned her, pulling the van into the shelter parking lot.

"Are you kidding me? This is huge. Huge! And my head is the perfect size for my body, thank you very much."

Stepping out of the van, she smoothed her skirt across her legs and looked around at the people filtering in and out of the building.

My adoring public, she thought with a smile, immediately chiding herself for being outrageous. How many of those people had completed the survey, though, and chosen her as the favorite? The majority, at least.

"Just tell me when you're ready, Kenny."

She stood in front of the shelter and fluffed her hair a bit behind her shoulders, pondering her phrasing. Her quick wit was one of the things people seemed to like about her, so she thought it best to have some cute phrase prepared.

"Whenever you're ready, Harley."

Shaking her shoulders a bit to loosen up, she raised the microphone to her face and said a few words about the kindness of the city, and what people had to be thankful for. As she finished, Kenny lowered the camera and looked at Harley thoughtfully. "What was that, a stump speech?"

"That will be great after we get a couple interviews and give the basic information. Let's just find a couple people to chat with, okay?"

Kenny followed Harley through the door to the shelter, where she gave him some instructions on getting a shot of the food preparation area and spoke briefly with the shelter's director, who gave her a simple interview with information about the times, expected numbers, and how much food they would serve.

Afterwards, Harley glanced around the building to see if she noticed anyone who captured her interest. Her eyes rested on the spokesperson for Cooper Corporate Financial, who was co-sponsoring the food drive and had also co-sponsored the blood drive the month before. A few words from Madeline might be interesting, to see if she could determine the reason for the sudden philanthropic spirit of the company. Besides, when Harley met her at the blood drive, she was delightfully cute and a pleasant change of pace.

"Over here, Kenny," she waved her hand. "I think I see a familiar face." Stepping toward the young woman with the mass of auburn-tinted hair, Harley watched as she stacked a couple cans of green beans. "You're from Cooper Corporate Financial, right? Madeline, wasn't it?"

"Yes, that's right," she agreed politely. "Madeline Heard."

"I'm her mom!" a slightly robust blonde woman stated from the young woman's right. That kind of enthusiasm would look bizarre in her serious "heart-of-the-city" news piece, so Harley decided to ignore her.

"Could we get a few words?" Harley continued, glancing at Kenny to make sure he was prepared.

"Actually, I'd rather not."

Harley was about to calmly question the reason for the refusal when Madeline's mother decided to force her way in again.

"I could do an interview!"

Ugh, if I wanted a crazy fan interview I could get one of those every day of the week. I want to be a serious reporter, lady, not a walking sideshow.

"Why don't you interview the staff here at the shelter?" Madeline wanted to know. "They know more about what's going on than I do."

"Oh, we already have," Harley assured her. "I'd like to get the rest of the story, and this will just take a minute." Straightening her blazer, she motioned to Kenny and held the microphone up towards her lips.

"Ready," Kenny confirmed.

"Madeline Heard is the spokesperson for Cooper Corporate Financial, co-sponsor of the food drive—"

"Hold up," Kenny interrupted, tilting his camera to the side. "The old lady's in the shot."

"What?" Harley sighed, finally making eye contact with Madeline's mother. "Ma'am, will you move, please? You're in the camera line." *Seriously, why do I always get these crazies?* Letting out a quick calming breath, she tried again. "Okay, one more time. Madeline Heard from Cooper—"

"No, Harley, I decline an interview."

For a split second, Harley was confused. Sometimes politicians declined interviews, or defense attorneys, or even the occasional upset-after-a-loss sports player. Company spokespeople, though? That wasn't good business. Madeline was young enough, maybe she didn't realize how the game was played.

"Like I said," Harley brought her voice down to a whisper, "it will just take a minute, and then we'll be done here."

"And like I said," Madeline reiterated, "I decline."

If Harley was confused before, she was nearly incensed now. She was trying to make things easy on Madeline, and she wasn't cooperating. The last time she met her, she felt like they were slightly similar—nearly the same age and taking the torches from the last generation. It was rather refreshing that such a young woman was the spokesperson for the large corporate giant, but she was obviously not taking her position seriously.

"You're refusing to talk to me?" Harley assessed, feeling a blush creep into her cheeks.

"Yes, I believe so," Madeline answered curtly.

It was a betrayal, right? She had covered the ludicrous Halloween-themed blood drive graciously, ignoring the preposterous costumes and the corny clichés they used throughout the event. Now the other woman wouldn't give her the slightest courtesy by providing an interview?

"I...I don't know what to do, Harley," Kenny bumbled behind her.

"Here's an idea," Madeline stated, glancing about the room. "Run a story about the shelter without looking for an angle. You've got enough footage for today."

I'm going to kill her.

"How dare you insinuate that I'm looking for an angle," she stated a little too loudly, unaware of the other people around her. "I don't look for angles in my stories. Have you never seen me on the air? Do you have any idea how rude that is?"

"I'm honestly not that familiar with you," Madeline retorted, not backing down.

"I'm the top reporter in this town," Harley insisted. "Number one most popular newscaster, in fact."

"Oh, come on now. Why would Channel Six send the hottest reporter in town to a volunteer food drive?"

"Because I'm good with people," Harley blurted. "No one else could possibly make these crummy little unimportant stories seem interesting. What would you know about it, anyway?"

Whirling on her heel, she stormed toward the door, feeling tears building up in her eyes.

Why would Channel Six send the hottest reporter in town to a volunteer food drive? Because Summer is entrenched and I can't dethrone her.

"Kenny!" she called when she realized he wasn't following her.

Throwing the door to the shelter open, she stood in the cold wind and brushed angrily at her eyes. She could probably piece together the story from what she had, but it still wouldn't do to begin crying. And to have a meltdown in public like that—it simply wasn't like her. Turning around the side of the building, she saw a very familiar face sitting on the curb. Lowering herself next to him, she sniffed quickly.

"Duke?" He turned at the sound of her voice and gave her a reserved smile. "Is there something I can do for you?"

"No ma'am, I'm right as rain. You don't look your usual chipper self, though."

"Just having a bit of an emotional hiccup," she assured him, pasting a smile on her face. She placed her hand on his arm and took a deep breath. "Do you remember when you told me that you don't have to be important to make a difference?"

"Of course I do. When we had dinner together."

"Sure. Sometimes I really need that reminder, you know?" Pausing to brush away an escaped tear, she looked down at the pavement.

"We all do, I suspect. You make a difference to me, simply by caring. Just like the people here today are making a difference by donating their time or their food. It only takes a spark sometimes to shine a light so bright that it can't be hidden."

"Thank you," she muttered, leaning over and wrapping an arm around his shoulders. "Kenny, are we good to go back to the station?"

"Sure thing, Harley."

"See you Friday?" she asked Duke, who simply nodded in agreement.

Denton lowered himself into the chair beside Harley's desk and stared solemnly at her, not even bothering with his normal flirty banter. She had spent the entire afternoon pondering her "favorite reporter" status and her meltdown at the shelter, and she felt like such a fraud. Shaking her head, she offered a slight smirk.

"What is it, Denton? Shouldn't you be headed home for some turkey or pie or something?"

"Eventually. What about you? You headed home?"

Sighing, she glanced at her desk. "I have to work, and besides, I haven't been home in two years. I'll just spend my day here, filling in for Summer."

Laughing, Denton placed his elbows on her desk. "I knew you wanted the desk, but that interview you did today...I mean, talk about hardcore. You're a great actress, Harley Laine. Well done. Keep it up, and you'll be sitting beside me in no time. No wonder you didn't need my help. Got your own plan, right?"

Harley's face nearly went white as she thought about someone catching her meltdown on camera. If Mitch got ahold of that, she'd be done. He had already banished her to the outer realms of journalistic nothingness—what remained? County fairs and pie eating contests?

"What are you talking about?" she asked hesitantly.

"Mitch showed me the interview."

Without another word to Denton, Harley rose from her chair and went directly toward Mitch's office, not bothering to think about what her impulsive action could cost her. If he was angry in that instant, would he throw her out? She stood in his doorframe, heart pounding and giant lump in her throat, but as he looked up at her, he merely grinned.

"Louisville's number one reporter!" he exclaimed, rising from his seat. "Wow, Harley, this is fantastic. Just great."

"It is?" she muttered.

"Don't tell me you haven't seen it since Kenny brought it in," he expressed, setting the video to play.

Harley watched as her face appeared on the screen, standing next to the director of the shelter.

"As you probably know, every year there is a food drive and Thanksgiving meal given here at the shelter for those who have nowhere else to go for the holiday, and I'm here today with Doug as the program enters its seventeenth year with its most effective results to date."

She observed as she asked Doug a couple questions about capacity and expectations, and then she appeared a little more sober. "Do you think people realize the importance of their actions in assisting with something like this?"

"Small statements are so important, Harley, which is why one little donation can turn into thousands, and one idea can start a movement."

The picture changed to outside the shelter, with Harley sitting on the curb, her legs tucked underneath her as she sat next to the man with the full, graying beard. Instinctively she raised her hand to her lips as she watched the two of them on camera.

"Duke, do you remember when you told me that you don't have to be important to make a difference?"

"Of course I do. When we had dinner together."

"Sure. Sometimes I really need that reminder, you know?" Her likeness on the video brushed away a tear and glanced at the ground.

"We all do, I suspect. You make a difference to me, simply by caring. Just like the people here today are making a difference by donating their time or their food. It only takes a spark sometimes to shine a light so bright that it can't be hidden." The camera caught Duke looking at her like he was proud.

The shot faded, and Harley was back in front of the shelter, giving the speech she prepared before she walked inside. "Fellow citizens, it's been a difficult year for many of us. For one person that might mean having suffered a loss, and for another that might mean falling on hard times. It might mean lost love, or dreams shattered, or hearts broken. We have a great deal to be thankful for, though: the breath in our lungs, the sun shining on this clear, cold day, and the huge heart of this city we live in for our neighbors and our friends. There is no greater example of this heart than what I am witnessing behind me here today, with so many turning out to volunteer their time simply to make sure that the less fortunate among us receive the same love and affection on Thanksgiving that most of us receive at home. My heart swells with pride to count myself one of you, and to think of you all as my friends as we meet here every day. Louisville, you have become my family, and today I'm your proud daughter, sister, and friend."

Mitch stopped the video, and Harley simply stared at the frozen screen.

"That was outstanding. You cried with a homeless person, Harley. Simply breathtaking." Standing to her feet, she didn't say a word as she prepared to walk back out into the hall. "You've got the desk tomorrow, with Summer gone."

"Yeah, I know," was all she replied.

With the day firmly behind her, Harley headed out the door and to her BMW, ready to drive home and sit alone in her bedroom. Maybe she'd watch some old episodes of *The Office*—that always cheered her up. Or, she could call Annie and see what she was doing, but she probably had some family-related Thanksgiving obligations.

Unlocking her car, she glanced up at the windshield and saw a single red rose there on top of the wiper blade, a paper tucked beneath. Her fingers protested as she grabbed the half-frozen flower and jerked the paper loose, sliding into the driver's seat and rubbing her hands together quickly to warm them. As she started the engine and set the defroster to high, she stared at the words written on the outside of the paper: *Harley's Song*.

Immediately Ryan's face popped into her thoughts, using that totally cute drumstick trick just to pull her closer and then winking. Reliving the memory made her entire body grow warm. Every time her phone rang at work she would feel a jolt of anticipation that he might have sought her out at last. When she stopped to put gas in her BMW, she watched the other patrons to see if one might look familiar. Even when she was sitting in traffic, she found her eyes darting around looking for the man who had captured her attention, but she hadn't received even a glimpse since the night at Bonham Station.

He had the advantage, too, because he knew where to find her. She only knew that he occasionally worked at Tiny's, and since he hadn't even done that lately, she was lost in her attempts. Two subsequent trips to Bonham Station had left her searching, too, when she found no trace of him. She had nearly given up hope that he wanted to find her at all, but in her hand rested Harley's Song. She could probably come up with a handful of people who would leave a rose on her car, but a song? Her heart told her it had to be Ryan.

She hesitantly unfolded the paper, looking down at the words.

> Have you come down?
> This angel above where I am now
> I'm trying to breathe but forgot how
> 'Cause I know now
> Who you are
>
> You're the highlight
> That radiates brightly in my life
> So perfectly wrong that we're so right
> 'Cause you can't hide
> Who you are

So while you say that we're worlds apart
I'm kneeling before you presenting my heart
Living without you feels too hard to start
Right now
Now that you've come down

So I send through
A prayer that I might prove enough to
Hold you as near as a tattoo
And be close to
Who you are

Holding her fingers over her mouth, she hastily scanned the parking lot searching for any sign of movement. It wasn't signed; no indication of who wrote it, or phone number, or request to meet her somewhere. Simply the offer of a heart and a prayer, but enough to cause her to place her hands over her face and let the tears pour out in the station parking lot.

Chapter Ten

Working the desk on Thanksgiving wasn't like working the desk on a regular day. First of all, she wasn't sitting next to the handsome Denton Price, playing off his witty banter. Instead, she was sitting next to the very ordinary Bill Triplett, the elder sportscaster who always seemed to wear his suits a size too big and couldn't tell a joke to save his life. Second, it was pretty much a given that no one would be watching the local news. They might tune in for a few moments to catch the weather, but everyone would either be stuffing their faces, catching a football game, or preparing for Black Friday shopping.

Still, Harley did her best to sell it, and then she settled for her Thanksgiving dinner of microwaved turkey pot pie that she picked up from a convenience store on her way home. The glamorous life of Harley Laine, eating gas station delicacies on a bath rug in her bedroom with the wires exposed in the wall, reading an old copy of *Bridget Jones's Diary*. She decided her life must truly have been pathetic if she was slightly jealous of Bridget, grouching about her cigarettes and drinking too much alcohol as she shuffled around having "Uncle" Geoffrey grab her bum while she tried to peddle gherkins to the unsuspecting masses. So what if Mark Darcy had on a horribly tacky Christmas sweater and said she dressed like her mother? At least she knew where to find him.

The day after Thanksgiving Harley found herself exactly where she expected to be—reporting on Black Friday sales as though that were the most important topic in the universe. It was slightly warmer than it had been the previous couple days, so she left her heavy down coat in the van while she spoke to shoppers, opting instead for a peach-hued blazer over her white button-down shirt and black pencil skirt.

They had already been to two shopping malls and were headed to a third shopping center when they heard sirens, and Harley ordered Kenny to follow the sounds to find out what was happening. In no time they pulled up to within a block of where a small warehouse was on fire, with firefighters pulling a man out of the building. Harley told Kenny to grab his camera quickly, as they were the first on the scene, and she began to rush into the fray.

"Miss Laine, I'm sorry but you've got to stop there," a burly middle-aged firefighter instructed, putting his hand out so she couldn't pass.

"Can you tell me what's going on?" she asked, craning her neck.

"Some kind of mechanical fire, ma'am, but it's not safe for you to go any closer." Nodding her understanding, she turned to wait for Kenny, who was just beginning to make his way back from the van. A quick scan of the crowd told her that a couple people must have been in the building when the fire started, because there were several onlookers and the paramedics were already on the scene. The gentleman who had just been pulled from the building was sitting on the curb as a couple of the men dressed in blue paramedics' uniforms huddled around him. In fact, one of the paramedics...

Startled, Harley broke loose of the fireman's arm and ran a few steps toward the building, trying to get a better look at the men on that curb.

"Harley!" she heard Kenny yell, but she didn't look in his direction. Lifting her head a little higher, she took a couple more steps.

A loud, booming explosion rocked the ground she was standing on, and almost knocked her to her knees. The sound must have caused her body to react in shock, because she had an unbelievable cramp running across her abdomen. Reaching over to clutch at her stomach, she pulled her fingers back when she felt something very unfamiliar hit her fingertips, noticing herself begin to shake.

"Harley!" Kenny yelled again, this time pulling up behind her and placing his hand on her back. "Please God, somebody help us! We need help over here!"

Daring to glance down, Harley saw the broken shard of metal protruding from just below her rib cage on the right side of her body, and before she had time to think about reacting the fireman who had ordered her away earlier scooped her up in his arms and was carrying her over to the ambulance.

"Can we get some medical here?" she heard him ask loudly as the material of his uniform shifted under her cheek. "Louisville's sweetheart," he said to her. "Why'd you have to go maiming yourself on my watch? I'll be drummed out of town."

There was a flurry of attention around her, enough that she couldn't determine who was talking to her, where they were taking her, or even whose hands were touching her. By the time they had her in a reclining position and were shoving her into the back of an ambulance, she could see Kenny's stricken face beside her, white and panicked.

"Harley…" he said as he was shoved back and a young man with skin the color of caramel stepped in beside her. She happened to glance down and saw that the wound was packed with gauze around the metal, which was still firmly in place. Closing her eyes, she told herself she would be all right.

God, please…

"Let me in there," she heard, and she imagined Kenny fighting with the firemen, trying to get close to her. "What happened, Miguel?"

"Large puncture wound, but she's stable. Getting ready to get fluids into her, and then some morphine."

"Harley?" the voice continued, and she felt a warm hand enclose her own. "Baby, can you hear me?"

Forcing her eyes open, she glanced at her fingers and followed the hand that held them up a strong arm that disappeared under the blue paramedic uniform. When her eyes continued upward across his neck and to his chin with the little strip of dark facial hair that led up to his lips, she drew in a quick breath.

"Ouch," she whispered, wincing. "Ryan?"

His hair was pulled into an elastic at the back of his head so it wasn't hanging on the side of his face, but the blue eyes were the same. "I'm here, baby."

Pulling her eyes away, she glanced at Miguel. "He must think I'm going to die."

"Why's that?" Miguel asked with a short laugh.

"Why else would he keep calling me baby?"

"You two know each other?" Miguel asked as he placed the needle for the IV in her arm.

"We're old friends," Harley offered with a slight smile as she looked up at Ryan again. "In fact, I do believe his heart aches for me, if I'm not mistaken."

"That's clearly the morphine talking," Ryan interrupted, continuing to grasp her hand as his thumb brushed across her knuckles one by one.

"And…getting ready to administer the morphine," Miguel said, shaking his head.

"Is the story that important to you, that you'd risk your neck?" Ryan continued, staring intently at her face. "They said you ignored their orders and went running towards the building."

"It was an accident," she muttered.

"You running was an accident."

"Yes, I thought I saw someone."

"You thought you saw someone," he repeated again, his eyes locked on hers.

"Yeah, and I did, didn't I? Because here you are."

"Oh, man," Miguel said as he continued to work to her left. "The lovely lady has impaled herself while looking for you, my friend. Lucky dog."

"Why do I feel warm?" Harley wanted to know.

"The morphine's kicking in," Miguel answered simply.

"You were looking for me?" Ryan grasped her fingers tighter as he said the words.

"Hmm, yeah," she breathed, beginning to relax a bit more. "I look for you everywhere. Tiny's. Bonham Station. Even at the gas pump."

"Why wouldn't you just give me your number?" he asked, shaking his head.

"Did you come to the station Wednesday?" she responded, wincing again as Miguel adjusted her carefully.

"Wednesday?" He looked up as though he was giving it some thought. "Wednesday... I can't seem to remember."

"You're a terrible liar."

"Could you tell what kind of damage it did internally?" Ryan wanted to know, looking at Miguel as he continued to rub her hand. "Stomach, intestines..."

"Don't think it's as deep as it looks, but can't be positive about anything," Miguel answered. "Hanging in there, Harley? We won't be much longer."

Suddenly, she laughed and squinted her eyes closed. "This is so embarrassing. Definitely not how I pictured our next meeting."

Staring at the inside of her eyelids, she fought the urge to pry them open and gawk at Ryan. She had been thinking about him for so long, now that he was in her presence, she was having a hard time figuring out a proper reaction.

"How was our next meeting going to go?" Ryan asked. That caused Miguel to chuckle, and Harley focused on the feel of Ryan's fingers against her own.

"I was definitely going to make you sing the song," she said, opening her eyes and meeting Ryan's boldly. "Will you sing me the song now?"

"No," he answered quickly, peeking at Miguel.

"That's a huge mistake," she informed him. "What if I'm mortally wounded and you just refused my last request?"

"You're not mortally wounded," Ryan argued.

"And you don't want to hear this guy sing," Miguel added. "Dude's tone deaf, big time."

The vehicle came to a stop, the back doors were thrown open, and suddenly Harley was being hustled into the hospital.

"Ryan!" she called weakly, and he appeared to her right almost instantly, grasping her fingers again. "Don't leave me."

"I have to go," he informed her sadly, concern crossing his features. "They'll take good care of you, and I'll be back."

"Promise?" she asked as he released her hand.

"Promise!" he called.

As soon as Harley arrived at the hospital, she was rushed in to inspect the damage, and surgery was performed to repair the muscle and close the wound. To her great relief, the impact hadn't caused damage to any of her organs, so she was resting comfortably and under observation. The hospital gave her a very bland dinner and she watched a report about herself on the news. Thankfully, Kenny hadn't had the camera going when she had her unfortunate incident, so that embarrassment wasn't being spread far and wide.

"Our very own Harley Laine was injured in an attempt to bring you the first look at the warehouse fire and explosion today," Summer stated. "We wish Harley the speediest of recoveries and await her return to the newsroom most anxiously."

A large bouquet of fresh colorful blooms rested in the corner of her hospital room from the Channel Six staff, but it meant so much less to her than that half-wilted rose she had discovered partly frozen on her windshield that was at home in her bedroom.

Running towards the building was completely crazy, she realized, but that paramedic looked so much like Ryan that she couldn't help herself. Her surprise at finding him in the ambulance with her hadn't passed, and she was still in a state of disbelief. Nothing about him made sense. If he was a paramedic, why was he working at Tiny's and living with his parents?

All kinds of wild thoughts went through her mind. Drinking problem, maybe? Gambling? Sold all his possessions because he wanted to be a rock star? Each presumption was a bit more preposterous than the last, and eventually she just gave up and focused blindly on the television, trying to numbly pass the few hours before time to sleep.

"Awake?" she heard from the doorway, and she glanced over to see the object of her most-likely misguided affection standing there with a brown paper bag and a huge smile on his face.

"You came back," she stated, trying to sit up a bit straighter but finding it impossible to move without straining her abdominal muscles. He crossed over to the bed and placed the bag on the rolling table, lowering himself to a seated position next to her thigh.

"I have a captive audience, and you definitely can't run away this time," he told her with a wink. "I wanted to check on you and make sure you were okay, naturally."

"That is very kind and noble of you," she assured him.

"Well, don't go too heavy with the noble business yet. The truth is, I might have an ulterior motive in coming over here tonight."

"Which is?"

He traced his index finger across the back of her hand, and she felt goose bumps spread up her arm.

"I would really love to ask you to go out with me, but I probably can't afford to treat you the way you're accustomed to being treated. In fact, I know I can't. But tonight, you've got no other plans, right?" He looked confident for a split second, and then slightly unsure. "I mean, you don't, do you?"

"I'll cancel all of them," she assured him as he drew his eyes up to her face.

"I brought you a burger from Tiny's," he whispered, glancing back at the door. "Tiny wanted to shut down the whole place and come over here to take care of you himself, but I assured him I could handle it."

"Thank you."

"I hope you don't mind that I brought one for me, too. Maybe we can do dinner and a movie?"

"What's the movie?" she wondered, glancing towards the brown bag.

"Confession," he stated, rising to retrieve the bag, "you are notorious about not giving people your number. Your friend Annie, though? She doesn't have that problem. She gave Matt her number right away. He gave it to me."

"You called Annie?"

He smiled as he walked to the door and pulled it closed after glancing out into the hall to be certain they weren't being watched. When he returned to her side, he removed a cheeseburger from the bag and placed it on the tray in front of her.

"Annie says you love *The Office*, and you're in luck because my parents happened to have it at their house."

"Yes, I will admit that we've been known to pull all-nighters."

"That's what she said," he informed her as he retrieved his own burger. "Did you like what I did there? That's what she said?"

"You're very clever," she told him with a laugh. "But if you insist on this being a date, I feel like I should be completely honest with you."

"Shoot."

"If at any time you request that I remove myself from this bed during the evening, I will have to decline."

"Because?"

"I have no idea where they took my clothes."

"Just a guess, but I'm saying you probably won't want to wear those clothes again," he insisted, trying to figure out how to work the portable DVD player he had smuggled in.

She watched him silently as he stood in front of her—the way his back filled out his T-shirt, the bottom edges of his tattoo visible on his arm. She couldn't put her finger on what so intrigued her about him, but she couldn't seem to pull her eyes away as he studied the buttons and eventually had Steve Carell's face on the screen. As he turned, he grabbed his burger and settled in the nearby chair.

"Hold on," she said, giving him a bit of a glare. "I thought you said this was a date?"

"Uh-huh," he agreed as he unwrapped his burger.

"So if you took me to Tiny's, would you sit at a different table than me?"

"Definitely not."

She struggled to move herself over in the bed and managed to scoot over only a couple centimeters. "Okay, if I could move my body, I would insist that you sit here with me. Unfortunately, I currently seem to be paralyzed."

"I can remedy that, if you're okay with it." He rose from his seat and prepared to slide his arm under her knees.

"No, don't touch me! I wasn't kidding about that whole no clothes thing."

Laughing to himself, he wrapped the blanket around her to protect her backside and then slid his arm under her knees, scooping her up and moving her over about a foot. She winced slightly as her muscles stretched, but tried not to let him see. He then returned and placed himself beside her on the bed, their arms touching ever so slightly. Feeling rather self-conscious with him so close to her, she turned to look at the small DVD screen.

"So, we should talk about something, right?" She smiled as she picked up her burger. "Oh, I know. Have you gotten any more tattoos since you inappropriately showed me your naked torso?"

"Was that inappropriate?" He took a giant bite of his burger and turned to face her, giving her a teasing stare.

"You're nearly always inappropriate, I'm afraid, but I find you fascinating."

"That is quite a coincidence, because I likewise find you fascinating."

"Enough so to write a song about me?" She snuck in a bite of her burger as his face tinted slightly red.

"I may or may not have written a song, depending solely on whether or not you liked it."

"If I say no?"

"Then I have no idea what this conversation is about, obviously." He finished off his burger as though he was making a point, and she took another small bite as she considered her words.

"So, if I say yes?"

"Then I meant every word."

"You forgot how to breathe?" she prodded, enjoying his discomfort. She took another quick bite of her burger before she placed it in front of her.

"You have that effect on me, I guess. I'm having a bit of trouble breathing right now."

"It's because you ate your burger too quickly," she joked, having a bit of trouble breathing herself. "That can cause problems, you know."

He rose and threw the cheeseburger wrappers and remains in the garbage so they wouldn't be discovered, and then he lowered himself beside her again, even closer this time so their arms were pressed against each other.

"Tell me something no one else knows," he said gently, relaxing his head against the pillow as he looked at her. She turned her head toward his so she was looking into his eyes, making sure not to twist her torso and inflict pain on her abdominal muscles.

"No one else knows?" she repeated, gazing at him.

"Yes, a secret we can share."

"Kind of like when you called me 'baby' in the ambulance?"

"I was clearly upset and delirious," he countered with a bit of a grin. "Come on, give me some inside scoop on what makes Harley Laine tick."

Almost transfixed by his gaze, she forced herself to think. "Well, I don't like motorcycles."

"I got that vibe the night at Tiny's," he stated, widening his eyes.

"But it's not really the bikes themselves I don't like, it's more the idea. My dad fixes them, you know. That's his job—his passion. So much so that he saddled me with it for life."

"Your dad named you after his motorcycle," Ryan said, wrinkling his brow a bit.

"Yes, exactly like everyone has teased me for my entire life." She sighed quietly as she gave her eyes a quick roll. "So, your turn. Tell me something no one else knows."

"I can't get you out of my mind, Harley. And it has nothing to do with motorcycles." Her heart fluttered a bit as his fingers spread across the palm of her hand and then intertwined with her own. Letting out a shaky breath, she wrapped her fingers tightly around his. With a start, she realized she was staring at his mouth, thinking about what it would feel like to kiss him, so she lowered her head to his shoulder and closed her eyes briefly when he rested his head against hers.

"Don't forget me when you go home tomorrow," he whispered.

"You're not so easy to forget," she admitted, smiling to herself.

Ryan remained there next to her on the bed while they laughed at *The Office* for a couple hours, until her breathing evened out and he looked down to see that her eyes were closed. Pressing a kiss to her temple, he paused near her hair, allowing her scent to linger in his mind for a moment longer. He had to go home and get some rest for work the next day, and she would likely be gone by the time he could come back to see her. Pausing near the edge of the bed, he grabbed the marker off the dry erase board on the wall that held the nurses' instructions.

"Forgive me, Harley," he whispered, pressing the tip of the marker to the inner section of her upper arm right beneath her armpit.

Harley was woken at midnight by a nurse checking her vital signs, and she quickly glanced around the room to realize she was alone. The television was off and the room was quiet. Aware that she had apparently dozed off and Ryan had disappeared, she sighed audibly.

"Everything okay?" the nurse wanted to know.

"I feel like I just woke up from a dream. It's rather disappointing."

The nurse checked the IV line and then gave Harley an understanding smile. "Well, maybe when you fall asleep you can go back to your dream. Sorry I woke you up."

The nurse walked to the door and back out into the hall, closing Harley in the quiet. Reaching her right arm up, she attempted to rub her eyes and happened to notice a dark mark from the corner of her eye. Stretching her arm forward, she glanced down at her newly drawn ink that stretched from the inside of her armpit halfway to her elbow. Ten numbers, drawn carefully. With a quick laugh, she brought her left hand up carefully due to the IV line and traced the numbers on her arm with her finger.

Her heart swelled, and she relaxed back against her pillow as she closed her eyes to let sleep overtake her again. She wouldn't escape without Ryan's phone number this time. He was so insistent about that fact, he had tattooed it on her arm.

Chapter Eleven

The sun spread through the horizontal blinds as Harley reluctantly sat up and gingerly placed her bare feet on the floor. She wasn't in excessive pain; the worst portion seemed to be as she was rising from a reclining position, or alternately lowering herself. As long as she was upright and moving around, she could almost forget that she had been wounded at all, until she accidentally brushed against the stitches. Still, she felt almost fortunate to have ended up in the hospital, simply because she had spent time with Ryan.

Glancing at her arm again, she rummaged through her purse until she found her phone and could program his number safely inside. Since he had taken care to make certain she had it, she didn't want it accidentally sliding down the shower drain.

"Up and around this morning?" her doctor asked as she walked into the room.

"Yes," Harley stated cheerily. "This has been a delightful bed and breakfast, but I do believe I'm ready to return to the real world."

"I hardly blame you. Just let me get a quick look at the stitches to verify that there's no infection, and I'll sign your discharge papers so you can be on your way. Someone give you a serial number?" She motioned to Harley's arm as she helped her back into the bed.

"Handsome EMT wrote his number on my arm while I was asleep," Harley told her, laughing. "Think I might get stab wounds more often."

"I certainly wouldn't recommend that," the doctor said with a knowing smile. "Your stitches look good, though. We'll have you out of here in no time."

Grinning, Harley struggled to right herself in the bed and placed a call to Annie, begging her to come pick her up and bring some comfortable clothes. Naturally, Annie grilled her about why she hadn't been answering her phone, scolded her for not calling sooner, and said she was scared to death when she saw the story on the news. Harley could barely get in two words edgewise before Annie said she was on her way and hung up.

Believing she should at least ask for what she could salvage of her clothes from the day before, she stepped up to the doorway, peering into the hall as she held the back of her hospital gown closed with her fist. While she craned her neck to try to locate a nurse, she happened to lock eyes with a girl two doors down who was doing the very same thing. Smiling rather guiltily, she gave a quick wave with her right hand. The girl responded by shyly retreating a couple inches. Peeking back and forth down the hallway, Harley cinched the back of her gown a bit tighter and crossed over to the other girl's room.

"Hey," she said breezily as she stepped up to the young woman, who looked to be about fourteen or fifteen. "Are you trying to break free, too?"

"Actually, I was just looking for my mom," she stated, glancing down the hallway again.

"Want company?"

She nodded shyly and stepped back into her room. As she retreated, Harley couldn't help but notice that her movement was hampered by several lines and tubes that she had to drag with her. As the girl settled herself carefully back onto the bed, Harley pulled the back of the gown tightly beneath her legs and lowered herself on the light tan armchair.

"I'm Harley Laine," she began, smiling at the younger woman, who pulled the pole containing all the cords closer to her bed in order to make herself more comfortable.

"I recognize you from the news," the girl stated, glancing at the door again.

"So you're clearly at the advantage here. You know who I am, but I don't know you. What's your name?"

"Kelsey," she added, self-consciously tucking a strand of dishwater blonde hair behind her ear. "Kelsey Andrews."

"Pretty name." Harley crossed her legs under her gown, feeling a little absurd simply due to the knowledge that she wasn't wearing proper underclothes. "Do you come here often?" She meant the comment as a teasing joke, but Kelsey seemed to shrink a bit before answering.

"Quite a bit lately, yeah." Fiddling with her cords, she avoided making eye contact with Harley.

"How old are you?" Harley dared to ask quietly, gazing at the girl. She was quite pretty, but her coloring was slightly off and she had dark circles under her light brown eyes.

"Seventeen."

"I remember seventeen," Harley said, staring up at the ceiling as she reminisced. "My biggest worry was whether or not I'd fail trigonometry and physics. Oh, and whether Brent Dillard would ask me to prom. He didn't, by the way. I ended up going with Rick Dillard, his cousin. He only asked me because his dad was friends with my dad, and somehow they guilted him into it. I hadn't really come into my own back then. Really skinny, no curves at all. Not that I have many curves now, but padded bras do wonders in that department."

Kelsey tittered a bit and placed her hand over her mouth.

"I'm sorry. You probably think I have no filter."

"No, that was funny," Kelsey insisted. "Did you scribble all over your arm?"

Harley glanced down at the two numbers that were visible under the sleeve of her gown. "Oh, can I tell you a secret?" She grinned slyly at the younger girl, who nodded hesitantly. "I was rescued yesterday by this completely handsome EMT, and he wrote his phone number on my arm."

"That sounds like a romance novel," Kelsey told her with a sigh. "Do you have to stay here long?"

"They're getting ready to release me as we speak." Harley hesitated as Kelsey's eyes drifted to the door. "I was poking my head into the hall looking for my clothes."

"Kelsey, what are you doing up?" Harley heard the unfamiliar voice behind her right shoulder, and she twisted and pulled her stitches, causing an unavoidable grimace. "Did something happen?"

"No, Mom, I was just looking for you. And then Harley Laine came to visit me."

"Oh." The older woman nearly jumped, glancing over at Harley. She quickly smoothed her dark brown shoulder-length hair and looked a bit self-conscious. "Goodness, what a surprise! What brings you by?"

Glancing down at her hospital gown, Harley stifled a giggle. "I'm just down the hall, actually. Managed to injure myself yesterday, rather stupidly I'm afraid. I was peeking into the hallway at the exact time Kelsey was doing the same."

"Goodness, where are my manners?" Kelsey's mother stepped forward and extended her hand towards Harley. "Regina Andrews."

"Very nice to meet you," Harley added, not getting up because she didn't want to have to readjust her backside.

"We like watching you on the news," Regina said, settling on the edge of Kelsey's bed. "Well, when we watch TV, which isn't very often."

Harley hesitantly glanced from mother to daughter. "Kelsey said you've been here a lot lately."

"Yes, but we're praying that things will look up for us soon."

"Do you mind if I ask…" Harley hesitated, torn between not wanting to pry and wondering what could be wrong with the pretty teenager.

"Kelsey has cirrhosis of the liver," Regina began, placing her hand on Kelsey's against the bed.

"I'm sorry, Mrs. Andrews," Harley said quietly, unsure what that meant but knowing from their exchanged looks that it couldn't be good.

"She had a blockage of the bile duct, which started the disease a couple years ago," the mother continued, recognizing

Harley's quizzical expression. "The healthy liver tissue is replaced with scar tissue, which keeps the liver from functioning the way it should. She takes diuretics but occasionally we still find ourselves here due to fluid retention."

"And what will they do?" Harley asked, referencing the doctors and the hospital.

"She's on the transplant list," Regina offered bluntly but calmly. "She's always tired, and she rarely wants to eat. And you can see she has a bit of jaundice and bruises easily."

"Does that mean no prom for you?" Harley attempted to smile at the blonde teenager.

"Most likely not, but there was no Brent Dillard for me, anyway," Kelsey admitted with a shy grin. "Besides, I'd be just like you and wouldn't fill my dress out."

"If you were going to prom, I'm sure you'd be better dressed than I was in my old prom bomb—it was a blue poofball nightmare. It belonged to Rick Dillard's older sister, and my mom had to put a couple seams under my arms just so it wouldn't fall off. Good times."

Kelsey smiled a bit as she looked down at her fingers, tugging at Harley's heart.

"So, Harley, what happened to you yesterday?" Regina presented the question as she adjusted Kelsey's pillow behind her. "How did you wind up here?"

Giving a guilty, conspiratorial grin to the teenager, Harley giggled for a second. "Can I be perfectly honest?"

"I like honest," Kelsey told her.

Harley began to lean forward, but thought better of it when a draft hit her backside. "I came upon this fire at a warehouse, and my cameraman and I were trying to get the exclusive first look. The fireman had just told me I couldn't go closer, but I was watching where they had taken this man they pulled out of the building. He was sitting on the curb with the paramedics. As I'm looking, I notice that one of the paramedics looks familiar. He looks just like this guy I know, in fact. I started moving closer, not even realizing what I was doing." She raised her eyebrows at Kelsey, who had a small grin on her face.

"So, if anyone ever tells you that looking for cute boys can be hazardous to your health, Kelsey, I am proof that it's the truth. I was looking for a guy, and I got caught in an explosion. Luckily for me, the metal just sliced into my skin and muscles and not into anything else."

"It seems kind of funny, you looking for a guy," Kelsey piped up, not bothering to stifle her laugh. "I would have thought guys would be looking for you."

"We are in total agreement." Harley attempted to appear serious. "Where was a friend like you in high school when I needed her? I could have used the morale boost."

"For Brent Dillard?" Kelsey wanted to know.

"I'm sure now he's totally kicking himself," Harley stated with a wink. "Actually, he probably has no idea I'm alive anymore. Not that he realized it then, either."

"Did you grow up here, Harley?" Regina piped up, eyeing Kelsey to make sure she wasn't overexerting herself.

"A couple hours away in a really small town. I went to the University of Kentucky School of Journalism and then worked in Little Rock for a year before I came to Louisville." Glancing guiltily at Kelsey, Harley mentally told herself to stop being so self-centered. "What do you want to do after high school, Kelsey?"

"Oh," Kelsey muttered, glancing at her mother. "I don't know..."

"We just try to focus on the short-term and keeping her healthy," Regina said quietly.

"But you have dreams, I can see it in your eyes." Harley noticed the quick snap of Regina's head in her direction, but she continued to focus on Kelsey. "Sometimes it's nice to dream, even if you don't know if your dreams will come true. I like to dream that one day I'll be in New York on the morning news programs, even though my boss seems to enjoy sending me out to chase chickens and report on world record attempts." Harley made certain she smiled at Kelsey after her little joke, who responded by giving a slight grin of her own.

"You promise not to laugh?" Kelsey asked, leaning back against her pillow as she drew in a ragged breath. Harley nodded her head solemnly as she waited for the younger woman to speak. "I really want to be a missionary—to help in places where people don't have basic medical care."

Harley was rather surprised by the answer…enough so that she hesitated to speak for a moment. Kelsey mistook her silence for judgment, and she allowed the corner of her mouth to tilt up just a bit as she looked down at her hands.

"You think that's crazy," Kelsey assumed, continuing to stare at her fingers.

"No," Harley insisted. "No, I don't think that's crazy at all. In fact, I think that's pretty amazing."

"Harley?" she heard from behind her. Turning slightly, she saw Annie in the doorway. "Oh, hey. I've been looking for you. Everything okay?"

"Just making some new friends," Harley stated as she rose, taking care to hold tightly to her gown. "Annie's here to take me home, but would it be okay if I came back to visit you sometime?"

Kelsey nodded slowly as Regina rose and told her goodbye, after which Harley backed into the hallway, protective of her posterior.

The phone rang four times, and Harley was about to hit the end button and drop it against her bed when there was finally a sound on the other end.

"Yeah," was the one-word greeting.

"Ryan?" she asked hesitantly. "And if this isn't Ryan, when were you in my room and how did you manage access to my arm?"

"Wait, I think I need to sit down." She heard a rustling on the other end of the phone, and she smiled to herself as she rested her fingers on the bedspread beneath her. "If I didn't know better, I might be tempted to think that the lovely miss Harley Laine lowered herself from her pedestal long enough to dial my number. Surely I'm mistaken."

"You're right. What was I thinking? I'm sorry, but I have to go."

"No, no," he pleaded, suddenly serious. "How are you feeling?"

"Fairly good, all things considered. A little sore, but otherwise on top of the world."

"On top of the world, huh?" She heard him chuckle on the other end of the line as the rustling returned again, and she imagined him settling onto his own bed and lying there the same way she was. "Why is that exactly?"

"Oh, no reason. In spite of being stabbed and stitched and bleeding all over myself, and traipsing about in the hallway this morning with my backside hanging out, I can't seem to stop smiling."

"Because?"

"I have no idea. It's the strangest thing." She couldn't stop the grin from spreading onto her face as she stared at the ceiling, and she wondered if he could sense it through the phone.

"I know it's late, but I think maybe I should check on you. Do you want me to come over?" His voice sounded rather tentative, almost a whisper.

"Um..." Harley stalled, glancing around at her crude bedroom walls. "No, that doesn't seem like a good idea. Where are you? Maybe I could come see you? So you can see for yourself that I'm okay, I mean."

"Oh," he stammered, clearing his throat. "I would say yes, but my dad's already asleep, and..."

Ew. I nearly forgot he lived with his parents.

"Yeah, another time then," she surmised, sitting up on the bed and grimacing as her stitches stretched a bit. "What did you do tonight?"

"After work, I did a bit of landscaping."

"Landscaping?" She pressed her lips together as she gave that response a bit of thought.

"Yeah, I've got a buddy with a landscaping business, and he let me help him for a while tonight for the extra cash. Spreading gravel by hand—who needs to go to the gym, right? Tomorrow we're stacking stones along a driveway. Some day off, huh?"

"You always work on your day off?" She bit her lip as she studied her fingernails. "Don't you ever have any fun?"

"Yes, at work," he stated with a short laugh. "I'm finding myself in a bit of a quandary lately, though, and it's your fault."

"My fault?! Please explain yourself."

He hesitated a moment, making Harley wish they were face to face so she could see his expression.

"Well, I really need the extra work, and I've had a couple offers for next weekend, but I'm contemplating turning them down. I know I shouldn't, but there's this girl..."

"What sort of girl?" Harley wondered quietly, sensing his smile on the other side of the phone.

"I'm not completely sure yet, hence the problem."

Clearing her throat a bit, Harley decided to change the subject. "So, I'm hoping you will tell your friend Miguel how grateful I am for his assistance in the ambulance. He's fantastic at his job."

"Is that a thinly veiled insult?"

"Well, to be fair, I didn't witness you doing much of anything, unless you count fawning all over me and calling me baby."

"Come on! Did you call me just to insult me?" He hesitated a second, and then continued more gently. "You're mad that I wrote on your arm, aren't you? I defaced your flawless canvas."

"Actually, it's the most beautiful piece of art I've ever seen."

"Ladies and gentlemen, I do believe the fair princess might have a soft spot for the pauper after all."

"Why do you have to go and make it weird?"

"It's self-preservation," he remarked, letting out a slight sigh that made her think he was adjusting his spot on the bed. "As long as I keep reminding myself that you hold a small amount of disdain for me, it won't hurt as badly when I see you out on the town with Junior Trust Fund."

Pausing, she allowed her brow to furrow as she reworked his words in her mind.

Spoiled brat.

Think you're too good for me.

Only after guys for their money.

"Still there, Harley?"

Was she? She suddenly felt a bit isolated.

"Yes, I'm just wondering why you wanted me to call since you so obviously desire to throw jabs at me."

"I'm sorry," he assured her, voice quieting. "That was rude. The thing is…I've got a lot on my plate, and adding you to it is just going to make things more complicated. Not that I'm complaining. You're like the dessert that's just out of reach, because I can't touch it until I take care of the rest of the meal. You know what I mean?"

"You're comparing me to chocolate cake?"

"It was a horrible metaphor."

"Maybe you should just relax a little," she said, staring at the ceiling. "You're always working."

"Trust me, I wish that was an option," he admitted as he expelled a breath he was holding.

"Listen, my friend Annie is worried about me, so she's dragging me to church with her in the morning. I'm kind of feeling weird about it, and you seem pretty in touch with your spirituality, with all the Bible ink and such. I wouldn't be totally opposed to you just popping up while we're there."

"You make such a tempting offer," he stated sarcastically.

"This is really unnatural to me, okay? I normally don't have to do this." Instantly worried that he would think she was comparing him to other men, she softened her tone. "Will you come with me tomorrow?"

"You have no idea how badly I want to say yes, but I can't, Harley. I've got work to do."

"On the ambulance?" she asked, trying not to let his rejection sting.

"No, the landscaping, remember?"

"Is it really that important?" Pausing a second, she closed her eyes. "If it's about money, I will pick you up, and you don't have to spend a dime."

"That's equally insulting and flattering. I'm sorry, really. I'm not trying to hurt you."

"You're not," she insisted, forcing the words past a lump in her throat. "I was just trying to be nice, since you went to the trouble to leave me your number and everything. I don't want to disrupt your meal, being all cakey and stuff, so no worries. Forget I asked."

"Please don't do that."

"Do what?" Tears filled her eyes, and she angrily willed them away. "You're the one sending me mixed signals here. You beg me for my number every time I see you, but then you pretty much call me decadent but useless, with the weird dessert reference. Don't toy with me. Why did you come to the hospital last night? What was that, exactly?"

"That was me wanting to be with you," he said in a hushed tone.

"Well, this was me wanting to be with you, so I guess we're even," she said while a tear slid out of the corner of her eye and made its way down the side of her face. "Good night, Ryan."

Chapter Twelve

Annie stood with her hands on her hips, giving Harley a slight glare from just inside her apartment door. Gazing at her friend's tattered jeans, Harley glanced down at her own skirt and felt rather foolish.

"You might have mentioned not to dress up," she said, stepping through the doorway.

"And you should have waited until I came to pick you up, lady. It doesn't seem like you should be driving."

Harley considered using one of her tried-and-true excuses for not allowing Annie into her home: *I didn't have time to clean yesterday. It's such a long way out of the city. It's easier for me to drive so I can run errands on the way home.* Luckily, today she had an easy excuse.

"I took a cab," she said breathily. "I had to pick up my car at the station, so it was just easier that way."

"And how are you feeling?" Annie wondered, still half-glaring at her friend.

"Well enough that you can back off, warden," Harley assured her with a slight laugh. "I don't feel completely wonderful, but I'll manage."

"Did the doctor tell you to stay in bed or anything like that?"

"Only to take it easy, which I am. Anyway, I have to go back to work tomorrow. I've got the momentum of being named favorite reporter, and I can't lay low and let that slide. I have to capitalize on it while I can."

"Of course, Harley the vicious career-driven newswoman has returned."

"And Annie, the snarky friend, has decided to rub my face in it today. What's with this weekend and people giving me a hard time?"

"What are you talking about?"

Closing her eyes and rubbing her fingers across her forehead, Harley pondered telling Annie about Ryan. "Nothing. I've been stabbed. I'm obviously not having a stellar holiday."

"You should have done Thanksgiving with me like I asked."

"I had to work that day, remember? I don't want to worry about it. Let's just have a good time today, okay? If that can be achieved in church."

"Something tells me you're rather hostile to the whole idea," Annie assessed as she walked down the hall, throwing the words over her shoulder.

Harley paused next to the couch and settled her backside on the armrest, careful not to slouch in a way that would involve her abdominal muscles. "I'm not hostile!" she called, staring into Annie's kitchen. "I'm not exactly a newbie, you know. My parents forced me into attendance every Sunday. I've had my share of hellfire and brimstone and rigid rules that I could find nowhere in the sacred texts, which I looked at until my eyes were crossed."

"You're jaded because of a people problem," Annie stated as she returned from her bedroom, stopping midway in the hall to pull her second black boot over her calf muscle. "Forget about people and just give God a chance for a change."

"Very clever, until you factor in the little tidbit of information that those individuals are God's spokespeople. If I was all-powerful, I would choose someone to speak for me who was... I don't know, intelligent and kind, perhaps?"

"Ah, but God uses the foolish to confound the wise," Annie told her, lifting her pierced eyebrow.

"That makes sense, because there's an abundance of foolish, and I'm usually confounded." Harley took a moment to give her friend a slight smile. "I'm sure your church is nothing like the ones I'm used to, okay? First of all, I'm pretty sure that group wouldn't have allowed you through the door, which would have been a colossal mistake, because they have no idea what they're missing."

"Aww, you made me feel all warm and fuzzy inside," Annie said sarcastically, grabbing her coat. "Come on, let's go find the foolish so you can bestow your mighty wit upon them."

The atmosphere in the room was more casual-friendly than solemn when Harley entered the rather plain building, and Annie fell into easy conversation with each person who walked by. Every one of the other individuals greeted Harley as though they knew her, which Harley had come to expect as a strange side effect of appearing on the nightly news.

One particular person she bumped into startled her enough that she could barely contain her gasp as she stared into the bearded face with the gray eyes.

"Duke? I didn't expect to see you here."

"Well, I'm mighty glad to see you. I was worried about you Friday night. Tiny was beside himself."

"You and Fletcher know each other?" Annie inserted herself into the conversation.

Responding to Harley's questioning glance, Duke stretched out his hand. "I'm sorry, it appears we haven't been formally introduced. Fletcher Marion."

"What's going on?" Harley muttered, looking skeptically at Duke's outstretched hand. "Did I fall in the rabbit hole or something?"

"No, hon," Duke admitted with a chuckle. "People started calling me Duke because of my last name, Marion."

"I have no idea what that means." Eyeing him warily, Harley folded her arms across her abdomen, accidentally pushing in on her wound. Sighing slightly, she relaxed her posture.

"Generation gap," Duke continued. "John Wayne's real name was Marion, and people called him the Duke, so…"

"I had no idea you had a nickname, Fletcher," Annie said, causing Harley to turn to her with wide eyes.

"The guys gave me the name back when we used to ride together, and it stuck. I never felt like a Fletcher, but a name is a name."

Harley blanched a bit, because she certainly knew what having an unfortunate name entailed.

"So how do you get here on Sundays?" Harley wanted to know, glancing around at the others who were finding their seats.

"On my Harley," he stated quickly.

"Fletcher… I mean Duke." Annie giggled for a second. "I think I like that—I'm going to use that from now on. Duke is our recovery group leader for people dealing with addiction."

Stunned into silence, Harley only stared at the gentleman she had shared chocolate with every Friday night for months.

"People dealing with anything they need recovery from, really," Duke inserted. "Luckily, so far I haven't felt a need to repent of my chocolate addiction. Or my friendships with pretty reporters."

With a jolt, Harley shook herself from her stupor. "I'm sorry, this is baffling me. You're driving around on a Harley, and yet you're…"

"I'm what?"

"You know," she hissed, glancing around her again. "Homeless."

"Who said I was homeless?" His lips tilted slightly upward under his mess of facial hair.

"Um, circumstantial evidence?"

"You made an assumption."

"Yeah, because you sit on the park bench outside Tiny's every Friday night."

"I have a recovery group just down the block from there on Friday afternoons. I like to sit outside Tiny's afterwards and pray for the people in my group."

"He gives you free food."

"You too, if I'm not mistaken."

"That's beside the point," she said, shaking her head. "What about being at the shelter?"

"I volunteer there."

"This is all very perplexing," Harley stated as the music began and Annie grabbed her arm to pull her toward a chair. They stood in front of their seats as the guitars began to play, and Harley felt Duke reach over and touch her arm from the aisle. She glanced at him, and he leaned close enough to be next to her ear.

"Sometimes people aren't what they seem," he whispered, "but when God gives me friends, I figure it's for a reason." Giving him a quick scowl, she turned back towards the musicians. "Don't judge a book by its cover." With that, he positioned himself next to her and began to sing.

Trying to concentrate on the music, her mind began racing. All the time she spent treating Duke like a homeless person, and he was just sitting on the bench to pray. She felt the warmth rising in her neck thinking about her mistake and how she'd jumped to conclusions. What a colossal imbecile she had proven to be!

And what did he mean, saying sometimes people aren't what they seem? If referring to the friends he made he was referencing her, then she found that fact practically an insult. Why would he accuse her of not being what she seemed?

Unless…

What if he was talking about Ryan? He was friends with Ryan, but how? It had to be from the recovery group, and if so, he definitely had some sort of problem. Whatever it was would explain the desperate need for money all the time. It was one thing to imagine herself wanting to date a man who lived with his parents and didn't have a car, but add in some sort of addiction, and it was simply too much.

Closing her eyes, she lowered her head and shook it a bit, the full realization of the fact that she absolutely could not date Ryan practically smothering her. Not that he even wanted to date her, since he seemed extremely wishy-washy about the subject in the first place.

She jumped a tad and glanced to her right when she felt a hand grasp her own, and Annie gave her a grin. No doubt she believed Harley was praying, and she found it encouraging. Squeezing her wild-haired friend's hand, Harley closed her eyes again.

"What the heck," she whispered inaudibly. "God, remember me? Harley?" Pausing, she bit her lip, trying not to allow the concern to spread across her face. "What do I do?"

After spending the morning at Annie's church, which Harley admittedly enjoyed and found amazingly non-pretentious, she drove to the studio and sat at her desk, going through her emails and jotting notes on what she wanted to accomplish during the week. When she saw several congratulatory messages about her piece the week before at the shelter, where she had talked with Duke, she guiltily placed her head in her arms on her desk. The number one rule of reporting was not to assume, but to get the facts. She hadn't bothered to get the facts on Duke, and she felt humiliated.

Two hours later, when she roused and realized she had fallen asleep with her head against her desktop, she sat up and rubbed a fist against her eyes. The entire weekend had been a jumble of mixed emotions. The two bright spots had been her evening with Ryan at the hospital, which was decidedly cloudy after the phone call the night before, and her meeting with Kelsey in the hospital room down the hall. Allowing a slight smile to touch her lips, she thought about the pretty blonde-haired teenager's sweet answer that she wanted to be a missionary.

Blowing out a deep breath and taking care not to stretch her muscles, Harley rose gingerly from her chair and grabbed her purse, pulling out her keys. She couldn't explain it, and it felt a bit impulsive, but she wanted to talk to Kelsey.

Chapter Thirteen

"Hello?" Harley called tentatively after knocking twice, and then waited until she heard a response before she peeked into the room.

"Oh, goodness!" Regina said, rising from her chair. "I'm surprised to see you again, Harley."

Glancing at the bed, Harley quickly realized that Kelsey was dozing.

"Did I come at a bad time? I don't have to stay."

"Of course not!" Regina insisted. "Please, have a seat."

"Thanks," she breathed, settling into a chair and glancing at the middle-aged blond man with eyes that matched Kelsey's, who sat beside the bed.

"Oh, where are my manners?" Regina asked. "Harley, this is my husband, Sam."

"It's nice to meet you, Sam," Harley stated with a smile.

"Same here," he informed her, rising and offering his hand. "Kelsey was real excited yesterday after meeting you. She told me as soon as I got here this morning."

"She's a great girl. I feel very fortunate to have stumbled upon her yesterday. Or I should say, it was quite astonishing that we were both spying into the hallway at the same time."

"Yes, she gets a bit restless," Regina stated with a sad smile. "She has so many things she'd like to do, but she gets tuckered out rather quickly nowadays."

"And there's nothing that can be done, besides the transplant?" Harley felt a bit rude for being so brusque, but Regina and Sam didn't seem to notice.

"Nothing of any consequence." Sam glanced at Kelsey before he continued. "Of course everyone here is doing what they can, but until a new liver is available, it's like patching up an old, bald tire. You can keep throwing new patches on there, but it's still worn out."

Harley grinned at the thought of the man describing internal organs as parts of a car.

"And how long will it take to have a liver available, or is that something they can't tell you?"

Twisting her mouth to the side, Regina tilted her head a bit. "Well, a living donor would be the best option for Kelsey, because she's not very far up on the list. She doesn't share a blood type with anyone but Sam, though, and he has a bit of a health problem, so he's ineligible at the moment."

"That must break your heart," Harley whispered, to which Sam only nodded.

"And you don't have any friends or other family members who would be willing to help you?"

Regina looked down at her hands in her lap and shook her head slightly. "How do you ask someone to do that? To look another person in the eye and ask them to lay down their life for you? There's always a risk involved, and it's not something to take lightly."

"But I know you want to ask, because she's your daughter," Harley continued quietly.

Regina glanced up with eyes full of moisture. "Of course, how could I not? She's my baby girl."

"Are you talking about me?" Kelsey wanted to know, her eyelids fluttering as a small smile touched her lips. "I heard baby girl. Either it's my mom, or it's Zac Efron."

"Zac Efron," her mother repeated, shaking her head as she swiped at her eye. "I don't suppose you know Zac Efron, do you Harley?"

"No, I can't say that I do."

Kelsey fully opened her eyes and directed her gaze toward Harley. "Hey, Harley. I'm surprised to see you. I figured your arm decorator would have swept you off to a distant land by now."

Clearing her throat, Harley tried not to smile. "Let's just keep that to ourselves," she whispered. "That is classified information, patient/healthcare worker confidence, HIPAA violations and all that."

"I hope it's not Zac Efron," Kelsey muttered, causing a loud giggle to erupt from Harley.

"You're full of life today, aren't you?"

"Yes," Kelsey admitted, stretching her arms to her sides. "I'm feeling a lot better, and I can go home tomorrow."

"Probably," Regina was quick to interject.

"Thank goodness I'm an optimist," Kelsey stated, wrinkling her nose. "Do you like Scrabble, Harley?"

"Scrabble? I can honestly say I have never played that."

"I'm quite good. I would probably beat you."

"Oh, honey, I'm sure Harley doesn't have time for that," Regina insisted.

"Actually, I've been looking for someone to school me in Scrabble-playing abilities. If Kelsey's up to the task..." Harley winked at her blonde-haired friend, and Kelsey positioned herself a little higher in her bed.

"Mom? Dad?" Kelsey's eyes seemed a little brighter, and both her parents agreed to play her game. Regina spread the board out on the rolling table that rested near her daughter's bed, and Harley shrugged out of her coat and stepped toward the three of them.

"You can sit by me, Harley," Kelsey insisted, so Harley sat down cautiously next to the girl on her bed and gave her a quick smile. "Do you want the full directions, or just the abbreviated version?"

"Abbreviated?"

"You get letters. You make words."

"Easy enough, I guess," Harley replied with a laugh. "So, do I get to go first?"

"Sure." Kelsey shrugged as Regina divvied up the wooden tiles and passed them around.

After much consideration, Harley finally placed the word TO on the board, followed by some teasing giggles from Kelsey. Harley shot her a playful warning glance and insisted that she try to do better, but Kelsey wanted her parents to go next. Sam hastily added N and O to the top of Harley's word to create NOT. Regina paused for a moment before using Sam's N to create the word AND.

When it was Kelsey's turn, she hid her tiles behind her hand and glanced over at Harley mischievously before using Harley's original TO and encompassing it with OC and PI.

"Octopi?" Harley blurted. "Are you kidding me?"

"It's just a simple word," Kelsey muttered.

With an exaggerated roll of her eyes, Harley dejectedly added an N to the bottom of the last letter of Kelsey's word to create IN.

Nearly an hour went by, with Kelsey soundly beating her three companions, when suddenly Harley shook her head.

"I call a foul," she stated, crossing her arms against her chest. "Zax? That's not a word."

"Dictionary," Regina simply ordered, and Sam brought out his phone.

"Zax," he said quietly, scanning the results. "A tool like a hatchet."

"Oh, come on, how do you know that?" Harley whined, causing Kelsey to giggle.

"Somebody's having a party without me," a voice sounded from near the door, and Kelsey tried to halt her giggling as Harley glanced up and felt her breath catch in her chest.

"You can take my place," Sam indicated, rising from his seat. "I need a break, and Kelsey's killing us anyway."

"Just like always," Regina agreed. "You finished a bit early today, didn't you?"

"Huh?" the newcomer muttered, attempting to drag his eyes from Harley. "Yeah, I suppose."

"We have a new friend," Kelsey stated with a smile, looking protectively at Harley, who realized in that instant that she was holding her breath and let it out in a slight rush.

"Yes, you hadn't talked to Kelsey yet, had you?" Regina asked him as he took another step into the room. "Harley, this is Kelsey's brother, Ryan."

Harley was vaguely aware that she should be saying something in reply, but as she stared at the man with his hair brushing his shoulders in front of her, she couldn't seem to force her brain into action.

"We've met," Ryan informed his mother, directing his gaze back at Harley. When his eyes locked on hers, she quickly looked down at her hands.

"Ryan is our rock," Regina stated emphatically, smiling warmly at her son. "I don't know what we'd do without him."

"Mom," Ryan said, shaking his head to discourage her.

"Our hospital bills were getting out of hand, and we were struggling financially, so Ryan took it upon himself to move back home and start paying all our bills so we could focus on getting Kelsey well again. He saves us every day."

Clearing his throat, Ryan gave his mother a silencing glance. "How are your muscles feeling today?" he directed toward Harley. "I guess your stitches are alright?"

"Yeah, thanks," Harley managed to squeak out as Kelsey gave her a quizzical look. "Ryan was in the ambulance with me the other day."

"Oh," Kelsey stated uninterestedly, before widening her eyes and really locking in on Harley. "Oh!" Leaning toward Harley, Kelsey gave her a little nudge in the shoulder. "Miguel is really cute."

Before she had time to think, Harley lifted her hands to her face and shook her head.

Not happening. Not happening. Not happening.

"Was Miguel in the ambulance with Harley, too?" Kelsey wanted to know.

"Yeah, he was there," Ryan stated, lowering himself into the chair next to the bed, positioning himself closer to Harley. "Why do you want to know?"

"Did he happen to mention anything about Harley?" Kelsey continued, giving her new friend a slight grin. "That he maybe has a crush on her?"

Dear God, make it stop!

"That Miguel has a thing for Harley?" Ryan repeated, allowing his eyes to rest on Harley's face. "My instinct is to say no, but since Harley's turning a muted shade of red, maybe you should ask her." He folded his arms across his chest, which dragged the top of his T-shirt down just enough that Harley glimpsed the top of his tattoo. The taunting nature of his stare made her even more embarrassed, but the desire to snap at him was tempered by the knowledge that Kelsey was at her side and there were other individuals in the room.

"I honestly don't know anything about Miguel," Harley told them, daring to glance at Ryan's eyes, sensing a hint of something. Disapproval? Distrust? Maybe disappointment? "Obviously, since he didn't reek of a trust fund, I probably wouldn't notice that kind of thing anyway."

Ugh, why did you say that?

"Wow." He pulled his eyes away and looked at his lap for a second. "I guess I deserve that. But I did tell you I was sorry, remember?"

"Sure," she stated as breezily as she could under the circumstances. "You're sorry, and I'm cake. I remember."

"And as far as this morning goes, I'm not necessarily saying I should have changed my answer last night, but I did kick myself a little about it after the fact. Just so you know, for the next time you ask."

"As if I would risk that again," Harley muttered, trying to ignore Ryan's hint of a smile.

"Oh, eww…" Kelsey added, wrinkling her nose. "Ryan? Not Miguel? Your story just got a whole lot less cool."

"What story is this?" Sam wanted to know, scraping the Scrabble tiles off the board and placing them into the box.

Rather than answer, Harley mentally cringed and glanced toward her coat, wondering if she could make a hasty exit without being completely rude. The fact that it was partially under Ryan's thigh was a problem, and the realization that he might confuse her coat-rescuing trance with an attempt to stare at those black jeans that were molded tightly against his thigh caused the blood to rush straight up into her cheeks once again.

Verbally explaining that she was not checking him out didn't seem like a great idea under the circumstances.

"Yesterday when Harley came in here, she had a bunch of marks on her skin, and she told me a totally smokin' hot guy on the ambulance got romantic and wrote his phone number all over her arm."

Harley's mouth fell open in sheer mortification. "I assure you, the majority of those words were not ever spoken by me."

"Maybe not," Kelsey giggled, looking at her mother. "She did have the numbers on her arm, though, and she was all smiley about it."

"And you did this, Ryan?" Regina asked with a laugh.

In response, he gave a lopsided grin. "Does that sound like something I would do?"

"You know what? I've stayed too long and I'm interrupting your family time, so I think I'm going to go," Harley said, rising to her feet and reaching for her coat. She had to lock eyes with Ryan to do so, as he tilted to one side so she could slide the coat out from beneath his leg. "Thanks for the schooling in Scrabble, Kelsey. Sam, it was nice to meet you."

"You don't have to leave," Regina told her as she settled near Kelsey on the bed.

"Oh, I think I do," Harley was quick to disagree. "Thank you, though, for allowing me to visit with you for a while. I enjoyed it."

"Maybe you can come over for dinner sometime," Kelsey suggested.

"Sure, maybe, we'll see." Harley allowed herself the slight agreement, albeit noncommittal. "Good night."

Stepping into the hall, she held her fist against her forehead and laughed contemptuously at her own stupidity. She could remain totally composed in the face of people wearing the most ridiculous outfits when she interviewed them for television. She had the presence of mind to take preposterous topics and somehow turn them into poetic pieces of fine art. She had spoken eloquently with sports figures and civic leaders and once even the United States Attorney General, and managed to appear unaffected and professional while standing in chicken dung or judging horrible city-wide talent competitions.

She was Harley Laine, for heaven's sake!

So why did the mere presence of Ryan Temple turn her into a blithering idiot?

As she neared the end of the hall, she punched the button on the elevator and the doors opened immediately, welcoming her into the waiting solitude. The moment they closed around her, she pulled the back of her hair through her hands and fought the urge to groan.

Ryan was completely unnerving. The instant he walked into the room, she felt like she wasn't in control of the situation anymore. And it wasn't simply his presence, because he had a way of speaking to her that drew her out of herself. Every word he said seemed like a challenge, or a taunt, or a prelude to something just over the horizon.

Leaning back against the handrail in the elevator, she let out a long sigh. The information she just learned washed over her slowly, and she felt tears unexpectedly fill her eyes. Ryan lived with his parents because he was paying their bills. He took on extra work and sacrificed his time so his family could focus on Kelsey.

The elevator doors shifted open, and she hastily brushed at her eyes to make sure no moisture had escaped as she slid her arms into her coat and pulled her car keys out of her pocket. Silently she walked past people milling about in the hospital lobby, keeping her head down in hopes that no one would recognize her. With the way she was feeling, all she wanted was the safety of her car and the isolation it would offer.

Meeting a blast of cold air as the automatic glass door slid open, she stuffed her hands into her pockets and made her way through the middle of the parking lot. The sun must have just set, because although the sky was a murky gray, it wasn't completely dark yet. Shaking her head to try to erase the jumble of thoughts amassing there, she stopped and hesitated at the end of the sidewalk.

"Harley!"

This is definitely not going to help the jumble.

Turning, she watched as Ryan stepped quickly across the parking lot behind her, wearing a heavy black coat with his hands shoved firmly into his jeans pockets. He didn't smile as he came near, and she tried to remain guarded as she steeled herself for whatever was to come. When he reached up and shoved his hand through his hair to push it away from his face, though, her mind fogged over and she felt an inexplicable heaviness, as though she had done something terribly wrong simply by stumbling upon his secret.

"I'm so sorry," she whispered. "I don't have a clue what to say." Pausing, she forced a breath into her lungs and attempted to slow down. "I'm sorry, Ryan."

"For something to do with my sister?" He had that look in his eyes again, chilling Harley a bit. "What are you doing here?"

"We met yesterday, and..." she began quietly, allowing her eyes to rest on his for a moment. "Kelsey seemed really remarkable, and I liked her, and I wanted to visit her today. I was feeling a little down. I didn't mean to push myself onto your family, Ryan. I had no idea."

"You had no idea," he repeated almost inaudibly. "Why did you get so uncomfortable when I showed up?"

"Because you make me uncomfortable?" she suggested, glad that he couldn't see her face tinting red in the impending darkness. "Because I would have never said anything to Kelsey about you and the ambulance had I known. I feel like a complete imbecile!"

"So this is just you being embarrassed?" he attempted to clarify, lifting his eyebrows in question and causing a wrinkle to form across his forehead.

"I'm sorry," she stammered again, pulling her coat tighter around herself and trying to shut out the cold. He removed his right hand from his pocket and extended it, stepping toward her and brushing a hair away from her face. Focusing on her eyes, he gingerly placed his palm against her side, careful to avoid the place where she'd been wounded. Her breath caught momentarily as he pulled her closer, wrapping the edge of his coat around her back. When he drew the other side of his coat around her, she found herself pressed against his chest. Her forehead touched his cheek, and she inhaled the fresh masculine scent of his body wash.

"I had a feeling you might fit here," his warm voice informed her. The cadence of his words against her ear almost felt like a caress, and her heart pounded in her chest. "Now will you please tell me what you're so sorry about, if it doesn't have anything to do with Kelsey?"

Bringing her hand up to rest near his neck, she allowed her fingertips to settle at the edge of the tattoo above his T-shirt. "Everything. For being selfish and worrying about my own feelings yesterday, when the whole time you were just trying to take care of your family. I misjudged you, didn't I?"

"No," he insisted, holding her a bit tighter.

"Yes, I did. You could have easily told me the truth. Why didn't you?"

"What, so you could feel sorry for me?" Turning slightly, he placed his lips just a hint away from her forehead, close enough that she felt his breath against her skin. "What I said last night—I didn't mean that the way it sounded, when I compared you to dessert. I was trying to say that life has thrown me all these things that I have to deal with, and responsibilities that I can't escape, and you're the beautiful storyline that's waiting just out of my grasp." She ran her finger over the neck of his T-shirt, and he let out a heavy sigh. "When I said that I wanted to spend time with you, you've got to believe that I meant that. If I was free, I'd be knocking your door down. But I can't ask you to share my burdens, Harley. It's not fair."

Closing her eyes, she lowered her head to his neck and rested against him, feeling the movement of his chest as he breathed.

"Harley?"

"Can I have a minute?" she wondered, a smile playing about her lips. "I'm testing the fit."

His gentle laugh was enough to tide her over as she hesitated, wanting to break the moment.

"Have you come down?" he sang quietly, rendering her frozen in the moment. "This angel above where I am now. I'm trying to breathe but forgot how…"

"Wow," she whispered, pulling back just far enough to look into his eyes. "You really are tone deaf, aren't you?"

Laughing, he released her from his coat and took both her hands in his, holding her fingers close to his heart.

"Completely honest confession…you've captured me, but that doesn't feel like enough. I can't drag you into my mess. I have nothing to offer you."

"Well, it's too late," she told him with a quick shake of her head. "I'm already in, and who says I want anything? Did I say that?"

"You deserve the world," he stated emphatically, squeezing her hands a little tighter. "I hope you get your dreams, Harley."

"That sounds like a sendoff," she grumbled, wrinkling her brow. "What is this, exactly?"

"It's whatever you want it to be," he assured her, offering a sad smile.

"Well, then," she stated mischievously, pulling her hands away from his and taking a step back. "Do you know what I want, Ryan?"

"No, tell me."

"I want a man who wishes he could knock down a few doors for me, even if he's not free to do so at the moment."

Grinning, she hit the button on her keys to unlock her car and retreated slowly backwards. Pulling open her car door, she waited and stared at him momentarily before sliding into the driver's seat. He moved towards her, so she closed the door and started the ignition, rolling down her window. Leaning down, he rested his forearms on the door as he bent so they were face to face.

"You pretty much just made my entire century, you know that?" Tapping his fingers against the door, he gave her a huge, bright smile.

"Ryan Temple, my heart aches for you," she said in a deep, teasing voice. "I mean it, you're killing me."

Laughing, he remained rooted in his spot against her car as she shifted into drive. "You might be making fun of me, but I don't care. Keep it up and I might call you baby when I dial you up tonight."

"Promise?" She added a grin for good measure. "You're not going to call me cookie or chocolate fondue?"

"I thought you were partial to cake," he stated with a slight smirk. "What if I can't get to dessert, anyway? What if I get stuck on the vegetables?"

"If you can't get to the dessert, I'll just have to present myself as green beans or something equally boring." She revved the BMW's engine a bit, and he leaned away from the car. "Thanks for the song, and you were right."

"About what?" he asked as he stepped back.

"The fit," she stated, daring to stare him in the eye. "It was pretty sweet."

Chapter Fourteen

Denton sat across from Harley's desk, staring at her over her computer with his polished news anchor look, trying to talk her into…something. So far, he had been rather vague and hadn't given her anything other than some lofty expectations about the future. More of the same old, same old. She wanted to believe his sentiment, but after a moment, her brain mentally replaced his words with *blah, blah, blah.*

"The truth is, I'm ready to share the desk with you. Between you and me, Summer is dragging me down."

Harley tried her hardest not to give Denton a wary glare, but it was proving nearly impossible.

"You and Summer seemed to be having a marvelous conversation this morning in your office, so how is she dragging you down exactly?"

"I like Summer, don't get me wrong," he continued quietly, placing an elbow on her desk. "The problem is, it's like trying to have a playful conversation with my mother. You and me, Harley, we have flirty banter. We sizzle. Imagine if the newscast sizzled."

"I'm not a strip of bacon, and I'm not exactly sure I want to sizzle."

"You're something else when you get on a roll, Harley—a fantastic actress. Just imagine the type of drama we could bring. You're already crying with the less fortunate, getting yourself blown to bits trying to get the story… If you and I were at the desk together, we have enough zing that people would always be wondering."

"Wondering what, exactly?" she questioned him, narrowing her eyes.

"Are they? Aren't they? People would talk, and talk is good."

Shaking her head, Harley fought the urge to reach out and slug him in the shoulder. She wanted people to marvel at her grasp of the political climate or the fact that she uncovered a scandal, not gossip about whether or not she and Denton were an item.

"I can't imagine being less interested in what you're saying," she finally said, glancing down at her computer to view the time.

"Then I'm not explaining it well enough," he insisted, rising from his chair and moving around to where she sat, leaning his backside against her desk. "Dinner tonight, eight o'clock. I'm thinking quiet, intimate. We can discuss everything in great detail."

"As tempting as that is, Denton, I have plans."

"Don't tell me Kip's back in the picture," he muttered, ducking his head and giving her a questioning stare.

"No, I have family plans. Even if I didn't, though, I'm not certain that fraternizing with a coworker is a great idea."

"Who said anything about fraternizing?" he countered, crossing his arms against his chest.

"Do you have no basic understanding of the word fraternizing?" Reaching under her desk to turn off her computer, she shook her head. "Socializing, hobnobbing, mingling—"

"I don't need a walking dictionary. Where are you going?"

"It's Wednesday," she stated succinctly, retrieving her purse and attempting to rise from her chair, while Denton partially blocked her escape. "I have a previous engagement."

"Where do you sneak off to on Wednesdays? You need to figure out another plan, if you're going to be at the desk with me."

"If and when that happens, I will," she agreed, waiting for him to move. When he realized she wasn't changing her mind, he moved a couple inches and she brushed past him.

"You want me to call you tonight?" he tried one more time. Walking away, she shook her head and tried not to laugh at his persistence.

"No, Denton. I have plans, remember? See you tomorrow."

The back door of The Revolving Closet opened slowly, and a sheet of purple tresses poked into the opening. Harley simply stared at her friend without saying a word, stunned into silence.

"Cat got your tongue?" Annie wanted to know, shoving the lavender hair behind her shoulder.

"Your hair is a lot longer than I thought," Harley stammered, shifting her purse to the other shoulder. "And it's purple."

"Thank you, Captain Obvious," Annie grunted, shoving the door open further. "Human Barbie came in two days ago, so you're in luck."

"I don't know," Harley muttered, glancing at the beautiful clothes Annie had on the counter. A pair of Valentino heels with lace trim on the side sat on the end, and Harley mentally sighed as she stared at them. "It feels a little callous to be decking myself out and spending money on frivolities when there are people suffering."

Stepping forward, Annie placed a cool hand against Harley's forehead. "Girl, are you ill? Is it an infection from the stab wound? Should I take you back to the hospital?"

"Oh, be serious," she said with a slight laugh, shaking her head and pulling Annie's hand away from her skin.

"I am serious. You don't sound like yourself. What gives?"

Dropping her purse on the counter, Harley ignored the clothes and placed an elbow by the Valentinos as she leaned against the wood trim.

"You remember Kelsey, the girl I was visiting at the hospital the day you picked me up?"

"Sure. Blonde, sweet, kind of pale."

"She needs a liver transplant."

"Ouch."

"Yeah, and she's Ryan's sister."

"Your Ryan? The drumming fry cook EMT with the weird hair and body art?"

"First of all, he's not *my* anything," Harley protested a bit sheepishly. "Secondly, I can't believe you just described someone as having weird hair, when you look as though you've fallen into a vat of grape juice."

"Touché," Annie retorted, twisting her mouth to the side. "So you feel bad about being frivolous while Kelsey's in the hospital, is what you're saying?"

"Partly, but more than that," she admitted heavily. "The reason Ryan lives with his parents and doesn't have a car is because he pays all their bills. What kind of person would I be if I listened to him tell me how hard he works every single night and then went out and spent all my disposable income on shoes? It feels a bit crass."

"Every night?" Annie prodded, and Harley grinned.

"Uh-huh, he's called me every night since he got my number."

"Oh." Annie crossed to the counter and began folding the clothes, since Harley didn't seem interested. "So you're still talking to him? I guess I sort of thought you'd…you know…get it out of your system or something."

"Why would you say that?" Harley picked up a black sweater and held it aloft for a couple seconds before placing it back on the counter.

"I guess I'm just in the 'Harley and Denton' camp."

That remark felt so off, Harley placed her arms across her chest. "You want me to be with Denton?"

"Not want to, really, I just expect it. You two have sparks between you."

"No, we don't. It's an act." Blowing out a long breath, Harley glanced at the ceiling. "Maybe Denton's right—maybe I am just a great actress. Ugh."

"Forget that," Annie told her, poking Harley in the shoulder. "Tell me about Ryan. He calls you every night?"

"Yeah. I can't figure him out, Annie. He makes me excited and nervous at the same time. I know it sounds crazy, but for the entire duration of our phone conversations, my heart is practically pounding out of my chest."

"What is it about him? 'Cause I got to tell you, girl, he's not the best looking guy I've ever seen."

"Shut up."

"I'm not dissing him," Annie quickly countered. "He just doesn't seem like a Harley match, that's all. He's ordinary."

Sliding down the side of the counter, Harley lowered herself all the way to the floor, pulling her knees up to her chest. Annie walked around the counter and plopped onto the floor as well, facing her friend.

"Last night, we were talking about him paying his parents' bills, which he doesn't like to bring up. But of course I did, because I'm a pain in the rear. I told him I didn't know many people…anyone really…who would do that, and he brushed it off. I might want to be important and make a difference in the world, but he's already doing that. He's changing the world from his little corner, and you know what he told me?"

"What did he tell you?" Annie asked quietly.

"He told me he's not trying to change the world, he's just not allowing the world to change him."

Grabbing a fistful of her purple hair, Annie began braiding it absently.

"That's pretty cool."

"Pretty cool?" Harley repeated, leaning her head against the cabinetry. "In a world where basically everyone is concerned about themselves—and I'm definitely including me in that stat, just so we're clear…"

"He's different," Annie completed Harley's sentence.

"No," she protested, staring at the wall as she considered her words. "It's not him, Annie. He makes me want to be a better version of myself. When he talks to me, I feel challenged to be something more than I am. Does that make sense?"

"Sure. In that case, then, I can totally understand why you're dating him."

"We're not dating," Harley said. Annie gave her a sideways glance, and she couldn't help but laugh. "He doesn't have the time or the funds to date, so we're just—"

"Talking on the phone."

"It's stupid, I know. I feel like a twelve-year-old."

"Not stupid, necessarily, just old-fashioned."

"Well, even though it might sound a bit silly, it's enough for me right now. And I'm sorry that I can't buy any shoes today. Really sorry, because those Valentinos are gorgeous. I should have told you not to stay here and wait for me."

"No," Annie stated, placing her hand on Harley's arm. "I would have stayed anyway, because it's good to see you. Do you want to go to church with me tonight?"

"Can't," Harley answered with a sigh, smiling while she looked at Annie's purple braid that reached just to the top of her shoulder. "I'm having dinner with Kelsey and her parents."

"Not Ryan?"

"Nope. Kelsey called me at the station today, so how could I say no? Anyway, Ryan's always working, so I'm sure he won't be there."

"You must have a real rapport with this girl," Annie decided, rising to her feet and taking Harley's hand. Careful to protect her sore abdomen, Harley rose and grabbed her purse.

"She's awesome," Harley agreed. "I just wish there was something I could do to help her."

"Hmm...that's quite the statement." Annie's eyes twinkled, and Harley placed her left hand on her hip.

"I sense something behind your words, Annie the purple."

"Sure. I mean, what could you possibly do to help her? How could Harley Laine possibly help anybody, right? It's not like you have a giant platform or anything."

Harley pulled her BMW into the driveway of the small brown ranch-style home and double-checked the address, making certain she was in the correct place. She guessed the house to be less than half the size of her own, although in living area the family surely used more than the three rooms Harley inhabited in her own home. One of the first things she noticed were the twinkling multicolored lights through the window on the Christmas tree, and she allowed a smile to cross her face.

If anyone needs a little Christmas, it's Kelsey, she thought as she opened the car door. She had considered driving straight over a little early when she finished visiting with Annie, but decided instead to make a run home and change into a more casual outfit. Her jeans and boat neck sweater made her feel a bit more comfortable, and she hugged her coat tightly around her as she walked to the door.

Knocking quietly, she waited on the simple porch and shoved her hands into her coat pockets. Merely a few seconds later, Regina swung the door wide and gave her a smile.

"Hi, Harley," she said, stepping forward to offer a hug. Harley accepted it cautiously and was ushered inside, where she shrugged out of her coat. Regina draped it across the back of the couch and pointed toward the kitchen, where a rather small table rested with four curved-back wooden chairs.

"Harley's here!" Kelsey said excitedly when she saw her guest, not rising from her seat at the table.

"Hey!" Harley settled next to Kelsey and reached over to take her hand. "How are you feeling today?"

"I've been better," she began with a smile, "but I've also been worse."

"She's feeling pretty well today, which is why she wanted to ask you to come by," Regina said, placing a glass pan on the table. "I hope you like meatloaf, Harley."

"I usually eat ramen noodles, so meatloaf sounds like heaven to me," Harley assured her. Kelsey chose that moment to push her hair over her shoulder, and it reminded Harley of Annie. Stifling a giggle, she attempted to look away.

"What's funny?" Kelsey prodded, looking at her mischievously.

"I was just thinking about my friend Annie. I saw her after work, and she usually has fiery red curls. Tonight her hair was straight and purple."

"Purple?"

"Yes, purple. Sometimes I don't know what goes through that girl's head."

"Sounds like she'd fit right in with those musician friends Ryan has," Regina added, calling for Sam to join them at the table. He appeared from the hallway, looking freshly showered and wearing a blue flannel shirt with faded jeans.

Regina pulled her chair up to the table, with Sam settling next to her. The group was perfectly staggered about the round table in the four chairs, and Harley politely bowed her head as Sam began to pray over their food. The simple action reminded her of the dinner she shared at Tiny's with Duke, and she fought a blush at her still-fresh embarrassment over her mistake.

"I saw you already have your Christmas tree in the window," Harley stated after everyone began passing food.

Regina nodded as she smiled at Harley. "We love the holidays. We'd leave the tree up all year if we could."

"I liked the story you did about the Thanksgiving meal at the shelter," Kelsey stated as she helped herself to some meatloaf. "I watched it yesterday."

"Yesterday?" Harley asked in surprise. "Did they replay it or something?"

"I don't think so." Kelsey passed the glass dish to Harley, who took a slice of the meatloaf for herself. "Ryan records the news every night, so they were loaded on the DVR."

"He must like to watch the weather," Harley muttered, glancing at Regina as she handed off the main course.

"He definitely likes something about the news," Sam stated, wrinkling his brow and trying to hide a smile. "It's only Channel Six, though—strangest thing."

"It's Denton and Summer," Harley quickly assessed, giving Kelsey a sly grin. "They're enigmatic, you know."

"You should have tried to use enigmatic during Scrabble the other night, instead of in and it and to." Kelsey giggled and quickly looked at her plate, spooning some mashed potatoes into the corner.

"I must say, Kelsey, you're quite the Scrabble snob." Harley softened her statement with a wink as she accepted the mashed potatoes. "It's been a long time since I had home-cooked food. Other than when I eat at Tiny's, but that's not really the same."

"Mom's a great cook," Kelsey piped up, giving her mom a smile.

Regina seemed uncomfortable with the praise, and smiled very quickly as she turned her gaze to Harley. "Do your parents still live where you grew up, Harley?"

"Yeah, still the same place. They don't change much."

"You see them very often?" Sam wanted to know.

"No. I saw them a couple years ago before I took the job at Channel Six, but we don't really keep in touch."

"Did they know you were in the hospital?" Kelsey asked, ignoring the green beans to the point that her mom placed some on her plate before passing the dish to Harley.

"No," Harley answered quickly. She considered explaining, but decided it was too embarrassing and complicated. "There's really no good way for me to keep in touch with them, because they don't have a phone."

"How does anyone not have a phone?" Kelsey wondered.

"You sound like a teenage version of Harley." She took a helping of green beans and then stared at her plate momentarily, hoping they would change the subject.

"Sam works at the phone company," Regina informed her, which inexplicably caused Harley to giggle. Kelsey quickly caught on, and after a couple seconds they were all chuckling quietly.

A loud noise deep within the house caused Harley to jump slightly, and Kelsey smiled. "Ryan always sneaks in the back door and takes a shower, just in case he has any germs. He doesn't want to make me sick." She paused and giggled again. "He's going to be a little surprised. He had no idea you were coming over for dinner."

"Ryan usually doesn't come home for dinner," Regina added. "He normally has something else lined up as soon as he's finished working."

Harley was conflicted, between her sadness that Ryan had to work so hard and the excitement running through her veins at the thought that he was in the house. On the odd chance that she was getting ready to blurt something ridiculous, or make the butterflies in her stomach obvious, she concentrated on shoving her fork into her meatloaf.

"This meatloaf is really phenomenal," she stated, realizing about halfway through her sentence that she probably shouldn't talk with her mouth full. Would they recognize her blatant attempt to put the focus on something other than Ryan? Was that even worse than talking about him, so obviously trying to change the subject?

"Thanks," Regina said, leaving it at that. Harley decided Ryan's mother definitely sensed her hesitation, and that made her even more uncomfortable.

"So, Harley, what do you like to do for fun?" Kelsey stabbed a couple green beans and held them aloft on her fork. "I bet you go to all kinds of cool places with your reporter friends every night."

"Um, no," Harley countered with a short laugh. "I usually stay at work too late, then go home and sit on my bed reading chick lit novels while I watch horrible reality television. Except on Fridays—on Fridays I go to Tiny's."

"By yourself?"

It never occurred to Harley that her life sounded so pathetic until the seventeen-year-old was looking at her with pity.

"Well, not really. Tiny's there, and my friend Duke."

Sam began to laugh, and Harley swung her head in his direction.

"Sorry," he offered, wiping his mouth with his napkin. "The way you said that, it just sounded like you were going to a saloon with John Wayne."

"Duke actually does like John Wayne," Harley said, and then furrowed her brow a tad. "I think? He's nicknamed after him, anyway, and I'm sure he must like him or he wouldn't allow people to call him that."

Although people call me Harley...and I'm not particularly a fan.

"Hey, meatloaf night and nobody bothered to mention it?" Ryan called down the hall as he appeared to Harley's right, sporting wet hair and a green t-shirt. He had a hooded sweatshirt in his fist, which he tossed over the couch as he stepped to the table.

"Harley's here." Kelsey decided to state the obvious.

"Yeah, I thought I heard angels singing," Ryan teasingly shot at Harley, who shook her head and averted her eyes from his. He grabbed a chair from the desk along the wall in the living room and carried it over to the table, plopping it down between Kelsey and Harley. He didn't have to bother getting himself a plate, because Regina had already taken it upon herself to go to the kitchen and retrieve everything he needed.

As he sat down in the chair, his arm brushed Harley's and he let his eyes linger on her face for a moment.

"Hi," she stated quietly.

"Hi yourself," he repeated. "What are you doing here?"

Rather than implicate Kelsey by talking about the dinner invitation, Harley shrugged and looked at her plate, lifting her fork in his direction.

"Green beans." It was a simple answer, but the instant it crossed her lips, it took on more meaning than she intended.

"Sweet," he answered, a slight smile tugging on one corner of his lips. "Kels, pass me the green beans."

"Green beans?" she answered skeptically. "You hardly ever eat green beans."

"I am all about the green beans tonight," he stated, not removing his eyes from Harley's face. "In fact, I may never eat anything but green beans ever again."

At that, she began snickering and turned her face to stop his intense gaze.

"You get out of working tonight?" Sam directed at Ryan, who quickly piled his plate with potatoes and meatloaf.

"Nope. Just had a few minutes and I wanted to pick up your car. It's gonna be really cold tonight to ride home on the bike."

"What are you doing tonight?" Kelsey wanted to know.

"Valet for a party at a hotel," he answered between mouthfuls of potatoes. "Hopefully it won't last too long so I can get some sleep before my shift in the morning."

Harley placed her fork on her plate and took a long drink of her water, trying to slow her pulse a smidge. She removed her hand from the glass and placed it in her lap, pressing against her jeans with her palm.

"Do you always eat this fast?" Harley muttered, a bit shocked at the rate at which he was shoveling in his dinner.

"No, but when you only have five minutes, you do what you gotta do." He looked at her and winked, and she gave him a slight smile. Her breath lodged in her chest as she felt warm fingers sliding across the back of her hand under the table, intertwining with hers as Ryan's hand completely encapsulated her own. His thumb brushed gently across the top of her hand while he continued thrusting his fork into his meatloaf and green beans with his right hand.

"Everything okay, Harley?" Regina asked, glancing at Harley's uneaten food and her fork resting on the plate.

"Oh, of course," she stammered, hoping the embarrassment wasn't registering on her face. Attempting to pick up her fork with her left hand, she clumsily began sampling her food again.

"So, are you and Ryan...?" Kelsey began, looking imploringly at Harley.

"What?" She knew she looked guilty, and she allowed the skin between her eyebrows to fold together in consternation.

"You know, dating?"

She dared to glance at Ryan, and even as he squeezed her hand under the table, he shook his head slowly. For whatever reason, his refusal felt almost like a dare.

"Yes," Harley said succinctly. "I mean, maybe, if he ever sits still long enough."

"And I have to go," he announced, rising from his seat and allowing his hand to slide away from Harley's. As he took his chair back to the desk, she already felt his absence like the warmth next to her was fading away. "See you in the morning, okay? I'll gas your car up before I come home."

"Don't work too hard," Regina said sadly.

"Hey, Harley, can you bring me my sweatshirt?" Ryan called from the hall. "I threw it on the couch."

Shaking her head at Kelsey's knowing grin, Harley rose and walked to the couch, taking the shirt in her hand and moving a few steps into the hallway.

"This is the epitome of laziness," she muttered as she neared him.

Without even grabbing for the shirt, he took her hand and held one finger up to his lips to implore her to be quiet. Narrowing her eyes, she watched as he drew her hand palm-up and traced the outline of a heart, never taking his eyes off hers. When he was finished, he closed his fist around her fingers and pulled her hand up against his chest, leaning closer until his mouth was near her ear.

"Green beans are my new favorite," he whispered, leaning back and offering a smile. "'Night, Harley." Sweeping the sweatshirt over his head, he offered a quick smile before he disappeared from her view.

Returning to the table, Harley lowered herself onto her chair and avoided Kelsey's eyes as she returned to eating her dinner, not certain she could hide the feelings that were almost certainly crossing her features.

"So..." Kelsey began, pausing as though she couldn't see the others at the table around the elephant in the room. "Ryan seems to like you."

"Oh, Kelsey, leave her alone," Regina muttered, shaking her head quickly as though she were trying to remove the thought from her mind. Harley watched in mortification as her face contorted a bit and tears filled her eyes.

"I'm very sorry if I've upset you," Harley stated hesitantly.

"No, of course not," Regina was quick to answer, reaching out and placing her hand on top of Harley's on the table. "Ryan works so hard, and it's just nice seeing his face light up, that's all. He's in the prime of his life, and he should be out making his way in the world and chasing girls, but instead he works himself to death. I suppose it makes me a little sad."

"He obviously cares very deeply about all of you," Harley responded, not sure how to react to the tears. "And Kelsey is certainly fortunate to have a brother who would go to such lengths to protect her."

"You're pretty eloquent when you're not playing Scrabble," Kelsey said, causing Harley to giggle again. The somber mood effectively broken, everyone went back to eating their meatloaf.

After dinner, Kelsey ushered Harley into her bedroom, where she showed her a couple spelling trophies that suddenly helped the Scrabble make perfect sense. After Harley gave her a sufficient tongue lashing about being a con artist, the two sat on the bed and Kelsey pulled her legs up near her chin.

"So, do you really like Ryan?" The younger girl asked the question quietly as though it could soften the edges of her words.

Smiling at her companion's directness, Harley slowly nodded her head. "Yeah, there's something about him, you know?"

"No, he's my brother," Kelsey answered succinctly, rewarding Harley with a smile of her own. Afterwards, she took a deep breath as though she was preparing to say something unpleasant, and Harley waited patiently. "Please don't hurt him, Harley."

The words sliced into Harley like a knife, and she swallowed past a lump in her throat.

"Why would you say that?"

"Because I can tell he likes you." Leaning her head back against the wall behind her, Kelsey looked down at her bedspread. "I don't think he wants to, though. I think he wants to help us so much, he thinks if he's distracted that he's doing us a disservice. I think that's why he won't say he's dating you, and he doesn't talk about you to us."

"I absolutely don't want to hurt any of you."

"I know."

"So you think I should stop talking to Ryan?" Harley wondered, slightly confused.

"No, that would crush him."

Harley laid back on the bed, staring up at the ceiling.

"I remember when my only worries were what shoes I was going to wear and how many people I would impress that day."

"When you were in high school?" Kelsey asked, causing Harley to emit a sharp laugh.

"No! Last week."

Kelsey lowered herself beside Harley and stared across the bed. "When you talk to Ryan tonight, please don't tell him anything I said."

"What makes you think Ryan will call me tonight?"

Giggling, Kelsey pointed to the other side of the room.

"I can hear through the wall, Green Beans."

Chapter Fifteen

Staring absently at her computer screen, Harley told herself to focus. She had been typing and deleting the same words into an email over and over, pondering the best way to approach the topic. Annie was right—she had a huge platform, and she desperately wanted to help Kelsey. Unfortunately, the how was giving her a measure of trouble.

"I'm glad you're sitting down, because you're getting ready to be the most excited woman in all of Louisville," Denton announced as he placed himself onto the chair in front of her desk.

"If this is a new twist on asking me out, I'm still not interested, Denton."

"Very funny." He narrowed his eyes a bit, relaxing against the chair and taking on an offended air. "Am I really that terrible? We seem like a pretty good match to me."

Letting out a heavy sigh, Harley looked away from her computer and placed both elbows on her desk, folding her arms across one another.

"Denton, it's not you," she insisted. "You are an intelligent, attractive, articulate, well-dressed guy. Any woman would be lucky to have you."

"Every woman minus one," he corrected. "Never mind—more tension for when we share the desk, right?"

She thought about making a snide comment, but decided it was best to say nothing about their relationship, or lack thereof.

"So, why exactly am I going to be the most excited woman in Louisville?"

"I nearly forgot," he said, straightening himself in his chair and giving a pleasant smile. "Guess who's going to be giving an interview to Trent Bauer tomorrow?"

"Trent Bauer? As in *the* Trent Bauer of New York morning show infamy? Wow! Denton, that is so awesome for you. Really, congratulations."

"Honestly, Harley, sometimes you're so clueless," Denton stated, shaking his head as he straightened his tie. "Bauer wants to talk to Louisville's hottest reporter...the one who's willing to get herself blown up to get a story."

"You're teasing me now, aren't you?" She wanted to give him a correcting glare or wrinkle her nose or something, but instead she sat there, looking stunned.

"Nope. Mitch was talking to his people just a few minutes ago. I'm sure he'll be rushing this way any second now, but I happened to overhear and beat him to it. I had hoped that being the bearer of good news might soften you a little on the idea of having dinner with me."

Jumping to her feet, she barely took notice of her abdominal stitches as she rushed around the desk and pressed a loud, smacking kiss to his cheek.

"Denton Price, I could just kiss you!" she blurted. "And I guess I did, didn't I? This feels like a turning point." Stopping abruptly, she straightened and pondered the situation. "It is, isn't it?"

"Of course it is!" he insisted, rising to his feet and wrapping his hands firmly around her upper arms. "It's going to be you and me, Harley, just like it's meant to be. We're a great team."

"Get a room, you two," Kenny muttered as he strolled by Harley's desk. "Oh, and next time you plan to talk about the two of y'all being a great team, you might want to make sure Summer's not standing behind you."

Summer chose that moment to clear her throat, and Harley spun herself around, staring guiltily at the blonde newswoman who happened to be wearing an unfortunate lime green boxy blazer.

"Summer," Harley muttered. "Hey, how are things?"

"Don't worry, the fact that Denton has his sights set on you was not lost on me. Although you could stop being so pathetic, Denton—she doesn't have any better offers, trust me. She made a big mistake with the way she treated Christopher Stanton, and I'm sure the Stantons have spread the word among their friends."

Harley inwardly seethed, but she forced herself to remain calm. "I certainly hope so. I wouldn't want any of their slimy politician friends thinking they had any inroads with me."

"I shouldn't worry about that now," Summer assured her with a fake smile. "You won't be finding yourself near any politicians anytime soon."

"Harley!" Mitch called, abruptly rushing himself toward her desk. It didn't escape Harley's notice that the action left him a bit winded, and she glanced down to notice some sort of food stain near the buttons on his shirt, as usual. "Trent Bauer wants to interview you in the morning about the accident last week. You're making national headlines, young lady. And that firefighter on camera afterwards calling you Louisville's sweetheart is just the icing on the cake! I'll get you all the details. Fantastic!"

Harley didn't bother answering as he turned to walk away, instead glancing at Summer, who had narrowed her eyes a bit.

"Oh, and Harley…" Mitch continued, facing her again, "they're having some pension debate at the capital tomorrow. After the interview with Bauer, get yourself over to Frankfort and cover it for me, would you? Talk to anyone you can, even the governor if possible."

"Sure, Mitch," she stated professionally and politely, even though she was inwardly squealing with delight. "Sorry for the interruption, Summer…you were saying?"

"Denton, when you have a moment, come see me," Summer ordered, pausing as she stared intently at Harley. "You know the difference between you and me? This is my home, and our viewers are my people. You can't wait to get out of here."

"Partly true," Harley admitted, "but one shouldn't be punished for having talent and ambition, correct?"

Summer appeared to be pensive, but she quickly looked back to Denton. "Just come see me." Turning, she strode away.

"I'm going to pay for this," Denton murmured. "You know what would make up for it? Going to dinner with me tonight. I'll even make it strictly a business dinner, if you want. How can you protest that?"

Laughing, Harley threw her head back in defeat. "Denton! I can't protest that, and I do appreciate the offer, but I just can't go to dinner with you, even as a business thing. I would feel really guilty."

"Is this about the fraternizing again?" he wanted to know. "Because Summer just made it clear that people are already talking."

"No," she was quick to interject. "The truth is, I'm sort of seeing someone."

"Another politician? Is that why Mitch is sending you to Frankfort?"

Unable to stop herself, Harley reached out and pinched him in the upper arm. "You deserve that. What a rude thing to say! No, he is not a politician, and I really don't want to talk about it, okay? Now, if you'll excuse me, I have lots of work to do. Really important pension-related research."

"Fine," he added with a smile. "In case anyone wonders, I will be going to my own Summer-directed funeral now."

"Have fun," she stated, providing a smile of her own.

Harley awoke at four o'clock in the morning, flipped on the light in her bedroom, and blinked her eyes really hard a few times. She had been nearly too excited to sleep, and her eyelids felt like they were covered with glue on the inside. Plodding down the hall and into the bathroom, she quickly fished out some eye drops and pried her eyes open to try to give them some life.

"You look terrible, Harley Elaine," she whispered to the mirror, where her hair was sticking up awkwardly on one side and plastered to her head on the other. As she brushed her teeth, the ringtone of her phone sounded from her bedroom, and she hurried across the hall, stepping on a jagged spot in the floor and hobbling the rest of the way across the wood.

"Ouch!" she exclaimed around her toothbrush, realizing too late that she'd already hit the button to accept the phone call. "Hello?"

"Harley? You okay?"

Ryan.

The mere realization sent her into a tizzy of emotion. She nearly forgot about the pain in her side from the pull of her stab wound, and could have almost looked past the fact that her rush through the hall had landed her a sizable splinter in the heel of her foot.

"Yeah, fine, just clumsy." She glanced up through the window into the pitch black night sky, and alarm bells began ringing in her brain. "Why are you calling at this hour? Is it Kelsey?"

"No," he quickly answered. "Wow, I'm sorry, I wasn't even thinking. I had a late shift, and I just wanted to call before I fell asleep. I probably woke you up."

"You didn't." Pulling her leg up, she glanced at the bottom of her foot to try to locate the offending splinter of wood. "I have an early morning, actually." She pondered telling him about Trent Bauer, but decided he might be tired.

"So...I had a message from Tiny that he might need me tomorrow night. Actually tonight, I guess. Score one for me because it's Friday, right?"

"Yeah, TGIF and all that," she muttered, concentrating on grabbing that tiny bit of wood with her fingernails.

"TGIF?" he attempted to clarify, laughing quietly. "I really don't care that it's Friday, other than the fact that there's this incredible girl who comes by Tiny's on Friday nights."

"Really?" Suddenly, the splinter became a lot less interesting. "Tell me about this girl."

"She's stunningly beautiful, wicked smart, and she has a heart of gold."

"Sounds like you made her up," she teased, standing up and placing weight on the splintered heel, nearly causing another fall. Carefully lowering herself to the bed, she made sure she lifted her foot to the bed as well so she wouldn't make that mistake again.

"Oh no, she's very real."

"If that's the case, then she must be way out of your league."

"Totally and completely." He paused a moment, and she wondered if she should say something. "So, what are you doing tonight?"

"Me?" she asked innocently. "Oh, I don't know. I'm very busy and I have to go to the capitol today, after which I'll try to interview the governor. But perhaps this evening I might drop by Tiny's—so I can get a peek at this girl."

"If you're lucky, I'll make you a Caramel Delight."

"I know what this is," she said, biting her lip to keep from giggling. "You've got a new tattoo and want to show it to me, don't you? Last time you tempted me with the Caramel Delight, you just wanted to show me every inch of your torso."

His laugh was so rich and resounding, she imagined Kelsey was probably waking up in her bedroom from the sound.

"Yep, it says Harley, and it's on my—"

"I don't want to know," she insisted. "The last time I ate at Tiny's, it was with another gentleman who indicated that he might have my name tattooed on his arm. What is it with you people?"

"Are you kidding me?" he asked with a sigh. "Please tell me you don't take dates to Tiny's. And especially not that Denton guy from TV who always winks after your reports."

"No he doesn't!" she protested, mentally wondering if he was correct. "I think someone's jealous."

"I'm telling you, that guy has the hots for you. I'm surprised he hasn't already tied you down, to be honest."

Unable to hold it in, Harley let out a short, loud laugh. "Denton asks me out every day, practically. He asked me to go out with him last night."

"Did you?" he asked quietly.

"No, I didn't," she informed him slowly and deliberately. "I'm waiting for someone to knock the door down."

"Someone?" His voice was rather hesitant, and she felt the butterflies begin fighting in her stomach.

"Yeah, one specific person, really."

"Green beans," he whispered. "Green beans, green beans, green beans..."

"What are you doing?" she asked, on the verge of laughing.

"Convincing my head to keep my priorities straight."

"Is it working?"

"Not one bit," he admitted. "I'll look for you tonight...and for any guys who have Harley tattoos, so we can toss them from the establishment."

"You won't have to look far," she stated with a slight grin as she stared at her bedroom wall. "You'll find him on the bench outside. Get some sleep, Ryan."

Dropping her phone onto the bed, she rose again to head to the bathroom and try to make herself presentable, resorting to a limp as she once again put pressure on the splinter. Stepping into the bathroom, she propped her leg up on the counter as she retrieved her tweezers.

"You're a mess, Harley Elaine," she whispered at her reflection again, allowing a grin to spread across her face. "Why that guy, huh? And stop smiling at yourself like an idiot."

Sitting in the black director's chair in front of a huge Channel Six Action News logo, Harley had to admit she felt oddly glamorous for such an early morning interview. Wearing a pale green fitted button-down shirt and a simple black pencil skirt, she knew she exuded confidence and sophistication. It didn't hurt that she had convinced Annie to let her borrow the Valentino shoes she viewed Wednesday night, with the lace on the sides.

"You're a rock star," Kenny had informed her when he sidled up to her desk right before the interview.

Yes—yes, I am. A news reporting rock star. Today I will chat with Trent Bauer, and then interview the governor.

"A week ago today, Channel Six Action News reporter Harley Laine from Louisville, Kentucky was the first person from the media on the scene at a warehouse fire," Trent Bauer began. "Little did she know, a few moments later she herself would be the news story as an explosion rocked the area and landed her in the hospital. She is here with us today. Harley Laine, good morning. This Friday is looking better than your last, I take it?"

"Right now it is, Trent, but it's still early. I'm headed to the state capitol today, and who knows what kind of fireworks I'll face."

"None that would send you to the hospital, let's hope," he stated with a smile. "Let's go back to last week, because I really want to know what happened in the moments leading up to that fateful explosion. Can you tell us what was going through your mind?"

Definitely not. Hmm...a cleaned up reporter version perhaps?

"It was the day after Thanksgiving, and my cameraman and I were doing some routine stories when we heard the sirens and saw that the warehouse was on fire. When we came closer and realized they had pulled at least one gentleman from the building, we hurried onto the scene. A very kind firefighter tried to persuade me to stay back, but being quite stubborn, I stepped closer trying to see what the paramedics were doing."

"And that's when the explosion happened?"

"Yes. I heard it and felt the shaking a bit, but almost immediately I noticed a cramping sensation in my abdomen. When

I reached for my stomach, that's when I realized that I had been hit with a piece of debris from the building."

"A piece of metal that effectively sliced into you like a knife..." Trent attempted to clarify.

"...and it was still protruding from me at that moment. Since the paramedics weren't certain what damage had been done internally, I was taken by ambulance with the metal still in place."

"We have a picture of you being carried to the ambulance by the firefighter you mentioned, Lieutenant Ken Burris. Have you and Lieutenant Burris spoken since that day?"

"No, I haven't had that pleasure, but I would love to tell him thank you."

"He called you Louisville's sweetheart," Trent continued, and Harley laughed quietly.

"He was probably referring to a poll that went out in the newspaper that same morning listing me as the most popular reporter," she assured him, playing it down. "He was very kind to me, and I'm grateful for his quick action."

"You probably never considered that morning that something could happen to you that day," Trent suggested.

"Of course not, but isn't that the way it is with most of life's momentous occurrences?"

"So a clean bill of health after the hospital trip, though?"

"Good as new, with some battle wounds, of course."

"So, Harley, I have to ask you another question," Trent interjected. "A lot of times when people have a traumatic experience, it serves as a turning point. Have you gone through anything like that this week?"

With a pang of guilt, Harley thought of her hospital stay and peeking across at Kelsey down the hall.

"Actually, Trent, something about my hospital stay really affected me deeply," Harley began, taking a second to regroup her thoughts. "When I was about to be released to go home, I was peeking into the hallway looking for a nurse, and I happened to lock eyes with a seventeen-year-old girl who was doing the same. We wound up becoming very quick friends, and I can't stop thinking about her. She needs a liver transplant, and her situation just forced me to think about life and what's important. It's so easy to become obsessed with *things*, especially during the holidays, but it's *people* we should care about...people like Kelsey and her wonderful family who are just struggling to keep themselves afloat through difficult circumstances."

"Such an important message during the holidays," Trent agreed.

"I would just encourage people—don't take those around you for granted. There are people in your circle of influence who are in need. Also, Zac Efron, there is a seventeen-year-old girl in Louisville who would love to meet you."

"Equally important," Trent stated with a laugh. "Harley Laine, it is a pleasure to speak with you. Take care out there, and no more explosions."

"I promise you, I will do my best to avoid explosions. Thank you for having me."

"Harley Laine, expecting a call from Zac Efron. Back in a minute."

Chapter Sixteen

Being on morning television with Trent Bauer had a way of making a small-time reporter pretty irresistible, apparently, because Harley had no problems making inroads with the governor's office when she contacted them that morning. In fact, she pounded out details for a sit-down exclusive before she ever left Louisville to head towards Frankfort.

On her way there, she also received a phone call from Mitch.

"When you're finished with the governor, hurry back here to do a story on that girl you brought up in the interview this morning," he ordered.

"What? Why today? Give me some time to talk it over with them."

"No time, Harley," he insisted. "Summer already contacted them, but the mother is refusing to talk to anyone but you. People have been calling the station, and we set up a fund at the bank for people to donate to her cause. We need to get the story out there so they stop calling the station."

"Mitch, I can't just rush something together—"

"Just hurry back." He hung up so quickly, Harley fought the urge to scream at the phone in her hand.

"Probs Harl?" Kenny muttered.

"Talk much?" She lashed out at him before she measured her words, and with a quick sigh, she stared over at him in the driver's seat. "Sorry, Kenny. I don't know, possibly. Mitch wants us to hurry the governor's interview and rush back."

"Figures."

"Why is that?"

"You know, we finally get the good story and can't even enjoy it. At least you had the Bauer interview this morning. Summer's shakin' in her boots, I bet."

"Oh, that's ridiculous," Harley informed him. "Summer doesn't wear boots. Always kitten heels."

"There's the sassy Miss Laine. Where ya been hidin'?"

"Behind a giant wall of self-loathing," she acknowledged with a bit of a scowl. "Anyway, forget that. The pensions they're talking about today are a real problem. I'm vaguely aware that I should care, but now I'm worried about Kelsey. How did Summer find her contact information? I didn't even give her last name."

"You mean that girl you talked about this morning?" Kenny wondered, glancing at his passenger. "Oh, that's easy. One of the gals said the teenager called you the other day, and they still had her phone number on the message books."

"Why did everyone know about this but me?" she responded angrily.

"Um, because you were busy hobnobbing about Bauer, and then reading up on your pension stuff. No biggie, you said you wanted to help her, right? Well, people's helping her now, just like you wanted."

"But this isn't what I wanted," she complained. "I want to help her myself, not enlist a faceless mob. This just feels weird."

"Then give her your liver."

"Excuse me?!" Not quite believing what he just said, Harley stared at him, open-mouthed and eyes wide.

"They said she was looking for a living donor, right? You're alive, ain't ya?"

"Regina, I am so sorry," Harley let out in a rush as the door opened to her. "If I had ever wanted to do a story about you all, which I'm not sure I would have, honestly, this absolutely is not the way I would have gone about it."

"You meant well," Regina stated as she wrapped an arm around Harley. "Anyway, your station set up the fund at the bank, and it's already blessed us so much more than we could have imagined. I don't even know what to say."

"Just say you're not angry with me," Harley pleaded. "I wish I could go back in time. I'd change everything I said."

"Oh, don't fret so much. Come on, Kelsey's just checking on the 'help Kelsey meet Zac Efron' webpage."

Even with the somber mood in which she had shrouded herself, that statement made Harley laugh out loud. She stepped over to the computer, where Kelsey sat in her pajamas staring at the aforementioned website.

"Hey, Harley. Looks like the movement is gaining some traction, although part of me hopes it fails. What would I say to Zac Efron, really? I would probably pass out with fright."

"Or he would call you 'baby girl' and you would burst of sheer excitement," Harley teased. "How are you feeling?"

"Tired."

That one-word answer from Kelsey told Harley more than enough. She had learned in their short acquaintance that Kelsey's attitude was pensive and cautious when she wasn't feeling well, and bubbly and talkative when she felt better. That day obviously wasn't a banner day health-wise for the teenager.

"I can tell my boss that we can't do the interview," Harley suggested. "It's okay, really. There's been so much going on today already..."

"No, it's alright," Kelsey insisted, rising to her feet. "Can I get dressed first?"

"Yes, of course," Harley told her with a sigh. As she watched Kelsey shuffle away, she lowered herself to the couch. "I really am sorry, Regina. I never meant to ambush you like this. That's why I told Kenny to give me a few minutes."

"Kenny?" Regina attempted to clarify.

"My cameraman." Gazing at the Christmas tree with its blinking lights, Harley swallowed past the lump in her throat. "Actually, there was something I wanted to talk to you about."

"Anything," Regina assured her as she sat beside her on the couch. Harley hesitated, feeling her heart beating a bit erratically.

"Well, I…" she began, then reassessed. "Could you tell me…if someone wanted to find out if they would qualify as a donor for Kelsey…?" Harley nervously licked her lips, fighting her jittery emotions.

"I doubt if Kelsey would be comfortable taking that kind of stance in an interview," Regina quickly stated.

"Oh," Harley said with a slight flinch. "I didn't mean to insinuate that. It's just that if I was a match…if I *am* a match, I mean, would you take me? Do you think Kelsey would take me?"

Placing her fist against her mouth, Regina focused sad eyes on Harley and stared at her for a moment. Then, without a word, she removed her fist and placed her hand over Harley's arm, squeezing it gently. The two sat silently regarding one another until they heard Kelsey's bedroom door open, and the teenager emerged wearing jeans and a gray t-shirt with black lace detailing.

"Thank you," Regina whispered. "Thank you, Harley. You've been such a Godsend to us."

"Do I look appropriate?" Kelsey wanted to know as she sank between her mother and Harley on the couch.

"Like a million bucks," Harley acknowledged with a sigh. "Should I get Kenny?"

"She's bringing boys?" Kelsey glanced at her mom.

"Cameraman," Regina told her with a smile.

"Please, Mitch, wait to run it," Harley begged, standing in front of his desk with her hands folded together.

"Why would I want to do that?" he asked, rising to his feet and squinting his eyes as he faced her across his desk. "We need to go with the story, because we've been getting calls. I don't need my staff running interference for some kid."

"I'm not asking you to run interference, I'm just asking for a little time to make the story right."

Stepping around his desk, Mitch placed his hand on Harley's shoulder, giving it a fatherly squeeze.

"I don't understand why you're fighting this. The piece makes you look like a saint."

"It shouldn't be about me at all. It should be about Kelsey. Please... With everything that's happened today, can't you give me this one favor?"

"Are you kidding? You want me to make it less flattering to you, when that's the last thing I want. You're suddenly a celebrity with the national exposure and the governor today, so we need to capitalize on your spotlight while we can."

"To Kelsey's detriment?"

Anger surged through her veins, and she felt the prick of hot tears stinging her eyes. Vowing not to let them fall, she squeezed her hands into fists at her side.

"The story won't hurt the kid, and you know it."

As Mitch stepped out of the room, Harley felt the weight of the world come down on her shoulders.

It was nearly nine o'clock when Harley drove her car past Tiny's, locating a parking spot and then strolling toward the front of the restaurant in her boyfriend jeans and her black pea coat. She had taken the time to go home and strip off all her makeup, even though she might run into Ryan, and she wrapped her hair into a loose knot at the back of her neck.

Rather than his usual spot on the park bench, Harley spotted Duke just inside the window sitting at a table meant for two, where his companion was Tiny. She stood near the curb for a moment and watched them conversing with one another, wishing she could be a fly on the wall. She certainly didn't feel like being Harley Laine that evening, but it seemed unavoidable.

Crossing over to the door, she pulled it open and stepped inside, allowing the smell of fried food to waft over her senses. She quickly settled at a two-top in the corner and concentrated on pulling her coat off and straightening it along the back of her chair so she wouldn't have to glance around the room. When she finally looked up, she met Duke's gaze as he waved her over and motioned to a chair next to him. Bracing her heart for a possible emotional onslaught, she retrieved her coat and stepped over to the table, sitting at the edge of the table between Tiny and Duke.

"Hello there, little lady," Tiny stated softly. "I sure was worried about you last week. I was glad when Ryan came in here and said you was okay, 'cause I was 'bout to go make some noise at that hospital."

"Thank you for not making noise," Harley told him solemnly. "I was embarrassed enough as it was."

"What can I get you tonight, hon?" Tiny placed his large hand on her shoulder, and she attempted to smile.

"You know, I'm not really that hungry. Thank you, though."

"I think you're right, Duke," Tiny said. "She does seem sad. We need to cheer her up a bit."

Patting her on the back, Tiny rose from his chair and stepped away toward the kitchen. Harley reluctantly turned her eyes to Duke, and he shook his head as he gave her a slight grin.

"I don't suppose you saw the news today?" Harley wondered, staring at the table.

"I was busy and wasn't by a television," he assured her. "But, nowadays people don't even need the television, with all the phones with the gadgets and other nonsense."

"So you did see it," she surmised.

"No, but Ryan's sister called him about it." He paused and she took the opportunity to glance up at his face. "You don't seem pleased."

"Oh, Duke," she muttered with a sigh, folding her arms across the table and dropping her head against them. He placed his hand against her back and let it rest there without saying a word while she took a moment and tried to steady herself.

"Harley," she heard behind her, and she knew immediately it was Ryan. Straightening, she rose to her feet slowly and turned to face him. He seemed taller than she remembered, and broader somehow although she knew it wasn't possible. Reluctantly drawing her face to his eyes, she unwittingly held her breath.

"Popular lady," he stated simply, and then he glanced around at the others in the dining room. "I have a minute, if you want to talk."

"Okay," she squeezed out, not bothering to move after she stood. His fingers gripped her elbow, pressing her forward as he drew her through the kitchen entrance and into a storage closet, flicking the light on overhead. She glanced around at the small space, imagining that it would be a good location to commit a murder and hide a body.

"Look, I know what you're going to say, and before you even get started, I'm sorry," Harley offered. "I completely understand why you're angry with me, but I had no idea your mom was going to do that—"

"Can you just give me five seconds?" Turning his body away from her, he placed his hands on the back of his head and linked his fingers together, staring at a wall of brooms.

"Right," she whispered, leaning back and knocking over a spray bottle of some type of cleaner. Bending over to set it aright, she raised to a standing position at the same time he turned to face her.

"I'm not going to pretend that I wasn't a little angry, okay? I'm handling things…maybe not in the best way possible, and definitely less than perfect, but we were doing okay. I'm not a charity case."

Harley nearly flinched at the extent to which his words startled her. "What are you talking about?"

"The thing at the bank," he said, folding his arms across his chest. "There was already over five thousand dollars in there by the time my mom called to talk to me about it."

"Ryan—"

"Don't patronize me, Harley. I know you meant well, but you should have talked to me about it first. If you just wanted to help my family, then it's nice of you, granted. And if you're trying to free me up so I can take you out or something—"

"I cannot even believe you just said that!" Widening her eyes, she replicated his stance, placing her arms across her chest. "I had nothing to do with the account at the bank. I was on my way to Frankfort when people at the studio were setting that up. And where do you get off thinking I'm so desperate that I would go around setting up bank accounts just so I could get myself a lousy date?"

"Nobody called you desperate," he answered with a sigh, dropping his hands into his pockets.

"You did," she disagreed, grabbing the handle to the door.

"Wait a minute, what did you mean about my mom?" he asked as she opened the door, stepping into the hallway.

"Good night, Ryan," was all she said as she walked back out into the dining room, stepping up to Duke's table and grabbing her coat from the chair.

"Hey, where you think you're going?" he asked, those intimidating gray eyes focused on her beneath his black baseball cap.

"I need some air. I'm sorry, Duke. Maybe I'll see you next week."

Flinging the coat over her shoulder, Harley threw the door open and stepped into the cold night, making it only a few paces before she stopped to shove her arms into her outer garment. She began to rifle through her pockets for her keys, and once she found them, she slumped onto the bench in front of the restaurant, placing her head in her hands.

I didn't ask for any of this, she thought. *This day should have been a culmination of so many things I've wanted, but instead I'm conflicted and worried.*

"Mind if I sit down?" She glanced up to see Duke offering her a piece of chocolate, and she shook her head with a sad laugh. "You know, it's probably not as bad as you think."

"This time it is," she stated without emotion.

"Because a fund was set up to help Ryan's sister with her medical expenses?" he wondered. "I know his male ego might have been bruised momentarily, but he'll get over it."

"That's what you think is bothering me?" Smiling, she glanced up at the sky. "If only that was it, Duke."

"Well," he said with a sigh as he sat beside her, "I can't rightly help if I don't know the problem."

"I'm not sure you can help." Fishing her phone out of her pocket, she pulled up the Channel Six website and easily located her story from earlier that evening, holding it out in front of Duke as he scratched his beard absently.

"Our own beloved Harley Laine spoke this morning during her interview with Trent Bauer about her chance meeting with a teenage girl at the hospital last week," Denton intoned, looking newscaster perfect as usual. "Tonight, she brings you the rest of the story of the remarkable young lady and her struggle."

"I never imagined something like this would happen to me, but since it has, it's never occurred to me to handle it with anything but gratitude," Kelsey stated on the tiny screen. "I'm not owed health, or even breath in my lungs, but I took them for granted for a long time. We all do, really."

Harley's voice could be heard coming through the phone as photos of Kelsey flickered across the screen. "Kelsey Andrews is seventeen years old, a beautiful young woman who schools everyone she meets in Scrabble, but while other girls her age are considering colleges and thinking about prom and graduation, Kelsey is wondering when she will receive a liver transplant."

"The health problems started a couple years ago," Regina explained, "but she's only been on the transplant list a short time."

"But for all the health problems, I have never met someone with a more upbeat spirit," Harley's voice continued. "Despite her difficulties, her optimism and faith in the face of adversity shine brightly. Even though I only met her a week ago, my life has been changed by knowing this young woman."

"Of course thinking about the past or the future aren't going to get me anywhere, so I focus on the now," Kelsey stated, looking demure and pretty on the camera despite the visible circles beneath her eyes. "We all have a purpose in this world, and I refuse to believe that mine is to sit around feeling sorry for myself and waiting to feel better. This is the life I've been given, and I've never wanted to live with regrets."

"Kelsey's always been such a bright, happy girl," Regina added. "She refuses to let her circumstances define her."

"Does this add a wrinkle to the type of future I imagined?" Kelsey continued. "Of course, but when was I in charge of my future anyway? I didn't wake myself up this morning or remind myself to breathe through the night."

"Ideally, what is the best thing that could happen right now for Kelsey?" Harley continued on the camera, sitting across from Regina and her daughter.

"Due to Kelsey's placement on the transplant list, her ideal match is a living donor," Regina stated, glancing at her daughter. "Unfortunately, we don't have a good candidate right now."

Harley watched as pictures of her speaking with Kelsey and Regina came on the screen, followed by her own voice. "But Kelsey doesn't lose hope, and so she is an inspiration to everyone lucky enough to cross her path. In just a short week she has changed my own outlook. Where I would have looked at my unfortunate accident last Friday as a hindrance, I have come to consider it a blessing, simply because I now know Kelsey Andrews."

Harley recognized the end of the video she crafted, but then the added part began playing—the part Kenny recorded while she was in Kelsey's bedroom and the section Mitch repurposed onto the end of the interview.

"We have been so blessed by Harley this past week," Regina stated, looking slightly teary. "We were talking a couple days ago about finding a living donor, and I said that it was difficult to ask someone to put their life on the line for your own."

"Harley cares about Kelsey a great deal," Kenny's voice agreed on the video.

"Yes, she does," Regina acknowledged, "enough so that she asked me if she could be a donor for Kelsey. She can't possibly know what those simple words mean to a family that is always searching for hope. To know that there are people in this world who would be willing to make that sacrifice—well, it's touching."

"Indeed, it is," Denton agreed, back at the studio. "If any of you are interested in helping the Andrews family, a link has been set up on our website to the fund for Kelsey's medical expenses. An interesting day for our own Harley Laine…talking about her harrowing explosion experience, covering pension talks with the governor, and offering a gift of life to someone in need. Louisville's sweetheart, indeed."

Clicking the video off and dropping her phone to her lap, Harley stared down at her fingers. Hearing it again didn't soften her feelings. The entire thing still made her feel dirty and selfish.

"Sweetie, it's not that bad," Duke muttered, sensing her hesitance.

"It is, though, don't you get it?" she asked with a sniffle, suddenly fighting tears. "I care a great deal about Kelsey, and I do want to help her, but for her sake, not for mine. Today I got a taste of the Harley Laine Show, and it made me sick to my stomach." Wiping a tear away with the back of her hand, she turned to face her friend. "The whole thing is so very opportunistic, Duke. I tried to talk Mitch into letting me rework the story, after they added that bit on the end. You know what he said? He needed to 'capitalize on my spotlight.' It's sick."

"Harley," he answered, placing his arm around her and pulling her against his side. "Little lady, God sees your heart. He's not judging you because of what this Mitch chose to do with the story. And you can see on that video there that Ryan's mama is right proud of you."

"Yes, I can see it, and I don't want anyone to be proud of me. Least of all any of them."

"Well, I think you'll find we're a bit stubborn and don't take kindly to being told what to do," a voice to her right stated. As she glanced up, she saw Ryan kneeling beside her at the bench. "Please forgive me. My head's not in the right place right now, but that's no excuse. I'm sorry, Harley."

"No, I'm sorry." She slowly rose to her feet while he did the same, and his hand slid around her waist beneath her coat, drawing her closer. Allowing his warmth to envelope her, she dared to look up into his eyes.

"You would really do that for Kelsey?" he asked, face expressionless. "I mean, you have pretty much zero chance of being a match, but you actually asked my mom about that?"

She didn't answer as she focused on the deep blue of his eyes, noting the dark flecks that rested within and wishing she could immerse herself in them.

"You're not allowed to be sad," he continued. "You're the one who draws me out of myself, remember? Now you're dragging yourself right into the mess."

"Ryan..." she whispered, blood heating in her veins as his warm lips touched the skin of her temple right next to her eye, sending a wave of longing over her. She realized in that moment that she had never cared for any man the way she felt about Ryan, and the thought scared her more than she wanted to admit.

"I have to go back inside," he murmured, moving his lips to the swell of her cheek just below her eye. She instinctively tilted her head up, expecting the trail of his kisses to find its way to her mouth. The thought caused her to shiver.

"Do you want to wait for me?" He pulled away and reached for her hand. She bit her lip as she glanced at his mouth, wondering what his kiss would taste like.

With a slight chuckle, he took a step back. "You seem distracted and tired. Why don't you turn in early? I won't call you and wake you up, okay?"

He's not going to kiss me.

A heavy sigh escaped her lips involuntarily, and he stopped cold. "Please tell me I didn't completely screw things up, Harley. I know I'm stubborn as all get out sometimes."

Stepping toward him, she lifted her hand to his face and gently traced her finger down the strip of hair beneath his lip, reaching the bottom of his chin right as his hand clasped hers and a huge smile spread across his face.

"Duke, brother, can I get you some more chocolate when I go inside?" Even though Ryan was clearly not addressing her, his eyes never left hers.

Stumbling backward, she instinctively lifted a hand and placed it against her heart. She had completely forgotten that Duke was sitting there with them. The memory of her desire to kiss Ryan flew into her mind again, and she felt her face heating up at the thought of sharing such an intimate first moment in front of the grizzly old biker.

"I'm good," Duke answered simply. "Anyway, I think you've got your hands full."

"Yeah," Ryan agreed, taking both of her hands in his. "I have a completely booked workday tomorrow, but if I happened to pop up at Duke's church Sunday, would you be opposed to that?"

"Completely," she murmured, regaining some of her composure. "Why would you want to spend your day off hanging out with Duke?"

"I only have a few hours Sunday, actually."

"Even worse."

"I so can't tell where I stand with you," he whispered, shaking his head.

"About eighteen inches away," she stated, raising her eyebrows. Leaning toward him, she placed her face beside his and rested her mouth by his ear. "Just for the record, you could stand a lot closer. A lot. I completely forgot Duke was here." Stepping back, she watched the heavy rise and fall of his chest and hoped she was causing that reaction. With a smile, she turned and pulled out her car keys.

"You don't play fair!" he called after her.

"Good night, Duke. 'Night, Ryan."

"Forget what I said before. I'm definitely calling you tonight, baby!" Ryan yelled as she rounded the corner.

For a few seconds, she thought about giving him a witty response. In the end, she decided against it, just so the sound of him calling her baby would be the last thing ringing through her ears.

Chapter Seventeen

Ryan nearly jumped out of his skin when he turned on the light in the kitchen and saw his mother sitting at the table. Placing a hand over his chest, he leaned against the wall and let out a shaky breath.

"Something wrong?" he asked quietly. "You haven't waited up for me since I was a teenager."

"No, honey, nothing's wrong. I just wanted to catch you before you went to bed."

He reached for a wooden chair and cringed at the scraping sound it made when he pulled it across the floor, glancing down the hall at where Kelsey was sleeping. As he lowered himself to the seat, the pace at which he had been pushing himself seemed to catch up, and exhaustion overwhelmed him. Slouching slightly, he rested his head on the back of the chair as he glanced at his mother.

"How's Kelsey?" he wanted to know, blinking his eyes and then pulling them open again with some effort.

"She's okay. It was a pretty full and exciting day for her, so she went to bed early." She paused as she tapped her fingernails gently on the table, staring at her son. "You seem worn out."

Letting out a quick rush of breath, he nodded his head. "It's my own fault. Sometimes I just can't help but be an idiot."

"This is about Harley?" Regina guessed.

"Why Harley, Mom? And why now, of all times?"

"Why not Harley?" she questioned him. "Why shouldn't it be Harley?"

"A host of reasons. Number one, she's too good for me. And before you begin telling me how special I am or any of that, it's not me saying that. Harley thinks she's too good for me. She basically told me that the first time I met her, and while I think she's softened on it a bit, that's only because we've never been in public together. I can't fit in with her crowd, and I'm not really sure I want to, to be honest."

"She's a lovely girl."

"Yeah, she's lovely," Ryan agreed with a sharp laugh. "Watch her on the news, Mom. That Denton is constantly flirting with her, and she's schmoozing with the politicians... The night I met her she had just been on a date with one, in fact."

"But has she been dating anyone lately?" Regina pried. "Sweetie, I'm not trying to pressure you into anything, but she seems to like you, and I can see how you feel about her."

"How I feel about her is the other side of the problem. I don't have the time or the energy to nurse a broken heart right now. When I look at Harley, I see a broken heart coming my way."

"You can't possibly know that, Ryan. God knows what we're going through, and I can't believe He would have sent Harley into the midst of everything simply to break your heart."

Without replying, Ryan placed both his elbows on the table and clasped his hands together.

"Kelsey said you call her every night," Regina pressed, causing Ryan's eyes to widen.

"How would she know that?"

"She says she can hear you through the wall."

Clearing his throat, Ryan shook his head. "That's pretty humiliating." Glancing at his hands, he took a second to ponder his words. "The truth is, I do really like her. I like the way I feel when I'm with her, like I'm slightly on edge and this excitement is always there building under the surface. But I really don't think either one of us is capable of having any sort of relationship right now."

Regina drew her eyebrows together, and Ryan sighed as he leaned back against the chair again.

"Tonight, we were talking at Tiny's," he began, staring at the wall across the room. "I was just kind of thinking out loud, and I happened to say that I couldn't tell where I stood with her. She was very literal about it, and said I was about eighteen inches away."

Regina laughed, and Ryan paused a second to smile to himself. "After she left, though, I realized that was the real problem. She holds me at arm's length, and I do the same to her. Neither one of us wants to let the other too close."

"Have you talked to her about it?"

Rising to his feet, Ryan picked the chair up instead of scooting it across the floor. "No, and I can't. Not right now. Go to sleep, okay? You need your rest, and so do I."

Her breath came out in a puff of frost as Harley knocked on the door of Annie's apartment, hugging her coat around her body. She had gone to sleep excited about the prospect of going to church with Annie, mainly due to the possibility of being close to Ryan, but she was decidedly less enthusiastic at the moment. Her phone had buzzed at five o'clock in the morning with a simple text message from Ryan:

Work stuff came up. Sorry. Rain check.

If the text had come from any other man, Harley might have taken the news with a grain of salt. With Ryan, though, rain check didn't mean *I'll see you in a couple days.* Rain check meant *I might see you in a month, if you're lucky.* She wasn't feeling especially lucky.

She allowed her disgust to show on her face as she thought about Ryan, and to her detriment, Annie chose that precise moment to open the door.

"Wow, are you that thrilled about going with me? Because I've got to tell you, I'd rather go alone." Annie allowed a hint of a smile to spread across her features, and Harley laughed a bit halfheartedly.

"Sorry, I was just thinking on my face, I guess."

Annie's hair was still a shade of violet, but it was back to its curly former glory. She stepped aside as Harley entered her apartment, closing the door behind her.

"I'm guessing you're doing some heavy thinking to have a facial expression like that one," Annie said without hesitation. "What gives?"

Dropping herself on Annie's couch, Harley plopped back like she owned the place, draping her skinny jeans-clad legs and her knee-high boots over the arm of the couch.

"Ryan was going to meet us at church today, and he backed out," she admitted reluctantly. "I'm pretty sure he's angry with me. I insulted his manhood, he thinks."

"Whoa, girl, that sounds like a juicy story." Sitting across from Harley on an ottoman, Annie pressed her elbows against her knees and wrapped her hands around her chin. "Spill."

"You saw all the stories about Kelsey on the news Friday?" Harley attempted to verify, to which Annie nodded. "The studio set up that fund for Kelsey, and suffice it to say that Ryan wasn't too pleased about it. He told me he wasn't a charity case."

"Yikes."

"He is just so exasperating! He practically went off on me about the bank thing Friday night, and then he came outside acting like he wanted to kiss me or something. Of course he *didn't* kiss me, just made me insane, and then told me he would call me that night and even yelled 'baby' at me as I walked away."

Annie attempted to hide her giggles behind her hand, but Harley gave her a silencing glare.

"Of course it sounds funny to you," Harley continued unabatedly. "He didn't call me, in case you were wondering. I barely slept at all because I kept checking the phone, but nothing. He called me last night and pretended that nothing happened, and then suddenly this morning something came up. Rain check."

"The nerve."

"It's not funny," Harley insisted as she set her animated eyes on her friend. "How would you like it if some guy treated you that way?"

"Well," Annie stated, sitting up a bit straighter, "first of all, I would have just kissed him myself, if I wanted to that badly. And second, if he blew me off like that, I would tell him to take a hike. I'm not in love with the guy, though, so that's easy for me to say."

"In love," Harley scoffed. "We haven't even been on an official date, because he's married to his work. Not even his work—just working. And he only does that to help his family, because he's a saint. Do you see why this is so perplexing?"

"No," Annie answered, rising and grabbing Harley's purse. She began rifling through it until she found her phone, and then held it out to her friend. "Dial the man's number. 'Ryan, I am interested in you. I want to date you.' Enough said."

"I don't see how that's particularly helpful!" Harley expressed as she snatched the phone from Annie's hand.

"The poor guy doesn't know where he stands with you, and you're freaking him out."

Stunned, Harley dropped the phone to her lap and pulled her legs around to sit on the couch properly. The fact that Ryan said those exact same words to her Friday night was not escaping her.

"What made you say that?"

Dropping her head, Annie let out a sigh. "You know I love you, but you're not exactly easy to get close to. We're pretty good friends, and I've never been to your house. I've never been inside your car to see what type of music you're listening to. You don't talk about your family, or where you grew up—"

"Because I don't want to bore you to death."

"Is that it, Harley? Truly? Because it feels like more. And if I can't seem to break a barrier with you, when we're relaxed and chummy, how is Ryan supposed to feel? He's probably all tense and nervous around you."

"People don't have problems talking to me," Harley countered. "That's what I do all day, isn't it?"

"Sure, reporter Harley. Not this Harley, the one I see on Wednesday nights. You hold yourself back. I know because I used to do it myself."

Unable to stop the laugh from bursting forth, Harley shook her head. "Annie Jessup holding herself back? Now that I'd have to see to believe."

"There are things about me that you don't know. Many, many things. I'm quite a mystery."

Annie reached behind Harley and grabbed her coat before snagging her purse and slinging it over her arm. Harley followed suit and rose, placing her phone back into her own purse.

"Okay, then, tell me about the mystery that is Annie. Inquiring minds want to know."

Opening the front door, Annie shook her head solemnly.

"Sorry, but no. You open up to me and I'll do the same, but not before. And if I find out you opened up to Ryan before me..." She stopped and gave Harley a warning glare. "Girl, you best not, that's all I got to say."

Walking into the office on Monday afternoon, Harley dropped her purse to the ground as she slumped into her chair. Her momentary popularity had taken on its own life form, and she wished she could escape. Without a clear exit route in sight, she placed an elbow on her desk and dropped her chin onto her hand.

Testing to see if she was a match for Kelsey was nerve-wracking enough, but because of Mitch she was living out the nervousness on camera and with a microphone in her hand. That day more than any other, she felt like she was using others for her own advantage. Not even for her advantage, really—for the betterment of Channel Six and the powers that be.

In addition to initial testing to determine whether she was a match for the liver donation, she had followed up on her bone marrow registration by submitting some blood for the National Marrow Donor program. She had been a possible match, they said, so they needed some bloodwork. Ordinarily she would have ignored it, since she had only registered for the little boy's benefit in the first place, but since Mitch saw fit to accompany her on the story, he gently suggested that she "give it a go." Her instinct was to spin around and tell him that he should "give it a go" himself, but she decided against poking the bear at that moment.

Initial observations acknowledged that Harley did share the same blood type as Kelsey, so additional tests would be completed. That tidbit of information alone sent her into a moment of panic, because she hadn't clearly thought the situation through. If she was found to be a match, how long would she be off work? Would she herself be terribly ill?

Forcing the thoughts out of her mind yet again, Harley focused on her computer screen. Her email inbox held four messages from state politicians responding to her requests for comments on the pension issue, along with questions on a couple local issues that she had slipped in since she had the opportunity. Making herself give them attention seemed futile, though, because her heart wasn't in any of it.

No, her heart was far away, thinking about things she hadn't really considered in years.

Chapter Eighteen

The workweek passed in a haze with constant distractions, and Harley struggled to keep her head above water. She decided she was too busy to see Annie on Wednesday, and she purposely turned off her phone when she went to bed at night so she couldn't take any late night telephone conversations.

Kelsey contacted her at the station a couple times during the week, and while she spoke with her young friend, she wavered between sincerely hoping she was a match so she could help her and secretly wishing she wasn't. Although she wanted to be altruistic and offer Kelsey whatever help she could, she was internally terrified.

As she walked up her own front porch steps on Friday evening, fumbling with her keys in the darkness, Harley glanced down the street at the homes of her neighbors. Twinkling Christmas lights shone through their windows, and some had lights adorning their garages and rooflines. Her own home was dark and imposing at the end of the cul-de-sac, absolutely devoid of any sort of Christmas cheer.

Normally upon entering her home, Harley went straight up the stairs and locked herself inside her bedroom. For some reason, though, she felt compelled to walk through the unused portions of her house. Leaving the front door ajar, she took a couple steps across the hardwood floor of the foyer and pushed open the door to the kitchen. A stark space met her, devoid of appliances but instead boasting empty holes in the cabinetry, which had some doors hanging precariously askew. The area was clean, but hardly livable.

Stepping to her left, she pushed open another door into the living room, flipping on the light switch to her right. The large window in the front was where she would put a Christmas tree, if she had one, but the curtains were tightly drawn to keep the world out. If they weren't drawn, any passerby might realize that her living room had a vacant fireplace along the wall, no furniture for lounging, and staples sticking out of the floor as reminders that a carpet once rested in that space.

"Hello?" she heard echoing behind her, and her body instantly froze with the unwelcome sound. Turning, she stomped across the kitchen, the sound of her clicking heels reverberating through the empty room.

"Harley? The door was open."

She crossed the threshold of the kitchen as quickly as possible and threw the door closed behind her, wide-eyed with surprise.

"How do you know where I live? And why are you here exactly?"

She hadn't intended her words to come out so harshly, but she wasn't surprised when Ryan's eyebrows rose in surprise.

"Take it easy," he responded. "I'm not a serial killer, alright? You wouldn't answer my phone calls, and I was starting to worry, so I did a little of my own research. I would have knocked like a normal person if the door had been closed. While we're at it, the fact that you blindly left your door open makes me a little nervous for your sanity."

"I live on Wonder Lane," she said, folding her arms across her chest. "Nothing happens here. This is the most boring street on the planet."

Well, relatively speaking.

"You live in the *biggest* house on Wonder Lane," he corrected, "so it's probably the biggest target."

"It's just a house."

"Sure, Scarlett O'Hara. Just a house. Does it have a name?"

"A name?"

"You know, like Tara?"

"Sure, I like to call it home."

Ryan closed the door behind him to shut out the cool night and shifted his hands to his pockets. The waft of air from the force of the door came towards her, and a cologne-scented breeze drifted across her face. She shivered slightly, but realized it wasn't from the chill. The fact that he had sought her out in her home, and had taken the time to put on cologne, sent her emotions in overdrive.

"I'm not working tonight," he announced, as though he wanted to confound her conflicted feelings. "I wanted to ask you if you would go out with me, like an official date. I need to figure out what this is for my own sanity."

"You want to ask me out for your sanity," she repeated dubiously.

An easy smile spread across his face, and she allowed her gaze to sweep over him. Black jeans, boots, inky blue button-down shirt open at the collar...

"Do I meet with your approval?" he asked cautiously.

Drawing her hand up to her neck, she felt her face growing warm as he watched her reaction. "Always," she answered simply.

"I don't want to ask you out for my sanity," he finally added. "I want to ask you out because I can't get you out of my head."

"That's a pretty good reason." Glancing down at her skirt and heels, she smiled ever so slightly. "Do you mind if I change first?"

"Nope. I'll just have a look around."

"No." The word came out so quickly, she instantly felt a prick of guilt at its abruptness. "I mean, just wait right here, and I'll be ready in a minute, okay?"

He moved toward her, and she froze in place, worried that he was going to touch her and unsure whether she wanted him to do so. When he was close enough to be just inches from her, he brushed past and placed a hand on the kitchen door.

"You left the light on," he stated simply, shoving the door open. As he did so, he paused, holding the door as though in a trance.

Harley's breath halted in her chest as he took a step into the room, glancing around. When he moved farther into the kitchen and didn't bother to speak, she squeezed her eyes closed and mentally cringed. The click of a light switch alerted her to the fact that he had traveled through the kitchen and made it to the living room, and she shook her head in disbelief. The urge to follow him and attempt to explain herself grew stronger, but what would she say?

Ryan, it's all about appearances.
I intend to fix it...someday.
Isn't the outside gorgeous?

He began to move in her direction, and she waited for his questions like a statue. Instead of stopping before her, though, he flipped the lights off in the kitchen and continued walking, making his way to the front door. Her heart constricted as she realized he might be disappearing into the night, and she squeezed her hands into fists at her side.

Turning abruptly, he swung open the door at the bottom of the stairs, glancing into the corridor. The sound of his boots hitting the wood on the steps assaulted her senses, and within seconds she was on his trail, flying up the steps behind him, trying not to trip in her heels.

His eyes swept across the clothes she had on racks in the first bedroom she utilized as a closet, and then he took a couple more steps to her modest bedroom. She stood motionless in the hallway, biting her lip and feeling the heaviness of his silence as he remained in the entry to her bedroom.

Say something, she willed herself, but couldn't manage to squeeze anything out of her throat. Finally, he turned and focused on her and her alone, not taking his eyes from her face.

"You are such a hypocrite," he whispered.

"No." She shook her head, fighting the urge to crumble.

"A fraud, then."

"Ryan—"

"Your floor..." he began, glancing down. "You don't have a kitchen. Where is your furniture?" When Harley hesitated, he widened his eyes. "Harley, there are holes in the wall. I can see exposed wires. Is the rest of your house like this? No wonder you never eat!"

"I do okay," she tried to convince him.

Undaunted, he marched into her spare bedroom, looking over her clothes. "But you have the important things, right? You've practically got your own designer storefront in here."

"You have to dress for the life you want," she told him, aware of the worried expression crossing her features.

"What do you want?" he asked, clearly frustrated. "Do you even know what you want?"

No. Do you?

"I want to change and meet you downstairs."

Nodding slowly, he strolled past her and trudged down the steps, stepping out the door and closing it behind him. She leaned back against the wall, letting out a reluctant sigh. For a second she wondered if she should even change, because he would probably be long gone before she reached the bottom of the steps. In case he did stick around, though, as crazy as it sounded...

She stood amidst her clothes, pondering her choices. She could opt to dress down and go the jeans and T-shirt route like she usually did on Friday nights, but this might be her only chance at a date with Ryan, especially after what he had just seen. He had obviously taken time to try to look good, and he smelled incredible.

Yeah, he definitely smells incredible.

Shoving aside a couple hangers, Harley located a dress she hadn't worn in a long time. It was one of the first she bought when she arrived in Louisville, and it never felt appropriate for the newsroom. Crossing over to the bathroom, she stepped out of her skirt and slid the dress up over her hips, pausing to unbutton her white blouse. As she drew the three-quarter length sleeves of the dress over her arms, she glanced at herself in the mirror. Simple, elegant black fabric hugged her frame and skimmed her legs, draping against her neck. Twisting her body, she fought to zip the back of the dress, finally finding success.

After smoothing her hair around her shoulders, she crossed back to her spare bedroom and located a pair of simple black four-inch heels.

Completely ready, she remained in the hallway as she took a deep breath.

He's probably not even here, she thought. Instead of dwelling on the thought, though, she made her way down the steps. When she emerged into the foyer, she found him leaning against the wall, staring towards the kitchen. His eyes darted toward her as he stood erect and took a step toward her.

"You're still here." Sounding stunned probably wasn't the best strategy, she realized, but she couldn't stop the words from tumbling out.

He swallowed hard before he answered. "I should probably be angry with you or something, but I'm having a hard time sorting it out."

"Why is that?"

"Because my heart is overriding my head."

He moved even closer, and she reached for her coat, but he drew it out of her hand, holding it in front of him. Turning her back, she allowed him to drape it over her shoulders. Spinning, she found herself within inches of his face, and she lifted her eyes to his. They were nearly the same height due to her heels, and she didn't dare remove her eyes as he stared at her. Unable to resist the urge to touch him, she lifted the tips of her fingers to his cheek and pushed a strand of hair behind his ear.

"How did this happen?" he wanted to know. "You shouldn't be walking down those stairs in a dress like that for me."

She wanted to say a million things, but they all felt too inappropriately intimate, so she simply allowed a smile to spread across her face.

"Where are you taking me?"

He shook his head quickly, as though clearing his mind. "Hadn't thought. I was just planning on taking you on your Friday Tiny's run, but—"

"Sounds perfect."

The smile he gave her was enough to melt her heart, and she reached for her purse and held it in her hand. He pulled a set of car keys out of his pocket, presumably for his mom's car, and Harley responded by handing him her own.

"Sweet...you're going to let me drive?"

"It would appear so, handsome."

He held out his arm, opened the door, and ushered her into the evening air. As he reached the BMW, he opened the passenger door and took her hand as she slid into her seat. Once she was closed safely inside, he crossed to the driver's side and slowly lowered himself onto the seat, placing his hands on the wheel and getting a feel for the car.

Harley couldn't resist teasing him. "Does it meet your approval?"

"Not bad. What happened to your seat?"

Harley's mind flashed to the duct tape, and after what he had seen inside her house, she thought it best to be brutally honest.

"Drug deal gone bad. For the person who owned the car before, not me. I got it for a steal." Since Ryan had no visible reaction to her statement, she decided to continue. "Just like my house. The people who owned it were trying to unload it because of all the improvements they needed to make. Obviously I didn't have enough capital to make them myself."

Ryan brought the car's engine to life and began to back out onto Wonder Lane, and Harley twisted her mouth to the side.

"I get all my clothes at The Revolving Closet—that's my friend Annie's resale shop. But you're right, the public Harley, that's not who I really am, although I would be hesitant to call myself a fraud or a hypocrite."

"This is a pretty smooth ride." He glanced over, giving her a wink, and she realized suddenly how comfortable it felt to have him so near.

"You should have asked me out a long time ago," she breathed, letting the words hang in the air between them.

"You're kidding me, right? How many times did I try to get your number?"

"I'm sorry about that," she insisted. "Thank you."

"For what?"

"Figuring out where I live. Driving to my house. Smelling phenomenal."

He didn't say a word, but his fingers grazed her left thigh, moving their way across her hand slowly enough to give her goose bumps.

She wasn't sure what she had expected out of her evening only moments before, but it hadn't included sitting in her car holding hands with the man she couldn't manage to remove from her thoughts.

"Good evening, Duke," Ryan stated as he neared Tiny's and rambled up to the bench, his arm circling Harley's waist.

"What's this?" Duke had a definite twinkle in his eye.

"This is a long overdue date," Harley told him, enjoying the sensation she felt as Ryan hugged her closer.

"I can't imagine a better couple," Duke informed them. "You'd best get her inside so you don't freeze. And share your chocolate with Ryan tonight, Harley—I'm okay."

"Thanks," she whispered as she allowed Ryan to pull her towards the front of the building. Ushering her inside, he located a table to one side that seemed mostly secluded and moved in that direction, pulling out her chair and pausing to help her shrug out of her coat.

"Oh, mercy." Tiny rambled over to their table and paused, his large frame looming over them as they both tried not to smile. "Don't tell me this is a date? 'Cause Miss Harley already went and made me a promise about any date that brought her here."

"Nobody made any promises," Harley assured him.

"Tiny, I have to thank you, because if I hadn't been working in the kitchen I might have never met this beautiful woman, who consequently *is* on a date with me right now. That's important to note, since she made a promise...?"

"...that if any date brought her here, she'd marry them on the spot."

Harley's eyes widened as she stared at Tiny, unable to believe he'd just divulged that tidbit of information. Ryan chuckled quietly and cleared his throat.

"Well, I'm not quite sure I'm at that point yet, but good to keep in my back pocket for another time." Ryan winked at Harley for good measure, and then turned back to Tiny. "What's your specialty tonight?"

"I've got a mean chicken fettuccine alfredo if you have a hankering for that. Or there's always the standby favorites."

"That sounds good," Harley told him.

"Yeah, me too." Ryan paused to smile at his companion. "Thanks, Tiny."

Staring across the table at Harley, Ryan suddenly picked his chair up, moving it around the side so he was directly next to her. Settling himself back in the seat, he reached for her hand. A sweeping sensation rushed across her abdomen as he lifted her fingers and gently pressed his lips against her skin.

"So, the public Harley is not who you really are?" His eyes rested on hers, searching. "I want to know you...the real you."

Staring at Ryan, she imagined the wall she had built crumbling before her, and although it was intimidating, the fact that he was sitting on the other side made it seem almost possible.

Letting out a huge sigh, she reached into her purse and retrieved her wallet, pausing a second to close her eyes. "Okay, just so we're clear, this is between you and me, right? You're not going to go off telling Kelsey or your mom?"

"You think I discuss my love life with either one of them? Not that they don't try, mind you."

Still firmly latched onto Ryan with her right hand, she used her left to flip through her wallet and pull out her driver's license, hanging her head a bit sheepishly. With trepidation, she held it out to Ryan with a shaking hand. His fingers slid around it, and as he held it for inspection, her heart pounded in her chest.

"Wow."

"Wow? That's all you have to say? Wow?"

"Sorry, I'm having trouble coming up with an appropriate reaction." Raising his eyebrows, Ryan continued to stare at her license. "It's just…when you told me at the hospital that your dad named you after his motorcycle, I kind of had a presupposed notion of what that meant. It wasn't this."

"Whatever you thought, it has to be worse."

"This is definitely worse. If you changed your name, why don't you have your new name on your license?"

"Because I never changed my name. My name is Harley Elaine, so I just shorten it to Harley Laine."

"Wow."

"Again with the wow."

"Sorry, what do you want me to say?" Staring at the license, he shook his head. "Harley Davidson. No wonder you hate motorcycles. I think I hate them for you, honestly."

"You don't need to worry about being polite about it. Trust me, if a joke can be made, I've heard it."

"Maybe I *should* marry you on the spot, just so you can rectify this injustice."

"Well, that one's new," she said, shaking her head. "Honestly, who sidles their kid with a name like that? It's cruel."

"He must have meant well."

"Oh, of course. My parents always mean well. They do the right thing until it drives you into a hole in the ground."

"Just an observation, but you seem a little bitter."

Sliding her license back into her wallet, Harley looked down at Ryan's hand over hers. She added her left hand to the pile, almost desperate to touch him.

"Is that enough opening up? You're probably sorry you asked."

"No," he insisted, adding in his free hand so that all their fingers were enmeshed together. "When I said I want to know you, I meant that. I really don't care how long it takes. I've got plenty of time."

"What about you?" She intently searched his eyes as she clung to his hands. "I want to know you, too. Like why tattoos?"

"Why tattoos? That's pretty blunt."

"Maybe, but you showed them to me the same night you met me, so you're not too intent on hiding them."

Two glasses of water appeared on the table, but the couple barely noticed.

"That's a hard one to answer, because if I'm really honest, I'm sure it will freak you out." He paused as Harley squeezed his hand, not removing her focus from him, and he gave a resigned shrug. "Maybe because there's such a big age difference between us, or because she always just seemed so small compared to me, but I've always been the most overprotective big brother you could imagine. It's hard not to be crazy about Kelsey, though, because she has such a genuine, sweet spirit. You know what I mean, obviously, since you're already so close with her."

"She's fantastic," Harley agreed quietly.

"But I'm not really her full brother, you know——I'm her half-brother. My mom was married before she met Sam, and even though he was only around until I was about six months old, I've always known that Jeff Temple was my dad. He moved to Arizona, but we've always stayed in contact.

"Well, when we found out that Kelsey needed a transplant, naturally there's no question…of course I'm going to be her donor, right? The tests were just a formality, until I wasn't a match. Kelsey is blood type B, just like Sam. Mom's blood type O. I'm blood type A. I was ranting about it on the phone to Jeff one night when he casually mentioned that he was blood type B."

"Meaning?"

"If they're O and B, then their kids have to be O or B." He watched as recognition of what he was inferring flickered across her face. "Jeff's not my dad, Harley. When they got married, my mom and Jeff had a pretty rocky start. They were really young, only eighteen and nineteen. Six months in, Mom had an affair. They worked through it until after I was born, but the stress took its toll on Jeff. He decided to leave, but they both chose not to let me know."

"Wow."

"That's all you have to say? Wow?" He smiled playfully. "Sorry, I couldn't resist."

"So Jeff's not your dad, but did I miss the part about the tattoos?"

"No, I didn't get that far yet. I was really upset, and I wanted to lash out. I think the thing that bothered me the most was, if I was really Jeff's son, chances are I could have been the donor. While I was having that internal struggle, though, I would sit with Kelsey and she would say these beautiful prayers of hope. She should have been angry, too, but she wasn't.

"So, every time I struggled with losing my own hope, I plastered it on myself. As you know from the night I met you, I struggled a few times."

"Do you think you'll get more tattoos?"

He smiled before he answered. "Time will tell, I guess, but I don't have plans for more at this particular juncture."

"Spoken like a politician."

"I can't believe you'd insult me after I shared such a personal story with you."

Tiny chose that moment to return with their plates, and Ryan reluctantly relinquished Harley's fingers and allowed her to pick up her fork.

"Is that why you take it upon yourself to pay your parents' bills?" Harley continued questioning. "Since you can't be the donor, I mean?"

Ryan wrapped a fettuccine noodle around his fork before lifting it into the air.

"Not really. I just love Kelsey and want to make sure she has the best possible chance of being healed. I wouldn't have done it for my mom, because I was pretty angry at her. In fact, I didn't talk to her for several months. That was a while ago, though."

Harley stared at her plate, thinking about how she could partially understand his predicament.

"I haven't spoken to my parents in two years," she said quietly.

"I'm guessing this doesn't have anything to do with your name, although that's certainly worth being angry about."

"No, but it's a really long story." When he simply shoved the fork in his mouth and lifted his eyebrows, she looked at her plate with a resigned grin. "I grew up basically in the middle of nowhere, about two hours east of here. My parents live on a half-acre piece of land in a trailer with two bedrooms and a dinky bathroom. My dad fixes motorcycles, as you know, and my mom is an unpaid secretary at their church. I grew up knowing I was dirt poor and having to work hard for everything I had."

"You haven't touched your food, Harley," Tiny interrupted, suddenly hulking over them. "Everything okay?"

"Huh? Oh, of course, just talking. I guess you're accustomed to me inhaling my food here, aren't you?"

"It's okay," he stated with a toothy grin. "I'll just leave you two alone then."

Ryan's left hand rested on the table, and Harley thought about taking it, but knew better than to try to eat the fettuccine with her left hand. Instead, she shifted her leg a little closer and pressed it against his.

Ryan cleared his throat as he gave her a knowing smile. "So, um, dirt poor... Please continue."

"Right," she said, glancing down and taking a breath to still the erratic beating of her heart. She liked to think of herself as calm under pressure, but the slightest hint of flirtation from Ryan rendered her practically useless. "My parents had me in church every waking moment, and my mom would go on mission trips every summer and leave me with my dad. It was almost like she had a second summer family or something. You can imagine the kind of childhood I had...oversized hand-me-down clothes, totally laughable name, overzealous religious parents, no telephone in the house, and a body that resembled a walking stick."

Ryan laughed, and she shook her head. "I'm not kidding— I was scrawny until college. Late bloomer. Anyway, I always wanted to be a newspaper reporter, and I knew I wanted to go to college. Since my parents couldn't afford it, I worked especially hard to earn scholarships and then I spent every night and weekend doing whatever jobs I could find to earn money. Every red cent went into a savings account for my college fund, and with my scholarships I even had some left over. Thus, the ridiculously large house I live in."

"I would have never figured you for the frugal type," Ryan assessed.

"Yes, well, surprise."

"And you haven't talked to your parents because…"

"Be patient, I'm getting there. When I was in college, I found out that I was really good at being in front of a camera, so I changed my focus. It was pretty tough for me, because I was working every night adding to the savings account while I went to classes during the day, and I never had a social life. That's not an exaggeration…zero social life. The whole thing was exhausting.

"I went directly from college to a job in Little Rock, so I breezed through and told my parents goodbye, and they agreed to write. A year passed and I spent the entire time working and looking for a better opportunity. When this job in Louisville came up, I was thrilled. It was closer to home and a much better gig for me, so I popped in at my parents' to tell them the good news. They were both out, so I let myself into the trailer to wait for them, and that's when I saw it sitting on the kitchen counter."

"Saw it?" Ryan wondered, widening his eyes as he took a bite of his chicken.

"Their tax return." Focusing on the window at the front of the restaurant, Harley paused as she replayed the memory in her mind. "I had worked my tail off from the time I was fourteen, doing every kind of job imaginable. We didn't have a phone. I never had clothes that fit, and when I saw that tax return…"

Peeling her eyes away from the window, Harley looked directly at Ryan. "Over half of their money they sent overseas to my mom's 'second summer family'. They had been funding another 'daughter' for years, while they watched me kill myself trying to make my own way. I was crushed, and I didn't even wait for them. Left them a note: *Got a job in Louisville.* I guess..." She looked at her food again, feeling self-conscious. "I guess that's what set it off, really—the desire to prove that I could be wildly successful, in spite of them. Dressing for the job I wanted. I haven't had time to go home since then, and I really don't want to anyway."

Squinting his eyes a bit, Ryan tilted his mouth to the side. "That's a really horrible story," he offered, adding a slight laugh at the end.

"How is that funny, exactly?" She sat up straighter and pulled her leg away from his, but he responded by moving over and pressing his leg to hers once again.

"Oh, it's not, I was just picturing you as a human walking stick."

She giggled along with him before they launched into more lighthearted topics, eventually moving their way from their fettuccine to a shared piece of chocolate cake. A couple hours piled on top of one another, until finally Tiny showed up at their table again.

"Well, kids, the place has cleared out. Ryan, if you want to lock up, I won't have to kick you out just yet."

"Sure, I can do that."

Harley watched Tiny's retreating back as he went toward the kitchen, and then she turned to focus her eyes on Ryan. Rising from his chair, he reached for her hand and pulled her up to meet him. His right hand skimmed against her dress at her waist, settling just above her hip. She felt a physical skip of her breath as she sensed the heat of his fingers through the fabric, and she hesitantly lifted her hand to his chest as his eyes danced over hers, keeping her hostage.

"Have you figured it out?" she asked, her voice sounding shallow and fragile in her own ears. "What this is, I mean?"

His left hand found the other side of her waist and wrapped around to the small of her back, moving her forward until she was solidly against him. Her eyes slowly drifted from his eyes across the sweep of his eyelashes, past the contours of his cheek, resting on the corner of his mouth. Her fingers reached up to settle on the hair under his lip, and he visibly swallowed.

"You did that last week, and you were lucky Duke was there to save you," he whispered.

"Save me?" She pulled her eyes back up to his. "What if I don't want to be saved?" Tilting her face toward him, she lightly brushed her lips against his before pulling back slightly. His arms tightened around her as he brought his mouth down to meet hers, giving in to a slow, all-consuming kiss that more than melted anything standing between them. She was unsure whether she was leaning towards him or he was pulling her closer as she memorized the feel of his mouth against hers, fingers locking around the long dark hair at the back of his neck.

Reluctantly he drew his lips away, taking in a shuddering breath as she moved closer, claiming his mouth again as she pushed her fingers farther into his hair. His hand drifted up her back, tugging at her as he stepped backwards, bumping awkwardly into a table. Undeterred, he lowered himself to lean against it as she moved with him, kissing him hungrily. Bringing his hand up to the back of his head, he wrapped his fingers around hers, dragging her hand down against his chest. A soft moan escaped her throat, and he struggled to push her back. As their lips parted, he glanced at her mouth, and she wondered how she had waited so long to kiss him.

"Ryan." She sounded hoarse and breathless, but she didn't care. "I'm in love with you. Do you feel what's happening between us? Is it only me?"

Pausing, he brushed a hair away from her face as he assessed her searching eyes. "I think I'm pretty solid on what this is."

"And?" Hesitance framed her features, and he let a slight smile appear on his face.

"I'm in love with you. All in. Over my head."

Climbing out of the BMW, Ryan threw the keys to Harley, who caught them midair and gave him a knowing smile. Hands in his pockets, he sauntered over to where she was standing, rocking on his heels as he waited in front of her.

With a laugh, she turned toward her house and began walking towards the porch, carefully maneuvering the steps. When she reached the top, she fumbled with the keys a bit, staring at the man who followed her to that spot.

"What are you doing tomorrow?" he asked, taking her hand.

"I don't know. You tell me."

"Christmas shopping? I haven't gone yet, and I took the whole weekend off."

"The whole weekend?" Squeezing his fingers a little tighter, she offered a mischievous grin. "Merry Christmas to me."

"I'll have the bike because my mom will need her car—"

"So I'll just swing by the house and we can take my car." Stepping closer to him, she drew the tip of her house key across his abdomen playfully. "Unless you have objections."

"No, ma'am." Grabbing her keys, he pulled his hand back slowly so hers would follow, until she was pressed against him. "See what I did there?"

"You're very clever," she whispered.

"Thank you for a perfect night," he told her as he rested his lips near her mouth, his warm breath fanning her cheek.

"Thank you for being a stalker," she teased. "And for the delicious kisses."

He didn't answer as he tilted her face up and ran his finger down the center of her chin. When she laughed, he responded by silencing her with an unhurried, lingering kiss. She felt the effects of his action in the pit of her stomach, and she answered by wrapping her arms around his neck.

"Merry Christmas to me," he mumbled, pulling away and pressing his lips against her forehead. "I should go now, before I get myself into loads of trouble. I'll see you tomorrow, Harley Davidson."

"Hey, that was mean."

"Don't worry, it's our little secret." He let a smile cross his face, and Harley waited for his teasing remarks. "Anyway, you know how I feel about motorcycles."

Chapter Nineteen

Harley squinted her eyes against the sunny day as she closed the door to the BMW, staring at the unassuming little house. A smile tugged at her lips as she placed her keys in the pocket of her boyfriend jeans, strolling toward the front door. With only minimal makeup and her hair pulled into a ponytail, she felt really free for the first time in ages. Breathing the cool, crisp air into her lungs, she rapped her knuckles on the door.

Ryan answered, wearing a white T-shirt and distressed jeans and once again smelling fabulous.

"Harley Laine from Channel Six Action News," she began, holding her fist in front of her mouth like a microphone. "Would you mind answering a few questions?"

"Are there cameras?" he asked playfully, peering over her shoulder.

"No cameras. Off the record."

"In that case..." Trailing off, he pulled her forward and placed his arms around her, but she wiggled away and closed the door behind her.

"Stop, please. I'm a consummate professional, and this is a serious interview."

"A serious interview?" Ryan raised one eyebrow as he backed himself to the middle of the room. "My apologies, then. Please continue."

"Mr. Temple, do you make it a practice of professing your love to vulnerable young women?"

Fighting a laugh behind his hand, Ryan cleared his throat.

"I would have to say...no."

"So is it safe to assume, when you do make such a profession, that it isn't made in jest?"

"I would never do that."

"Yet you were overheard expressing this emotion last night in the company of...someone I know."

"She said it to me first."

"I'm sure she was overcome by the heady scent of your cologne. It can render a person quite defenseless, frankly."

"I've got to say, Denton's flirting usually annoys me, but I'm starting to feel for the poor guy. How exactly is he supposed to resist you?"

"Commenting about Denton's flirtatious nature is an obvious attempt to change the subject to avoid your own admission of guilt. And he doesn't resist me, as I've told you before. He asks me out constantly, and I tell him no. My heart is otherwise occupied, thank you very much."

"Otherwise occupied?" he wondered, reaching for her again. This time she didn't protest, but allowed him to pull her closer.

"Uh-huh. Doing an intensive case study on one particular subject."

"Ryan, are you heading out?" they heard Regina yell from down the hall. Harley backed away guiltily and gave Ryan a slight smile. "I was going to use the car..." She emerged a few seconds later, pausing when she saw their houseguest. "I didn't know you were stopping by, sweetie. Kelsey's still sleeping."

"As if I could sleep with you yelling," Kelsey muttered, stepping up behind Regina, T-shirt half tucked into her pajama pants and her hair sticking up on one side of her head. "What's going on? Darn it, Ryan, why didn't you say we had company?"

"Harley doesn't care that you have bedhead," he stated with a laugh.

"Are you going to be here for a while?" Kelsey wanted to know, attempting to smooth down her errant locks. "Maybe we could watch a Christmas movie or something."

Glancing between Regina and Kelsey, Harley's forehead wrinkled slightly. "Actually, I have a date, so…"

"Oh." Kelsey looked a smidge dejected, and Harley instantly felt a twinge of guilt. "Well, it was nice of you to drop by on your way to your date, anyway."

"Yeah, I was in the neighborhood because I have to pick him up," Harley added. "Maybe after, though? I'll be back around later."

"Sure." Kelsey followed Ryan with her eyes as he reached for his coat and shoved one arm into the sleeve. "Where are you going?"

"My girlfriend's here to pick me up," he said simply. "She has a sweet BMW, and she's really hot." Stepping up behind Harley, he wrapped his arms around her waist.

"Is he playing a joke on me?" Kelsey directed her words to Harley, who leaned her head back against Ryan's shoulder.

"No, he's not kidding," Harley assured her. "I am really hot." Adding a wink for good measure, she retrieved her keys from her pocket. "You driving?"

"Absolutely." Plucking the keys from her hand, he straightened his coat as he took a step back. "I'll try to have her home in time to watch your movie, Kels."

"Have a good time!" Regina called as they stepped out the door.

Ryan crossed to the car quickly, pulling open the passenger door and blocking Harley's path.

"I can't believe you think you're hot," he whispered.

"I can't believe you called me your girlfriend. That's pretty presumptuous on your part."

"So sorry," he stated, allowing a smile to spread across his face. "After last night, I just assumed—"

"That I wouldn't be dating other people? That I want to be in a committed relationship? That there's no other person I'd rather be with right now?"

"Well, yeah."

Squeezing between him and the car, she placed her hand on his shoulder and pressed a feather-soft kiss to his neck.

"You were right. And I don't care what you call me, as long as you do."

Christmas music rang out overhead as Harley strolled through the mall with her hand firmly clasped in Ryan's, staring at the storefronts. The scenery exuded a winter wonderland, albeit rather dingy and fake-looking, but she hardly noticed as she glanced at the man beside her.

A strange sensation filled her chest, tingly and exciting, and she bit the inside of her cheek to keep from smiling as she glanced away. She had never been so enamored with anyone in her life, and the thought was both thrilling and terrifying. For the moment, she decided to focus on thrilling, since she could feel the flesh of his fingers warm against her own.

"Have you done any Christmas shopping yet?" he questioned, interrupting her thoughts.

"No, but I never do, really. Unless you count shopping for myself."

"Which you do a lot." He cast a sideways glance in her direction, and she squeezed his hand harder.

"Only on Wednesdays, and not recently. I'm guessing you haven't done any shopping?"

"Been too busy. Anyway, I've had a lot on my mind, and I wasn't really in the mood."

"Are you in the mood today?"

"For what?" he asked mischievously. "I would probably consider it a lot more tedious if I wasn't with you."

"I'm glad I could make your day less tedious, then."

Ryan paused at the entrance to a coffee shop, taking a deep breath. "That smells great. Maybe we should just stay here."

"We could, but you'll never get your shopping done." Pulling on his hand, she coerced him back into motion.

"Harley Laine? Is that you?"

Stopping in her tracks, Harley twisted her neck to see who had addressed her, and found her eyes locked on Denton Price. His gaze roamed over her from head to toe, and he never bothered to wipe the surprise from his expression.

"Wow, it is you. You look different, and…shorter."

Ryan pulled his fingers away from hers, and she nervously wiped her palms on her jeans. "I'm sure it's because I'm not wearing heels," she said. "Ryan, have you ever met Denton?"

"No, I've not had the pleasure," Ryan stated hesitantly, extending his hand. Denton reluctantly took it while looking at Harley questioningly.

"Nice to meet you," Denton finally added, dragging his eyes back to Ryan. "I take it you're the guy she's sort of seeing?"

"I don't know how one would go about 'sort of' seeing another person, but I guess you'd have to take that one up with her."

Harley's nervousness ratcheted up a notch as she glanced at a passerby who was eyeing them curiously. "So, are you Christmas shopping, too?"

"Yeah, trying to anyway." Denton drew his eyes to Ryan again, sizing him up. "I'm sorry, you're just not Harley's usual fare—not to be rude. Merely an observation."

"O-kay," Ryan answered slowly. "I have no idea what to do with that."

"He's right," Harley stated, shrugging her shoulders. "I'm pretty sure Ryan already knows that." Stepping closer to Ryan, she wrapped her arm around his waist and looked up at his profile. "This guy is so selfless and poetic and truly amazing, and I'm really lucky that he's willing to date me. I'm proud to be the girl on his arm."

Ryan dropped his head and grinned as he protectively circled Harley's shoulders, resting his fingertips against her arm.

"Well, if you've got Harley in your corner like that, you must be a good guy." Denton reached out to pat Ryan on the shoulder. "Take care of this girl. I need her for the witty banter."

"Good to meet you," Ryan stated as Denton walked away. He turned to Harley, resting his eyes on hers as a lazy half-smile formed on his face.

"Shopping?" she suggested, feeling rather self-conscious.

"You really meant that, didn't you?" Removing his arm from her shoulders, he took her hand as another shopper bumped him, forcing him closer.

"We're going to be trampled." She knew she needed to move, but the blue of his eyes seemed brighter than normal, and she didn't want to look away. With a resigned sigh, he continued walking.

"So you really don't have any shopping to do?" He lifted his eyes back to the retail displays.

"No. The truth is, my parents never really celebrated Christmas this way, so it's kind of foreign to me."

"When you say 'this way' you mean..."

"Gifts, mostly."

Pausing at a candle shop, Ryan stepped inside.

"You like smells, don't you?" Harley added. "First the coffee shop, now the candles."

"Yes, ma'am. You do too, though—at least you seem to like my cologne. Or were you being sarcastic earlier?"

"Trust me, you smell amazing."

Grabbing a candle, Ryan held it behind his back and lifted his eyebrows. "A game, perhaps? Close your eyes and tell me what you smell."

She glanced around to make certain no one was watching before she did as he asked, gently closing her eyes. Within seconds one aroma was overwhelming all the others, and she inhaled as she tried to place it.

"Apples and brown sugar?" she guessed.

"Nice, apple pie. Okay, wait for the next one."

Continuing to hold her eyes closed, she tried to block out the sounds of the other shoppers as she waited. A fresh floral scent greeted her, and she smiled.

"Lilacs. I adore lilacs. There are lilac bushes behind my house, did you know that? No, of course you didn't know that. Sorry."

"Maybe you can show them to me in the spring," he stated quietly. "How about this one?"

Having her eyes closed was beginning to make her feel strange, since she couldn't glance around to be certain there were no prying eyes.

"Some sort of citrus? Orange, maybe?"

"Orange and vanilla," he corrected. "How about now?"

She waited, eyes still closed, taking in the scent of Ryan as he stood before her, presumably choosing another fragrance. A smile crossed her face, and she couldn't stop herself.

"Yummy boyfriend? I smell yummy boyfriend."

His lips gently touched hers, and she drew her eyelashes upwards as she caught his eye, continuing to gaze at him as her stomach fluttered. Rather than say anything, she stepped toward him and placed her cheek against his t-shirt as he wrapped his arms around her. The rhythm of his heartbeat tapped against her skin, and she melted into his warmth.

"I sort of feel like I'm living someone else's life," he muttered. "What are you doing with me, gorgeous?"

Leaning back, she looked up at his face. "You just feel…right."

"I will definitely take that," he told her with a grin. "Come on, we're never going to get any shopping done with you looking at me like that." Sliding his fingers through hers, he walked back into the throng of people, merging into the flow of foot traffic. "So, no gifts? Tell me what Christmas was like growing up."

"We had a tree," she began thoughtfully, wrinkling her brow. "Dad would cut one. Sometimes they were big and full, and other times they were scrawny as all get out. We had two strands of lights, because one wasn't enough and three were too many.

That's what my dad used to say. Mom and I usually spent one Saturday stringing popcorn, and we would cut out snowflakes from the back of my school papers. Those were our decorations."

"Sounds almost normal." Releasing Harley's hand, Ryan wrapped his arm around her shoulders and pulled her close. "What else?"

"Christmas Eve they would read the Bible aloud, and then they would let me fall asleep on the couch staring at the lights on the tree."

"You slept on the couch?" Ryan glanced down at her, concern crossing his features. "Did you ever catch Santa in the act?"

"No worries, Santa didn't come to my house. On Christmas morning, we would make pancakes, stick candles in them, and sing happy birthday to Jesus. Then we would read our annual Christmas message from Mayowa."

"Mayowa?"

"The Nigerian girl that my parents...you know. 'Thank you Davidson family for the wonderful gifts you bestow upon me. God blessed me with your generosity.' Blah, blah, blah. Then it was time for my present."

"One present," he clarified.

"Yes, one present. Usually chocolate. One time it was a caramel apple. Oh, and one year they gave me a notepad. That was stellar, and I was really excited. I can't believe how naïve and idiotic I was as a kid." Harley halted to look at the contents of a jewelry counter. "Ryan, look at this! Tell me it's not absolutely perfect for Kelsey."

He obligingly glanced into the display, seeing a gold necklace surrounded by letter tiles of all varieties.

"It looks like a Scrabble board," he agreed.

"Right? It just fits her so well!"

Ryan glanced first at the price tag, and then at Harley. "I can't afford that."

"Neither can I," she answered sheepishly. "Sorry, let's keep moving. What was Christmas like in your house, since I've bored you to death with my memories?"

"Good," he answered simply. "We had a fake tree covered in millions of lights, and all sorts of decorations. Christmas Eve we'd go to a candlelight service at church, and then we'd rush home to set out the cookies and milk for Santa. We definitely didn't sleep on the couch." He paused and glanced down at Harley before continuing. "Then, basically, we'd wake up and find our presents from Santa, along with a few from our parents. It was simple and good, that I can remember."

"What kind of presents did you get?"

"Umm...no apples. Let's see...drum set one year. Usually some sort of cool toy when I was a kid. As I got older, electronics. Last year was pretty subdued because finances were tight. I guess this year will be, too. Although I've got to say, things are looking a little brighter since we had that medical fund set up at the bank. I should apologize to you about that again."

"No, you shouldn't, and don't give me credit for it, either. It really wasn't me; it was the station. They got tired of people calling."

"Well, to tell the truth, I don't even want any presents this year."

"Why is that?"

Hugging her tighter, he smiled to himself. "I already have what I really wanted."

Chapter Twenty

Saturday afternoon, Harley rolled down Wonder Lane, unable to wipe the smile off her face. Spending the day with Ryan had been a sheer delight, and afterward they watched *Home Alone* with Kelsey. In the middle of the movie, Ryan received a phone call about working an unexpected evening shift on the ambulance, and he reluctantly left with promises to see Harley in the morning. When Kelsey drifted to sleep at the end of the movie, Harley kissed her on the forehead and slipped out, pausing only to say goodbye to Sam.

As she rounded the final bend toward her home, she noticed a ladder against the house closest to hers, with a gentleman atop the roof making some repairs. Slowing to a stop, she glanced at the woman standing in the front yard, watching a little girl ride a tricycle in circles on the driveway.

"You live here?" she called as she opened the door, and the young woman turned at the sound of her voice. She looked to be roughly the same age as Harley, with dark hair that hung from a ponytail at the back of her head.

"Yes, I live here." She gave Harley a wary glance and then jerked her eyes back to her daughter in a protective fashion.

"I'm your neighbor," Harley quickly stated. "That's my house, at the end of the street. Harley Laine."

"The news lady?" she asked, giving Harley a dubious once-over. "Sorry, I didn't recognize you. Alexis Jennings, and this is my daughter, Bailey."

"Nice to meet you." Her eyes darted back to the guy on the roof. "Having repairs made?"

"Just a little leak—nothing major."

"Oh."

Alexis wasn't the most forthcoming person she had ever met, and for whatever reason, Harley was feeling awkward with the conversation.

"I'm actually needing a little work done on my house, too. Is he reputable?"

"Who?"

Giving her neighbor a curious glance, she directed her eyes back to the roofline. "The guy up there fixing your leak."

"Oh, yeah, I guess. He's Bailey's dad, so…"

"I'm sorry," Harley blurted. "I didn't realize he was your husband."

"He is definitely *not* my husband," she assured Harley, employing a stone-faced expression.

"Sorry again," Harley told her, mentally chiding herself. The man began his way down the ladder, and she wished she could make herself vanish without being rude.

"This is my neighbor, Harley Laine," Alexis said loudly. "She needs some repairs on her house."

"Hey!" Whatever hesitance Alexis imparted, this guy more than made up for with his pleasant smile. "Nice to meet you. I've done my share of pretty much everything you can imagine construction-wise, so I'm your guy. Oh, Jake McAuliffe." He extended his hand, and Harley took it with a smile.

"Jake," she repeated, noticing the warmth of his hand in hers. This guy was definitely easy on the eyes, but his touch didn't light a fire in her the way Ryan's did.

"So, what is it that needs fixing?"

"A ton of things, really, but for now I've just got a couple holes in the wall that I need repaired. To be honest, I don't know much about that kind of thing, but could I have my boyfriend talk to you?"

Jake blinked a couple times before he answered, as though he were thinking it over, before he gave her a rather cocky smirk. "Sure, have your boyfriend call me. That's fine. You want my number?"

She nodded, and he stepped over to a red truck with Tennessee plates, pulling open the passenger's side door. Within a few seconds, he was headed back with a business card for a place called River Rock Bed and Breakfast. Flipping it over, he showed her where he had scrawled his number on the back.

"Call me sometime," he stated with a slightly crooked grin that showcased a dimple in his left cheek. "Or have your boyfriend call me, if you want."

"Thanks." She tapped the card against her hand before turning and strolling back to her car.

"Nice wheels!" Jake called after her. She acknowledged him with a wave of her hand, opening the door and sliding inside.

She could have been wrong, but Jake seemed to be just a friendly, neighborly type until she mentioned the boyfriend, and then his demeanor went up a notch to flirtatious. Was she imagining that? So strange.

And obviously there was a story there with Alexis and her animosity toward him...intriguing.

Walking up the steps to her house, Harley was glad she couldn't see any other homes from her vantage point. Popping open the door, she paused in the foyer as she slipped off her coat, remembering Ryan's appearance the night before. When he had confronted her about the condition of her house as they stood upstairs...

His impassioned state crossed her mind, and she felt the heat creeping into her face. He had been rightly annoyed with her, but when his eyes flashed as he stood upstairs and asked her if she knew what she wanted, she had known immediately that it was him.

Once she really thought about it, she realized it had been there all along. She'd seen it in the way he fiercely fought for his sister by working constantly. He'd expressed it by marking his body every time he wavered. And when he kissed her at Tiny's the night before... Well, Ryan Temple didn't do things halfway. He had passion, and that was exciting.

Pulling out her phone, Harley pressed the button and waited as it rang, taking a deep breath.

"Hey girl," Annie answered. "I'm just closing here. What's up?"

Dropping to the floor, Harley sat cross-legged in the foyer, staring at the wall.

"I'm in love with Ryan."

"You cracked, didn't you?" Harley could almost imagine Annie shaking those curls. "I knew you would open up to him first. You calling me to hurt my feelings now?"

"No, actually..." Glancing at the floor, Harley studied the lines in the wood. "Do you want to come over?"

"I imagined a lot of things, honestly, but this never crossed my mind." Annie stood in the middle of Harley's living room, staring at the stark walls and the neglected fireplace.

As though she wanted to protect herself from the harsh reality, Harley wrapped her arms across her abdomen.

"So Ryan was angry with you? Not that I blame him. Girl, this house is the end all, for real. I cannot believe you live here. I mean, you could step out the front door all covered in velvety green drapes with your hair rag-curled, yelling at Miss Sue Ellen, and I'd be like, 'Yep. She's Scarlett O'Hara, alright.' You can't do this to your poor house."

"I know," Harley muttered. "I should have never bought it, but I was just so...stubborn and insistent on proving a point, I guess. But I can't fix it. I barely make enough to afford the payments."

Stepping up to the window, Annie threw back the drapes, letting the last remains of afternoon light shine against the wall.

"How many bedrooms do you have again?"

Biting her lip, Harley glanced up at the stained ceiling.

"Five."

"Five!" Annie repeated. "And you're not even using the good ones, sentencing yourself to the first two so you don't have to make any effort. The master bedroom is a really cool room. What do the stairs at the end of the hall lead to up there?"

"The sitting room and the library. Oh, and the door that leads to the hothouse."

"'Hey, Annie, what sort of place do you have?' I'm glad you asked. It's a great studio with one bedroom and quite a roomy bath. You? 'Oh, it's a charming old plantation candidate with a library and a hothouse.'" Giving up the southern accent she had proffered for her little speech, Annie placed her hand on her hip. "You snooty, hoity-toity little twerp."

"Hey!"

"The way I see it, there's really only one solution to your problem." Stepping across to the fireplace, Annie wiped her finger across the dust on the mantle and wrinkled her nose in disgust.

"What is that, exactly?"

"I'm moving in."

"Just put trash bags over the hangers in the closet, and we'll take out whole stacks of them at once."

Harley stood in the corner of Annie's bedroom feeling slightly shell-shocked. When Annie said she was moving in, she believed she was being sarcastic, or at least was referring to a future date.

No—when Annie said she was moving in, she meant *she was moving in*. As in that very night.

"You know…it might make more sense to wait until after the holidays, right? I mean, you probably have to give your landlord a month's notice or something?"

"Nah." Annie dismissed her words with a wave of her hand, pulling open a drawer. "My landlord is my dad's business colleague, so no worries. Besides, why wait when you are in desperate need of some Christmas spirit in that palace?"

"But we can't move your furniture. And where are you going to put it, anyway? As I'm sure you noticed, the place is a bit...unfinished."

"So we put it in an unfinished room and move it around when your handyman is working in there."

"My handyman?"

"You know, the guy you were telling me about earlier? Studly dude working on your neighbor's roof?"

"Annie!" Stepping aside to avoid a shoe that Annie threw in her direction, Harley planted herself resolutely with her hands on her hips. "Number one, I can't afford to start paying a handyman to redo all the rooms in the house. Number two, just because a guy happens to be slightly good looking doesn't mean I'm just going to give him free roam of the place. I know nothing about him!"

"He's your neighbor's kid's dad, right?"

"Yeah, but she didn't seem too keen on him, you know what I mean? Almost hostile, in fact. So the knowledge that he is that kid's sperm donor gives me no confidence in his uprightness."

"Make him give you references, then," Annie said, tossing another pair of shoes. "And when I give you rent, you can spend the entire thing on the repairs. Then you can just do whatever repairs you can afford each month. That's a simple solution and you can start bringing your house back up to livable conditions."

"I suppose."

"Unless you don't want me living in your house," Annie suggested quietly, lowering herself to the bed. Harley sat beside her and studied her friend for a few seconds, noting her smooth, creamy exotic skin and those purple curls held back by a black comb. How could she deny her request, when Annie had practically let her run roughshod over her at The Revolving Closet for as long as the two had known one another?

"Of course you can live with me, if that's what you want. I just never gave the idea any thought before, and it's taking a while to settle on me, so to speak."

Harley was surprised when Annie's eyes filled with moisture, and she instinctively reached out for the other young woman's hand.

"Sorry," Annie whispered, wiping at her eye. "It's just...I've been having a rough time, and I could use somebody in my corner right now."

"I'm solid in your corner," Harley assured her. "Solid."

"I know. The truth is, Daryl called me yesterday."

Daryl. This knowledge added nothing for Harley, because that name was totally unfamiliar.

"And Daryl is?"

"My ex." Another tear escaped, and Annie brushed at it hurriedly. "We were a couple for a long time—most of college, and two years after. He played college football, and I loved being with him. He made me feel really special."

"So, why is it so bad that he called you?" It was only a gentle prod, but it sent Annie into a fit of tears. Moving over slightly, Harley wrapped her arm around her friend's shoulders.

"Because he never wanted me to change," Annie stated through shaky intakes of breath. "When we graduated, I cut six inches off my hair, and he dragged me down to the salon to get extensions to make it the way it was. He would inspect my refrigerator and cabinets constantly to make sure I was only eating things he approved, because he didn't want me gaining or losing a pound."

"Sounds like a nice guy," Harley added sarcastically.

"When he asked me to marry him, I thought it was because he was finally convinced that I was good enough as I was. I should have known he wouldn't follow through until he believed our lives were perfect. We moved in together, and that's when things started going over the edge. The man controlled every aspect of my life—what I wore, how my makeup looked...even when and where I could see my friends or my parents. Finally, one day I had enough and called him on it. He slapped me so hard he left a handprint on my face."

"Oh, Annie…"

"But I left. I left and I didn't look back. Not until he called me, because the man can be very convincing. And I did love him."

"Sweetie, that's not love."

"See?" she asked, rubbing her nose with the back of her hand. "This is why I need you, okay? I need someone to knock some sense into me when I'm having a low moment."

"Get some sense, then," Harley said quietly.

Laughing in a hushed tone, Annie focused on Harley's eyes. "I think that's why I always do the crazy things to my hair, really. If I do run into Daryl, surely he won't want me with purple hair."

"I'm surprised anybody wants you with purple hair."

"Harley!"

"It's a joke. I was just trying to lighten the mood."

"Thanks." Rising to her feet, Annie shook her entire body as though she was trying to rid herself from her thoughts. "So, I guess I should slow down, huh? I'm being unreasonable."

"I don't think so," Harley insisted, picking up a shoe. "Get to work, lady, we have a lot of stuff to move. If we're going to get that plantation house back in shape, it's going to take at least two Scarletts to make it happen."

"I'm looking for Jake…" Harley stated into the phone, glancing again at the little picture of River Rock Bed and Breakfast. Quaint and charming…a little like her own house, actually.

"You got him. Who is this?"

"This is Harley Laine, your…um, neighbor to Alexis."

"Right. I thought you were going to have your boyfriend call."

Ugh, why didn't I? I should have let Ryan talk to him.

"I just had a second, and dialed while I was thinking of it." Harley looked down at the number again, wondering why the man had such an odd card in his possession. "Look, I'm very seriously considering using you to do some work in the house, but I was wondering if you had any references? Someone I could call, maybe?"

"Oh," he stammered, suddenly not sounding very sure of himself. Merely a guess, but Harley imagined that he didn't find himself in that spot often. "Yeah, sure. I'm not really doing that kind of work at the moment here in Kentucky, but I did back in Tennessee. I could give you the names of a couple guys I worked with back there."

"That would be great."

Harley grabbed a pen and waited patiently until he began rattling off the names and numbers. *Artie Randolph...got it. And Cole Parker.*

Wait a second...Cole Parker? That name sounds familiar.

"Thanks, Jake, and I'll call you when I know exactly what we want to do."

He made his goodbyes and hung up the phone, and Harley barely hesitated before she went to the Internet to see why that name sounded so familiar.

Cole Parker...found him. College baseball phenomenon... Huh, really adorable, with that smile. Husband to Camdyn...

Camdyn Taylor, go figure. The writer she tried to ambush at that conference. No wonder his name sounded familiar.

So much for checking the references. It looked like hiring the contractor would definitely be a job for her boyfriend, after all.

Chapter Twenty-One

The BMW knew precisely where it was going as it turned onto the unassuming road, heading toward the unremarkable house that contained the most remarkable person in Harley's life. She almost smiled to herself at that thought, but held it in so Annie wouldn't think she was a raving lunatic.

Annie, who sat in the passenger seat, simply stared out the window and studied the scenery. When Harley told Ryan she would pick him up for church Sunday morning, she didn't mention Annie. To be fair, that was before Annie had visited Harley's house…before she had decided that crashing with her friend was the best option. It was before Annie's things had been piled into Harley's empty living room like a giant leaning tower of random junk.

When she pulled into the driveway, Harley prepared herself to give Ryan the news gently as she knocked on the door, but Annie bounced out of the car and strolled up the sidewalk like she owned the place, robbing Harley of the opportunity. Resigned to a couple guilty grimaces and apologetic glances, Harley prepared to greet Ryan.

One knock on the door was all it took, and the hinges squeaked as the thing was thrown open. Rather than Ryan standing at the door, though, the two young women were faced with a brightly beaming Kelsey.

"Hi, Harley!" she belted, not bothering to soften her grin. "Ryan said I could come with you guys and we could take Mom's car."

"Oh," Harley mumbled, nearly laughing at her young friend's level of exuberance over going to church. She thought it was ridiculous, really. "Great, because Annie wanted to come, too. I hope that's okay. You remember Annie?"

"Hi, Annie."

Kelsey's demeanor took on a note of shyness, and Harley stepped inside to save the three of them from any awkwardness. Her concern for Kelsey diminished almost immediately, however, when she was grabbed from behind by two strong arms around her waist.

"I'm getting used to seeing your face," he whispered against her ear, not taking notice of Annie or Kelsey.

Fighting the blush that she could feel creeping across her neck, Harley smiled and tried to act unaffected. "And here I thought you probably dreamed about me every night."

"I wish. I'd script those dreams."

"So...church?" Peeling herself away from Ryan, Harley turned to focus a pleading gaze on him. "Are we ready to go?"

"I call shotgun!" Kelsey stated cheerfully.

"Then Annie's driving," Ryan added, a mischievous twinkle in his eye.

"Aw, heck no," Annie complained. "I am not driving around a make-out mobile, okay? My behind will be firmly planted in the back seat, thank you very much."

"Your friend obviously thinks very little of your self-control." Ryan playfully nudged Harley, who poked him in the ribs and gave him a slight glare.

"Annie and I can ride in the back," she informed him. "It will be good for my self-control."

During the twenty-minute car ride to the church, Harley informed Ryan and Kelsey about Annie's plans to move into her house, and it was quickly established that Ryan would be happy to help move the furniture across town that afternoon, if for no other reason than Harley would actually have something to sit on. This led to some disapproving descriptions of Harley's living conditions by both Annie and Ryan that left Kelsey gasping in response.

"No worries," Annie assured the occupants of the sedan. "Harley is already lining up the studly guy down the street to do some repairs."

"What?" Ryan's eyes popped up to the rear view mirror so quickly, Harley was afraid he might run off the road.

"I did call him to get his references, but I'm out of my league in that department. I was kind of hoping you'd talk to him."

"Me?" Although only his eyes were visible in the rear view mirror, there was definitely a smile evident in the upturn of the lines around them. "Actually, I know a few guys myself. Homely fellas."

"Hey, I'm living in the house now, too!" Annie protested, lifting one corner of her mouth. "Don't deny me a little fun."

Ryan cleared his throat. "I'm already second-guessing this arrangement. Maybe you should get a different roommate, Harley. I'm thinking a nun, maybe? Or my grandma?"

Kelsey erupted in a burst of giggles. "Grandma would do nothing but complain about the dust in the house. And she would probably walk around calling the repair guy a cutie-patootie."

Glad for the slight change of subject, Harley tugged against her seatbelt as she leaned forward. "Cutie-patootie?"

"Grandma always says that to Ryan. She'll pinch his cheek first, of course. He hates that. 'Ryan, you're such a cutie-patootie. When are you going to get a proper haircut, dear?'"

"Kels!"

"She would love you, Harley. She thinks Audrey Hepburn is the most beautiful woman to ever live, and you have a Hepburn-esque vibe about you."

"Is she for real?" Harley asked doubtfully, jerking her thumb toward Kelsey. "What seventeen year old says that people are Hepburn-esque?"

"She is very Eliza Doolittle when she comes into my shop," Annie interjected. "Sometimes she disrobes in the middle of the store."

"What?!" Ryan let a laugh escape before he managed to bring it under control.

"Really, Annie, if you're going to insist on disparaging me, I might be rethinking this whole living arrangement myself."

"Please don't kick me out the plantation, Miss Scahlett," Annie pleaded. "I be's good, I promise!"

Ryan turned the car into the church parking lot, and Harley let her breath out in a huff.

"Thank goodness we're at church," Harley said. "You bunch of heathens need to repent."

The afternoon was proving to be unseasonably warm, which Harley believed was to their favor since they were having an impromptu moving day. When church was over, Ryan drove them to Wonder Lane so Kelsey could see Harley's house for herself, after which she asked to be taken home since she was tired. Annie stayed behind to begin unpacking her things while Ryan took Kelsey and Harley back to his parents' house.

Kelsey seemed to visibly weaken as the day went on, and by the time she was back in her own home, all she wanted to do was take a nap. Harley could see the worry etched on Ryan's face, and she quietly asked him if he'd like to stay with Kelsey. He begrudgingly told her there was nothing he could do, so he climbed into Harley's BMW and they headed back to Wonder Lane.

After parking in the driveway, Harley stepped out of the car and tossed a joke at Ryan as a red truck pulled up behind them. With a questioning glance, Ryan turned his attention to the man stepping away from the driver's side of the truck.

"You're the boyfriend, I take it?" Jake asked, stepping towards Ryan. "I was in the neighborhood dropping off my daughter, and I happened to see you guys pull up." Pausing to adjust his baseball cap, he extended his hand. "Sorry—Jake McAuliffe. Harley asked me about doing some repairs."

Ryan took his hand cautiously and gave Harley a wary glance. "Ryan Temple. Nice to meet you, man."

"Is now a good time to take a look? If not, I could come back later."

Ryan grimaced as he turned to look at the house. "Actually, Harley's friend just moved in, and we were going to pick up some of her furniture this afternoon."

"In a BMW and a Jeep?" Jake wondered, glancing from Harley's car to Annie's Jeep.

"Yeah, obviously we haven't really thought it through," Ryan told him with a slight laugh, reaching up to scratch the back of his head.

"Need a hand? I've got the truck, and nothing to do this afternoon."

"Seriously? That's really cool of you to offer. You sure?"

"Might as well," Jake stated, shoving his hands in his pockets. "Want me to follow you over there?"

"Just let me get Annie," Harley interrupted, heading toward the house. She didn't need to look far, because Annie suddenly burst through the front door, practically bouncing down the steps.

"Hey, we got help?" She smiled as she came closer to the new handsome face. "Ryan, I thought you said you were gonna round up some homely fellas?"

"You must be Annie." Jake took a second to smile, showcasing a dimple in his left cheek. "So, Ryan, you want to ride with me? We can talk about the repairs."

"Oh, absolutely not." Annie pulled open the door to the truck, launching herself up precariously into the cab. "I have massive ideas about those repairs, Jake. I'm sure it will take the whole of the ride over there to discuss them."

Jake shrugged before he turned towards the truck. "Fair enough. We'll meet you over there."

Laughing, Harley tossed Ryan the keys to the BMW. "Something tells me we won't need to bother checking that guy's references. Between Annie driving him half insane on the way to her apartment and watching him like a hawk when he's at the house, if he's up to no good, he'll disappear in a flash."

"Just as long as *you* don't disappear. I'm not sure I want a good looking guy hanging around my girlfriend's house all the time."

"Wow, you went from 'I'm not sure what this is' to jealous boyfriend in one weekend. Bravo."

The conversation lulled as they both opened their car doors, and Harley settled inside and fastened her seatbelt as the engine roared to life. She glanced at Ryan as he turned his face to look out the back window and pull out onto the sleepy street, and he offered a slight shake of his head.

"I'm not jealous...yet. Although you did get pretty fidgety when I put my arm around you at church."

Shocked, she allowed her mouth to gape a touch. "I did not!"

"You started tapping your foot, and then you slid your hands under your thighs. Oh, and then you were drumming your fingers against your jeans, don't you remember? I grabbed your hand?"

"That?" She let a laugh escape as she turned to gaze out the passenger window. "The sermon was just making me feel a little weird, that's all. That 'God ordering your steps' spiel."

"You don't believe it?"

Frowning slightly, she pondered a response far too long to remain comfortable. When she realized how long she had hesitated, she began to feel a bit defensive.

"It's not that I don't believe in God. That doesn't even really feel like an option...there's just this innate feeling in me that there's something more. Whether I think there's an all-powerful being that is orchestrating minute details of my life? No, I think that's crazy. Surely you don't believe that."

She dared to look at him just in time to see a crooked smile appear on his face.

"Actually, yeah."

"With Kelsey and everything that's going on? Honestly, that would make me even less likely to believe that, I would imagine."

He rubbed his neck, and Harley sensed that she was making him uncomfortable. Whether it was from her stance or from his own misgivings, she couldn't tell.

"I'm not going to pretend that I have a great handle on theological things, but there are a couple things I know. First of all, this is a fallen world. I can't tell you why Kelsey is sick, but I've been there on the days when her faith's all that's gotten her through. My best evidence, though, is you."

"Me? What do you mean?"

"Earlier this week, I was having a conversation with my mom about you. Complaining about the timing. I said you seemed like a broken heart waiting to happen."

"Ouch."

"I meant that in a good way," he quickly added with a short laugh. "My mom said, 'Why would God send Harley into your life just to break your heart?' I didn't really have it worked out in my mind at that moment, but now I think I know."

She almost couldn't force herself to ask, "Know what?"

"Because of you, I actually had a day off yesterday."

"Until you got called in."

"Yeah, but I had part of a day. I got to go to church today. Before that fund was set up at the bank, I would have felt like taking five minutes would sabotage everything."

"So you think God brought me into your life so you wouldn't have to work so hard?"

Bringing the car to a halt at a stop light, Ryan turned and looked her directly in the face, only a touch of a smile playing about his eyes.

"No, Harley. I think I finally have the chance to slow down a little because God brought you into my life to love me. To love all of us. Because He knew we needed you."

Chapter Twenty-Two

Mitch was parked at Harley's desk when she came back from an assignment Monday morning, wearing an evergreen-colored shirt that wasn't straining against the buttonholes for a change. He even had a tie around his neck. It was a bright blue monstrosity that clashed with his shirt, but it appeared that he was making an attempt. That mere fact filled Harley with a measure of dread.

"There's my star reporter!"

His sing-song voice gave her the desire to roll her eyes, but she kept her emotions under control. It wasn't that long ago that he was prohibiting her from covering politics and sending her after fowl, so she remained leery and wasn't going to allow herself to become comfortable.

"Good morning, Mitch. To what do I owe this greeting?"

Rising from her chair, he strolled around her desk and placed his hand on her shoulder protectively, like a father figure might.

"Do I really need a reason to say hello? Just a friendly visit to tell you to keep up the good work, kiddo. Oh, and you'll have the desk tonight."

"What?" Her hackles rose significantly, because even though those words filled her with excitement, they were also intimidating. "What about Summer?"

"I gave her the night off." He waved his hand dismissively, as though Summer was an afterthought. "It's good to have a new face there now and again. And Denton's been bugging me to give you a shot. Of course, the powers that be were a little hesitant until all the recent success you've had."

Capitalizing on her accidental popularity?

All of her hard work and research and the hours she spent on her stories, and the reason she was finally getting a shot at the desk boiled down to the fact that she thought she saw a boy, and she made a stupid decision. Ryan might have believed everything that was happening to him was because of her, but in a weird twist, everything that was happening to her was because of him.

Well...Ryan and Kelsey, to be more precise.

"So, what do you want me to do today?" Shifting uncomfortably in the Valentino heels that Annie let her keep for allowing her to move in so quickly, she twisted her mouth to the side. "Before the desk, I mean? What would you have Summer doing?"

"There are going to be some basketball players visiting children at the hospital. I want you to get in the middle of that."

"Basketball...that sounds like Trip's gig. I don't want to step on anybody's toes." The sportscaster might have been getting up there in years, but he surely wouldn't want the pretty little upstart reporter stealing his fluff stories.

"Don't worry about it. It's more a human interest story, and that's right up your alley. Besides, you do the stories, and let me get paid to do the thinking."

Right. Do the stories, not the thinking.

This is a proud moment for women everywhere.

"I'll figure it out," she informed him with a sigh, crossing to her chair and lowering herself. "Anything else?"

"Nope. Just try not to injure yourself today."

Very funny.

She watched his back as he walked away, wishing she had the nerve to speak her mind. That action would inevitably lead to not working the desk, at the very least, and possibly an extended Christmas vacation.

Straightening in her chair and resolving to forget about Mitch, she nearly jumped when Denton pounded his knuckles on her desk.

"Paging Harley Laine. I hear she's supposed to man the desk with me tonight. Or woman the desk, perhaps?"

"So I've been told. It's your lifelong dream come true."

Rather than give her a smirk and continue on his way, Denton pulled up a chair in front of her. Inwardly cringing, she readied herself for taunting.

"So...strangest thing happened to me this weekend. I ran into a coworker at the mall."

"I can't think of anything strange about that, unless you *literally* ran into your coworker, and in that case you definitely owe him or her an apology."

"Ever the comedienne." Denton lifted one foot from the floor and set it atop his knee, bouncing it slightly as his eyebrows arched upward. "I was beginning to feel a little sorry for myself that you would date that boring Kip Stanton and couldn't even be bothered to go to dinner with me, but I didn't know you secretly liked...rockers? Bikers? I'm not sure what category that guy even falls into."

"Ryan's an EMT." She wasn't sure why she felt she needed to throw that into the mix, but it was hanging between them, and she couldn't take it back. Not even when Denton eased himself back in the chair and gave her a smug grin.

"Ah, so it's the Florence Nightingale scenario." When his statement prompted no response, he leaned forward and pressed his fingertips together. "You know, the patient falling for the one who nursed them to health?"

"I get it, but you're wrong in this case. I met him before I had the unfortunate accident."

"And where did you meet, exactly?"

Harley's mind flashed to that night on the back of Ryan's motorcycle, clinging to him only to arrive at Annie's apartment smelling like greasy food and masculine body wash.

"That's not important. What we should be talking about is work, since you managed to talk Mitch into letting me have a guest spot on the Denton show this evening."

"That's our show. At least, it should be."

The phone atop Harley's desk let out a chirping ring, and she glanced down to see an unfamiliar number. As she reached for the receiver, Denton offered a sly wink.

"Just don't let your guy get in the way of what we've got going, with the witty banter."

Shaking her head, she watched him retreat before she committed to wrapping her fingers around the phone.

"Harley Laine," she said succinctly, holding a pen above the notepad on her desk expectantly.

"Harley Davidson?" the voice clarified.

Glancing around conspiratorially, Harley slouched in her seat slightly. "Yes, this is Harley."

"We have your results back from the recent donor testing, and you're a match. Is there a good time for you to return to our offices? We'd like to see you right away."

The room practically started spinning, and for a moment, it was as though she had forgotten how to breathe. All the thoughts she and Ryan had wrestled through the day before came rushing back, about whether God had planned for Harley to be part of their lives. Was this the answer all along? Had she been drawn to Ryan because she was the match for Kelsey?

"Does Kelsey know?" It came out as not much more than a whisper, and Harley could barely hear her own voice through the pounding of her pulse in her ears.

"Kelsey?"

"The girl who needs the liver."

A couple of her male coworkers chose that moment to stroll past her desk talking about a sports score, and it seemed so odd that someone could be having such a blasé conversation at a moment that was so pivotal.

"Oh, dear." The voice on the other end of the line sounded almost apologetic. "I never paused to think that you might have been waiting on other results. This is for the National Marrow Donor program. We have a match on that, honey."

The National Marrow Donor program. Right.

Not for Kelsey.

An odd sense of disappointment washed over her in that moment, but not for the reason she expected. It had nothing to do with Kelsey, really. For a split second, she thought there really might be a divine plan for her life, and the idea filled her with hope.

So much for blind faith.

She wrote dates and times on her notepad without really listening, plugging out the numbers like her hand was working separate from her brain, unattached and doing the bidding of another individual on the opposite end of that phone line.

"We'll see you then. Sorry again for the mix-up."

Even after she heard the dial tone on the other end of the line, Harley sat a minute with the phone cradled to her ear, marveling at how easy it was for the other woman to simply label something a mix-up that caused her to go through the gamut of emotions in the span of seconds. The fact that she didn't know her own heart was troubling, and it pricked her conscience that her immediate sympathies weren't for Kelsey, but for herself.

The truth was, it would be nice to think her life had a purpose. All those years of wanting to be important to the world paled in comparison to wanting to matter to one person, or even a few people.

She didn't have time to think about that, though. She had basketball players to greet, and sick children to hurt for, and precious few hours to prepare herself for Denton's flirty banter.

Harley pressed her fingers against the hand extended to her, lining up her cold palm to one that was significantly warmer. She stretched her fingers to their longest state, but still barely reached the back of his knuckles. Turning to her little audience, she opened her mouth wide to express her shock.

"You guys were right! His hand *is* bigger than mine!"

The good-natured young man laughed as he shrugged his shoulders, and a mischievous-looking boy in the front placed his arms across his chest.

"Could you bench press Harley?"

"My goodness, what a question!" Harley widened her eyes in exaggeration for the other children as she smiled at the boy.

"She's pretty small, so yeah."

Harley shot the power forward a quick glance that begged him not to attempt it, and he grinned shyly.

"But could you pick her up with one hand?" the boy pushed, tilting his chin up rather smugly.

"I don't know, should we find out?"

The children cheered, so he centered his palm on the top of her head, his fingers gingerly cradling her skull. As he lifted his hand ever so slightly, she followed his lead and slowly rose to her tiptoes, giving the appearance that he was drawing her upward. A couple of the children looked visibly shocked, until the boy in the front realized what was happening and called them on the hoax.

"Do you think I should challenge him to a one-on-one matchup?" Harley suggested, glancing from face to face and settling on one little girl who was peeking from behind another child. She wrinkled her nose just enough that the girl managed a smile.

"Definitely not," the boisterous boy spoke up. "He would smash you like a bug."

"Well, I definitely do not want to be a bug, so I guess our friendly game will have to wait for another day."

The amiable giant pretended to be disappointed as they said their goodbyes to the children, and Harley turned to Kenny, who said he was going to grab a few more background shots. Stepping into the hallway, she strolled towards the main entrance, checking messages on her phone. Pausing before the elevator, she pulled up a text from Ryan.

Thinking about you.

Smiling privately, she glanced up to see a nurse walking toward her.

"Harley? I hope you don't mind, but I saw you come in and thought I'd catch you before you left."

"Sure." Dropping her phone in her purse, she took on a professional air, assuming the woman wanted to ask her something related to Channel Six.

"Do you have a moment? I have your test results back."

Again with the test results?

Nodding slightly, Harley simply stood there until the nurse motioned her towards a more private area.

"We ran the antibody screen." When that news was met with nothing but a blank stare from Harley, the nurse took a deep breath. "An antibody is made by the body's immune system in response to an antigen...a foreign substance such as a blood transfusion or a transplanted organ. Antibodies attach the transplanted organ, so the white blood cells of the donor and the serum of the recipient are mixed to see if the antibodies and antigens react."

"And?"

The fact that the nurse felt she had to place her hand over Harley's told her everything she needed to know.

"I'm sorry, but you're not a match."

Rubbing her right hand across her forehead, Harley peered at the nurse through squinted eyes. "Does Kelsey know yet?"

"I thought you might want to tell her."

"Yeah, of course," Harley said, straightening as she caught a glimpse of Kenny coming down the corridor. "Thank you."

The nurse turned and strode in Kenny's direction, passing him as he checked a strap on the bag he was carrying. Harley watched him continue toward her with purpose, looking very much like a man without a care in the world.

"So, we good?" he wanted to know.

Good. So many implications wrapped up in that one little word, spinning through Harley's mind in a torrent of thoughts that she couldn't pinpoint, let alone process. Ryan's unanswered text remained in her purse—an electronic reminder that she was on his mind. As she thought about what he would think of her news,

Kelsey's beaming face the day before flashed unbidden through her memory, and she wondered if she had the strength to disappoint her friend.

With a slight air of defeat, she shrugged her shoulders. "Sure, Kenny. We're good."

"The week of Christmas? But that's next week. Does it have to be so soon?"

Harley listened for the voice on the other end of the line, heart pounding in her chest.

"Those are the only auditions we're doing at this time. If you aren't available, perhaps there will be other opportunities in the future."

"Oh no. I'm definitely available."

I will make myself available.

"Very good. I'll email you the details, and look forward to meeting with you soon."

Dropping the phone back into its protective cradle, Harley felt the blood pumping through her veins. The day was proving to be one of extremes, and she wasn't likely to forget this high for some time. Giggling under her breath, she paused to pick up her cellphone, hitting the contact info for Annie.

Just got phone call. Trent Bauer needs cohost. Audition in New York week of Christmas. Dying!!!

With trembling hands, she dropped the cellphone to her lap. Working the desk with Denton was a nice thought, but cohosting with Trent Bauer? Hers would be the face millions stared at as they drank their coffees every morning. The most important international news stories of the day would cross her lips as people readied their kids for school or themselves for work. And to think they had contacted her simply because Trent Bauer was intrigued and wanted to see how she handled herself in person.

Her phone buzzed in her lap, and she hastily retrieved it and touched the screen.

Girl, shut up! That is sweet!

Laughing, Harley hesitated as another buzz vibrated her fingers.

If I could be happy for you, which I can't. You are not allowed to leave.

Of course chasing her dreams would mean leaving, but she never intended Louisville to be a long-term situation in the first place.

But if you leave, I get the house. Just sayin'.

The house. Did she want to leave the house? Wonder Lane? Annie?

Ryan… He believed that God sent her to his family—how would she manage to break the news?

Chapter Twenty-Three

Tossing in bed, Harley pounded her pillow with her fist and sat up in the darkness. Sleep had evaded her, and it seemed like a fight she wasn't going to win. Something was guiltily gnawing away at her, but she couldn't decide what it was.

After coming home Monday evening and chatting with Annie about the thrilling possibility of a move to New York, she couldn't manage to force the words past her throat when Ryan called. She hadn't found the nerve to tell him about the news she received at the hospital, either. Instead, she talked to him about her stint that night at the news desk, her visit with the basketball players, and the fact that Annie had already allowed Jake into the house that day to patch up a few holes in the wall.

"Oh, by the way, I have a job interview halfway across the country," didn't seem like something she wanted to interject into the conversation.

Staring at the illuminated 3:04 on her phone, she deemed that silence a failure. He might have been disappointed, but the unspoken words wouldn't be haunting her.

Stretching her body, she pulled her shorts-clad legs out from under her comforter and shivered as she moved to the window, placing her fingertips against the cold glass. A streetlight up the road illuminated her sleepy section of Wonder Lane, dotted by darkened houses and one home still ablaze with Christmas lights. The blue and white alternating bulbs stretched across the front of the roofline, and a giant candy cane glowing bright white and red rested just beyond the mailbox.

One and a half more weeks until the holiday, which she now had planted firmly in her brain thanks to the fact that her audition was next week. She had studied the calendar after the phone call, and realized that she only had a few days to prepare herself for the possibility. Was she ready to take on such responsibility? Enough research had been conducted during her dreaming phases that she knew those anchors were practically married to their jobs. Was that really the life she wanted?

A couple months before, she wouldn't have given leaving Louisville a second thought, but in the last few weeks, she had grown roots. Not deeply planted roots, but small, short roots that were tangled with the dirt and trying to grasp onto something solid.

Sighing, she glanced upward from the street, out into the distant night sky, focusing on a light she saw in the distance. Through the dewy fog against the window she couldn't tell if it was a star or a satellite or an airplane, but she supposed it didn't matter. Rubbing the damp glass, the smears from her fingers caused the glow from the Christmas lights to shoot off in all directions in the reflection of the window. Allowing herself a slight smile, she shook her head.

"God?" Nervously licking her lips, she drew her brows together in slight discomfort. "God, if You're listening, it's Harley Davidson. Remember me? I was the kid who memorized all the Bible verses at church summer camp? Skinny, lanky kid who the other kids made engine noises at when they came near?" Clearing her throat, she forced her eyes to remain trained on that light in the distance. "I've always been the inquisitive one, remember? I would spend my time studying the giant Hebrew to English dictionary from Dad's dresser, just to see if the Bible was translated correctly?"

Allowing a slight laugh to tumble out at the thought of dragging around that huge book, she bit her lower lip, feeling a tear slide down her cheek. "All I've ever wanted was to find the truth, and I've worked hard for as long as I can remember. There hasn't been anything I've received in life that I haven't struggled to obtain on my own, and now the culmination of every ounce of that effort is just on the horizon. When I think about the difference I could possibly make with that platform..."

Wrapping her arms tightly across her chest, she lowered her forehead to the glass. "If You really are as involved in our lives as Ryan thinks You are, then I'm asking for Your help. Help to find myself in the place where I can make the most difference. If I'm here for a reason, then to find myself fulfilling that purpose."

The distant light in the sky disappeared suddenly from her view, and she let out a heavy sigh.

"Figures. The wise men had a star to follow, but all I have is a forgotten trail of Christmas lights and a vast expanse of darkness, left to fumble around like a blind man."

Feeling another hot tear slip down her cheek, she closed her eyes.

"When I consider your heavens, the work of your fingers, the moon and the stars, which you have set in place, what is mankind that you are mindful of them, human beings that you care for them? You have made them a little lower than the angels and crowned them with glory and honor." Pausing, she opened her eyes to the darkness. "See? I still remember, even though my crown slipped off somewhere between there and here."

"Next week? Harley, that's not much notice."

Squeezing her hands together, she forced a deep breath into her lungs. The protest from Mitch was pretty weak, and she knew he wouldn't take much convincing.

"I know it's pretty sudden, but just think about the positive publicity. The chances of Trent and the team there actually choosing me are slim to none, but I can put our station on the map a little bit and bring focus to the Louisville area."

Lifting a hand to his chin, he scratched it absently as he stared past her at the door. "Well, you haven't taken any vacation since you've been here, and you're certainly due. Just take those five days right through Christmas, and then come back after."

"Five days?" she repeated a little dazedly.

"Sure. You do know how to take a week's vacation, don't you?"

Laughing, Harley shook her head. "I'm not familiar with the idea, but I'll figure it out. Thanks, Mitch."

"Just do us proud," he insisted as she rose and exited the office.

Pausing to adjust the zipper on her boot in the hallway, Harley hesitated as she knelt near the door to Denton's office. Hushed voices rose from inside, and she immediately recognized Denton's tone as the voice he used when he wasn't particularly pleased. Wondering who he was arguing with, she remained crouched there, hidden from view.

"Because she wouldn't do that, and you know it," Denton's agitated voice insisted.

"Don't pretend that she's a little saint," the feminine voice said, and Harley immediately knew it was Summer. "She's been gunning for the top spot since the moment she got here, and there's no reason to think she wouldn't do whatever it took."

"What you're insinuating is beyond dirty, and I don't like it."

That perked Harley's ears up even more, and she glanced behind her as she slowly rose and pressed herself against the wall.

"It's some kind of scam, Denton. That girl's brother is dating Harley, and they're funneling money into something with that medical fund."

Even as the assertion caused Harley's heart to pound wildly in her chest, she twisted her mouth sideways in an effort to mask her consternation. For someone who couldn't manage to do her own research, Summer had certainly sleuthed out Harley's love life quickly. The mere thought was enough to humiliate and infuriate her simultaneously.

"Be careful what you throw around, would you? That's a terrible thing to accuse someone of, if it's not true."

"Then let's find out if it's true."

"No way. You're on your own with that one."

Summer emerged from Denton's office, and Harley quickly straightened and attempted to act nonchalant as she faced the senior newswoman, whose face tinted slightly red beneath her blonde hair.

"Harley," came the hushed acknowledgement, as she guiltily tried to brush past her.

"Summer," Harley answered without emotion, glancing at the woman's back when she passed. "Is that a new pantsuit? It's very...you." Taking a step forward, Harley shook her head at Denton.

"Hey, you were great last night, Harley. Listen, about that—"

"No worries," she said, letting out a sigh. "Thanks for defending me. Of all the horrible things she could have thought up, that really ranks up there."

"She feels threatened, and for good reason. She's practically a goner, and she sees it coming a mile away."

Sitting in the sterile gray room, Harley allowed her eyes to roam over a poster of the human body on the wall before she dropped her gaze to her hands. She had interviewed countless doctors for her news features, but this time she was out of her element. Rather than feeling in control and self-assured, she struggled to find her voice and calm her nerves.

"We'd like to start the filgrastim injections tomorrow," the mostly bald doctor said, staring at her thoughtfully. "You'll need to have those for the five days leading up to the PBSC donation, to increase the number of blood stem cells in your bloodstream."

Five minutes ago, she would have felt like she was hearing a foreign language, but from her short interaction with the doctor and previous blood testing, she was already familiar with peripheral blood stem cells. Letting out a shaky breath, she squeezed her fingers together tightly.

"Tomorrow," she repeated robotically.

"Yes, and that would put you in Dallas Monday morning."

"Wait, Monday?" Slowly drawing herself from her stupor, she shook her head. "I'm supposed to be in New York Monday, so that's not a possibility. Maybe after the holiday we could work something out."

Leaning toward her from his stool, the doctor placed his hand over her own, forcing her to halt the twisting motion of her fingers. "Harley, what if 'after the holiday' is too late? The patient is in dire need, which is why they want to send you to Dallas."

She dared to look up and caught his sympathetic eyes, dark brown like her own father's, and she felt a tear surface at the corner of her eyelashes, releasing itself to move down her cheek.

"There's nothing to be afraid of," he attempted to soothe her. "There will be one apheresis session, a couple needles in your arm, and full recovery usually takes seven to ten days." When that didn't seem to change her countenance, he tightened his grip on her fingers. "You're not obligated to do this, Harley. If it's causing that much fear..."

Shaking her head, she pulled one hand loose to swipe at her eye. "I'm not afraid of the procedure. I'm afraid of..." Letting out a short laugh, she looked at the wall past the doctor's head. "I'm afraid of my life, and what it looks like. Of my conscience, of holding a mirror up to myself. Who is this person?"

"Who are you?" the doctor attempted to clarify.

"No, who needs the donation? Is it someone like my friend Kelsey, who is seventeen and lovely? Or is it a criminal on death row?"

Giving a heavy sigh, he patted her hand again. "You know I can't give you any patient information."

"Which is exactly why I can't tell you yes," she muttered, squeezing her eyes closed.

"Go home tonight and think about it. I'll set up the appointment for you tomorrow morning. If you don't show, I'll know your answer."

Nodding, Harley rose from her chair and looped her purse over her shoulder.

"Sorry," she whispered. "You must think I'm a horrible person."

"No," he insisted, giving her a sad smile. "I think you're human."

Chapter Twenty-Four

As her car rolled forward toward the end of Wonder Lane, Harley squinted her eyes, thinking her mind was playing tricks on her. In the large front window of her home, where she normally kept the curtains pulled tight, she saw twinkling lights.

Closing the door to her BMW, she hugged her coat closer around her as she stood outside her home witnessing the foreign sight. Of all days to introduce the Christmas spirit, it felt like a giant affront to her senses. A huge black sheet over the window would have been a more appropriate welcome.

Stepping up to the front door, she cautiously pushed it open, half expecting Annie to be waiting with a giant smile on her face, or reindeer antlers on her head. When she found nothing, she hung her purse on a coatrack peg and glanced over at the mirror against the wall, reflecting a young woman wearing a red dress, her dark hair falling in waves across her shoulders. Staring at her own reflection, she found it impossible to smile.

"Harley?" she heard from up the stairs. "Hey girl, 'bout time you got home. I was starting to worry."

Slowly dragging her feet up one step and then another, Harley managed to find herself on the second floor, standing in front of her closet/bedroom. The holes in the wall had been repaired, thanks to Annie's quick friendship with Jake. Stepping out of her shoes, she stretched her arm behind her as she tried to unzip her dress.

"I made salad," Annie announced, stepping up behind her. "I left some in the kitchen for you, provided the rats haven't carried it off."

"Thanks," Harley muttered.

"Either you have something on your mind, or we need to have a serious conversation about the rat problem. I thought I was making that up. Until now I haven't noticed any, so is there something you want to tell me?" Stepping forward, Annie grabbed the zipper and gave it a tug, pulling it to the small of Harley's back.

"No rats, as far as I know. I saw your Christmas lights."

Grabbing a long-sleeved T-shirt, Harley tugged it on as she allowed the dress to fall to the floor. She reached for a pair of faded jeans as Annie placed her hands on her hips.

"The place needed some Christmas spirit, at least that's what Jake and I decided."

"You and Jake are becoming quite the pair."

Annie laughed and shook those purple curls briefly. "Not that kind of pair. Don't get me wrong—he's a total doll. I could stare at him all day. His heart's not available, though. Totally messed up over somebody."

"Alexis?" Thinking back to the forceful way she refuted being Jake's wife, it certainly seemed possible.

"I don't think it's her…he only came here for his daughter. No, that man has a heartbreaker in his past, I can tell."

"Well, maybe you can help him rebound," Harley teased, facing her friend with a hint of a grin. The sound of a motorcycle engine drifted in from outside the window, and she wrinkled her forehead slightly.

"Oh, surprise! Ryan's coming over." Annie gave a little shrug, looking towards the door.

"Thanks for the warning, and how do you know this?"

"He stopped by a little bit ago, but said he'd come back. He's fantastic, you know. I think I finally get it."

"Get it?"

"You know, why you're in love with him."

"Annie!" Swatting at her friend as the knock sounded on the door, Harley simply gave her head a quick shake. "Sometimes I'm tempted to give you a time-out."

"Don't worry, I'm unpacking my room, so you can have the entire downstairs to yourself, roomie. It's like a self-imposed time-out."

Giving a sly wink, Annie continued down the hall as Harley began taking the steps, careful to avoid splinters. Socks might have been a good idea, or even slippers, but it was too late and Ryan was standing outside. Taking a deep breath, she pulled open the front door.

With his helmet under his arm, a slight smile spread across Ryan's face. His cheeks held a pink tint from the ride across town, and the blue of his eyes seemed brighter than normal. A forest-green beanie held his hair away from his face and covered his ears, which were likely pink from the night air as well. Studying his features, Harley's heart pounded a little harder.

"Are you going to make me stand on the porch all night? 'Cause I'm a little cold."

Moving back, she watched Ryan step inside and press the door closed, bending down to place his helmet on the floor. When he straightened, he locked his eyes on hers while he shrugged out of his coat, hanging it on the coat rack.

"You know it might snow tonight?" she asked quietly, folding her arms across her chest to ward off the chill that permeated the entryway.

"I know I wanted to see your face. I didn't get much farther than that." He closed the distance between them and placed a cold hand against her cheek. "You okay?"

She attempted a small smile as she wrapped her fingers around his hand and pulled it away from her face. "Yes and no, and your hand is freezing. If the fireplace worked, I'm sure that would be helpful. It hasn't been used in so long, though, I'd probably burn the house down. Or at least smoke us out of the room. Just...wait here, okay?"

He lifted his eyebrows expectantly as she turned and disappeared up the stairs, heading into her bedroom to pull the comforter off her bed. Stopping before going back down the steps, she grabbed a pair of wool socks, pulling them over her bare feet.

As she emerged from the stairwell, comforter billowing about her like a fluffy cloud, Ryan laughed.

"What are you going to do, smother me?" He laughed, giving her a wide smile.

"The intent is to warm you up, but since you'll have to go back out into the cold, I don't know what good it's going to do."

She didn't give him a chance to answer as she stepped through the dining room and pushed open the door to the living room, which was stained a dark brown from the dining room side but looked rather faded and dingy from the other. She didn't stop to turn on the light as she peered at the tree in front of the window, which was rather small and looked like it had only been bedecked with the lights to that point. Crossing to Annie's couch, she paused and waited for Ryan to join her.

"This will be the first time I've ever sat in this room," she remarked casually as he rubbed his hands together before crossing his arms and placing his fingers beneath his armpits. "Sorry we don't have Annie's TV hooked up yet, and mine's upstairs."

"Believe it or not, I didn't come here to watch TV."

Shifting uncomfortably from one foot to the other, she glanced at the couch. "Did you take off early?"

"It's 8:30. That doesn't exactly feel early to me, but yeah, I finished up a little before I expected."

"Sorry. I guess I've lost track of time." Peering at the couch again, she lifted one corner of her mouth in a teasing smile. "Are you going to sit down, or are we just going to stand here awkwardly staring at one another?"

"I'm going to sit down. Any other instructions?"

He lowered himself slowly to the corner of the couch, reaching out for her hand.

"You're too cold for that," she protested with a grin. "Why don't you pull your boots off and make yourself comfortable?"

"Making myself comfortable is likely to put me to sleep. And with that giant comforter, I'm a little afraid you're tucking me in for the night."

Dropping the comforter onto his lap, she sat beside him, looping her arm through his and leaning against him. "Like I told you, I'm just trying to get you warmed up. Why you'd be out driving around on your bike on a night like this is beyond me."

"I'd imagine you have a pretty good idea," he said, allowing her to snuggle against him. "You want to tell me what's bothering you?"

Although she felt safe and welcome sitting next to the man beside her, she hesitated briefly, wondering if she should share her deepest thoughts. Closing her eyes, she focused on the fact that she could feel the coolness of his skin beneath his shirt, and the thought that he would go to such lengths to see her caused her to relax slightly.

"I'm not a match for Kelsey," she began softly. He didn't make a move as she leaned further against his arm, dropping her head to his shoulder.

"I never expected you to be a match," he finally said. "The mere fact that you were willing to make such a sacrifice for Kels is wonderful, so don't let your disappointment take that away." Letting out an audible sigh, he placed his head against hers. "Can I put my arm around you now?"

"Not if your hands are cold." Smiling to herself at his annoyed grunt, she focused on the sound of him breathing beside her. "That's not all. Summer was making some allegations about me today...completely ridiculous things, but they set me on edge."

"Did anybody believe her?"

"Not that I know of." Forcing herself to remain calm, she tried to ignore the pounding in her chest. "There's something else. Trent Bauer's looking for a cohost, and they called me about having an audition Monday in New York."

"The morning show guy?"

Harley didn't dare look at him, but the change in his tone told her everything she needed to know. Squeezing her eyes closed, she tried to ignore the tightening around her heart as she nodded her head.

"You're telling me you might be moving to New York," he whispered, clearing his throat. "How long have you known about this?"

"They called me yesterday, and I couldn't figure out how to tell you last night."

He grew silent, and she chewed nervously on the corner of her lip. She had expected telling Ryan about New York to be difficult, but she never imagined her heart would feel so conflicted.

"And that's what you want?" he asked, catching her by surprise.

As she pondered his question, the day's events came rushing uninvited through her mind. "Today I met with a doctor who told me that I was a donor match."

"But I thought you said—"

"A marrow donor match. They want me to start injections tomorrow and go to Dallas Monday."

"The same day as New York?"

The emotions of the day overwhelmed her, and she sniffed quietly as she felt tears prick her eyes. "How do I justify New York in my mind now? If I follow the forward trajectory of my life, and try to bring about the plans I made, someone could die." Succumbing to tears, she gulped with difficulty. "Someone could die, and I have no way of knowing... Is it someone like Kelsey? It's one thing to imagine sacrificing for someone you care about, but for a random person you'll never meet?"

Pulling herself away, she turned to face him, drawing her legs up toward her on the couch. "Greater love has no man than when he lays his life down for his friends, right? That I can comprehend, but a stranger? Tell me something that makes sense. I feel like everything's falling down around me."

His eyes focused on hers, barely discernible in the dim Christmas lights, but she could see that a wrinkle formed between his eyebrows. "Greater love... What you're talking about isn't human love at all. That's a love that can only come from God. It's against human nature to sacrifice for someone you don't know."

Rubbing the back of her hand across her cheek, she leaned her head against the couch cushion. "Then I'm not the person," she stated almost inaudibly. "Right? How can I be that person?"

Ryan watched as Harley rested the back of her head against the couch, obviously conflicted about her feelings. He had always known inside that she wouldn't be a match for Kelsey, but her selflessness in suggesting the idea had made her even more lovely in his eyes, if that was even possible.

Focusing on her beautiful face, he rubbed his hands together to try to force some warmth into his fingers, almost desperate to touch her. He wanted to hold her...tell her everything would work itself out somehow, even though he doubted it himself. When the words New York slipped off her tongue, he felt as though he'd been punched in the gut.

Still, she needed his reassurance, and he longed to give her something, even if it meant offering himself up for a broken heart.

"Do you remember the night we met? You told me you wanted to be important."

She exhaled loudly without looking at him as she closed her eyes against his words, and he took the opportunity to study the contours of her face, his eyes following the smooth skin of her cheek down to her chin and her shapely neck. To him, she was absolute perfection, and the thought of being so close to her and losing her made his heart physically ache.

"It sounds so childish, doesn't it?" she asked. "Wanting to be important."

Moving his eyes to her mouth, he watched as she swallowed and then pulled her bottom lip between her teeth, looking so young and unsure of herself. Above every other instinct that was flowing through his veins, at the moment all he wanted was to protect her.

"You are important," he offered quietly, not taking his eyes off her face. "You're important to me, and you're important to Kelsey. You're important to more people than you realize."

Dragging her gaze upward, she stared deeply into his eyes, igniting a fire inside that he forced himself to ignore. "What was it you told me?" Pausing to sniff softly, her chin quivered just enough to betray her lack of self-assurance. "You weren't trying to change the world?"

With a sad smile, he pulled his hands out from under the blanket she'd given him, squeezing them into fists as he placed one against his mouth and tried to blow some warmth into his fingers.

"It's not about changing the world. It's about refusing to let the world change you."

"Refusing to let the world change you," she repeated, eyes locked on his. "What if I don't know who I am? I'm not sure I've ever known."

Reaching up, she grasped the corner of his beanie and slid it away from his head, bringing it down to her lap. Her fingers grazed the corner of his ear before her fingertips pushed gently through his hair. His breath grew heavy almost immediately from the simple, intimate act, and she seemed to notice as she brought her other hand up to his hair.

As her fingers came to rest against the back of his head, she allowed her eyes to drift towards his mouth. He swallowed self-consciously as she studied him, sweeping her eyes across every inch of his face in a way that made him feel that she was memorizing him. Maybe because she believed she wouldn't see him again?

The thought brought such instant sorrow, he fought to keep the discomfort from his face, afraid to give away his feelings. Harley had said she was in love with him in the heat of the moment, but if she understood the depth of his feelings for her, he feared he might drive her away.

His lips parted slightly as he prepared to say something, but his attempts were cut short as she let out a slight sigh, keeping his hair twined between her fingers.

"What did I do to deserve you?" she whispered, her hands tracing paths down the sides of his face. "You are so out of my league."

Unable to stop a short burst of air that expelled from his lungs, he forgot about trying to warm his hands as he reached for her waist, drawing her closer. A trail of moisture still glistened against her cheek in the dim light of the Christmas tree, and he brought his thumb up to gently wipe it away, marveling at the softness of her skin beneath his hand. As he thought about the beautiful woman in front of him expressing that he was too good for her, his eyes welled up with tears and he gave a quick shake of his head.

"Harley..."

His voice sounded hoarse in his own ears as he tried to fight back emotion.

"What should I do? You always have everything figured out."

The urge to laugh presented itself at her erroneous assumption, but instead he offered the beginnings of a smile.

"I don't know anything," he admitted. "I'm trying not to think so much with my head, and just follow my heart for a while."

"Is it working?"

The light from the tree illuminated the right side of her face, and for a second he thought she looked like an angel, slight wisps of her hair catching the glow and framing her face.

"No. Right now it's close to breaking." She dropped her eyes, but he placed his hand against her chin and forced her focus back to his face. "I thought I had things going really smoothly, up until the night at Tiny's when you needed a ride. Once I knew there was a void in my heart that only you could fill, how could I keep it empty? I don't know how to go back to the way it was, without destroying it. It's too full of you."

"What do you mean?"

"I mean I can't go to New York, not with Kelsey..." Sighing, he paused to rein in his emotions once more. "It means I don't want to lose you—not now. It means that I love you with everything in me, so when you make your decision, you know what's on the table."

The instant he released the words, he caught himself holding his breath, hesitantly awaiting her response. She still hadn't removed her hands from his face, and as she drew her eyes downward, she traced a line from his mouth to his chin with her thumb.

"Can I lay my cards on the table?" she asked quietly. Rather than respond, he simply nodded. "My heart belongs to you, so completely that I don't think I can follow it anywhere, because it's not moving. And if you loved me even half as much as you just said you did, you should have kissed me by now."

He laughed almost inaudibly, hardly believing his ears as a wave of relief washed over him, and he couldn't stop the grin from spreading across his face. "Maybe I'm waiting for you to kiss me."

She leaned into him as he wrapped his arms around her, tilting her lips upward in expectation. For a second he hesitated, simply closing his eyes and feeling her breath against his skin while he allowed their noses to touch, inhaling the scent of her hair.

"Stop torturing me," she whispered.

Needing no further inducement, he closed his mouth over hers, feeling the results of the simple act coursing through his body and tying his insides in knots. As she relaxed in his embrace, he deepened the kiss, pushing all thoughts away from his mind except the marvel of the woman whose soft lips were responding to his at that moment. Of all the traits Harley possessed, above all the physical attraction he felt for her, he knew that she had a big heart and was caring. He also knew she was passionate, and would go after whatever she wanted.

As if in response to his thoughts, a soft, breathless moan escaped her lips, and he felt the heat of her fingers against his abdomen, locating the bottom of his T-shirt and moving across his skin. Instinctively his muscles tightened, and he pulled back, exhaling heavily as he glanced behind them at the open door to the dining room.

"Are you afraid of me?"

He was fairly certain her words were teasing, but the way she said them in his ear, they sounded almost suggestive.

"Should I be? Bringing a blanket down here, trying to get inside my clothes... Are you trying to seduce me?"

He returned his eyes to her, and she responded by assuming a rather shy posture. "Can I see your tattoos again?"

"What? That's not a very effective argument, asking me to take my shirt off. Besides, I thought you wanted me to be warm, not freeze me to death."

"Oh, never mind," she complained, eyes narrowing. "You're a very frustrating man, willing to be an exhibitionist for someone you just met, but won't even respond to a simple request from the woman you love."

The woman I love, he thought, unable to stop a smile. "Hmm, but I already had a huge crush on you when I showed you my tattoos."

"You had known me five minutes. When exactly did you develop this huge crush—instantaneously?"

Toying with the bottom of his shirt, he lifted his eyebrows, offering his most mischievous smile. "You were covering a benefit rock concert, interviewing this real bonehead who kept saying the most idiotic things. That was the first time I ever saw you, and it's like I was mesmerized by how poised and beautiful you were in that crazy situation." Pausing, he chuckled at the memory. "Then, you turned to the camera and I expected you to say something about charities or throw it back to the studio. Do you remember what you said?"

She looked rather self-conscious before she answered. "No, what did I say?"

"You said, 'Guys, I don't know what to say except...rock on, Louisville. Rock on.' Then you stuck your tongue out and made a weird hand gesture."

"I remember that," she added with a laugh. "That was right after I came here, nearly two years ago."

"You mean I've been dreaming up fantasy meetings with you for two whole years? That's crazy."

"You're clearly insane." She grabbed his T-shirt, threatening to attempt to pull it up while he held it in place. "Come on, I wanted to inspect them the first time you showed me, but I really couldn't. You were turning my insides to mush, and there was no way I was getting too close to your chest."

Smiling at her admission, he jerked his shirt up, sliding it over his head. "This is totally against my better judgment."

He sucked in a breath as her fingers rested on the anchor against his ribcage, studying it intently, tracing a line around each letter in "hope" as though she would be able to feel them. While she looked at the design, her hand drifted up to her mouth, absently touching her lips. Leaning back against the couch, he willed his breathing to remain normal.

Her actions made it even more difficult, though, as she leaned closer and stared at the cross on his arm, allowing her hair to fall gently against his shoulder. He winced, the restraint required not to touch her almost proving painful. As she lined herself up in front of him again and placed her palm against his pectoral muscle while she inspected the word across his collarbones, his pulse started racing and he let out a low chuckle for self-preservation.

"Okay, nosey. I think that's enough."

"I'm not finished."

She hovered directly in front of his face, and he caught her fingers in his hand. "I'm trying really hard to be a gentleman here, babe. You're finished, or I'm finished, one or the other. You get what I'm saying?"

Acknowledging defeat, she sighed and slid away from him on the couch, allowing him to pull his shirt back over his head. Her gaze flitted to the Christmas tree, and he took the opportunity to study her profile, noting how innocent and vulnerable she seemed. Her eyelashes swept over her cheek as she blinked quickly, peering at the tree more intently, as though she was counting every light on the branches.

Allowing his own eyes to travel to the tree, Ryan's first thoughts were that it was pretty small for the area, and the lights looked like they were hastily strewn across the branches. Not too many of them, either—maybe two strands.

Because one wasn't enough and three were too many...isn't that what she told me her dad said?

Judging by the faraway look in her eyes, he assumed that she had gone back home in her mind, and she was imagining those same Christmas lights herself.

"You okay?" he asked, placing his hand over hers against her leg.

"Huh?" Her shoulders rose as she took a deep breath, finally acknowledging him with the turn of her head. "Oh, sure. Just a million thoughts going through my head."

Pressing his hands to his thighs, he slowly rose from the couch. "I guess I should probably go. No worries about getting cold, since you practically lit a fire under me." She extended her hand, filled with forest-green knit, and he pulled his head covering from her fingers with a smile.

"It's snowing," she said almost inaudibly, returning her attention to the window. "You can't ride your motorcycle home in the snow."

He took a step closer to the window, staring out into the dark night, catching a glimpse of snowflakes dancing past the street lights on Wonder Lane.

"It's snowing," he repeated as she stood next to him. Reaching out to pull her into a hug, he brushed the hair away from her face with the back of his hand. "Hopefully it's not too slick yet."

Shaking her head, she looked up at him. "You can stay. On the couch, I mean. I wouldn't want to tempt you to be anything less than a gentleman."

Staring back into her amber eyes, inspecting every fleck and color highlighted by the Christmas lights, he tried to think clearly.

"I don't know, Harley. It doesn't seem like a good idea."

"I'll go upstairs right now, and you'll have the place to yourself. Please? If something happened to you on the way home, I'd never forgive myself."

Deep inside, a gut instinct told him to kiss her the way he desired and see what happened. Who knows how long Harley would want to be with him, especially if she decided to choose New York. She wanted him to stay the night? Why shouldn't he try to use that to his advantage? He was pretty certain most able-bodied young men his age wouldn't waste an opportunity to be with Harley, in every sense of the word.

Not that she was propositioning him. Far from it, if he was being completely honest with himself, but how much convincing would it take? Her vulnerability was staring him boldly in the face, daring him to see if he could push her over the edge. Her touch on his bare skin while she inspected his tattoos was still fresh in his mind, and he felt his breath thicken in his throat.

"Yeah, I'll stay," he heard himself saying, mouth suddenly dry. Moistening his lips, he hesitated, waiting for her to make the first move. She inched toward him, and he wondered in that instant if he could make any attempts at resistance, wanting every piece of her that she would give him. Her cheek touched his, warm and soft, and his anticipation heightened as he felt her shallow breath near his ear.

Do you really want to start your relationship this way? Maybe a forever kind of relationship?

Every muscle in his body tensed, and as though she sensed the change, she paused with her hand on his arm and her mouth near his ear.

"I love you."

The words were so quiet, he was confused for a split second whether he thought them, or whether she breathed them.

Harley stepped back, offering a shy smile. "Good night, Ryan. Sweet dreams."

"Love you, baby," he managed through his throat as he watched her retreating back disappear through the dining room door. Plopping down on the couch, he pressed his elbows to his knees and ran his hands through his hair, marveling at his complete lack of self-control. Letting out a frustrated breath, he looked around the room. He had the comforter and the decorative pillow from the couch, so he'd be fine, if he ever managed to drift off to sleep. There was the fact that he needed to use the restroom, though, and the only working one he'd seen while they were moving Annie's things was the one upstairs. He was definitely not going up there in his state.

Resigned, he rose to his feet and headed toward the back of the house, determined to do his business from the back porch. No chance of anyone seeing him in the darkness, and to be perfectly honest, the cold night air might do him a heap of good at the moment.

"Annie?" Harley whispered, holding her pillow to her chest and standing in the doorway of her friend's bedroom, looking nervously out into the hall.

"Hey, did Ryan leave?" Annie wondered, straightening up from the book she was reading as she reclined on her side against the bed.

"No, it's snowing, so he has my comforter and he's sleeping on the couch."

"So…what are you doing?"

Biting her lip, she glanced over her shoulder again. "I just… Can I sleep in here with you? He's probably going to come up here to the restroom any minute, and… Well, I'm having a bit of a self-control problem."

"Psst, Ryan."

Ugh, just when I had finally fallen asleep.

Peeling an eye open, he was surprised to find Annie kneeling in front of him by the couch. Jerking his other eye up, he bolted up on the couch, inexplicably worried that something had happened. Where was Harley?

"What time is it?" he asked, reaching up to scratch the back of his head.

He tried to focus on Annie, whose purple curls were sticking out every which way from her head, the look completed with what appeared to be Hello Kitty pajamas.

"It's 5:30, hon. What time do you have to be at work? I want to make sure I get you back to town in time."

The Christmas tree was still lit up, and there was no light to be seen outside, so he shook his head, trying to clear out the fuzz. "Are you sure it's 5:30? I feel like I didn't sleep at all."

"Join the club," Annie muttered. "Harley kicked me all night."

He gave Annie a puzzled expression as he shifted on the couch. "Harley?"

"She left at 4:00. Said she had a ton of work to get done for her big day. Interviews to line out and stuff."

Her big day. Interviews to line out. None of those words helped to ease the anxiety forming in the pit of his stomach. Unwilling to speak his fears to Annie, he managed a slight nod.

"I have to be at work at 7:00, but I can take the bike."

"In four inches of snow? Best to let me take you, okay?"

Shaking his head, he tried to rub the effects of sleep away from his eyes. "Sure, sounds good."

"I'll go get dressed." Annie rose to her feet and crossed the room, leaving him alone once again.

Leaning his head back to look at the ceiling, he swallowed past the lump in his throat. He felt a bit more comfortable as he went to sleep last night about Harley deciding not to go to New York, but Annie had just thrown him for a loop. Reaching for his cellphone, he knocked a slip of paper to the floor where it found a resting place by his boots. Gazing at the partially folded paper, he couldn't miss the simple word RYAN printed on the outside. As he spread it open with his palm, illuminating it with the light of his cellphone, a curious tightness possessed his chest.

Morning, baby. Sorry I had to leave so early, but I have a big day. I hope you don't mind that I asked Annie to take you home. You looked so peaceful, I didn't want to wake you.

After studying your incredible body of art last night, I'm actually trying to have a little faith today. Will you pray for me, that I've made the right decisions? Please?

My very own gentleman. I didn't even know those existed anymore. Until I see you...

Yours Alone,
Harley

Pressing the paper to his chest, he closed his eyes and smiled. "God, do you see this? Harley's trying to make the right decisions. I'm not really sure I can be trusted to pray about that with a clear conscience, because she just called my body incredible. By the way, thank You for the fact that she wrote that in a note and didn't stand here telling me that face to face, because I'm really not sure what to do with that. And she thinks I'm a gentleman! I guess I should be glad that You didn't make her a mind reader, because I was anything but a gentleman last night, right?"

Taking the paper in his fingers, he leaned forward and put both fists against his forehead, shaking his head slightly. "If she wants to make the right decisions, I'm asking You to ignore me here, because I'm not sure I'm on board with her best interests. I want her, completely and forever, so my own interests are winning out on my end. Please, give me Harley."

Pausing, he let the stillness of the room wash over him, sitting in the quiet.

"Um, Ryan? If you're finished wanting Harley, I'm ready to take you home."

Poised with her pen over her open notebook, Harley rested her elbow on the desk, phone shoved against her ear through the assistance of her shoulder. "Can I quote you on that, sir? Of course I agree with your analysis, but the words will have a lot more clout if they're attributed to a constitutional lawyer rather than a reporter."

Scribbling on the blank page, she hefted her purse up on her free shoulder, balancing it against the desk using her knee and her hip.

"Can I help you?"

Holding up her index finger, Harley motioned to the woman with dark-blonde hair that she would only be a second.

"Thank you very much. I'll be speaking with the judge later today, and I'm grateful for your assistance." Punching the button on her cellphone to end the call, she turned her attention to the woman in front of her. "So sorry. I'm trying to get everything lined out, and it's proving to be a challenge."

Taking a deep breath, she dropped her phone into her purse and stood resolutely in front of the reception desk. "Harley Davidson. Dr. Ramsey sent me over. I'm here for my first injection."

Chapter Twenty-Five

"I would feel infinitely better about the situation if you were going with me. I know it's silly, but I'm nervous. Not to mention the fact that those injections have given me a five-day headache, and I am completely ready for this to be over."

The minute the words left Harley's lips, she felt like a complete and total heel. How could she say such a thing to Kelsey, who was battling illness every day? As though she should feel sorry for Harley for having a simple headache.

"I'm so sorry," she breathed into her cellphone, glancing around at the other busy travelers who were sitting near her at the airport, their laptops open or reading on their tablets. "Of course having a headache is nothing, and I shouldn't have even mentioned it without considering your feelings. You must think I'm completely self-centered."

"Right now I just think you're crazy. How could you think that I would be anything other than super proud of you?"

"Oh, I don't know, I guess it's just the assumption that you have brains in your head." Glancing at the gentleman closest to her, who was wearing a tailored business suit and kept glancing in Harley's direction, she attempted to lower her voice. "You're not allowed to be proud of me. And besides, I think you know I definitely wouldn't be doing this if it hadn't been for you."

"Ryan told me about New York."

Feeling her chest constrict, Harley glanced at the businessman again, who gave her a flirtatious smile. Turning her body the other direction, she tried to swallow around the lump in her throat.

"Yeah, it's really no big deal."

"The thing you want more than anything is no big deal?"

Staring at her fingernails, Harley fought the tension rising through her body. She had spent the last five days convincing herself that she made the right decision, but part of her still wished she had boarded the flight to New York the day before and spent the morning trying out her banter with Trent Bauer. So much so that she hadn't had the nerve to tell Mitch the truth. When he called her wondering about her audition, she was prepared to tell him simply that things didn't work out like she planned. That wasn't a lie, in and of itself. As far as how the details would pan out...

"Sometimes the timing isn't right, and our dreams get put on hold," she attempted to convince herself along with Kelsey. "And the things I want are changing a bit, admittedly."

"You're talking about Ryan?"

The mere mention of his name caused goose bumps to form on her arm. Of course, there was Ryan. She had never loved anyone as ferociously as she loved him. It was exhilarating, but also slightly confusing.

"Lots of things are changing," Harley countered, not wanting to divulge her innermost feelings to Ryan's sister.

"I hope I feel okay the day you get married, because I want to stand beside you."

Even though no one else in that terminal could hear her conversation, Harley felt the heat creeping up her neck and into her cheeks. "Or maybe I can stand next to you when you're marrying Zac Efron."

"He's too old for me. I wouldn't mind having you for a sister, so I could beat you in Scrabble all the time. And, Ryan pretty much thinks you're a princess. He told me that you love him."

Allowing a quick laugh to escape, Harley slid down in her seat and tried to make her situation a little more private. "I do. Very much."

"When I found out about you and Ryan, I thought it was weird. You just don't seem the same, you know? But after hanging out with both of you, I think you're perfect."

"Really?"

"Well, mostly. I still think it's kind of strange that you're interested in my brother, but I'm happy about it."

Harley attempted to hide her grin behind her hand as she heard a call being made for boarding, and she glanced down at the carry-on bag by her feet. Since she was only staying one night, she chose to pack very light and only had one piece of luggage, which would save her time later.

As she drew her eyes back up, her gaze shifted to a small foil-wrapped, pyramid-shaped lump of silver on her knee. She couldn't remember the last time she had a Hershey's Kiss. With a heightened feeling of anticipation, thinking perhaps Ryan was there after all, she brought her eyes up to her right.

"Duke?" Her surprise at seeing her bearded friend was so sharp she could almost taste it. "Kelsey, I have to go." Slowly dragging the phone away from her ear, Harley pushed the end button and held it in her lap, reaching for the piece of chocolate.

"Hey, little lady."

The simple phrase nearly sent Harley into laughter. She knew next to nothing about John Wayne, but that certainly sounded like something he would say. While *that* Duke would have likely been wearing some combination of chaps, spurs, and a cowboy hat, her own Duke settled next to her wearing a black T-shirt, a leather vest, and a black doo-rag with flames shooting across the sides of his head. Taking note of his dark rolling bag with the Harley Davidson logo emblazoned on the front, she focused on the piece of chocolate in her hand.

"Did you come all the way to the airport just to share chocolate with me?" she asked mischievously.

"Come on, now. That would be crazy." Fishing in his pocket, he pulled out his own silver-wrapped piece of candy. "Just taking a little trip, that's all, and thought I'd come over and say hello."

"Going home for the holidays?" she wondered right before popping the chocolate into her mouth.

"Nope." He unwrapped his chocolate and sat quietly, as though he was savoring the flavor.

"So where are you going?" She made a point of rolling the silver foil into a tiny ball and staring at it between her fingers.

"Popping on down to Dallas."

"Dallas," she repeated dubiously. "You have family in Texas?"

"Nope." He focused his steely-gray eyes across the terminal, and she fought the urge to grow frustrated at his non-responses.

"So...why are you going to Dallas? Motorcycle convention? You want to catch a Cowboys game?"

"Just so you know, not everything needs to be dissected for the evening news."

Hearing another boarding call, Harley rose and reached for her bag on the floor, narrowing her eyes at Duke. "Just so *you* know, every time I ask you a question, I'm not necessarily trying to make it into a news story. Sometimes I'm just trying to make small talk. Turns out that's hard to do with a clam."

"Watch it," he said, giving her a stern look.

She carried her bag to the gate and waited, preparing to board the plane. To her surprise, Duke rose and ambled up behind her, standing with her in line.

As she was being told to enjoy her flight, Harley hoisted her bag to her shoulder and began walking slowly, intrigued by Duke's presence. Within just a few seconds, he was by her side in the jetway, looking ahead as though they were strangers. Unable to remain in suspense, Harley stopped abruptly and stood like a statue, causing Duke to glance over at her.

"Mr. Fletcher...Marion. Will you please tell me what you're doing, as a friend?"

Releasing a hint of a smile, he nodded his head. "A friend of mine is having a medical procedure, and I want to be there to help."

"What type of medical procedure?" she asked, softening her voice.

Appearing a bit uncomfortable, he reached up with his right hand and scratched his cheek, running his fingers across his beard. "I don't suppose I rightly know, but it doesn't much matter. See, I've got this friend…real nice guy, would do anything for you. Know the type? His girl is going to the hospital in Dallas, and it was just killing him that he couldn't get off work. So, here I am."

Shifting her bag, she moved to the side as another traveler made his way past her. "You're going all the way to Dallas because your friend couldn't get off work? And what about you, you don't have work to do today?"

"Mondays are my day of rest, so to speak. I don't have any group activities to organize at the shelter or with the church, so I generally take it easy. Besides, the way I see it, my friend is good people. He's a motorcycle man, just like me. If he's in a bind, the least I can do is keep an eye on his Harley on my day off."

Glancing at the floor of the jetway, Harley sniffed and tried to take a deep breath.

Duke reached out and touched her arm, causing her to look in his direction. "Suppose the first thing we need to do is make sure you get on that plane, right? And that won't happen if you're standing here sniveling."

Forcing a laugh, she nodded and looped her arm through his, standing up a little straighter.

"Such a sweet talker," she added mischievously. "Come on, cowboy. Looks like you and me are about to mosey on down to The Lone Star State."

Harley had wondered what she would do for the approximate eight hours of her apheresis, and she had an audiobook in case she needed the distraction. With Duke never leaving her side, though, she didn't need anything extra. Although they hadn't been seated together on the plane, simply knowing that he was onboard and in her corner gave her a heightened sense of confidence.

The fact that Ryan had cared enough to ask Duke to accompany her filled her with warmth from her head right down to her toes, and she spent the majority of her flight to Dallas gazing out the window and daydreaming with a slight smile crossing her face. The only thing that had kept Ryan out of her mind after the flight was Duke's attention.

Once they had been settled, and Harley found herself sitting in a cozy chair with needles in both arms, Duke located a chair nearby and kept her company. Since she was afraid they might not let him come with her, Harley lied at the desk and stated that he was her father. It wasn't such a stretch…he was probably older than her own dad, and obviously shared the same love of motorcycles.

Duke had looked on in amazement as the procedure was explained to Harley, soaking up the details. The blood would be removed through a needle in one arm and passed through a machine that would collect the blood-forming cells, and the remainder of the blood would be returned through a needle in the other arm. It seemed simple enough, and other than the fact that she was still experiencing some headaches and other soreness from the injections back home, things weren't too uncomfortable.

"I'm surprised your boss didn't force you to bring a camera along," Duke remarked, employing no emotion whatsoever in his voice. As usual, it was hard to tell if he was joking or completely serious.

"He has no idea where I am, and I'd like to keep it that way. The faster all of that buzz dissipates, the better." Allowing herself to relax slightly, she pondered her thoughts, trying to decide if she should vocalize them. "I was supposed to go to New York to interview for a morning show, but the truth is, I'm starting to wonder if that's really what I want."

"Well, now, I like Ryan as much as the next guy, but don't go giving up your dreams just because you might have found a good match."

Leaning her head back against the seat, she giggled as she stared at Duke, arms crossed against his leather vest and looking downright intimidating. If she had taken him with her to any of her appointments in Louisville, people might have believed that the local news reporter had employed a bodyguard.

"Honestly, do you think I'm as fickle as that?" she wondered, glancing at the tube running from her arm to the machine. "All I've wanted was to be someone important, and to make a difference. Through all of this, though, I've managed to see that being important and changing the world aren't so much about people looking at you as they are about people *not* looking at you."

When Duke raised his eyebrows in response, she knew she had spoken less than eloquently.

"What I mean is, being in front of a camera has all the appearance of making a person seem important, and it provides a huge platform for changing things. At least, it would if your boss wasn't always looking for a political angle on his stories. And I really do think I've done some good in my career, but the things that really matter? The things that make the most difference are the things that are done quietly, in the background, when no one is looking. Things where I might not get any recognition at all."

"Are you okay with that?"

She hesitated briefly, pondering the answer deep within, wondering if she could be.

"You know what? I'm not sure." Glancing at the ceiling, she shook her head slowly, letting all her concerns flood into her mind. "I keep trying to hold up that mirror and stare into it, but the fact is, I'm not all that impressed with what I see. As much as I hate to admit it, I enjoy the attention. It's gratifying to my seventeen-year-old self to say, 'World, do you see me now? You used to make fun of me, but look where I am.' When I see someone on the street and they call me Louisville's sweetheart, it makes me feel good. I like the idea that there are teenage girls out there looking to me to see how I dress, the way I carry myself. I even enjoy the fact that I can manage to coerce Denton into flirting with me just by the coy use of language. But everything I do is a show. Denton's right about that—I'm a great actress. Or, at least I've become one."

"But that bothers you."

Harley longed to put her head in her hands and take a slight breather, but the needles on either side reminded her to remain upright. "Of course it bothers me. 'Dress for the job you want, not the job you have.' That's what one of my professors told me in college. I've done that for so long, I've nearly lost sight of reality. I can't tell where Harley Laine leaves off and Harley Davidson begins."

"Harley Davidson?" he asked, a mischievous twinkle in his eye.

"Breathe a word of that, and I will end you."

"Wow, no need to be hostile." His words held a bite, but his laugh said otherwise. A smile began to spread across her face, and she bit her lip to keep it from growing.

"Sorry, nobody knows about that except Ryan, so if you don't mind keeping that to yourself…"

"No worries. If anything, it makes me like you even more."

"That doesn't surprise me," she complained, focusing her eyes on her knees. "Can I ask you a question?"

"I don't guess I'm going anywhere."

Drawing her eyes up, she focused on Duke, still sitting there calmly with his arms crossing his chest. No doubt anyone who saw them would think he was angry about something, but Harley knew it was an act, just like her high-class reporter shtick.

"When I was a little girl, I memorized a lot of scripture. A lot. Lately, one passage in particular keeps running over and over in my mind. I can't seem to make sense of it." She paused to gauge Duke's reaction, but since he seemed to have none, she soldiered on. "When I consider your heavens, the work of your fingers, the moon and the stars, which you have set in place, what is mankind that you are mindful of them, human beings that you care for them? You have made them a little lower than the angels and crowned them with glory and honor."

For a split second he just stared at her as though she might be crazy, but then he uncrossed his arms and shifted himself in his seat. "Psalm 8."

Startled, Harley blinked twice and twisted her mouth to the side. "What's Psalm 8?"

"You just quoted Psalm 8."

"Oh." Her heart sank slightly, and she almost wished she hadn't brought it up.

"What do you think of it?"

"Me?" Shrugging her shoulders, she shook her head. "I'm not sure what to think. I have no trouble seeing the beauty in the heavens, the stars. Those things are easy for me to appreciate, but the part about man... I guess I don't get it. Why would He care? Most people who are walking around thinking they have the crown are the ones who hurt everyone else."

"Says who?"

"Personal experience?" Forcing a deep breath, she couldn't coerce herself to even fake a smile. "I think even deeper than that, though, is the fact that I might be just as bad. I've been setting myself up as the queen, trying to wrestle the crown from everyone. I have to be the best on my street, at the studio, on television. What if that's the reason I'm doing this, too? Because I have to be the most altruistic? This whole time, have I only wanted to rescue Kelsey so I could set myself up as her savior?"

"Nonsense. You care about that girl, don't ya?"

"Of course I do."

Something inexplicable rose up inside her, and she fought to tamp it down, thinking about the subject in abstract rather than personally.

"Psalm 103."

"I think we've established that I don't know the numbers, so can you just give me the quotes and save me a headache?"

Rather than spout more scripture, Duke stepped away from his seat and moved toward her, kneeling down in front of where she sat, careful to avoid the tubes going into her arms.

"Psalm 103 is David praising the Lord, who 'redeems your life from the pit and crowns you with love and compassion.'"

"With love and compassion," she repeated, staring at him as he continued to kneel beside her.

"Love and compassion, darlin'. That's the crown I see when I look at you. Maybe glory and honor is something you desire, but the crown He's blessed you with is love. You love Kelsey, and your compassion for her not only drove you to want to help her, but it's driven you here. It's driven you to help someone you don't even know."

She felt herself tearing up, and she cleared her throat in an attempt to bring her emotions under control. Sitting in that chair with her blood going through the machine beside her, the absolute last thing she wanted to do was begin crying like an imbecile.

"Ryan thinks God is intimately involved in our lives, and I'm tempted to believe that myself."

"But you don't," he assumed gently, placing his hand over hers.

"I don't *want* to believe it," she admitted, realizing it herself for the first time. "Mainly for what it means for the past."

Duke carefully folded her hand between both of his, mindful of the needle in her arm. With a tender look in his eyes, he offered a sad smile. "Hon, just because somebody hurt you doesn't mean that's what God intended. And just because someone claims to be right with God, that doesn't mean they are. It certainly doesn't mean they talk for Him. There are a might lot of people who called themselves Christians who wouldn't allow me to darken their doorsteps years ago, because of the way I looked. I'm grateful that I didn't let them sway me from the truth."

Harley let her mind drift to a picture of the church that Duke and Annie attended, seeing the diverse crowd who seemed to have nothing linking them together. Nothing but their faith, at least.

"But…if things have been hard, and you've struggled, does that mean God wanted that? If someone did hurt you, didn't accept you for who you are, what does that mean? If God really is involved in our lives?"

Duke shifted to his other knee as he appeared to give her question some thought, narrowing his eyes as he patted her hand.

"You remember the story of Joseph, in the Old Testament?"

"Sure, the guy whose brothers threw him in a hole."

Her terse response caused Duke to chuckle. "Yeah, they threw him in a hole, and then they faked his death, sold him into slavery. He was wrongly accused, imprisoned, and forgotten by those who vowed to remember him. Not exactly learning experiences I would have chosen." He paused, peering deeply into her eyes. "But do you remember what he said when he finally told them who he was? Years later, when he was powerful, and they fell before him? He said that they thought evil against him, but God meant it for good. When he was young, he dreamed that he was elevated above them, and they hated him for it. But their actions wound up being the very thing that elevated him."

Glancing down at the ground, Harley attempted to digest what he had just said. *What they thought evil against him, God meant for good.*

"I don't know your history, darlin', and I don't know what you're wrestling with deep inside, but I can see this in your very own situation right this second. You remember not too long ago, when you and I were sitting on that bench in front of Tiny's, and you were upset about your boss using Kelsey to try to make you a star?"

"Yes, it shouldn't have been about me."

"But he made it about you, and what was different because of it?"

"It became a spectacle," she offered softly. "I think it gave us all false hope, because there was such a build-up on whether I would be a match for Kelsey. And it made me look like a martyr, volunteering to be tested for this and that and everything."

"Which you wouldn't have done if your boss hadn't insisted."

"Of course not. I would have done it quietly, and no one would have known except Kelsey's family."

"And you wouldn't be here now, as a possible answer to someone's prayers."

"Because God used Mitch's selfishness for good?"

Rising to his feet slowly, he reached over and tousled her hair a bit, as though she were a child.

"Well, here you sit, little lady," he said with an easy smile. "I dare you to doubt that."

Chapter Twenty-Six

The elevator doors opened, and Harley found herself bolting into the hallway before she reminded herself to calm down. An overabundance of haste wasn't going to help matters, and she needed to try to remain calm for Kelsey's sake.

When Ryan called the evening of her stay in Dallas to tell her that Kelsey had been admitted to the hospital again, she wanted to come home immediately. He was able to convince her that there was nothing she could do, and she should wait for her morning flight as she planned. To his credit, Duke talked another passenger on the flight into switching seats with him, and he allowed her to rest against his shoulder, fitfully dozing as they returned to Kentucky.

Dark splotches filled her vision, and she abruptly stopped, leaning against the cold, sterile wall. Although she felt mostly normal, she was a bit weak. Fainting in the corridor wasn't likely to assist anyone, and she should have known to take it easy. She had been tired and slightly sore ever since the procedure, and she knew recovery would probably take a week.

Feeling the blood slowly return to its proper place, she straightened up and began walking, albeit a little more slowly. The patient room loomed ahead of her, and she hesitated before stepping inside, forcing herself to look calm and unafraid for her younger friend.

She rapped on the door quietly, barely peeking her head inside, where she saw Kelsey lying on the bed. She appeared to be sleeping at first, eyes closed, dark circles resting underneath and her surrounding skin colored with the effects of jaundice. Her lashes slowly flitted upward, though, and she brought her eyes over to meet Harley's.

"Please tell me this isn't just a ploy to get my attention," Harley said, her lame attempt at a joke eliciting the slightest of smiles from Kelsey.

"I wish."

Regina rose from her seat next to the bed and stepped up to Harley, wrapping her in a warm hug. "How are you feeling, sweetie? Did your procedure go okay?"

"Of course, but I couldn't wait to get back, especially after Ryan called. I wish I would have been here."

"There was nothing you could do," Regina assured her as Harley settled on the bed next to Kelsey, taking her friend's right hand in both of her own.

"Is there anything I can do for you, Kels? Anything at all, you name it."

"Do you have any news on Zac Efron?" Kelsey asked weakly.

Harley laughed, placing her fist against her mouth to hold back the giggles and the tears that threatened. Shaking her head, she gave Kelsey a tremulous smile. "I love you, you know that? You inspire me, Kelsey Andrews."

"I inspire you?"

Nodding, Harley leaned down and pressed a kiss against Kelsey's forehead. "Absolutely, more than anyone I've ever met. You make me want to be a better person—not for my own benefit, but because I wish I was truly good, like you."

"But you do so many good things, Harley," Regina interrupted, causing Harley to turn in her direction.

"Sure, sometimes, when I'm dragged kicking and screaming in that direction."

"How was Dallas?"

Harley straightened up and smiled at Regina, sensing that the woman was trying to make things seem more normal instead of sentimental. "I don't know. I basically saw the inside of the room where I sat all day, and Duke and I had dinner at the hotel."

"The biker from church?" Kelsey asked quietly.

"Yes. I'm sure we looked like quite a pair. He accompanied me to give me moral support, and I was really glad he was there. Supposedly it was Ryan's idea."

"That's sweet of him, then," Regina stated. "So you didn't have to be alone."

"Will you stay with me, Harley?"

Harley drew her eyes back to Kelsey, attempting to give her a reassuring smile. "Of course, as long as you want me to."

Apparently satisfied with the answer, Kelsey closed her eyes to rest again, and Harley looked to Regina with questioning eyes.

"She's really tired, that's all. Everything will be okay." Rising to her feet, Regina placed her hand on Harley's back. "Mind if I take a few minutes to walk around? I'm getting rather restless."

"Take all the time you need."

As Regina stepped out of the room, Harley gently brushed the hair back from Kelsey's forehead, studying her peaceful countenance.

"I'm really glad you're here. I was afraid."

A flitter of pain shot through Harley's heart at that admission, and she squeezed Kelsey's hand in her own.

"Everything's going to be fine," she choked out, struggling to find words. "You need to keep your hope, sweetie."

"I know. I wasn't afraid for me. I was afraid for you."

"For me?" Despite her best attempts, a tear slid down Harley's cheek, which she let go unheeded, since Kelsey was still closing her eyes.

"Yes. Because I want you to know that whatever happens, I'm okay. And I love you."

Another tear streamed its way down her face, and Harley bit her lip to keep herself calm. "Please don't talk like that, Kels."

"Why? You don't know what's going to happen. Things happen to people every day, whether they're sick or not."

The truth of that statement rested on Harley as she stared at her friend, who looked unbelievably pale and fragile at the moment. Even in her state, she could be destined for the world much longer than Harley. Wasn't that evidenced the day of the explosion, when she found herself at the hospital?

"I don't have any regrets," Kelsey whispered, tilting her head to the side and letting out a small sigh, followed by the soft sound of her slumbered breathing.

Her face contorting, Harley smiled through a sheen of tears as she gazed upon Kelsey's sleeping form in that hospital bed.

"Nor should you, my friend. You're practically perfect."

Harley awoke a short time later, her body curled up next to Kelsey on the bed, and glanced up to see the most handsome EMT she had ever seen watching her with a coy smile. Making sure she didn't rouse Kelsey, she pressed herself up to a seated position, self-consciously pushing a strand of hair behind her ear.

"Not working?" she asked quietly.

"I snuck away for a few minutes." He reached for her hand, and she stood and stepped toward him. "You know, one of these days, I might ask you to run away with me."

"Promise?"

Tilting her chin upward with his fingers, he slowly and deliberately bent toward her, heightening the anticipation until his lips barely grazed her own, his mouth gently tugging against hers in invitation. She brought her hand up, wrapping her fingers around the back of his neck, the tender kiss threatening to undo her composure. Unable to resist, she yielded to the firm pressure of his hand at the small of her back, melting into him even as a tear rolled down her cheek. While he moved his lips delicately against hers, she tried to ignore the pounding of her heart.

This room was everything Duke had talked to her about the day before. Love and compassion—they were bursting to the seams and maybe even overflowing.

"Ryan, you 'bout ready?" came a voice from the hallway.

With a sigh, he pulled away, gazing into her eyes. "Yeah, just give me a sec, Miguel." Brushing against her cheek with the back of his hand, he gave her an endearing smile. "Everything's okay, baby."

"No," she protested, shaking her head slowly. "Everything's not okay. Some things are more than okay. Far and beyond more than okay."

With a slight nod, he continued to study her. "Tomorrow's Christmas Eve, you know."

"Yeah, I know."

"And I have the entire day off. I can't think of anything better to do with it than spend it with the woman who holds my heart."

The way Ryan looked at her and spoke with such sincerity had a way of making her want to wilt like those old-fashioned women swooned in the classic movies, but she forced herself to remain upright and not appear utterly ridiculous.

"You know, earlier Kelsey was talking about not having any regrets," she said.

"She doesn't have any?"

"No," she answered simply, placing her hand against his chest.

"And what about you?"

Unable to vocalize her thoughts, she nodded her head.

"So what are we doing tomorrow, Harley? What does our Christmas Eve look like?"

Running her finger across the patches on the sleeve of his uniform, she managed to offer a sad smile.

"I need to go home."

Chapter Twenty-Seven

Harley could have fooled herself into thinking going home wouldn't be particularly strange. Eighteen years she spent in the trailer halfway between Salt Lick and Hope, as the crow flies. That's what her dad used to say, anyway. She never argued, because it certainly felt like she was always halfway between something.

The closer they drew to that familiar place, though, the more her palms seemed to sweat and her stomach grew queasy. Had she left on better terms a homecoming might have felt comfortable or even sweet, but she wasn't proud of the way she abruptly departed from her family. Leaving a note was cowardly, and she was no coward.

Glancing over at Ryan, she gave him a half-hearted smile that reached no farther than the corners of her lips, and certainly didn't penetrate the icy chill surrounding her. As though he read her mind, he reached over and placed his hand atop hers on her thigh.

He certainly had taken pains to make sure he looked his best to meet her parents. Despite the fact that she showed up at his house fairly casual wearing dark-wash jeans and a loose sweater that hung off her shoulder, he met her at the door wearing a slim-fit long-sleeved purple dress shirt that was practically molded to his body. A henna-colored pattern scrolled across one shoulder and down the side of the chest, stopping where he had the shirt tucked into his distressed jeans.

Sitting in the car with him, studying him again, he nearly took her breath away. He had rolled his sleeves up to his elbows nearly as soon as they loaded into her BMW, and as her eyes traced the line of his arm up towards his face, she couldn't help but smile.

"Stop looking at me like that," he requested, keeping his eyes on the road.

"I'm sorry, but you make it nearly impossible. I can see every one of your muscles through your shirt."

"That seems like an exaggeration."

"Really?" she wondered with a smirk. Leaning towards him, she draped her fingers across his bicep. "Look at that. And you expect me to keep my eyes over here?"

"I'm warning you—torment me, and I will torment you later."

"I'm not scared," she insisted with a laugh, forcing her eyes to drift to the passenger window. It wouldn't be far now, and the thought sent a new wave of dread over her.

Resorting to silence, she watched as trees whizzed by along the side of the road. She had tried to view her childhood home from a satellite Internet map once, when she was feeling particularly nostalgic, but it had been impossible. The tiny little line of white led off the road, but it disappeared into a mess of green that was impenetrable. The trailer had always been nestled right into the woods, with trees precariously close to their dwelling, as though her father simply didn't want to bother with mowing a lawn. And he never had, as long as she had lived there.

When Ryan slowed the car and peered to the side of the road, noticing the DAVIDSON on the mailbox, he flipped on the blinker and gave her an encouraging grin. It gave her no solace. She was worried that they might be angry with her, naturally, but even worse, she feared they might not accept Ryan.

How many times had she heard her mother complaining to her father about the types of men who gave him their business? Men with tattoos and long hair, or the mother of all things evil— earrings. He couldn't turn down business based on peoples' appearances, he said. The truth was, her father had been different during the summers when her mother was overseas on her missions work. He and Harley seemed like allies during those times, understanding and accepting of one another.

She stopped thinking about tattoos as the trailer appeared in their view, resting in front of them like a ghost from the past, never updated and still boasting the damaged panel in the front from a hail storm.

Ryan didn't ask her if they were in the right place, because certainly he instinctively knew. If he couldn't tell from the haunted look on her face, he would have known from the rigid form of her body, or the fact that she was having trouble blinking.

Placing the BMW in park, Ryan let the engine continue to idle, gazing over at her.

"Think they're home?" he asked.

His words elicited nothing more than a shrug as she pulled on the door handle and stepped out onto the brown grass poking through the gravel, splattered here and there with the remnants of a snow that hadn't yet melted in the shadows. He allowed the engine to still and joined her in front of the car, staring up at the rickety-looking wooden stairs.

"I'm here," he whispered. "I don't care what happens—if you're worried and want to go back to Louisville, or if you're angry, or if you're upset. Whatever happens, I'm here."

"I know," she stated simply, placing her hand in his. "You're here to love me, because God knew I needed you."

She didn't allow him to respond as she marched carefully up the steps, testing each one to make sure it wouldn't crumble beneath her weight. It never occurred to her that something might have happened to her parents in the two years since she'd been gone, but the shoddy condition of her childhood home certainly made that seem like a possibility. Steeling herself, she rapped quickly on the door, feeling Ryan's hand make its way to her back.

"Elaine?" she heard her father's voice from somewhere deep inside, and an instant wave of relief washed over her at hearing his voice. The sound of the trailer creaking as he moved toward the door could be heard with each footstep, and Harley backed away a few inches, feeling the moment's impending closeness. As the door was drawn open, she was almost certain her heart stopped beating.

"Dad," she acknowledged, taking in the thin, lanky man with dark hair graying at the temples, plaid shirt rolled up to his elbows just like Ryan.

"Harley?" he managed, voice cracking. "Honey, that you? Ya look all grown up."

"Apparently that happens as one gets older," she said, noticing the deeper creases around his eyes. "You alright?"

"I do okay." Pausing, he motioned to the steps behind her. "Need to get the stairs fixed."

She nearly smiled as she recognized her father's familiar habit of deflecting questions away from himself by directing the subject to inanimate objects.

"Yeah," she agreed solemnly. "Dad, this is my boyfriend, Ryan Temple. He rides a motorcycle."

She had no idea why she felt like she should add that tidbit of information, but Ryan chuckled briefly behind her.

"Nice to meet you, Mr. Davidson."

"Call me Phil." The two men shook hands, eyeing one another cautiously, and Phil backed away from the door. "Come on in, y'all. Sorry we weren't expecting you."

Glancing around at the small living room, Harley took in the space that seemed virtually unchanged. Same old tan woven couch, worn out brown recliner that was nearly threadbare on the arms, and a solid bookcase shelf full of different versions of the Bible. She studied the carpet as she moved across the room, noting how it was loose in spots and wrinkled—identical in color to the Kentucky earth, just as it had always been.

"Elaine! Get out here, you're not gonna believe this."

Harley waited, nervously standing in front of her father as she heard her mother's squeaking footsteps coming down the hall. When the familiar face stepped into view, her countenance erupting into a smile, Harley was immediately put more at ease.

"Oh my goodness! My eyes must be deceiving me!"

"Hi, Mom." Harley kept her gaze on her mother, noticing the fact that she had gained a little weight and looked like she had aged ten years instead of two. Her lackluster chestnut hair was pulled back loosely at her neck, her appearance made worse by the fact that she was wearing an old-fashioned polyester blouse that Harley's great-grandma might have worn. It was impossible for her not to think that her mother would look at least ten years younger if she simply made an effort on her appearance.

"We got a phone, honey." She stepped over to the wall, plucking a handheld from its cradle. "See here? We thought maybe you might want to call us, but then we didn't know how to tell you."

"That's great, really." Staring at her mother's animated face, Harley wondered how she should react.

"You should take our number. Eight-five-nine—"

"Maybe you could write it down for me later."

"Oh," she muttered, placing the phone back in its place. "Yes, that sounds good."

"This is Ryan Temple, my boyfriend."

"You have a boyfriend?" she asked incredulously, finally looking at Ryan. "Well, I'm surprised. Hello."

"It's a pleasure to meet you, Mrs. Davidson."

"Just call me Elaine. Are you staying for Christmas? I wasn't expecting you."

"No, Ryan's sister is in the hospital, so we'll only be here for a little while."

Harley studied the way her mother wrung her hands together, looking for something to busy herself.

"Well, sit, both of you. Can I get you anything?"

"No, thank you," Ryan answered, sitting gingerly on the couch where he sunk a little farther than he expected, his knees winding up higher than his hips. Harley settled next to him and immediately grabbed his hand, as though she was clinging to him for dear life.

"Do you still live in Louisville? What kind of job do you have?" Elaine settled herself a couple feet from Harley, placing her hands together at her knees.

"Yes, I'm a reporter for Channel Six Action News."

"Oh, for the television?"

For the television? Every time I visit my parents I feel like I stepped onto an episode of The Waltons.

Ryan glanced at Harley and shifted uncomfortably. "Harley is Louisville's most popular reporter."

Harley watched the uninterested expression on her mother's face, wondering what it would take to impress her. "Really? That's nice, dear."

"So, Phil, Harley tells me you work on motorcycles?" Ryan smiled at Harley, and she squeezed his hand as a thank you for moving the conversation along.

"Yup, I've got a couple out back, if you want to take a look."

Ryan gave Harley a questioning glance, and she shook her head.

"Go on."

He quickly turned to kiss her cheek before he shoved himself up from the couch with difficulty, following Harley's father quietly out the door. As soon as he left, Harley twisted her mouth slightly to the side and gazed across the room.

"Your boyfriend seems...nice."

Swinging her head to the left, Harley tried to gauge her mother's meaning behind her words. "He is nice. He's wonderful, actually."

"He's not a troublemaker? He's good to you?"

A troublemaker, of course. What else would he be?

"The absolute best. I couldn't dream of better."

"Okay."

If Elaine wanted to say more, she held her tongue, and Harley didn't dare ask what she was thinking.

"You don't have a Christmas tree." That fact dawned on Harley suddenly, and she didn't filter it before it passed her lips.

"Oh. No, I suppose the only reason I ever bothered with that was for you. It just seems like a nuisance now that you're gone."

That admission caused Harley to lift her eyebrows as she stared at her mother. "You did that for me?"

"Well, sure." Twisting her hands together, she seemed to deflate right before Harley's eyes. "I never expected you to be gone for so long. We haven't seen you in years."

The statement wasn't exactly accusatory, but it pierced Harley with a guilty sting that she tried to fight. Hadn't she every right to be angry?

"How is Mayowa?" The question sounded terse and rude to her own ears, but Harley couldn't stop herself from asking while she reminded herself why she left.

"She's wonderful, would you like to see?"

No, I don't want to see. Would you like to be replaced, dear? Perhaps we can surpass our feelings for you by focusing on someone else? Would you like to gaze upon the face of the daughter we chose over you?

Instead of voicing her thoughts, she sat like a statue while her mother rose from the couch and began to search through a stack of envelopes on the bookcase.

"Here she is." A grainy photograph was placed on Harley's lap, and against her instincts, she reached out with hesitant fingers and plucked it up, staring at the young woman. She stood amid a group of children, all smiling and waving for the camera. Her grin shone bright white against her dark skin, and her closely cropped hair was accented by a pink flower on one side.

"What is this?" Harley wanted to know, motioning to the building behind the group.

"Mayowa's always dreamed of being a teacher. She's teaching the local children to read."

Anger mixed with sympathy warred hotly in Harley's chest as she thought about her mother's words. Mayowa had achieved her dreams? It wasn't the Nigerian woman's fault that her mother had doted on her all those years, but why didn't Harley's dreams matter? Why had they never mattered?

"Why, Mom?"

"Why? I suppose she wants them to be able to—"

"Not why does she want them to read. Why have you given so much of yourself to this random person? What hold does she have on you?"

Lowering herself next to Harley, Elaine stared at the photo as she sat silently, not answering for several seconds. Deciding her mother wasn't going to answer, Harley gave up and tilted the photo sideways, giving it another glance.

"Mayowa is the same age as you. When I went on my first mission trip, she was an orphan and she was very sick. All she needed was basic medicine that was readily available here." Pausing, she looked directly at her daughter. "Have you ever met someone and felt like your soul was connected with theirs?"

Immediately Harley's thoughts flew to Kelsey, back in Louisville in her hospital bed.

"Yes," she answered quietly.

"Well, all I could think was that we had a healthy daughter at home, and this poor girl needed such basic things. And as the both of you grew older, God made it easier and easier to help her. Now she's helping her entire village. Our church partnered with her local church, and they've been able to set up medical services and teaching services."

Harley continued to stare into the dark eyes that looked back at her in that picture. Human beings just like her who certainly deserved their own chances at happiness, and she couldn't begrudge them some blessings in their meager lives. However deserving, though, their circumstances didn't change what her mother had done. What her father had allowed her mother to do.

"So the church talked you into this?" Harley asked. "That's it, right? Just like when you refused to let me speak with my best friend Beth anymore, because she was an unwed mother? Or when I couldn't go to Susie's wedding with Grandma, because they might have a champagne toast?"

"We were trying to protect you."

"From what, exactly? Life?"

"The wrong choices."

Pulling her eyes away from the photo, Harley turned to look at her mother. "The wrong choices, or the wrong people? Because I've got to tell you, everyone makes wrong choices. You've made your share."

"I know that, Harley. All have sinned and fallen short——"

Cutting her mother off by rising from the couch, Harley walked to the small window near the front of the trailer, looking down at the little hand crank that could be turned to press it open. From the looks of it as it sat askance, it had long since stopped being functional.

"You know what I never quite grasped, Mom? The thing that always gave me a hang-up as a kid? The whole sin thing. I sat in church with you week after week, year after year, and I knew about every type of sin imaginable. Don't sin and you can be close to God, I heard. Keep yourself clean so you can be close to Jesus. You can't go to church unless you're trying to be perfect. But now I know the whole thing was absolutely backwards. I did everything according to the rules, and I never felt any closer to God."

Elaine furrowed her eyebrows at Harley, but she merely shook her head and continued. "My friend Annie has purple hair and a pierced eyebrow, and she takes me to church with her on Sundays where I sit by a biker who counsels people with addictions. There are no perfect people in that place—just a bunch of messed up people willing to give everything because of Jesus. They are willing to give everything because He says, 'Come as you are.'"

"But then Jesus changes their lives," her mother protested.

"Yes, Jesus changes their lives. Not the pastor at the church, or another Christian who thinks they have it together enough to judge them." Letting out a sigh, Harley returned to the couch and lowered herself slowly. "I always thought God didn't care about me...that somehow I didn't quite measure up to His expectations, and that was why nothing ever worked in my favor. I poured over scripture after scripture trying to figure out which quality I was missing, did you know that?"

"No," Elaine whispered.

Hesitating, Harley peered at the long line of Bibles against the wall. "What did you mean, that God made it easier to help Mayowa as I grew older?"

"Oh," her mother muttered, crossing her arms against her abdomen. "Well, you were just so good at everything, Harley. You were such a hard worker, and a fast learner…so smart and quick thinking. I always figured God knew what He was doing, giving me a daughter that could make her own way in the world, so I would have room to help when I was needed. And you loved being with your dad so much, it was easy to take off in the summers. You made everything easy."

Laughing to herself, Harley pinched the bridge of her nose to stop the tears from forming. "So the reason I had to work so hard was because I worked hard. That's a bitter pill to swallow."

"You were a blessing." The words were spoken quietly, but to Harley they sounded loud and clear, both uplifting and hurtful in one blow.

Glancing at the photo where it rested beside her on the couch, Harley thought back to Dallas and wondered who she had helped with her donation. She had discussed the matter with Duke while they waited that day, and had come to the conclusion that it didn't matter. Her priorities were right and she was doing her best, and the rest was out of her control.

If she was willing to sacrifice for someone she didn't know, shouldn't she be able to manage some slight empathy for the woman who raised her? She didn't understand her logic, and would likely never agree with the way she had gone about things, but to obsess about it now would only drive her crazy.

Anyway, didn't Duke say that she was crowned with love and compassion? She certainly wanted to believe that.

Turning to her mother, Harley reached out and placed a hand on her arm, offering a sad smile. "Sometimes what others mean for evil, God can use for good."

"That's from Genesis."

Squeezing her mother's arm, she let out a sigh. "Yeah, from Genesis. I suppose if he can use what people mean for evil, he can use what they meant for good, right? And I think He will, in the end. Even if the execution may be a little shortsighted."

Pondering her words, Elaine gave her daughter a puzzled look. "I'm not sure what you mean, dear."

"Nothing," she muttered, allowing a sigh to escape. "Merry Christmas, Mom. Maybe we should string some popcorn and cut out snowflakes, for old time's sake."

Harley watched as her mother straightened, eyes widening. "But I only have my good stationery for writing letters. I can't cut that up."

The protest struck Harley as so absurd, she immediately started giggling, even as her mother looked slightly horrified. "Heaven forbid, I wouldn't want you to destroy your good stationery. Forget it. Is the peanut butter safe? Maybe we can make some cookies."

"Is the peanut butter safe," Elaine chided, shaking her head as she rose. "What a question."

Yes, indeed, Harley thought, watching her mother step before her into the kitchen, making note that she hadn't answered, which brought a fresh round of giggles. Perhaps her mother would have some misgivings about the waste of peanut butter as well.

"You have our telephone number, right?" Elaine asked Harley as she stood at the foot of the wobbly stairs, a tan sweater wrapped around her shoulders.

"It's in my pocket," Harley assured her, patting her hip for emphasis. She had nearly burst into laughter again when her mother pulled out her fancy paper and tore off the tiny corner for the phone number, but was able to control herself. Apparently giving her daughter her phone number made it higher on the importance scale than making Christmas snowflakes.

"Land sakes, Ryan, you have a fancy car," Elaine continued, peering at the BMW.

Ryan smiled at Harley before answering. "Actually, that's your daughter's."

"Oh. I never did understand why people wanted flashy cars, but I'm sure it's nice."

Glancing around for her father, Harley noticed him by the side of the trailer, motioning to her. Reluctantly turning in his direction, she peeked her head at her mom to make certain she wasn't following.

"Dad?" Harley whispered as she reached the end of the trailer. "Something the matter?"

"Not that I reckon," he answered, scratching his head as he examined the front yard for signs of movement. "When we were messing around with those motorcycles, I saw that your friend has a tattoo."

Laughing, Harley threw her hand over her mouth. After a moment, when she managed to calm herself, she pretended to be serious. "Yeah, he does. Lots of them—everywhere."

"Oh." Phil stretched his neck and looked towards the front of the trailer once more before he allowed a crooked smile to grace his face. "Well, don't worry. I won't tell your mother."

She bit the inside of her cheek to keep from smiling too wide at his remarks. "Thanks, but maybe you should tell her. I'd love to see her face."

"Maybe tomorrow," he added with a chuckle. "She's had too much excitement today already."

He managed to work in a wink before Harley wrapped her arms around his neck, giving him a squeeze before they stepped back toward Ryan and Elaine.

"Take good care of my girl, Ryan," Phil said.

"I intend to, sir."

"Come see us in Louisville," Harley added as she reached the passenger side of her car. Her mother nodded, even though Harley knew she didn't mean it. Her mother would go halfway across the world every summer, but Harley doubted she would ever grace the front door of her home. "Dad, maybe you can ride with Ryan sometime. Come see me, okay?"

Her father gave enough of a grin that she felt he might be considering the idea, so she considered that a solid accomplishment. Pulling open the passenger door, she slid into the car and waved at her parents.

The engine roared to life and Ryan turned and placed his hand against the top of her seat, eyes focused on the back glass as he placed the car in reverse.

"What were you whispering about with your dad?"

Choosing not to answer, she allowed her eyes to drift to the facial hair below his lip, and then drug her eyes back to meet his as slowly as possible. In response, he smiled and shook his head, and as soon as they were out of sight, he placed the car in park in the middle of the driveway.

"What are you doing?" she asked.

"I told you not to torment me." Twisting in the seat, he leaned across the center of the car, pressing his lips against hers before she had a chance to protest. For a split second she thought it might be funny to try to resist, but her body decided otherwise, relaxing against him as she wrapped her fingers around his forearm. As he tried to pull away, she rose from the seat and followed, as though she was magnetically drawn in that direction.

"Okay," he muttered, "don't get carried away."

Pretending to pout, she leaned back in her seat and wrapped her arms around herself protectively. "'Don't torment me, but it's okay for me to torment you.' You're so cruel."

"Okay, I'm sorry." Shifting into reverse once more, he gave her a charming smile. "What were you whispering about with your dad?"

"You and your alarming mass of body art. I tried really hard to convince him that you were a respectable young man, but the second we're out of sight, you park the car and pounce on me."

"Wow. I thought your dad liked me."

"Of course he liked you," she said, laughing. "He liked you enough that he wasn't going to tell my mom about your tattoo. And besides, it doesn't make any difference to me whether they like you or not. I've pretty much already made up my mind about you."

"And?" He glanced at her as he pulled onto the road, pressing on the accelerator.

"And…I think you're pretty amazing."

Chapter Twenty-Eight

Stepping up to the heavy wooden door separating her from those she loved, Harley took a deep breath before knocking three times, gently pushing it open.

"Anybody home?" she asked expectantly, peering around the corner. Kelsey was sitting alert in her bed, looking much better than she had a couple days before. Regina was next to her on a love seat, and Ryan was on the opposite side in a large armchair.

"Harley!" Kelsey spoke up, a huge smile adorning her face.

"This is absolutely not where I planned to spend my holiday," Harley complained, stepping up to Kelsey and taking her hand. "I wouldn't want to be anywhere else in the world, though. Merry Christmas."

"Merry Christmas," Kelsey repeated. "They're having turkey and stuffing in the cafeteria if you want some."

"You know what? I think I'm good. I'll just wait until the next time, and your mom can fix me a good old-fashioned turkey dinner."

"Sounds like you're planning on sticking around." Ryan stepped up behind her, placing a hand on her waist.

Turning, she lifted herself to her toes and planted a sweet, quick kiss to his lips. "I'm sure I could be persuaded easy enough."

"Man...that sounds like a dare. Did you all think that was a dare?" He lifted his palm to the side of her face, cradling her cheek in his hand as he stared into her eyes, the hint of a smile forming at the corner of his mouth.

"I think you should quit flirting," Kelsey interrupted. "It's Christmas and we should be exchanging gifts. Where's Dad?"

"The doctor wanted to speak with him," Regina stated. "He should be back any minute."

"Well, he won't care if I give Harley her gift." Reaching to her left, Kelsey picked up a rectangular package wrapped in red, holding it out to Harley. "Here, this is for you."

Harley took the package from Kelsey's hands, unable to ignore the mischievous look crossing the teenager's face. She was definitely not the kind who could keep secrets. Suppressing a laugh, Harley pulled back the paper to reveal a gray, worn out copy of Webster's Dictionary.

"She thinks I'm vocabulary-challenged," Harley presumed, showing the book to Ryan. "That's just plain mean."

"No, it's helpful," Kelsey insisted. "This is my old dictionary, and now you'll be able to study all kinds of words for when we play Scrabble."

Heart full, Harley smiled at her blonde-haired friend. "I love it, really. And the fact that it's yours makes it even more special."

"I autographed it for you."

"Okay, show-off." Shaking her head, Harley settled on the bed next to Kelsey, casting a glance at Ryan. The blue of his shirt was drawing out the color of his eyes, which were focused on her so intensely that she had to force herself to look away.

"Is it okay for me to give you your present?" Harley asked her, watching her face light up as she pulled the small, flat box from her purse.

"It's okay Mom, right?"

Regina smiled as she nodded her head at her daughter. "I'm not going to stand between someone and a present."

Harley held it out and watched Kelsey delicately take it into her hands. "It's from both of us—me and Ryan."

Giving her a quizzical look, Ryan leaned forward in his chair, placing his elbows against his knees as Kelsey pulled at the ribbon adorning the white paper with the gold foil scrolling. Her eyes sparkled as she pulled out the small black box, hesitating only a second before plucking the top of the box from the bottom.

Letting out a sharp gasp, she carefully inspected the gold chain and the letter tiles that hung from the necklace, spelling HOPE.

"Oh, Harley, I love it so, so much. Thank you. Thank you, Ryan. It's beautiful."

Harley took the necklace and shifted forward to help Kelsey fasten it around her neck, nearly unable to keep her eyes from her friend's beaming face.

Totally worth it.

"Mom, isn't it perfect?" Kelsey asked, sharing a toothy grin with her mother.

"That is really something," Regina said, nodding her head.

Harley fought the instinct to become emotional by taking a deep breath and reminding herself to be calm.

"Harley, can I talk to you for a second?" Ryan rose from his chair and stepped toward the door.

She attempted to offer Kelsey a reassuring smile, but something in his tone told her he wasn't pleased. Following him out the door, she halted when he stopped abruptly a few feet into the hallway. Turning to face her, his expression appeared to be one of confusion rather than disappointment, which was immediately a relief.

"I know how much that cost," he began, "and I know that I had nothing to do with that. How did you get that, babe? And don't tell me it was from Annie's rent money, because I saw you pay Jake for the work he did."

"Does it really matter?" Taking a step toward him, she placed her arms around his waist.

"Yes, it matters." He placed his hands on her shoulders, but didn't move to pull her any closer.

"Okay," she breathed, glancing down. "I took some things to Annie's store."

"What things?"

"Gucci sandals," she admitted, giving a shrug. "Jimmy Choo boots, Prada handbag, Burberry jacket—"

She could have gone on naming the other couple items she had taken to The Revolving Closet, but she found herself unable to talk once Ryan's lips were on hers, his hands moving to either side of her face, holding her captive while he kissed her tenderly. When he slowly pulled away, he rewarded her with a sincere smile.

"Merry Christmas," he whispered, reaching around to his back pocket. She released his waist and stepped back, accepting the CD case from his hand, where she saw HARLEY'S SONG written across its length.

"You mean I finally get to hear the entire thing?" she asked, giving him a smile of her own before a worried look crossed her face. "You're not the one singing, right?"

"Very funny. No, it's Matt."

"I can't wait to hear it." Pulling a folded paper from her pocket, she held it out to him shyly. "Merry Christmas."

He looked nearly as giddy as Kelsey had been while he unfolded it, and then he glanced up at her in surprise. "Is this what I think it is?"

Nodding, she watched a woman stroll past, eyeing them curiously. "I now have a helmet, and it's red and sparkly. I can't very well have a man with a motorcycle and never get to ride it with him, can I?"

"No, I guess not." Reaching for her, he nearly crushed her in a hug, holding her so tightly she could barely breathe. "I told you I didn't want anything for Christmas except you."

"And you got me," she answered, wiggling slightly so he would loosen his grip. "Now I'm going to be plastered to your back everywhere you go, like a bad nightmare."

"More like a dream come true. Come on, Kelsey and Mom will think I'm mad at you, and that couldn't be farther from the truth." Tugging on her hand, he coaxed her toward the patient room, throwing an arm around her shoulders as they stepped through the door together.

As soon as they entered the room, they were stopped by the appearance of Sam, looking as though he might have seen a ghost. Harley's heart sank almost immediately, knowing that he had just been talking to the doctor.

"I have news," Sam stated stoically, placing a hand on the edge of the bed to steady himself. Harley instinctively drew herself closer to Ryan, who stood unmoving.

"Sam?" Regina squeaked, the color draining from her cheeks as she rose and placed her hand on Kelsey's arm.

"I've just spoken to the doctor, and I've been cleared." Releasing a quick laugh, he looked at his daughter as he fought tears. "I've been cleared with my health, and I can be a donor for Kelsey. He wanted me to know as soon as possible, since it's Christmas."

Regina bent over her daughter and began to cry as Sam rushed over to hug the both of them, tears flowing freely. Ryan wrapped his arms around Harley, kissing her forehead while they both succumbed to tears together. She was spending Christmas Day crying in a hospital room, and for Harley, it was hands-down her favorite Christmas yet.

Chapter Twenty-Nine

Settling at her desk and filtering through her mail, Harley tried to force herself back into normal mode after her week away from work. When peering at her news stories in light of her time spent in Dallas and with Kelsey, fluff pieces about Christmas returns and post-holiday blues seemed almost a nuisance in comparison. There were life and death scenarios in countless places, but Channel Six wasn't focused on those. No, the hot topics were reviews on the holiday box office, fashions for New Year's parties, and the best remedies for hangovers.

Rather than immediately flinging herself headfirst into the assignments she had been given by Mitch, which were to interview a couple wedding planners about a bridal extravaganza and to taste-test four new flavors of cola made by a local company, she thoroughly reviewed her notes about the state's pension matter and penned out a detailed analysis of her findings.

Rising from her chair, she straightened her skirt and tugged at the bottom hem of her jacket near her hips, trying to appear as poised and professional as she normally managed to be. For some reason, the act wasn't proving as easy in her current state.

"Hey," she heard as she strolled past Denton's office, causing her to pause midstride and stare at her coworker. "You got a sec?"

"Actually, I was just going to talk to Mitch and..." Stepping into the doorway, she allowed the earnestness of Denton's face to pierce her protests. "Sure, I have time."

Glancing down the hallway anxiously, she sighed as she entered Denton's office and lowered herself into the chair facing his desk, placing her papers on her lap.

"You okay, Harley?" Placing his hands together on top of his desk, Denton leaned forward. "I'm worried about you. You seem different."

"Different how?"

"What happened with New York?" he whispered, compelling her to lean toward him. "I can't believe you would show up for the tryout and they wouldn't even put you on the air. Did you and Trent have some sort of disagreement before the broadcast or something?"

As she pondered her response to his question, she took a second to glance around his office. Sports memorabilia dotted two walls, including two signed photographs that she knew he treasured. Behind his desk, there was a single portrait of Denton with his parents, in front of the beach house where he took them the summer before as a surprise anniversary gift. His college credentials rested in frames on his bookshelf, proof of his education, and he sat there confidently before her, looking like he could have easily stepped out of the pages of GQ. If there had been any doubt in her mind, the realization suddenly hit her that Denton was the absolute perfect guy she would have imagined herself with not long ago.

That was the old Harley, though—the one who existed before she met her improbably perfect version of a tattooed rocker EMT with a heart of gold.

"It has something to do with Kelsey, doesn't it?" Denton continued. "Did you turn down the audition for her?"

Shrugging, Harley tugged at her black sleeve, gazing at her lap. "To be absolutely honest, the timing was just off. To everything there is a season, and this isn't my season."

"Mumbo jumbo designed to talk me in a circle and not give me an answer."

"Come on, isn't that what we do here?" she teased, sobering a bit when he didn't laugh. "Please don't make a big deal of it, okay? I struggled with the decision, but I did what was best and I'm fine with the consequences."

"What if Mitch is so annoyed that he doesn't give you the desk? He was pretty surprised when he started watching Trent's show last week and you were nowhere to be seen."

"It's out of my hands, Denton." Smiling, she rose to her feet and smoothed her skirt once again. "Let's just leave this one to God, shall we?"

"I liked you better when you took matters into your own hands," he called after her as she stepped into the hallway.

Shaking her head, she firmly gripped the papers she carried and marched forward to Mitch's office, mentally preparing herself with a pep talk that made it to her ears but not all the way to her heart. As she stopped in front of his doorway, she peered inside, witnessing him staring at his computer, pale blue shirt actually missing a button at the point where it was straining, causing Harley to wonder if it finally managed to loosen itself to the point of being a projectile.

"Miss Laine," he commented without emotion, not even looking in her direction. Stepping forward, she lowered herself to the chair before him, nervously squeezing her hand into a fist. "I trust you enjoyed your vacation."

"Yes sir, thank you." Wishing he would at least make eye contact, she swallowed with difficulty. "About New York——"

"I keep telling you that your persistence on digging into political scandals would make things difficult for you. It doesn't matter what a pretty face you are, Harley, if you insist on bringing up uncomfortable subjects."

"Pardon me?"

"I assume you wanted to talk about the real news stories with Trent, but he only wanted you as the pretty sidekick? It's no matter, because we weren't ready to lose you. Did you get the assignments I sent to you?"

Leaning forward, Harley stretched the papers in her hand out before her and placed them on his desk. "About that...I finished the research on the pension issue, and I have the piece I've been working on."

Finally dragging his eyes from his computer, Mitch spread his palm across the top paper and drew it closer by sliding it across his desk. After looking at it for several seconds, he simply shook his head.

"I have sources willing to go on the record," Harley quickly inserted.

"No, we can't run this. Do you know how many people would be breathing down my neck?"

"Everything in that story is a substantiated fact."

Giving her a stern look, he shoved the paper back in her direction. "Fact or not, we're not taking on that can of worms. Just get down to that wedding thing and take care of business, Harley. It's a busy time of year, so you're off vacation mode."

Her throat burned angrily, but she forced herself to retrieve her papers and retreat from the office, heading back in the direction of her own desk. Passing Summer in the hall, she held her head high as the blonde newswoman neared her, sporting a green blazer atop her cream-colored camisole.

"Harley, good to have you back."

"Is it?" Harley muttered, unable to bite back her words. "Or did you suspect I might not come back, since I was making so much money milking the citizens of Louisville through my fake charity?"

Continuing on toward her desk, Harley sensed Summer behind her, trailing her down the hall. Rather than looking, though, she pretended she wasn't there, going so far as to greet her other coworkers by name when she passed them. When she resumed her position behind her desk, Summer stepped up to the front of her office space, looking a bit confounded.

"I realize I was a bit harsh, alright? I had no right to make the assumptions I did. After talking with Denton, he assured me I was off base."

Still seething from the words Mitch had spoken, Harley peered up at Summer. "Why did it take having a talk with Denton? Am I really that bad?"

Offering a slight compensatory grin, Summer made obvious work of pondering a response. "Not bad, exactly, just…ambitious."

"And ambitious equals dishonest, I suppose?"

Placing herself in the chair across from Harley, Summer gave a wry smile. "No, which is why I'm apologizing." She allowed the words to hang in the air between them for a moment before continuing. "I don't want to be at odds with you. There's no reason we can't get along. The fact is, you remind me a bit of myself, back before I was jaded. This industry is fickle, you know."

"Tell me about it." Sighing, Harley looked down at the papers that had been so uninteresting to Mitch just moments ago. "How do you do it, Summer? Keep smiling up there year after year? Don't you ever get tired of talking about the same things day in and day out?"

Nodding her admission, Summer tilted her head to the side. "I focus on what I love, instead of the things I don't like. For me, that's Louisville. I grew up here, it's my city, and I like being the hometown girl. What do you love about this job?"

"That might be the million dollar question," Harley admitted, finally allowing a smile.

"You sure this is what Mitch had in mind?" Kenny attempted to clarify, giving Harley an almost comical grimace. "I think he just wanted you to come down here and talk to the people in charge, ya know? This is out there, even for you."

"Really, Kenny? Because I'm pretty sure we've stepped in poo together."

"Not on purpose."

"Let me focus on the story, and you just concentrate on your camera, okay?" When he didn't relax his posture, Harley placed a hand defensively on her hip. "Listen, I've been thinking a lot this morning about what I love about this job, and you know what I've decided? It's a combination of the people I get to meet and the witty remarks I conjure up for even the most ridiculous assignments. So we're going to have fun from now on, okay? I don't care if he sends me to Siberia to judge a hot dog eating contest—we're going to make it sound like the only place to be is with us, having the time of our lives. You on board?"

"Will you still gripe once in a while? 'Cause I like hearing your little rants."

"You want me to complain for comical relief?" Shaking her head, she laughed as she glanced down at her dress, straightening her posture.

"Hey, you missed that HR meeting last week. Trust me, there's a lot worse things I could have asked ya. A lot worse."

"Oh, I've no doubt." Shrugging her shoulders, she gave him a grin. "Why not? I promise to complain at least once a day, in the confines of the van, mostly to entertain you."

"And you'll still act all holier-than-thou?"

"If you insist. I'll even correct your grammar and enunciation."

Giving her a crooked grin, he extended his hand slowly. "It's a deal."

Sitting next to Annie on the sofa, Harley glanced into her bowl of ramen noodles and then to her friend, unable to keep the smile from spreading across her face.

"What?"

"Oh, nothing, just..." Harley bit her lip to try to hide her smile. "This will take some getting used to."

Annie self-consciously reached up to touch her black curls. "Leave it to you to be shocked when I look like everybody else. You're a special kind of strange, you know that?"

"I know that this is a delicious dinner, and I'm glad you have your TV set up to entertain us."

Apparently giving up, Annie shook her head, focusing on her own bowl. "So, what was that message from the hospital?"

Wrapping noodles around her fork, Harley brought her feet up to the couch, drawing her knees close to her chest.

"They're having a benefit on New Year's Eve, and their speaker had to cancel at the last minute. They wanted to know if I'd be willing to fill in."

"So you gonna do it?"

Pretending to think for a moment, Harley nodded. "Sure, why not?" Shoving the fork in her mouth, she looked across the room at the Christmas tree, which now boasted several paper snowflakes along with the lights. She and Annie had cut them up on Christmas night, using only the best paper they could find, having quite a laugh in the process.

"Shall we watch my lovely friend on the news? I finally got the DVR set up, and I have a feeling you had an interesting day, judging by your attitude tonight. Am I right?"

Harley simply smiled as she made an obvious effort of continuing to eat while ignoring her friend. Giving an exasperated sigh, Annie grabbed the remote. The TV blinked on, coming to life on a reality show, which Annie quickly remedied by going to the recorded items. Settling on the evening news, she leaned back against the couch and relaxed as Summer and Denton began saying their introductions.

"So, this benefit—is it a formal thing? Because Faith Cooper brought this dress in last week...custom-made, rose-colored Grecian-style gown with one shoulder. It's absolutely gorgeous. She was complaining about it being a bit shoddy for her tastes, and said she had to unload it because it was for her daughter's canceled wedding. I made a big play of it and agreed with her about it being shoddy, so she gave it to me for next to nothing."

"Annie, you're terrible!"

"And she hadn't even worn it yet, so you won't have to worry about anyone else knowing it was hers. I guess she would know if she ran into you, but she wouldn't dare say anything."

Laughing, Harley placed her bowl on the floor and leaned back against the couch, facing her friend. "That sounds lovely, but I'm not sure it's in my clothing budget right now."

"As if you need a budget to borrow a dress," Annie retorted. "Yes, I said borrow. And just think how easy it will be for me to sell after I say, 'This dress was worn by Harley Laine at the New Year's Eve benefit.'"

"Ah, so you have an ulterior motive."

"I have to make a profit." Discarding her bowl next to Harley's, Annie folded her legs beneath her while a mischievous grin spread across her face. "What about Ryan? You taking him with you?"

"He thinks he has to work, which is just as well. Can you imagine Ryan dressing like the people at those things? I'm sure he would laugh just thinking about it. But Kelsey wants to go, if she's feeling up to it. Her last big outing before the surgery."

"Then we'll have to find her something to wear, too," Annie said, looking genuinely excited. "Oh, Denton just said your name. Stop talking."

Suppressing a giggle, Harley stared at the television, listening to Denton introduce the bridal expo. "...Channel Six Action News sent our very own Harley Laine to cover the festivities."

"Louisville might be known for the Kentucky Derby, Louisville Sluggers, and Kentucky Fried Chicken, but for its romance? Today I'm popping into the bridal expo to see what we have to offer lovers, dragging my unwilling cameraman Kenny along for the ride. He's already rolling his eyes, so we must be on the right track. Come on!"

"Oh dear," Annie muttered next to Harley on the couch.

"So I'm sure you all know about throwing rice at weddings, or blowing bubbles, but did you know you could release butterflies?

Talk about every fairy-loving little girl's dream come true. Or what about releasing doves? Personally, I have an adverse reaction to birds that stems from a previous news story, but for somebody else this might be an awesome idea."

"She's gone crazy," Annie stated to the television.

"But what if you haven't gotten to that step yet? Guys, you're thinking about proposing, but not sure how to impress your lady? This is the place to be. There are tons of ideas, and we are testing every one of them. Testing them how, you might ask? Kenny has proposed to me fourteen times today. He's not a very happy camper, but some day his girlfriend will thank me."

Harley laughed as she verbally heard Kenny sigh on the camera.

"By the way, Kenny liked the billboard best, which we only simulated through a design on the computer. What he wrote would definitely *not* have gotten an acceptance from me, but in his defense, he was already a little irritated. Piece of advice, Kenny— when proposing to someone you actually like, never use the words 'annoying' or 'bossy' in your speech."

The camera panned to Kenny, sitting at a makeshift nail station, where a dark-haired woman was bent over slightly with his hand in hers. A bit unsteady, the camera bobbed as it focused on the lanky, scowling cameraman.

"Kenny's having his nails buffed, and he's thoroughly enjoying himself, aren't you Kenny?"

"I'm going to kill you."

The camera trained on Harley once again, walking between the vendor stations wearing her black suit and carrying a bouquet of roses. "I've seen loads of hair design ideas for wedding styles, and I'm actually getting ready to be a hair model. Wish me luck!"

Her face once again appeared on camera, this time with her hair swept into an updo, only a couple pieces framing her features. "I think it's pretty stellar. Elegant, classy, sophisticated...but totally clashes with the suit. Shall we remedy that, Kenneth?"

An audible groan could be heard as Kenny once again made his thoughts known on camera. A shot of the floor took center stage, the camera slowly trailing upwards until it found its way to Harley, wearing a white dress with trails of beading down the bodice leading all the way to the train. "It's intoxicating, really, all this romantic talk of weddings, finding myself standing here completely looking like a bride. My boyfriend is probably watching at home, trembling in fear. I couldn't convince Kenny to pretend to be the groom. Too bad Denton couldn't have gone on assignment with me. He would have totally taken the bait. P.S. ladies, Denton is single and deserves to have a nice girl in his life. I'm pretty sure he gives the city's most eligible bachelors a run for their money."

Kenny pulled in closer with the camera, bringing Harley into the full frame, where she held the bouquet in front of her like she normally would a microphone.

"Perhaps there is an atmosphere of love in the air here, after all. Maybe it's just all the beautiful smells and sights that have my senses on high alert, causing me to feel amorous. Or, it could be that I'm coming back from a week of vacation and feeling rather cheeky." Pausing to tilt her flowers toward the camera, Harley offered a wink. "Regardless of the reason, I must admit that I enjoyed this bridal expo much more than I expected. I'm not sure I can say the same for Kenny, but there's no accounting for taste. I would stick around, but there are some cake samples right over there calling my name. Rock on, Louisville. Rock on."

The television flashed back to Denton and Summer, shaking their heads as Summer laughed. "Oh my, our own romantic Harley Laine outs Denton as an eligible bachelor. Should we set up a dating hotline, Mr. Price?"

"Thanks a lot, Harley," Denton added with a self-conscious smile. "Right back with the weather. Keep it here."

"Girl, you've gone completely bananas," Annie said, poking Harley in the shoulder. "What were you thinking?"

"Clearly not." Offering a shrug, Harley smiled. "I was annoyed because Mitch wouldn't let me do the pension story after I'd spent so much time working on it. No worries, though—I sent it freelance to a few nationwide newspapers. Maybe one of them will pick it up."

"Won't Mitch be upset about that?"

"How could he be?" Harley wondered, giving her friend a mischievous grin. "I used a fake name."

Chapter Thirty

Finishing the final touches on Kelsey's mascara, Harley leaned back to inspect her handiwork. She had been able to remove nearly all traces of Kelsey's sickness with makeup, and her hair looked fuller and shinier than normal. In the simple but elegant blue dress Annie had loaned them, Kelsey looked like she was preparing to go to her prom.

"I'm totally jealous," Harley breathed, staring at her friend in the mirror.

"Jealous of me?" Giggling, Kelsey gave Harley a doubtful glare. "Why would you be jealous of me?"

"Because when I was your age, the only blue dress I got to wear was that horrible prom bomb nightmare from Rick Dillard's sister. You look so perfect."

"Thanks." Kelsey looked down at her fingers, seemingly nervous, causing Harley to wonder if she was feeling run down. Instinctively, she put her hand on Kelsey's shoulder.

"Everything going to be okay?"

"Oh, sure. It's just...I hope I don't embarrass you."

"As if you could," she protested, lowering herself to the side of Kelsey's bed. "Aren't you the girl who can walk vocabulary circles around me? I should be afraid I'll embarrass you."

The doorbell rang, and Kelsey whipped her head around to look at Harley.

"Now who do you suppose that could be?" Harley asked, giving Kelsey a conspiratorial smile as she rose to exit the room. Kelsey stood behind her, grabbing her hand as they walked into the hallway, bracing herself against Harley as she stopped in the living room. "Well? Don't you want to answer the door?"

"No, I can't. You do it."

Laughing, Harley stepped forward and swung the door open, revealing a rather large bouquet of pink roses. She heard Kelsey gasp behind her, at which point the bouquet dipped down a couple inches, revealing a smiling Denton.

"Ladies," he said, stepping inside. "I apologize for not being Zac Efron, but I was wondering if I could escort you to the benefit."

"Is that the best you can do? Seriously, Denton."

Dropping the hand with the roses down to his side, he let out an exasperated sigh. "I'm sorry, Miss Laine, but I was not at the proposal exhibition with you the other day, so I'm not as up to date in my romance protocol."

"Denton!"

"Okay, okay." Dropping to one knee, he extended the roses to Kelsey with a beguiling grin. "Kelsey Andrews, would you do me the honor of accompanying me to the benefit this evening? We'll have to drag along your schoolmarm older lady friend, but I'm game if you are."

Shaking her head, Harley took the roses from his hand and carried them to the kitchen. "Poor form, Mr. Price. Kelsey, are you going to accept that sort of invitation?"

"I think I should," she answered quietly, lifting her fingers to her neck in a protective gesture. "Don't you think I should?"

"You definitely should," Denton interrupted, rising from his knee and taking her hand, bending over it as he made a huge show of placing a kiss on her knuckles.

"Regina!" Harley called into the hall. "You better bring your camera out here. I think Kelsey's being proposed to."

Regina burst into the hallway with her camera, beaming as Kelsey's face tinted a shade of red. "Aw, honey, you look so beautiful. Let me take your picture before you go. Mr. Price, it's nice to meet you."

"Please, call me Denton," he insisted, smiling at Kelsey. "I hope it's okay with you if I drive the ladies to the benefit this evening. As long as it's what Kelsey wants, of course."

"Mom, can I?"

"Absolutely." Smiling, Regina held her camera aloft. "You two get closer together so I can snap a quick picture. Harley? Why don't you join them?"

"And ruin a perfect photo op? I don't think so."

Regina directed the couple on where to stand, and then took the requisite photos. Afterwards, she stepped aside and reached for Kelsey's coat.

"Harley, if you need to call——"

"Of course," she answered, smiling at Regina. "Please don't worry. I promise we'll take good care of her."

"I know you will, sweetie." She blinked away the gathering tears and shook her head. "Have fun."

Kelsey allowed Denton to escort her out the door with Harley following behind, where she helped herself into the back seat of Denton's sedan. Her coworker assisted Kelsey into the front seat, ever the gentleman, making Harley extremely happy that she had enlisted his help. Kelsey wouldn't soon forget the evening.

The two in the front seat conversed easily on the way to the benefit, mostly due to Denton asking lots of questions. Harley couldn't help being proud of him as she watched him with Kelsey, further cementing his status as one of Louisville's most eligible bachelors in her mind. Some woman would be very lucky to wind up with Denton Price.

As they pulled up to the event, Denton gave his keys to a valet and helped Kelsey out of the car, tucking her arm safely inside his own to shield her from any unwanted attention. Harley followed a few steps behind, holding her rose-colored gown in her fist so she wouldn't step on the trailing hem. Soft music filtered through the building, and the hushed mumble of people talking just inside carried on the wind as they maneuvered up the large number of stone steps.

"How are you holding up?" Harley overhead Denton ask Kelsey, to which she replied that she was perfect.

Once in the door, Denton maneuvered through the throng of people with ease, brushing most of them aside in his attempts to guard Kelsey. Harley wasn't quite as lucky, being pulled in different directions by people attempting to gain her attention. When one of those who wanted to say hello turned out to be Christopher Stanton, she simply gave him a polite nod and continued on her way. She had heard no more about his political aspirations, but she still had no desire to converse with him or his family.

Her seats were near the front, since she was a speaker, and she chatted comfortably with Denton and Kelsey while she fought her nerves. When Kelsey glanced just above Harley's shoulder moments later, she turned and noticed a well-dressed man and woman standing directly behind her, the man gazing at her while the woman looked rather aloof.

Faith Cooper, Harley's mind suddenly realized, sending a shiver of fright through her veins. Was she going to call her out for the gown in front of all these people?

Searching her mind for some explanation for the dress, Harley rose and faced them, plastering a smile on her face.

"Good evening," the man said, nodding his head slightly. "I don't believe we've met, and we wanted to introduce ourselves. I'm Kent Cooper, and this is my wife, Faith. I own Cooper Corporate Financial."

"Of course, Mr. Cooper," Harley repeated, extending her hand. "It's a pleasure to meet you and Mrs. Cooper."

Orange and plastic, she mentally nicknamed them in her head. His artificial tan was a bit much, and his wife's facial expression under her blonde hair hadn't changed at all since they had been introduced.

"You look remarkably like a young woman I knew in college," Kent stated, offering a blindingly white smile.

"Well, they say we all have twins out there somewhere, right?" Harley glanced at Faith again, wishing the woman would smile or something...blink, maybe.

"Faith will only watch the newscasts when you're reporting," Kent added.

"The other anchors are so dreadfully frumpy," Faith inserted, gazing without emotion at Harley. "You and I have similar fashion tastes."

Forcing herself to swallow, Harley tried not to allow her feelings to register on her face. "I'm glad you think so," she finally said. "Your gown this evening is lovely."

Faith glanced down uninterestedly at her purple gown, which Harley was sizing up, along with her strappy gold heels.

"Thank you." Faith tilted her head slightly to the side as she stared at Harley. "You know, I had a custom-gown made that looked almost exactly like the one you're wearing. It's the funniest thing."

I am so busted.

"Kent, isn't that funny?" Faith continued. "We truly do have the exact same fashion sense, don't we? I believe we must shop at the same stores."

"I would say that is a definite possibility," Harley assured her, offering a pleasant smile.

"Well, you are a delight, my dear. It's a pleasure to meet you."

"The pleasure is all mine," Harley insisted as the couple strolled away. Lowering herself into her chair, she fished into her purse and pulled out her cellphone.

Alert! she texted Annie. *Faith Cooper sighting.*
She really does look like a Barbie.
Didn't figure out about the dress.

Dinner had been served and they were working through their desserts when Annie finally texted Harley an answer, instructing her to steer clear of Faith Cooper unless she wanted to give away her resale-loving secret identity.

Let me know if you like her dress tonight, though, Annie continued. *I'm sure I'll have it next week.*

The nerves began to settle more firmly on Harley after dessert, because she knew she would be speaking soon. While she realized that most of Louisville knew her voice, she wasn't accustomed to speaking to large groups. Her normal audience was a single camera, and on occasion a small group in the studio.

As they announced her name, the other members of the audience began to applaud, and she felt herself rising from her chair and moving toward the platform, instinctively grabbing the fabric of her dress to keep from tripping. Each step closer to the podium, she felt her heartbeat pounding out a rhythm in her chest: *Who are you? Who are you? Who are you?*

She tried to shake it off as she stepped forward, staring at the notes she'd prepared that were rolled up in her hand—points about the type of city Louisville should strive to be. As she looked out at the faces, though, most of them having lived a lot longer than she had, her words seemed flat.

Who was she to think she could give these people advice? She had nothing.

Forcing a deep breath, she focused on the back of the room and happened to see someone carrying dishes who had a doo-rag on his head. Her mind shot instantly to Duke. Staring down at the paper in her fingers, she placed it on the podium and ignored it.

"Good evening," she said, gazing at Denton for reassurance, who promptly gave her a thumbs-up. "My name is Harley Laine, and I'm a reporter for Channel Six Action News. A lot of you probably recognize me. In fact, I've heard tell that I'm the most popular female reporter in Louisville, but who's keeping score, right?"

She heard a few laughs, and she offered a smile. "Up until recently, I was. I told myself that all I wanted was to be important, but I failed to see that's what we all want, isn't it? It plays out in a million different forms, but it all boils down to that one ingredient. Whether it's from a boss, or a significant other, a great city, or even the creator of the universe, we just want to know that we matter.

"I happened to tell a very wise man that I wanted to be important not too long ago. I wanted the highest and biggest platform I could reach, so I could make a difference. He told me something that changed my entire outlook." Pausing, she glanced at Kelsey, who was sitting demurely staring at her, proud smile on her face. "He said that I didn't have to be important to make a difference. The truth is, to every life you touch during the day, you are already important."

Daring to look a few people in the eye, she swallowed hard. "To further prove his point, this man makes a huge difference to the people in his life. He changes the world around him each and every day, but he doesn't see it that way. Instead of trying to change the world, he insists that he simply refuses to let the world change him."

Grabbing the side of the podium, she leaned forward slightly. "What if we all did that? What if we dug down deep, looked into our best versions of ourselves, and refused to let the world change us? Imagine the city we could be if we all embraced kindness, honesty, and love for our fellow man." Taking a second to smile, she stepped back again. "It feels like an unattainable dream, doesn't it? But in baby steps, we can make a difference. That's my new goal for this year—to report what's happening in the world without letting it alter what I think or how I react. It's easy to be cynical and even self-preserving, but if we all stopped even once a day and decided to do one small thing the way it should be done instead of choosing the easiest path, just picture the difference in our city!"

Harley's eyes drifted to Kelsey again, who must have become cold, because Denton's jacket was placed securely around her shoulders. Allowing a smile to light her face, she took a deep breath. "Being in front of the camera or named Louisville's most popular reporter may have the appearance of making a person seem important, but it's not real. My job provides a huge platform, but if it's not joined with love and compassion in my heart, it's a warped crown of rusty metal that's going to fade away. The things I do on Channel Six Action News aren't that important in the grand scheme of things. The truly important things are the actions I take when no one is looking, in the background, silently and with no fanfare. The kinds of actions people at this hospital perform every day, receiving little or no credit."

Pausing to scan her eyes across the entire crowd, Harley felt herself begin to relax at last. "So I challenge you, as fellow citizens of this great city, to be important quietly and not in a spotlight. This year, find your importance not in someone's eyes, but in another's heart. Thank you."

As Harley returned to her seat, she caught a glimpse of a familiar face near the entryway, so she hastily made her apologies to Denton and Kelsey and told them she would only be a minute. Attempting a poised but brisk walk in her gown proved difficult, as she balled the fabric in her fist and brushed her hair away from her bare shoulder.

Rounding the corner, she paused as she stared at the few loiterers who stood in the corridor, most likely waiting for others to arrive. Allowing a puzzled expression to cross her face, she turned to her left, where she felt fingers against her arm and jumped in surprise.

"I thought you would have learned not to chase me by now," that familiar voice said. "Last time that didn't work out so well for you."

Ryan continued to hold her arm from behind, and she released the dress from her hand as her heart pounded.

"I would say that it worked out perfectly last time," she corrected. "I have absolutely no regrets."

"You are so beautiful," he whispered, his fingers skimming across her bare shoulder.

"Do you have any idea how happy I am to see you? I missed you."

"But pulling extra shifts on the ambulance is what allowed me to be here, so I think it was worth it. You did a great job, baby. I'm so proud of you."

He gently removed his hand from her arm, allowing her to turn to face him. She paused as he came into focus, her eyes trained near his chest, noticing his tailored suit jacket and a black tie. As she brought her gaze upward, sweeping across his familiar facial hair, she stalled when she reached his eyes. His dark hair was nowhere near his shoulders, mostly short with just a hint of a mohawk near the top, which he had taken care to smooth over for the evening. Unable to stop a gasp, she lifted her fingers to her lips as she studied his new hairstyle, decidedly more conservative but still undeniably Ryan.

"Annie offered to hook me up," he explained, placing his warm hand against her shoulder again. "You don't seem pleased."

Shaking her head quickly, she removed her fingers from her lips as she allowed her eyes to roam over him. "You look incredible, honestly, but..." Biting her lip, she forced herself to look in his eyes. "I can't believe you cut your hair. I'm in complete shock. Why did you do that?"

Smiling, he moved his hand to her neck as he brushed his thumb across her cheek. "This is me dressing for the job I want."

Tears formed in the corners of her eyes as she reached up and placed her hand against the back of his head, feeling the soft, short hair beneath her fingers. "You had the job," she insisted, gazing at him. "And you don't have to worry about losing it, because you're irreplaceable."

"Yeah?" He looked down at the floor for a split second before he returned his eyes to hers, furrowing his brow. "The truth is, I've been thinking about cutting it for a while. I just didn't want you to think I did it for you." Hesitating momentarily, he wrinkled his nose. "What I mean is, it was a lot easier to commit to it knowing that you would love me either way."

Stepping back, she reached for his hands, feeling their warm strength in her own. "Please don't change for me, Ryan. Not a single thing about you."

Gripping her fingers tighter, he nodded. "Nothing has changed, really. I'm still the same guy you met that night at Tiny's—a little too overeager, whipping my shirt off at inappropriate times, desperately wanting to kiss you." Smiling, he released her hands and placed his fingers at the side of her waist, drawing her closer. "I'm still wrapped up in the wrong package...twenty-six years old, living with my parents."

"I sort of love that about you," she whispered, tilting her face upwards.

Shaking his head, he delayed giving her the kiss she obviously wanted. Instead, he placed his forehead against hers, letting out a sigh.

"I love you, and my heart has no doubt that you're the only one. My head keeps coming back to this question I want to ask you, but I know it's not the time. And believe me, I've been through every argument in my mind trying to convince myself otherwise."

Wrapping her arms around his neck, she breathed in the scent of him, imagining that she was smelling leather, spice, and mint. Combined with the warmth of his arms, it left her feeling almost intoxicated.

"Marry me, Ryan."

Pulling his head down, she allowed everything she was feeling to go into their kiss, her fingers playing with the short hair at the back of his neck. He responded as though he was making up for lost time, holding her even closer as she leaned against him, melting his resolve. Drawing himself away, he forced a deep breath as she slowly opened her eyes, gazing at him with longing.

"I will," he stated, almost so quietly she couldn't make out the words. "I want to be the kind of husband you deserve—a man who will devote himself to you. No distractions and nothing holding me back, okay? I promise, I will marry you, but you have to let me ask you when the time's right. Can you do that? Because I've gotta tell you, I'm not sure how much pressure I can withstand when it comes to you."

Smiling sweetly, she gently ran her finger down his chin, pausing to leave it positioned there as she nodded her head.

"If you insist, then yes, I'll wait patiently. I'll even try to forget we talked about this, on one condition."

"Name it."

"When you do finally get around to asking me the question, try to act surprised when I say yes."

Chapter Thirty-One

Harley stepped into the room rather cautiously, not sure what to expect. When she saw Kelsey in the bed alone, with only an empty room surrounding her, she stepped forward to the bed and touched her hand timidly. Her eyes flew open, and a simple smile graced her lips.

"I knew you'd come."

Grinning at the words, Harley lowered herself to the bed and took Kelsey's hand in both hers. "Of course I'm here. I'd like to see someone try to keep me away."

"What did you bring?" Kelsey glanced at the messenger bag Harley had slung across her hip, and Harley removed one hand and patted it carefully.

"Laptop. The newspaper liked the pension piece so much, I'm working on something new. This one's a doozy, involving all sorts of people. I doubt the paper will have the nerve to print it, but I'll just find someone else. I've become resourceful." She winked at Kelsey, who simply continued to stare at her. "Of course, I really don't think I'll get much work done at all. I'll be going crazy thinking about you."

"Please don't worry."

"I won't, but I promise you'll be on my mind the entire time."

"It's going to take hours," Kelsey added with a slight laugh.

"Like I said, the entire time." Glancing behind her, Harley twisted her mouth to the side. "Where's your mom? And Ryan?"

"Mom's spending some time with Dad, and Ryan should be back in a minute. You can't stand to be away from him for five seconds?"

"No, it's like cutting off my right arm," Harley teased, shaking her head.

"You're in luck then, because I'm back." Ryan appeared to her left, placing a hand against Harley's shoulder. "I'm glad you're here. I know Kelsey's been looking for you."

"Because I wanted my whole family here," Kelsey said, watching as a nurse came in and began looking through her chart. "Hopefully it will only take a few months before I'm back up and around. Maybe by then Ryan..." Glancing between the two of them, Kelsey gave a mischievous hint of a smile. "I'm ready to be your sister."

Fighting back tears, Harley leaned down and pressed a kiss against Kelsey's forehead. "Silly girl," she whispered. "You already are."

Chapter Thirty-Two
A Few Months Later

Stepping up to the park bench in front of one of her favorite places in the entire city, Harley lowered herself to the wood without saying a word, stretching her long legs all the way from her denim shorts to her black Keds. Glancing to her left, she couldn't help but award her bearded biker friend with a huge smile.

"Hey," she said succinctly.

Shaking his head, he chuckled under his breath. "Somebody's in a good mood tonight."

"As I should be. It's a perfectly beautiful evening, and the weather is going to be incredible tomorrow for the wedding. When I bought the house, I would have never even imagined a wedding in the yard." Sighing, she looked at him wistfully. "It's going to be gorgeous."

He pointed to the red sparkly helmet beside her, raising his eyebrows.

"Oh, Annie dropped me off. Ryan's going to be meeting me here. We have big plans tonight."

"I can't believe that boy hasn't given you a ring yet," Duke said, folding his arms across his chest.

"It's because he wants to tattoo it on his finger after we're married." Shrugging, she turned her attention back to the street.

"How's his sister doing?"

"So good." Pausing as she pictured Kelsey's face the night before at the dinner table, Harley laughed. "Better than good. She's feeling far better than what they expected at this point, which is fantastic. I can't wait to see her reaction tonight at her surprise party. That reminds me, I had something I wanted to show you."

Pulling an envelope from her purse, Harley loosened the paper from its covering, unfolding it in front of Duke as she read across his arm.

Hi. I've wanted to write to you for a little while now, but didn't have the words. Everything I could tell you seems so inadequate for what you did for me. For my family.

I could say thank you, but that seems too easy to say. Instead, I want you to see through my eyes for a minute, just to know whose lives you've impacted.

My three-year-old is watching Sesame Street sitting next to me, leaning sleepily against my arm. She is learning to use the potty by herself, but she had an accident this morning. We cleaned it up and then read a book about potties...again.

My seven-year-old got on the bus this morning, after I made his breakfast and packed his lunchbox. We had a tiny argument about whether or not he should wear his karate uniform to school. He won. I was a little bummed about letting him on the bus like that, but he did look awfully cute.

My husband left for work two hours ago. He made sure I felt okay, gave me the sweetest kiss, and then told me not to worry about dinner. I will worry about it. We may only have fresh fruit and macaroni and cheese, but there will be something on the table when he comes home.

The truth is, sometimes I don't feel like I can handle much. Some days it is all I can do to get through until night falls. Some mornings I call my mother and spend the rest of the day in bed, wishing I could find a fraction of the energy or the strength I had before.

But do you know what's beautiful? I'm still here. I'm able to clean up potty accidents, have arguments with my son, and put horrible meals on the table. A year ago, I wasn't sure this would be possible.

Thank you for my normal. It might not look like much from the outside, but from where I sit, it's pretty much everything.

God bless you.

Harley watched as Duke swiped at his eyes and pulled a handkerchief out of his pocket.

"Duke, are you crying?"

"Nope," he answered with a sniff. "Dust got in my eye."

"I cried too," she admitted.

"What did Harley do to make you cry?"

They both glanced up at Ryan, sauntering towards them with a huge grin on his face.

"I showed him the letter," she said, rising to offer a quick kiss as he wrapped his arm around her waist.

"That'll do it," Ryan agreed, shaking his head as he pulled Harley a little closer. "What do you know, Duke?"

"I know your woman is all giddy about meeting you tonight, and all hyped up about that wedding tomorrow. She was almost making me sick."

"Women," Ryan stated with a laugh. "I thought I'd never get over here tonight, because Annie kept calling me with the checklist. She definitely does not have the temperament to plan weddings."

"I can't imagine," Duke inserted. "I like that Annie, though...have ever since she came to my support group."

"Annie was in your support group?" Harley wondered, mouth gaping as she stared at Duke.

"Once upon a time."

Shaking her head, Harley smiled at the thought of her own mysterious John Wayne and her roommate back home. "Duke, you fascinate me. Really."

"Thanks," he muttered, giving her a wink.

"You ready to go, Harley?" Ryan asked. "Keeping the secret has been killing me. I'll be glad to finally get it out in the open."

"Sure." She patted her burly friend on the shoulder before she walked away. "See you later, Duke."

Taking Ryan's hand, she strolled towards the motorcycle, offering him a flirty glance as they walked together.

"What's gotten into you? You're awfully feisty tonight."

"I don't know, just happy I guess."

They rounded the corner into the bright sunshine, and Harley squinted her eyes against the glare as Ryan pulled her toward his motorcycle, kissing her hand as they walked. Scooping his helmet up, he held it aloft as he smiled at her, unable to break their contact to strap the protective device on his head.

"I love you, Harley Davidson."

Laughing, she blew out a breath in mock anger. "That is so obnoxious." Dropping the helmet to his side, he moved closer. "For the record, I love you, too," she mouthed against his lips as he pulled her into him. After a quick kiss, he drew the helmet up and over his head. She did the same, strapping hers under her chin. Ryan straddled the bike, waiting for her, and she stared at Tiny's for a second, remembering the first night she and Ryan shared a motorcycle ride. The thought instantly made her feel even warmer inside.

Swinging her leg over the bike, she settled against him, wrapping her arms around him tightly. He paused momentarily as he placed his fingers across her arm, and she suspected he was thinking how far they'd come as well.

Kelsey had a new lease on life, Annie had been rocking a fairly normal hair color for months, the huge house at the end of Wonder Lane was looking much improved, she was calling her parents every Sunday afternoon, and Mitch was finally letting her use some of her own ideas at the station. Plus, she was on the back of a motorcycle that belonged to the love of her life.

As he brought the engine to a roar, she smiled to herself inside the helmet, thinking that things couldn't get much better.

Harley took the steps two at a time in front of Ryan, who laughed and jogged to catch up with her.

"Wait for me," he pleaded, managing to grab her hand and slow her down.

"I don't want to miss the surprise," she insisted.

"You won't. Hey, just stop for a minute will you?"

Pausing near the door, she looked up at him expectantly.

"Is there something you'd like to say, Mr. Temple?"

"Yes," he said, pulling her into his arms. "There are a lot of things I'd like to say, actually."

"And they can't wait until a little later?" She gazed into his deep blue eyes, feeling her stomach perform a gymnastics maneuver.

Lowering his head, he placed his lips against her neck, kissing the soft spot right below her ear. She shivered as he leaned back, keeping his arms firmly around her waist.

"I don't think I'll ever get used to the fact that you love me," he whispered.

"You might as well get used to it, because it's pretty rock solid," she assured him quietly, reaching her fingers up to his cheek and tracing a path down the side of his face. "Now, can we go inside already?"

With a sigh, he released her so she could open the front door and step quietly into the house, crossing to the kitchen slowly as she glanced around the room.

"Where is everybody?"

She knew she had a rather befuddled look on her face, but having a surprise party with only two people yelling surprise seemed a little preposterous.

"You worry too much, it's still on track." Pausing to shove his hand in his pocket, he pulled out his cellphone. "Annie's bothering me again."

"Why exactly is Annie calling you? It would make a lot more sense if she was calling me."

"You want me to make sense of Annie?" he asked, lifting his eyebrows. "Here, hold this a second."

She dutifully stretched her hand out, and he dropped the contents of his pocket into her palm. Fighting the urge to roll her eyes, she glanced at the mound he had dumped there—change, keys, something sparkly...

With a slight gasp, Harley stared at the items in her left hand.

"What's going on?" She brought her right hand up to fish a princess-cut diamond out of his loose change. "You're walking around with a ring in your pocket?" Trying to slow the beating of her heart, she glanced around the room again. "There's not a party for Kelsey, is there?"

"Not exactly," he answered, watching her study the ring.

"And what about the surprise?"

"That'll be me, remember?" Scooping the contents of her hand back into his own, he shoved the change and keys back in his pocket. "You told me that when you said yes, I had to act surprised. Marry me tonight, Harley."

Tilting her head slightly, she offered a bit of a smirk. "How am I supposed to marry you tonight, exactly?"

"We head to Vegas. Right now."

"But the wedding tomorrow…I'm pretty sure you can wait one day."

"Baby, you're not listening to me."

"Oh, I can hear you," she said with a laugh, sliding the diamond onto her finger and holding it out for inspection. "You're just talking crazy. Be serious."

"I am serious," he insisted, dragging a paper from his back pocket and throwing it on the counter. Taking a break from peering at the ring, she unfolded the paper and glanced up at Ryan.

"This is a confirmation for a plane ticket."

"Two tickets, actually."

"To Vegas."

"Exactly, and if we don't leave soon, we might miss our flight."

Laughing, she self-consciously reached her hand up to touch her hair. "This is just…who's going to marry us?"

"I don't know. Elvis?"

She glanced up from the plane confirmation, unable to ignore the fire in his eyes. A burning reaction began deep in her stomach, threatening to overtake her.

"But the wedding—"

"We'll be back first thing in the morning. No one will even miss us."

"And Kelsey?" she asked, feeling slightly guilty.

"Do you honestly think Kelsey would let me get away with that? They're waiting at the airport right now." Taking her left hand, which now boasted the ring, he pressed it against his chest, the tip of her fingers pushing down his T-shirt enough to make his tattoo visible at his neckline. "Marry me. I don't want to go another day without being your husband."

The energy coming from him was so intense, she could almost feel herself trembling. Dragging in a shaky breath, she nervously moistened her lips.

"I'll have to pack," she whispered.

"Kelsey packed you a bag. I'm sure it's completely impractical, but it's waiting for you at the airport."

Giving her a disarming smile, he lowered himself to one knee, gazing up at her expectantly.

"You really don't have to do that," she informed him with a grin.

"No?"

"No, I'm in. All in. Over my head."

While retrieving the keys from his pocket, he slid one hand behind her neck, bringing his face within an inch of hers.

"Surprise," he whispered, his breath warm against her lips. "Maybe I should get a new tattoo to celebrate. I'm thinking 'Harley' right across my finger."

"I'm thinking I might spend hours studying your tattoos tonight."

"Scratch that, then. Looks like I'm going to be pretty busy...you know, being studied. I hope to become your new favorite subject."

"Do you offer a doctorate program? Because I'm very interested."

She had a couple more witty remarks running through her head, but they were cut short as he rewarded her with a leisurely kiss, his fingers moving to cradle the side of her face. When he finally released her, he motioned towards the door with his head.

"I should call Annie so she knows where we're going," Harley suddenly thought, pulling her phone from her pocket.

"Not necessary," he told her as he stepped across the living room, opening the front door. "Why do you think she's been bothering me all afternoon?"

"What a sneaky man you turned out to be." With a laugh, she stepped out onto the porch, pausing while he locked the door behind him. "What do you think of Harley Laine-Temple? I think it has a nice ring to it."

"That's a mouthful," he suggested, taking her hand as they moved toward the motorcycle. "How about I just call you baby?"

"I can deal with that." Pausing near the bike, she stopped to watch Ryan, thinking about the first time he asked her out. How she had managed to tell him no was a mystery, standing so close with her heart pounding. She could almost kick herself now for the time she wasted.

"You're staring at me," he said as he grabbed his helmet. "What's going through that head of yours?"

"Just thinking that Wonder Lane could use a lot more of you. I'll be doing the sleepy little street a great favor, won't I?"

Shoving his head into the helmet, he laughed through the open visor. "We'll have to come up with a great title for the house. A place like that deserves an awesome name."

Tugging the red helmet over her hair, Harley shoved her own visor up, allowing a smile to touch the corners of her eyes.

"The only name I'm concerned about right now is mine. I've thought about changing it a few times, but for some reason I never went through with it."

"Why not?"

Straddling the bike, he took her hand as she swung her leg over to sit behind him.

"You know, I'm not really sure. Maybe I was just hesitant to change who I was." Wrapping her arms around his waist, she smiled to herself. "Or maybe I was just waiting for a man who could handle a Harley."

About the Author

Christina Coryell is the Amazon bestselling author of The Camdyn Series and the Girls of Wonder Lane series. A resident of small-town southwest Missouri, where she lives with her husband and two children, she does most of her writing in unorthodox places and with lots of noise in the background. She's never really considered herself the queen of anything, but she once had a pretty snazzy car that she purchased after it had been wrecked. To her knowledge, there were no stabbings or drug deals involved in its past.

She loves to hear from her readers and welcomes interaction on Facebook, Twitter, and by email at her website, www.christinacoryell.com.

Independent authors rely on your support. If you enjoyed Crowned, please consider telling a friend and writing a review.

A Few Words

When you embark on an adventure like I have over the past year, it becomes pretty clear who has your back. For each of you supporting me faithfully, it does not go unnoticed, and I am grateful for you.

Thank you to my peeps at home for putting up with me. Mike, Reinah, and Truett—I love you. To Dad, for always asking how my books are coming along. To Mom, Cindy, and Karri for helping me hammer out the kinks in the story. To Linda, for being a perfect partner in this endeavor—couldn't do it without you.

Special thanks to my cover photographer, Kassi Hillhouse, for the fantastic images, and a huge thank you to Lexi for agreeing to portray Harley. I couldn't have asked for a better experience than working with you ladies.

To those of you who enjoy my books, your kind words inspire me to keep going. Thank you for your support!

It has been a crazy, unbelievable year, and I am grateful for every second I've been on this path. There have been bumps and turns in the road, but God has blessed me beyond my expectations. Can't wait to see how the next year unfolds!

Available Now
Girls of Wonder Lane

Book 1
Maddie Heard

Madeline Heard wants what many girls want—a little respect, a boost in her career, and to find a guy to share happily ever after. Can she find a way to have everything she wants, or should she be careful what she wishes for?

Book 2
Harley Laine

Louisville's hottest reporter appears to have it all—a perfect job, great car, beautiful house, and designer clothes. She's poised to set herself up as the woman at the top, until a gruff old biker, a teenage girl, and the absolute wrong guy threaten to derail her plans.

Coming Soon

Book 3
Alexis Jennings

Alexis has spent the past few years living someone else's life, but she's finally ready to make a fresh start. Outrunning her past might prove difficult, however, when Jake McAuliffe decides to follow her out of town.

And Don't Miss The Camdyn Series

Available Now:

A Reason to Run
A Reason to Be Alone
A Reason to Forget
For No Reason

Camdyn Taylor is a bestselling author hiding a bit of a secret—her identity. The victim of viral video proposal infamy, she heads out of town in the name of book research seeking a little anonymity. She never expects that a wrong turn could wind up not only changing her perspective, but possibly her entire life.

Equal parts romance, chick-lit, and women's fiction with a little history thrown in for good measure.

www.ingramcontent.com/pod-product-compliance
Lightning Source LLC
Chambersburg PA
CBHW030404180626
46812CB00005B/1923